LUKE SKYWALKER
and the
SHADOWS OF MINDOR

ALSO BY MATTHEW STOVER

STAR WARS

LUKE SKYWALKER
and the
SHADOWS OF MINDOR

MATTHEW STOVER

arrow books

Published by Arrow 2010

2 4 6 8 10 9 7 5 3 1

This book contains an excerpt from *Star Wars: Fate of the Jedi: Backlash*
by Aaron Allston. This excerpt has been set for this edition only and may
not reflect the final content of the forthcoming edition.

First published in Great Britain in 2009 by Century

Arrow Books
Random House, 20 Vauxhall Bridge Road,
London SW1V 2SA

www.randomhouse.co.uk
www.starwars.com

Addresses for companies within The Random House Group Limited
can be found at: www.randomhouse.co.uk

The Random House Group Limited Reg. No. 954009

A CIP catalogue record for this book
is available from the British Library

ISBN 9780099491996

The Random House Group Limited supports The Forest Stewardship
Council (FSC), the leading international forest certification organisation.
All our titles that are printed on Greenpeace approved FSC certified paper
carry the FSC logo. Our paper procurement policy can be found at:
www.rbooks.co.uk/environment

Printed and bound in Great Britain by
CPI Bookmarque, Croydon, CR0 4TD

The author respectfully dedicates this novel to the legendary Alan Dean Foster, and to the memory of the late, great Brian Daley, for showing us what it looks like when this stuff is done right.
Thank you, gentlemen. We are in your debt.

ACKNOWLEDGMENTS

The author wishes to gratefully acknowledge the following people, without whom this novel would not exist in its current form:

Mike Kogge, for suggesting that I look at the end of Luke's military career; Karen Traviss, for an opportune bit of translation; Sue Rostoni, Leland Chee, and all the folks at Lucasfilm for unflagging support and expert assistance; Shelly Shapiro, my editor at Del Rey, for leap-tall-buildings-in-a-single-bound encouragement, more-powerful-than-a-locomotive patience, and faster-than-a-speeding-bullet skill to shepherd this story from idea to hardcover; and Robyn, my beloved wife and periodic *Star Wars* widow, who accomplished the most heroic task of all: living with me while I slowly ground my way through this story.

THE STAR WARS NOVELS TIMELINE

5000 YEARS BEFORE STAR WARS: A New Hope

The Lost Tribe of the Sith:
  Precipice
  Skyborn
  Paragon

1020 YEARS BEFORE STAR WARS: A New Hope

Darth Bane: Path of Destruction
Darth Bane: Rule of Two
Darth Bane: Dynasty of Evil

33 YEARS BEFORE STAR WARS: A New Hope

Darth Maul: Saboteur*

32.5 YEARS BEFORE STAR WARS: A New Hope

Cloak of Deception
Darth Maul: Shadow Hunter

32 YEARS BEFORE STAR WARS: A New Hope

> **STAR WARS: EPISODE I
> THE PHANTOM MENACE**

29 YEARS BEFORE STAR WARS: A New Hope

Rogue Planet

27 YEARS BEFORE STAR WARS: A New Hope

Outbound Flight

22.5 YEARS BEFORE STAR WARS: A New Hope

The Approaching Storm

22-19 YEARS BEFORE STAR WARS: A New Hope

> **STAR WARS: EPISODE II
> ATTACK OF THE CLONES**

The Clone Wars
The Clone Wars: Wild Space
The Clone Wars: No Prisoners
Clone Wars Gambit: Stealth

Republic Commando:
  Hard Contact
  Triple Zero
  True Colors
  Order 66

Imperial Commando:
  501st

Shatterpoint
The Cestus Deception
The Hive*
MedStar I: Battle Surgeons
MedStar II: Jedi Healer
Jedi Trial
Yoda: Dark Rendezvous
Labyrinth of Evil

> **STAR WARS: EPISODE III
> REVENGE OF THE SITH**

Dark Lord: The Rise of Darth Vader

Coruscant Nights:
  Jedi Twilight
  Street of Shadows
  Patterns of Force

10-0 YEARS BEFORE STAR WARS: A New Hope

The Han Solo Trilogy:
  The Paradise Snare
  The Hutt Gambit
  Rebel Dawn

5-1 YEARS BEFORE STAR WARS: A New Hope

The Adventures of Lando
  Calrissian
The Han Solo Adventures
The Force Unleashed
Death Troopers

**STAR WARS: A New Hope
YEAR 0**

Death Star

> **STAR WARS: EPISODE IV
> A NEW HOPE**

0-3 YEARS AFTER STAR WARS: A New Hope

Tales from the Mos Eisley
  Cantina
Allegiance
Galaxies: The Ruins of
  Dantooine

Splinter of the Mind's Eye

3 YEARS AFTER STAR WARS: A New Hope

> **STAR WARS: EPISODE V
> THE EMPIRE STRIKES BACK**

Tales of the Bounty Hunters

3.5 YEARS AFTER STAR WARS: A New Hope

Shadows of the Empire

4 YEARS AFTER STAR WARS: A New Hope

> **STAR WARS: EPISODE VI
> RETURN OF THE JEDI**

Tales from Jabba's Palace
Tales from the Empire
Tales from the New Republic

The Bounty Hunter Wars:
  The Mandalorian Armor
  Slave Ship
  Hard Merchandise

The Truce at Bakura

5 YEARS AFTER STAR WARS: A New Hope

Luke Skywalker and the
  Shadows of Mindor

6.5–7.5 YEARS AFTER
STAR WARS: A New Hope

X-Wing:
 Rogue Squadron
 Wedge's Gamble
 The Krytos Trap
 The Bacta War
 Wraith Squadron
 Iron Fist
 Solo Command

8 YEARS AFTER STAR WARS: A New Hope
 The Courtship of Princess Leia
 A Forest Apart*
 Tatooine Ghost

9 YEARS AFTER STAR WARS: A New Hope
The Thrawn Trilogy:
 Heir to the Empire
 Dark Force Rising
 The Last Command

X-Wing: Isard's Revenge

11 YEARS AFTER STAR WARS: A New Hope
The Jedi Academy Trilogy:
 Jedi Search
 Dark Apprentice
 Champions of the Force

I, Jedi

12–13 YEARS AFTER STAR WARS: A New Hope
 Children of the Jedi
 Darksaber
 Planet of Twilight
 X-Wing: Starfighters of Adumar

14 YEARS AFTER STAR WARS: A New Hope
 The Crystal Star

16–17 YEARS AFTER STAR WARS: A New Hope
The Black Fleet Crisis Trilogy:
 Before the Storm
 Shield of Lies
 Tyrant's Test

17 YEARS AFTER STAR WARS: A New Hope
 The New Rebellion

18 YEARS AFTER STAR WARS: A New Hope
The Corellian Trilogy:
 Ambush at Corellia
 Assault at Selonia
 Showdown at Centerpoint

19 YEARS AFTER STAR WARS: A New Hope
The Hand of Thrawn Duology:
 Specter of the Past
 Vision of the Future

22 YEARS AFTER STAR WARS: A New Hope
 Fool's Bargain*
 Survivor's Quest

 ## 25 YEARS AFTER
STAR WARS: A New Hope

Boba Fett: A Practical Man*

The New Jedi Order:
 Vector Prime
 Dark Tide I: Onslaught
 Dark Tide II: Ruin
 Agents of Chaos I: Hero's Trial
 Agents of Chaos II: Jedi Eclipse
 Balance Point
 Recovery*
 Edge of Victory I: Conquest
 Edge of Victory II: Rebirth
 Star by Star
 Dark Journey
 Enemy Lines I: Rebel Dream
 Enemy Lines II: Rebel Stand
 Traitor
 Destiny's Way
 Ylesia*
 Force Heretic I: Remnant
 Force Heretic II: Refugee
 Force Heretic III: Reunion
 The Final Prophecy
 The Unifying Force

35 YEARS AFTER STAR WARS: A New Hope
The Dark Nest Trilogy:
 The Joiner King
 The Unseen Queen
 The Swarm War

 ## 40 YEARS AFTER
STAR WARS: A New Hope

Legacy of the Force:
 Betrayal
 Bloodlines
 Tempest
 Exile
 Sacrifice
 Inferno
 Fury
 Revelation
 Invincible

Crosscurrent

Millennium Falcon

Fate of the Jedi:
 Outcast
 Omen
 Abyss
 Backlash

*An ebook novella

A long time ago in a galaxy
far, far away. . . .

BRIEFING

LORZ GEPTUN STOOD OUTSIDE THE COMMAND CABIN door and tried to swallow. Really, this was too much: to be summoned before *Luke Skywalker,* of all people. A Jedi. Not only a Jedi, but the son of *Anakin* Skywalker. And now Geptun had to meet him. Face-to-face!

He tugged at the collar of his dress-blue uniform tunic, slid a finger behind it to try to stretch the fabric just a hair more. He grimaced at how difficult he found this simple task to be; surely his tailor had miscalculated—again—because he couldn't possibly have put on so much weight since he'd had this made. Could he? In, what had it been, three Standard months? A man of his admittedly advanced age—he would never see seventy again—should have settled on a size, and left it at that.

Geptun was not much in favor of dress uniforms, anyway. He'd left his own behind on his homeworld decades before, at the beginning of the Clone Wars, trading it in for mufti; in those days, Republic Intelligence had been a largely covert service, and had had no use for uniforms. He'd left Republic Intelligence not long after it had become Imperial Intelligence; his investigation of the so-called Jedi Rebellion had uncovered entirely too much of certain truths that the Imperial Executive had preferred to conceal, and for a number of years he'd been forced to make a living as a freelance broker of information while doing his best to avoid attracting any official Imperial attention.

Eventually, he'd offered his services to the Rebel Alliance. Though he had little interest in politics—his primary political conviction was a profound interest in his own safety and comfort—he'd recognized that the prospective government the Rebels planned to install would, owing to its youthful amateurish untidiness, afford him a great deal more opportunity for the freedom to make his own way in his own way. Which was another way of saying: to live and work in the lucrative shadows outside official scrutiny.

Which made his current situation all the more ironic.

He sighed. *Nothing ever works out how we wish, yes? Doesn't mean one can't turn it to one's advantage.* He sighed again and raised a finger to trigger the cabin's door chime . . . but before he could, the door slid open, and a voice that sounded a great deal older and wearier than Geptun had expected said, "Inspector Geptun. Please come in."

Geptun grimaced again. He'd become accustomed, this twenty-plus years past, to a galaxy without Jedi. He wasn't at all sure he was looking forward to their return.

He took a deep breath and waddled through the door. "General Skywalker," he said with a slight bow—no salute, as the Judicial Service was outside the military chain of command—and a pleasant smile. "How may I be of service?"

The young general sat on the edge of his desk, head lowered and hands clasped before him. He wore close-fitting civilian clothing of a somber black, very much in the style his celebrated father had made famous. Geptun reflected with a flash of annoyance that if he'd *known* Skywalker would be out of uniform, he would have come to this meeting in a comfortable blazer instead of this bloody jookley suit.

Skywalker lifted his head as though he had felt Geptun's annoyance—and he might very well have, Geptun reminded himself. Bloody Jedi. "Inspector Lorz Geptun," Skywalker said slowly. "I know a little about you, Inspector. You were a military governor and director of planetary intelligence for the CIS during the Clone Wars."

Geptun's too-tight collar suddenly seemed to tighten further. "Briefly. At the *begin*ning of the—"

"Then you were a Republic spy."

"Well—"

"And after that, you made your living tracking targets for bounty hunters."

"Not *specifically* for—"

"And now you're a JS investigator. Through all this, there's a running theme. You have a talent."

Geptun said carefully, "Do I?"

"You seem to be pretty good at finding the truth."

Geptun relaxed. "Oh, well, thank you for—"

"And at making money off it."

"Erm." He cleared his throat, but found he had nothing to say.

Skywalker pushed himself to his feet. His face was drawn, and far more deeply lined than Geptun had expected from a lad of twenty-four. He looked like he hadn't been sleeping for some few days now. His movements were slightly unsteady, and the shadows under his eyes were shading toward purple—but they were nothing compared to the shadows *within* his eyes. "That's what I know about you. What do you know about me?"

Geptun blinked. "General?"

"Come on, Inspector." Skywalker sounded even more tired than he looked. "Everybody knows stuff about me. What do *you* know?"

"Oh, well, you know, the usual—Tatooine, Yavin,

Endor, Bakura, Death Star One and Two—" Geptun realized he was babbling and shut up.

Skywalker nodded. "The usual. The stories. The press releases. The problem is that those stories and press releases aren't really about me at all. They're about the guy everybody *wants* me to be, understand?"

Geptun eyed him warily; he sensed that he'd been maneuvered onto dangerous ground. "I'm afraid," he said slowly, "that I *don't* understand."

Skywalker nodded with a slow, tired sigh. "That's because you don't know that less than a month ago, I murdered about fifty thousand innocent beings."

Geptun goggled at him, then blinked and cleared his throat again as he figured out what the young Jedi was talking about. "You mean Mindor?"

Skywalker's eyes drifted shut; he winced as though he were looking at something painful on the inside of his eyelids. "Yeah. Mindor. I say *about fifty thousand* because I don't know the real number. Nobody does. The records were destroyed along with the system."

"From what I've heard, your victory at the Battle of Mindor would hardly constitute *murder*—"

"From what you've heard. More *stories*."

"Well, I had heard—I, ah . . ." Geptun coughed delicately. "What is it, exactly, that you want me to do?"

"You're an investigator. I want you to investigate."

"Investigate what?"

"Mindor." Skywalker's face twisted. "Me."

He looked like something hurt. Or like everything hurt.

"Well, I, ah . . . erm." Geptun could think of several dozen ways to earn a tidy sum from such a project. "If you don't mind, may I inquire as to how *my* name came up for this?"

Skywalker looked away. "You were recommended by an old friend."

"Was I? And how did your old friend come to—"

"Not my old friend," Skywalker said. "Yours. His name was Nick."

"Nick?" Geptun frowned. "I don't know any—"

"He said to give you this." Skywalker held out a hook-shaped, curved, metallic-looking object. "Careful. It's sharp."

Geptun accepted the object gingerly . . . and as soon as it touched his palm, his mind was flooded with images of a dark-skinned man with tight-cropped hair, a cocky grin, and startling blue eyes. "Nick *Rostu*?" he breathed. "I haven't thought of Nick Rostu in . . . years. Decades. I thought he was dead."

Skywalker shrugged. "He probably is."

"I don't understand." But he did understand, at least a little. The object in his hand was from his—and Nick Rostu's—homeworld.

It was a brassvine thorn.

"So he was right about that, anyway." Skywalker nodded at the thorn. "He said you can read objects. That you can touch them and sense things about their owners."

Geptun shrugged. Why trouble to deny it? "It's a minor talent—but useful in an intelligence analyst."

"Or an investigator."

Geptun's nod was noncommittal. "What else did Rostu tell you about me?"

"He said you're vicious, venal, and corrupt. That you don't have a shred of decency, and about as much human feeling as a glacier lizard."

Geptun nodded abstractedly. "That *does* sound like Rostu . . ."

"He also said that you've got plenty of guts, that you're the smartest guy he ever met, and that once you get started on something, you never, ever quit. You don't like Jedi, and you don't much care who rules the galaxy as long as you can make a decent living. All of which makes you exactly the man for this job."

"And what job, if you don't mind saying, is this?"

"I want you to build a case. Talk to people. Everyone who survived Mindor. Get the facts, and make sense of them, and make a case."

"What sort of case?"

"War crimes," Skywalker said grimly. "Crimes against civilization, dereliction of duty, desertion. That kind of thing. Anything you can find out."

Geptun angled his head. "About whom? Who is the war criminal you wish to indict?"

"I thought that was obvious." The shadows in Sky-walker's eyes swelled as though they might swallow his whole life. "It's me."

Geptun said, "I'll do it."

STAR WARS

LUKE SKYWALKER
and the
SHADOWS OF MINDOR

*None of the stories people tell about me
can change who I really am.*

—*Luke Skywalker*

Six months after the destruction of the second Death Star and the downfall of the evil Emperor Palpatine, Luke Skywalker and the victorious Rebel Alliance still struggle against surviving Imperial forces, who remain as determined as ever to crush all that is good in the galaxy.

Black-armored stormtroopers under the command of the mysterious warlord Shadowspawn now raid the infant New Republic, taking up piracy, pillage, and destruction in the wake of the Empire's collapse. Attacking at will, they have shaken galactic confidence in the Republic's ability to maintain order and security.

In deep space along the Corellian Run, the Alliance's premier fighter squadron springs a trap on Shadowspawn's marauders . . .

CHAPTER 1

THE CORELLIAN QUEEN WAS A LEGEND: THE GREATEST luxury liner ever to ply the spaceways, an interstellar pleasure palace forever beyond the grasp of all but the galaxy's super-elite—beings whose wealth transcended description. Rumor had it that for the price of a single cocktail in one of the Queen's least-exclusive dining clubs, one might buy a starship; for the price of a meal, one could buy not only the starship, but the port in which it docked, and the factory that had built it. A being could not simply *pay for* a berth on the *Corellian Queen;* mere wealth would never suffice. To embark upon the ultimate journey into hedonistic excess, one first had to demonstrate that one's breeding and manners were as exquisite as would be the pain of paying one's bar bill. All of which made the *Corellian Queen* one of the most irresistible terrorist targets ever: who better to terrorize than the elite of the Elite, the Powers among the powerful, the greatest of the Great?

And so when some presumably unscrupulous routing clerk in the vast midreaches of the Nebula Line corporation quietly offered for sale, to select parties from Kindlabethia to Nar Shaddaa, a hint as to the route of the *Corellian Queen's* upcoming cruise, it attracted considerable interest.

Two pertinent facts remained concealed, however,

from the winning bidder. The first pertinent fact was that this presumably unscrupulous routing clerk was neither unscrupulous nor, in fact, a routing clerk, but was a skilled and resourceful agent of the intelligence service of the New Republic. The second pertinent fact was that the *Corellian Queen* was not cruising at all that season, having been replaced by a breakaway disposable shell built to conceal a substantial fraction of a starfighter wing, led by—as was customary in such operations—the crack pilots of Rogue Squadron.

IT WAS APPROXIMATELY THE MOMENT THAT R4-G7 squalled a proximity alarm through his X-wing's sensor panel and his HUD lit up with image codes for six TIE Defenders on his tail that Lieutenant Derek "Hobbie" Klivian, late of the Alliance to Restore Freedom to the Galaxy, currently of the New Republic, began to suspect that Commander Antilles's brilliant ambush had never been brilliant at all, not even a little, and he said so. In no uncertain terms. Stripped of its blistering profanity, his comment was "Wedge? This plan was *stupid*. You hear me? Stupid, stupid, stu*YOW*—!"

The *yow* was a product of multiple cannon hits that disintegrated his right dorsal cannon and most of the extended wing it had been attached to. This kicked his fighter into a tumble that he fought with both hands on the yoke and both feet kicking attitude jets and almost had under control until the pair of the Defenders closest on his tail blossomed into expanding spheres of flame and debris fragments. The twin shock fronts overtook him at exactly the wrong instant and sent him flipping end-over-end straight at another Defender formation streaking toward him head-on. Then tail-on, then head-on again, and so forth.

His ship's comlink crackled as Wedge Antilles's fighter flashed past him close enough that he could see the grin on the commander's face. *"That's 'stupid plan, sir,' Lieutenant."*

"I suppose you think that's funny."

"Well, if he doesn't," put in Hobbie's wingman, *"I sure do."*

"When I want *your* opinion, Janson, I'll dust your ship and scan for it in the wreckage." The skewed whirl of stars around his cockpit gave his stomach a yank that threatened to make the slab of smoked terrafin loin he'd had for breakfast violently reemerge. Struggling grimly with the controls, he managed to angle his ship's whirl just a hair, which let him twitch his ship's nose toward the four pursuing marauders as he spun. Red fire lashed from his three surviving cannons, and the Defenders' formation split open like an overripe snekfruit.

Hobbie only dusted one with the cannons, but the pair of proximity-fused flechette torpedoes he had thoughtfully triggered at the same time flared in diverging arcs to intercept the enemy fighters; these torpedo arcs terminated in spectacular explosions that cracked the three remaining Defenders like rotten snuffle eggs.

"Now, *that* was satisfying," he said, still fighting his controls to stabilize the crippled X-wing. "Eyeball soufflé!"

"Better watch it, Hobbie—keep that up, and somebody might start to think you can fly that thing."

"Are you *in* this fight, Janson? Or are you just gonna hang back and smirk while I do all the heavy lifting?"

"Haven't decided yet." Wes Janson's X-wing came out of nowhere, streaking in a tight bank across Hobbie's subjective vertical. *"Maybe I can lend a hand. Or, say, a couple torps."*

Two brilliant blue stars leapt from Janson's torpedo tubes and streaked for the oncoming TIEs.

"Uh, Wes?" Hobbie said, flinching. "Those weren't the flechette torps, were they?"

"Sure. What else?"

"Have you noticed that I'm currently having just a little trouble *maneuvering*?"

"What do you mean?" Janson asked as though honestly puzzled. Then, after a second spent watching Hobbie's ship tumbling helplessly directly toward his torpedoes' targets, he said, *"Oh. Uh . . . sorry?"*

The flechette torpedoes carried by Rogue Squadron had been designed and built specifically for this operation, and they had one primary purpose: to take out TIE Defenders.

The TIE Defender was the Empire's premier space-superiority fighter. It was faster and more maneuverable than the Incom T-65 (better known as the X-wing); faster even than the heavily modified and updated 65Bs of Rogue Squadron. The Defender was also more heavily armed, packing twin ion cannons to supplement its lasers, as well as dual-use launch tubes that could fire either proton torpedoes or concussion missiles. The shields generated by its twin Novaldex deflector generators were nearly as powerful as those found on capital ships. However, the Defenders were not equipped with particle shields, depending instead on their titanium-reinforced hull to absorb the impact of material objects.

Each proton torpedo shell had been loaded with thousands of tiny jagged bits of durasteel, packed around a core of conventional explosive. On detonation, these tiny bits of durasteel became an expanding sphere of shrapnel; though traveling with respectable velocity of their own, they were most effective when set off in the path of oncoming Defenders, because impact energy, after all, is determined by *relative* velocity. At starfighter combat speeds, flying into a cloud of durasteel pellets could transform one's ship from a starfighter into a very, very expensive cheese grater.

The four medial fighters of the oncoming Defender

formation hit the flechette cloud and just . . . shredded. The lateral wingers managed to bank off an instant before they would have been overtaken by two sequential detonations, as the explosion of one Defender's power core triggered the other three's cores an eyeblink later, so that the unfortunate Lieutenant Klivian was now tumbling directly toward a miniature plasma nebula that blazed with enough hard radiation to cook him like a bantha steak on an obsidian fry-rock at double noon on Tatooine.

"You're not gonna make it, Hobbie," Janson called. *"Punch out."*

"Oh, you'd *like* that, wouldn't you?" Hobbie snarled under his breath, still struggling grimly with the X-wing's controls. The fighter's tumble began to slow. "I've got it, Wes!"

"No, you don't! Punch out, Hobbie—PUNCH OUT!"

"I've got it—I'm gonna make it! I'm gonna—" He was interrupted by the final flip of his X-wing, which brought his nose into line with the sight of the leading edge of the spherical debris field expanding toward him at a respectable fraction of lightspeed, and Hobbie Klivian, acknowledged master of both profanity and obscenity, human and otherwise, not to mention casual vulgarities from a dozen species and hundreds of star systems, found that he had nothing to say except, "Aw, nuts."

He stood the X-wing on its tail, sublights blasting for a tangent, but he had learned long ago that of all the Rogues, he was the one who should know better than to trust his luck. He reached for the eject trigger.

Just as his hand found the trigger, the ship jounced and clanged as if he had his head trapped inside a Wookiee dinner gong at nightmeal. The metaphorical Wookiee cook must have been hungry, too, because the clanging went on and on and kept getting louder, and the eject still, mysteriously, didn't seem to be working at all. This mystery was solved, however, by the brief shriek of atmosphere through a ragged fist-sized hole in the X-wing's canopy. This hole was ragged because, Hobbie discovered, the fragment that had made this opening had been slowed by punching through the X-wing's titanium-alloy ventral armor. Not to mention the X-wing's control panel, where it had not only ripped away the entire eject trigger assembly, but had vaporized Hobbie's left hand.

He glared at his vacant wrist with more annoyance than shock or panic; instead of blood or cauterized flesh, his wrist jetted only sparks and smoke from overheated servomotors. He hadn't had a real left arm since sometime before Yavin.

Of more concern was the continuing shriek of escaping atmosphere, because he discovered that it was coming from his environment suit's nitroxy generator.

He thought, *Oh, this sucks.* After everything he had survived in the Galactic Civil War, he was about to be killed by a minor equipment malfunction. He amended his previous thought: *This* really *sucks.*

He didn't bother to say it out loud, because there wasn't enough air in his cockpit to carry the sound.

There being no other useful thing he could do with his severed left wrist, he jammed it into the hole in his canopy. His suit's autoseal plastered itself to the jagged edges, but the nitroxy generator didn't seem mollified; in fact, it was starting to feel like he had an unshielded fusion core strapped to his spine.

Oh, yeah, he thought. *The other hole.*

He palmed the cockpit harness's snap release, twisted, and stretched out his left leg, feeling downward with the toe of his boot. He found a hole—and the rising pressure sucked the entire boot right out the bottom of his fighter before the autoseal engaged to close that hole, too. He felt another impact or two down there, but he couldn't really tell if something might have ripped his foot off.

It had been a few years since he'd had his original left leg.

With the cockpit sealed, his nitroxy unit gradually calmed down, filling the space with a breathable atmosphere that smelled only faintly of scorched hair, and he began to think he might live through this after all. His only problem now was that he was deharnessed and stretched sideways in an extraordinarily uncomfortable twist that left him unable to even turn his head enough to see where he was going. "Arfour," he said quietly, "can you please get us back to the PRP?"

His current position did let him see, however, his astromech's response to the task of navigating toward the primary rendezvous point, which was a spit of gap sparks and a halo of sporadic electrical discharge from what was left of its turret dome. Which was slightly less than half.

He sighed. "Okay, ejection failure. And astromech damage. Crippled here," he said into his comm. "Awaiting manual pickup."

"Little busy right now, Hobbie. We'll get to you after we dust these TIEs."

"Take your time. I'm not going anywhere. Except, y'know, thataway. Slowly. Real slowly."

He spent the rest of the battle hoping for a bit of help from the Force when Wedge sent out the pickup detail. *Please,* he prayed silently, *please let it be Tycho. Or Nin, or Standro. Anyone but Janson.*

He continued this plea as a sort of meditation, kind of the way Luke would talk about this stuff: he closed his eyes and visualized Wedge himself showing up to tow his X-wing back to the jump point. After a while, he found this image unconvincing—somehow he was never that lucky—and so he cycled through the other Rogues, and when those began to bore him, he decided it'd be Luke himself. Or Leia. Or, say, Wynssa Starflare, who always managed to look absolutely stellar as the strong, independent damsel-sometimes-in-distress in those pre-war Imperial holodramas, because, y'know, as long as he was imagining something that was never gonna happen, he might as well make it entertaining.

It turned out to be entertaining enough that he managed to pass the balance of the battle drifting off to sleep with a smile on his face.

This smile lasted right up to the point where a particularly brilliant flash stabbed through his eyelids and he awoke, glumly certain that whatever had exploded right next to his ship was finally about to snuff him. But then there came another flash, and another, and with a painful twist of his body he was able to see Wes Janson's fighter cruising alongside, only meters away. He was also able to see the handheld imager Janson had pressed against his cockpit's canopy, with which Janson continued to snap picture after picture.

Hobbie closed his eyes again. He would have preferred the explosion.

"*Just had to get a few shots.*" Janson's grin was positively wicked. "*You look like some kind of weird cross between a starfighter pilot and a Batravian gumplucker.*"

Hobbie shook his head exhaustedly; dealing with Janson's pathetic excuse for a sense of humor always made him tired. "Wes, I don't even know what that is."

"*Sure you do, Hobbie. A starfighter pilot is a guy who flies an X-wing without getting blown up. Check the Basic Dictionary. Though I can understand how you'd get confused.*"

"No, I mean the—" Hobbie bit his lip hard enough that he tasted blood. "Um, Wes?"

"*Yeah, buddy?*"

"Have I told you today how much I really, really hate you?"

"*Oh, sure—your lips say 'I hate you,' but your eyes say—*"

"That someday I'll murder you in your sleep?"

Janson chuckled. "*More or less.*"

"It's all over, huh?"

"*This part is. Most of 'em got away.*"

"How many'd we lose?"

"*Just Eight and Eleven. But Avan and Feylis ejected clean. Nothing a couple weeks in a bacta tank won't cure. And then there's my Batravian gumplucker wingman . . .*"

"*You're* the wingman, knucklehead. Maybe I should say, wing*nut.*" Hobbie sighed again. "I guess Wedge is happy, anyway. Everything's proceeding according to plan . . ."

"*I HATE when you say that.*"

"Yeah? How come?"

"*Don't know. It just . . . gives me the whingeing jimmies. Let me get this tow cable attached, and you might as well sleep; it's a long cruise to the PRP.*"

"Suits me just fine," Hobbie said, closing his eyes again. "I have this dream I really want to get back to . . ."

"GOOD JOB, WEDGE." GENERAL LANDO CALRISSIAN, commander of Special Operations for the New Republic, nodded grave approval toward the flickering bluish holoform of Wedge Antilles that hovered a centimeter above his console. "No casualties?"

"*Nothing serious, General. Hobbie—Lieutenant Klivian—needs another left hand . . .*"

Lando smiled. "How many does that make, all told?"

"*I've lost count. How's it going on your end?*"

"Good and less than good." Lando punched up his readout of the tracking report. "Looks like our marauders are based in the Taspan system."

Wedge's brilliant plan had become brilliant entirely by necessity; the usual method of locating a hidden marauder base—subjecting a captured pilot or two to a neural probe—had turned out to be much more difficult than anyone could have anticipated. Shadowspawn seemed very determined to maintain his privacy; through dozens of raids over nearly two months, many deep inside Republic territory and costing thousands of civilian lives, not one of Shadowspawn's marauders had ever been taken alive.

This was more than a simple refusal to surrender, though the marauders had shown a distressing tendency, when they found themselves in imminent danger, to shout out words to the effect of *For Shadowspawn and the Empire! Forward the Restoration!* and blow themselves up. Forensic engineers examining wreckage of destroyed TIE Defenders hypothesized that the starfighters were equipped with some unexplained type of deadman interlock, which would destroy the ship—and obliterate the pilot—even if the pilot merely lost consciousness.

The brilliant part of Wedge's brilliant plan had been to conceal hundreds of thousands of miniature solid-state transponders among the flechettes inside Rogue Squadron's custom-made torpedoes, before giving the marauders a fairly decent pasting and letting the rest escape. Unlike ordinary tracking devices, these transponders gave off no signal of their own—thus requiring no power supply, and rendering them effectively undetectable. These transponders were entirely inert until triggered by a very specific subspace signal, which they then echoed in a very specific way. And since the only transponders of this very specific type in the entire galaxy were loaded in Rogue Squadron's torpedo tubes, drifting at the ambush point in deep space along the Corellian Run, and lodged in various parts of the armored hulls of a certain group of TIE Defenders, locating the system to which said Defenders had fled was actually not complicated at all.

Wedge's holoform took on a vaguely puzzled look. *"Taspan. Sounds familiar, but I can't place it . . ."*

"The Inner Rim, off the Hydian Way."

"That would be the less-than-good part."

"Yeah. No straight lanes in or out—and most of the legs run through systems still held by Imperials."

"Almost makes you wish for one of Palpatine's old planet-killers."

"Almost." Lando's smile had faded, and he didn't sound like he was joking. "The Empire had a weapons facility on Taspan II—it's where they tested their various designs of gravity-well projectors—"

"That's it!" The image snapped its fingers silently, the sound eliminated by the holoprojector's noise filter. *"The Big Crush!"*

Lando nodded. "The Big Crush."

"I heard there was nothing left at Taspan but an asteroid field, like the Graveyard of Alderaan."

"There's an inner planet—Taspan I is a minor resort world called Mindor. Not well known, but really beautiful; my parents had a summer house there when I was a kid."

"Any progress on this Shadowspawn character himself?"

"We've only managed to determine that no one by that name was ever registered as an Imperial official. Clearly an assumed identity."

"The guy's got to be some kind of nutjob."

"I doubt it. His choice of base is positively inspired; the debris from the Big Crush hasn't had time to settle into stable orbits."

"*So it is like the Graveyard of Alderaan.*"

"It's worse, Wedge. A *lot* worse."

Wedge's image appeared to be giving a low whistle; the holoprojector's noise filter screened it out. "*Sounds ugly. How are we supposed to get at them?*"

"You're not." Lando took a deep breath before continuing. "This is exactly the type of situation for which we developed the Rapid Response Task Force."

Wedge's image gave a slow, understanding nod. "*Hit 'em with our Big Stick, then. Slap 'em good and run like hell.*"

"It's the best shot we've got."

"*You're probably right; you usually are. But it'll sting, to not be there.*"

"Right enough. But we have other problems—and the RRTF is in very capable hands."

"*Got that right.*" Wedge suddenly grinned. "*Speaking of those capable hands, pass along my regards to General Skywalker, will you?*"

"I will do that, Wedge. I will indeed."

CHAPTER 2

THE SCHEMATIZED HOLOREPRESENTATION OF THE TA-
span system filled the entire command suite of the *Justice* with ghostly, translucent clouds of blue that ever so
slowly twisted and spun, merged and parted, moving
into and through each other. High in the center of the
room hung a dark disk, about the size of the last joint of
a human man's thumb: this represented Taspan itself.
The planet Mindor was a brilliant pinpoint that hung, at
this point in the simulation, about a meter in front of the
commanding general's nose. He barely saw it. Most of
his attention was consumed by glum contemplation of
the fact that he was the youngest in the room by at least
a decade.

The general in question was the newest, as well as the
youngest, general in the Combined Defense Forces of
the New Republic, popularly known as the NRDF. He
didn't look much like a general, or even a soldier. The
smooth curves of his face made him look even younger
than his twenty-four standard years; his sandy hair,
streaked blond by radiation from dozens of different
stars, was still shaggier than military-strict, and instead
of a general's battle dress he wore a simple, close-fitting
flight suit, like the starfighter pilot he had recently been.
Only the rank plaque on his chest marked him as a general, and only the remote, shuttered reserve behind his

clear blue eyes showed the price he had paid to earn his rank.

His unconventional appearance extended even to his sidearm, which was as far from an officer's blaster pistol as one could possibly imagine; no general had gone armed thus since the end of the Clone Wars.

He carried a lightsaber.

Seven of his twelve captains had had their own commands before the Battle of Yavin—three of them had been commanding ships all the way back in the Clone Wars, before he was even *born*—and Admiral Kalback, the fleet commander, was a distal pod-cousin of Ackbar or somesuch, and was at least sixty-something, not to mention T'Chttrk, who didn't even *know* how old she was, because her people, the insectoid T'kkrpks, hadn't started calculating time in Standard until their Great Reconciliation about a hundred years ago, at which time T'Chttrk had long been an adult, and a hereditary officer in their planet's defense forces.

Ordinarily being the youngest around didn't bother the new general at all. He barely even noticed. What bothered him this time was that all these seasoned veterans, among the best tactical-engagement commanders the New Republic had ever had, were all so deferential to his presumed wisdom that they wouldn't even *argue* with him.

Because he was a Jedi, they all assumed that he actually knew what he was doing.

If only it were true . . .

Right now, all he *really* knew was that he should never have let Han talk him into this.

"LUKE, LUKE," HAN HAD SAID, ARM DRAPED AROUND Luke's shoulders, "this general business, there's nothing to it." He probably thought Luke couldn't see that sly half grin of his. "If *I* could pull it off, you won't have any problems at all."

"If it's such an easy job, why'd you resign?"

"Better things to do, buddy." Han rolled his eyes at Leia. "The Princess's pretty important, but not so important the New Republic can afford having a full general play chauffeur and bodyguard."

"Bodyguard," Leia sniffed. "If you're my bodyguard, how come *I* keep having to rescue *you*?"

"It's how you prove you still love me." He grinned at her and turned back to Luke. "Seriously, Luke, you can do this. You're easily . . . uh, *almost* as smart as me— and you're a *lot* smarter than, say, Lando. All you've got to do is keep your mouth shut and listen to your officers. Don't let them squabble, and always pretend you know what to do next. Simple. Tell him, Chewie."

Chewbacca, reclining with hands behind his massive head on the couch by the gaming station, hadn't even opened his eyes. "Aroowrowr. Regharrr."

"Oh, *you're* a lot of help. Luke, ignore him anyway— he hates officers."

"I'm not exactly sure I like being one myself."

The offer of a general's commission had come as a complete surprise to Luke, and not a very pleasant one. A couple of months after the defeat of the Ssi-Ruuk, Luke had gone to Supreme Commander Ackbar and requested to be relieved of his duties as a flight officer. He'd been feeling for some time, he explained, that he might be of greater service to the New Republic as a Jedi than as a wing commander. Ackbar, canny old soldier that he was, had countered with an offer of joint command over the new Rapid Response Task Force that was being formed: a fleet-sized flying squad, able to bring military power against any point in the galaxy within a couple of days. "If you really wish to serve the New Republic, young Skywalker, this is the job for you. I suspect that your Jedi insight will be of more use in directing tactical operations than in meditation on the ways of the Force."

Luke had had no answer for this; he could only ask for some time to think it over. Faced with a decision that might very well determine how he would spend the rest of his life, he had retreated to the place that felt the most like home, and talked to the only people in the galaxy in whose company he could still, even now, really just be himself.

So he was stuck trying to explain how he felt to Leia and Han and Chewbacca as they all sat around the passenger compartment of the *Millennium Falcon*.

"It's *not* simple," Luke said. "I'm pretty sure nothing is simple anymore. Do you know they're producing *holothrillers* about me? And not, y'know, documentaries about the Death Star assault or anything—they're just making stuff up!"

"Yeah, I've seen 'em." Han grinned as he fished a handheld holoplayer out of the dejarik console and tossed it onto the table. "Bought it a couple months ago. Gives me something to do while I'm waiting for Leia to wrap up negotiations somewhere or just, y'know, finish her hair."

"No hair jokes, Solo," Leia said. "I'm not kidding."

Luke picked up the player and thumbed the controls over to the title page. *Luke Skywalker and the Dragons of Tatooine*. "Oh, will you *look* at this junk?" He shook his head disgustedly and tossed it back to Han, who snagged it neatly from the air. "That's what I mean. It's all—just so *stupid*."

"What, there's no dragons on Tatooine?"

"Sure," Luke said. "Krayt dragons. And they're dangerous enough, especially if they catch you alone— but *look* at that illustration! Not only have I never fought one with my lightsaber from bantha-back, I can flat-out *guarantee* that krayt dragons do *not* breathe fire!"

"Come on, take it easy, Luke." Han hefted the reader, smiling fondly. "These're for kids, y'know? And I gotta tell you, some of 'em are actually pretty good."

"Especially the ones about *you*," Leia muttered darkly.

Luke stared. "Are you putting me on?"

Han shrugged, flushing a little—but just a little; he was constitutionally immune to embarrassment. "You're not the only hero of the Republic, y'know."

"Han—"

"Ask him how much he gets paid," Leia said.

"You get *paid*?"

"Hey, I'm not a Jedi." Han's hands came up as if he was half expecting Luke to throw something. "I, ah, worked out a licensing deal with a couple holoshow producers. After Yavin. You understand."

"I do?"

"If he does," Leia said, "maybe he can explain it to *me*."

"It was Lando's idea." Han was starting to sound defensive. "All right, look, I got into this deal before I really knew what I was doing. The stuff's pretty bad, but it's harmless. *Han Solo and the Pirates of Kessel*, *Han Solo in the Lair of the Space Slugs . . .*"

"It's *not* harmless." Luke set his jaw. "Have you seen the one they call *Luke Skywalker and the Jedi's Revenge*?"

Han looked dubious. "I thought Jedi don't get into revenge."

"They don't—I mean, *we* don't. I don't know *what* I mean. They have me *slaughtering* my own *father*—to *avenge* the death of Palpatine! It's just—so *sick*."

"Take it easy, Luke. So the writers spice things up a

little. What's the harm? A little wham-bam just makes you look tough, you know?"

"That's not how I want to look."

"People *need* heroes—and stories like these are the way heroes *become* heroes."

"I thought heroes became heroes by doing something heroic."

"You know what I mean."

"Yeah, I do. And that's part of my whole problem. Everybody's *watching* me. It's like they're trying to figure out who I'll turn out to be. And trying to figure out a way to turn a profit on it."

Han spread his hands. "That's what keeps the galaxy spinning, buddy."

"Maybe it does," Luke said. "But I don't have to be part of it. Maybe that's what feels so wrong about being a general. It's like, I don't know, like I'm pushing myself forward. Like somehow I talked Ackbar into this so I could go on being larger than life."

"You *are* larger than life, Luke. That's what I keep trying to tell you."

"Being a general . . . sending other people into places where they have to take someone's life or get killed themselves . . ." Luke shook his head again. "Playing the hero when you're in charge just gets a lot of people hurt."

"Who's playing?"

"Luke, this commission is a wonderful opportunity, and not just for you," Leia put in. "Force powers aren't the only kind of power, and there are ways of helping people that are a lot more effective than hitting something with a lightsaber. As a Jedi, you might save the occasional, well, princess in distress or some such, but as a general, you can save *thousands* of lives. Millions. The Defense Force *needs* you, Luke."

"I can't beat you in an argument, Leia. I'm no politician, and the ag school in Anchorhead didn't have a debate team. But—I'm a Jedi. I'm *the* Jedi. Becoming a general . . . it just doesn't *feel* right."

"Well, y'know, I was only a kid at the time," Han said slowly, "and working for Shrike gave me, y'know, more *pressing* concerns than following the news, if you get me—but I seem to recall that your friend Kenobi was a general himself, back in the Clone Wars."

"I know. But he hardly talked about it."

"He was always modest," Leia said. "Obi-Wan was part of so many of the stories my fath—my, ah, adoptive father used to tell. He was a great hero of the Republic. That's why I turned to him when my cover was blown."

Luke shook his head. "It's just not the way I've always seen myself spending my life."

"Oh, is *that* all?" Han said. "C'mon, Luke—*nobody* ends up living their lives the way they expect."

"No?" Luke said. "I can think of this one guy—got his own ship, resigned his commission, got the military off his back, pretty much does whatever he wants to do, mostly just flying around the galaxy with his copilot rescuing princesses and such, accountable to no one but himself—"

"Accountable to *no* one? Are you kidding me?" Han looked appalled. "Luke, have you ever *met* your sister? Luke Skywalker of Tatooine, let me introduce Princess Leia Organa of *whouf*—!"

"Of the Extremely Sharp Elbow," Leia finished for him, having delivered the sharp elbow in question rather briskly to his short ribs.

"Yeah, okay, peace, huh?" Han rubbed his side, a wounded expression on his face. "All kidding aside, Luke, think about it. If you and me both had ended up living the lives we were expecting, we might still have flown at Yavin."

"You think?"

"Sure," Han said. "As TIE pilots. Working for *Vader*."

Luke looked away.

"Sometimes, things not going according to plan is a *gift*," Han said. "You gotta go with the flow, y'know? I mean, trust in the Force, right? Would the Force have brought you this chance if you weren't supposed to take it?"

"I don't know," Luke admitted.

"Why don't you ask Kenobi himself, the next time he shows up with that Force-ghost thing of his?"

"He's not a *ghost*—"

"Whatever. You know what I mean."

Luke shook his head, sighing. "He . . . doesn't come around anymore. It's been weeks since I've seen him. Like he's drifting away. Too far away to make contact."

"And maybe that means something," Leia said. Luke gave her a sharp look, and she replied with a shrug, "I know less about being a Jedi than you do about being a politician . . . but don't you think that your indecision itself signifies that you've been, well . . . leaning the wrong way? I mean, don't you usually just sort of . . . *know*?"

"Yeah," Luke said quietly. "Yeah, usually I do."

A saying of Yoda's came back to him so vividly he could almost hear the Master's voice: *If far from the Force you find yourself, trust you can that it is not the Force which moved.*

"I suppose," Luke said reluctantly, "it doesn't have to be a *career* . . ."

A broad grin rolled halfway onto Han's face. "You're in?"

Luke nodded. "I guess I am."

Han clapped him on the shoulder. "Thanks, buddy! You're the greatest!"

"Thanks for what?"

He turned his grin all the way on. "Ackbar swore if I

didn't talk you into this, he was gonna make *me* do it. *Han Solo and the Rapid Response Task Force* just doesn't have the right ring, you know?"

"Here is Mindor's effective gravitic radius." Commander Thavish, the task force's intelligence coordinator, was the next-youngest guy in the room, and he had five years on *Han,* let alone Luke. He keyed his thumbstick, and the pinpoint of Mindor grew into a sphere roughly a decimeter in diameter. "Standard englobement puts our Double Sevens here."

Three new pinpoints formed an equilateral triangle around the planet, roughly parallel to the system's plane of the ecliptic. The fourth and fifth pinpoints appeared above and below the plane. The five Double Sevens were the strike force's entire complement of CC-7700/E interdiction cruisers, each capable of projecting a simulated gravity well out to several hundred planetary diameters. When Thavish triggered the representations of the DS's gravitic influence, the overlapping spheres of effect filled an area roughly five light-minutes across—about ninety million kilometers—in which hyperdrives simply would not function.

"While the E series' weapons upgrades give the Double Sevens substantial point-defense capability, each of them will require a full squadron fighter screen, because we just don't have adequate intel on target forces. We could find ourselves facing anything from a few dozen to several thousand of those TIE Defenders; the records captured during the Spirana operation indicate that there are still over ten thousand verified-production Defenders unaccounted for. Plus, of course, we can't say for certain that the remaining loyalist territories contain no active production facilities. Not to mention that he might have Interceptors or other non-FTL fighters based in-system."

Captain Trent, commander of the *Regulator,* leaned closer. "And capital ships?"

"Shadowspawn's forces have never employed capital ships."

"Doesn't mean he ain't got any."

"Yes, sir. But there are elements of the system that suggest we will be facing primarily starfighters. It's just that there's no way to guess how many."

T'Chttrk chittered and clicked a question. Her D-series protocol droid, D-P4M, inclined its elegantly tungsten-coated head and murmured, "The commander respectfully requests to be informed of any *good* news."

"Commander," Thavish said, "that *is* the good news." He manipulated his thumbstick again. "The bad news looks like this."

The translucent clouds that had drifted through the simulation thickened as though they could become actually tangible. "These represent our best long-range scans of the debris field from the destruction of Taspan II. The Big Crush, as it is called, resulted from an accident at an Imperial testing facility for a new type of gravity-well projector. The planet was entirely pulverized, producing debris that ranges from pinhole micrometeors to asteroids several kilometers in diameter. This occurred only four Standard years ago; the debris has not yet settled into stable orbits. Worse, the planets were in conjunction at the time of the Big Crush, and Mindor was the inner planet of the two. So as the chunks of Taspan II spiral inward toward the star, Mindor's own gravity has captured great masses of them into eccentric, unstable orbits around itself."

Admiral Kalback leaned forward, chin palps twitching. "And there is no way to plot these orbits?"

"Commander, even if we could scan them all—which we can't—no computer could reliably plot their paths; even the word *orbit,* I'm afraid, suggests a much more settled situation than we'll be facing. They are constantly interacting with each other in every conceivable way, from gravitic effects to outright collision. If you'll direct your attention to these figures—"

Each individual cloud now sported glowing numbers that drifted right along with them. The numbers slowly changed, creeping up or down; when clouds drifted together, the overlap zones produced numbers of their own—higher ones. "These numbers represent our best estimates of the material density of each major debris cloud. Each figure reflects the number of tactically significant objects per cubic kilometer. By tactically significant, we mean large enough to produce substantial damage to a fleet ship, in spite of defensive fire and particle shielding."

Captain Patrell, the grizzled Corellian commander of the *Wait a Minute*, swore harshly enough that at least four of the other officers flinched. "Some of those numbers are in the *hundreds*!"

"Yes, sir."

The captains exchanged grim looks. The prospect of bringing cruisers that were themselves a respectable fraction of a cubic kilometer into that kind of asteroid storm was bleak.

"Let me put this another way." Another twist on the thumbstick produced new figures in the clouds. "These new numbers represent the estimated probability of catastrophic impact—one that results in significant degradation of combat function and crew."

Luke let his eyes drift shut. "Significant degradation of combat function. That means people dying, doesn't it? Ships crippled or destroyed?"

"Yes, sir."

"Then say so."

"Sir?"

"That's an order, Thavish. No euphemisms." He reflected sadly that five years ago, he hadn't known, really, what *people dying* meant—his first real taste of that had been the charred corpses of Uncle Owen and Aunt Beru, leaking smoke up into the Tatooine twilight . . .

He'd learned a lot since then. Not all of it was about being a Jedi.

"Yes, sir. Um, is this a Jedi thing, sir?"

"No," Luke said. "It's a General Skywalker thing. When you talk about someone as a set of degradable capabilities instead of a person, it's too easy to think about him that way, too."

"Yes, sir." Thavish turned back to the holoimage. "We used the Double Sevens as our baseline, as they're roughly median size for the task force. A DS at *this* point, for example, will have a one point eight five percentage chance of a catastrophic impact—"

"That's less than one in fifty!" Captain Patrell shook his head, chuckling. "For a minute, you had me scared!"

Luke said, eyes still closed, "What's the time frame?"

"Sir?"

"One point eight five percent in *how long*?"

"Oh, yes. That percentage chance is on, well, on insertion. That is, uh, instantly."

Captain Patrell stopped chuckling.

Luke nodded. "And after that?"

"Well—the statistical modeling is complex. It's a sliding scale, more or less; assuming you're not instantly, uh, destroyed, we have to calculate the—"

"Let's say, an hour."

When the numbers came up, the expressions got even more grim. After one hour, the probability was running over twenty percent. "So, basically," Luke murmured, "you're telling us that one hour into this operation, we'll have lost two ships. If the enemy does nothing at all."

"Well, the math is a bit more complicated than—"

"Basically."

Thavish nodded apologetically. "Basically. Yes."

"It's a graveyard," Patrell said. "It's where capital ships go to die."

"The Taspan system," Thavish said, "is an almost perfect starfighter base. In a starfighter, you're not only a smaller target for the asteroids, but you're maneuverable enough to dodge them. But to *hold* Shadowspawn there, we need the interdictors. Otherwise his entire force can simply vanish into hyperspace. But our interdictors are so vulnerable we can't afford to bring them in."

"Lord Shadowspawn," Luke murmured. "Not a stupid man. He knew what he was doing when he picked Mindor."

He looked up at the ceiling and took a deep breath, wishing mightily that he could steal an hour or two to rest and meditate and try to summon some of that Jedi insight he was supposed to have, but there just wasn't time. If only Ben—or Master Yoda, or even his father—would phase in right now with a word of wisdom . . . but whatever parts of them remained active in the Force apparently had business elsewhere. Just as they'd had for months now.

No insight from the Force. All he had for insight was his own.

It had better be enough.

He sighed. "Well, we can't wait them out, and we can't whittle them down. We can't even fight a pitched battle. That only leaves one option."

Admiral Kalback nodded. "Overwhelming force. Shock and awe," he said.

Commander Thavish tilted his head considering. "It might actually save lives, on balance. Ours, at least. Maybe even theirs. If we never give them a chance to think they can fight their way out, they might just sur-render."

"Saving lives is swell, if we can. Winning is more important," Luke said. "If we let Shadowspawn's forces escape, they could scatter. Go on the run—break up into small, independent units. We know better than anyone in the galaxy how much damage that kind of decentralized guerrilla insurgency can do—it's how we brought down the Empire. This might be our last chance to engage Shadowspawn force-on-force."

Luke looked around the table, meeting each commander's eyes in turn. "Every one of you needs to understand this. We hold nothing back except a small reserve force, to cover our exertion if things go bad. It's full commitment. All or nothing."

One by one, the commanders answered his stare with grim acknowledgment.

"All right," Luke said. "I want tactical readiness reports within the hour. We move in three."

CHAPTER 3

AEONA CANTOR LAY FLAT ON THE JAGGED HILLTOP, squinting through electrobinoculars that had gone foggy, their front lenses scored by too much exposure to the clouds of windblown grit that passed for atmosphere here on Mindor. The hunks of broken lava around her masked her silhouette, and she didn't have to worry about thermal imaging, because the rock around her was warmed by the noontime heat, and the jigsaw hunks of lava glued to her survival suit made perfect camouflage against visible-light sensors. All of which were necessary factors in her position, which was less than ten kilometers from a huge smoking volcanic dome.

The fact that this volcanic dome was huge and smoking was of no interest to her at all; she cared only about the double ring of planetary-defense turbolaser towers that surrounded it, and the gnat clouds of TIE fighters that streamed in and out of every visible cavern mouth on the mountainside.

Which was exactly how it had looked every time she'd gotten a glimpse.

She scowled, pushing a lock of burnt-orange hair off her forehead, and dialed the electrobinoculars up to a higher magnification. "I don't *get* it," she said. "Tripp, is he *sure* about the jammers?"

From a few meters below and behind her, a man who wore a similar outfit of lava-adorned survival suit answered with a shrug. "All I can tell you is what Boakie tells me. Subspace is clear. If we wanted, we could send a signal all the way to the Trigaskian Blur."

"Why would Shadowspawn turn off his subspace jammers? Right after a raid. Doesn't make sense."

"How would I know? Better you should ask *him*."

"If I ever get the chance," she muttered through her teeth, "we'll have other things to talk about."

"I *got* something!" This shout came from farther down the hillside, within the mouth of the cave where the rest of her men waited. "Hey, Aeona! Hey, I got something!"

Aeona flattened herself into the rocks and hissed, "Tripp! Tell that idiot to keep his bloody voice down!"

"What for? It's not like there's anybody around to hear."

"You're gonna argue with me?"

"Aw, Aeona, come *on*—"

"The blackshells could have seeded these hills with sonic probes. There might be a ground patrol. Do you know how the Melters keep finding us? Me neither. Till we do, the next guy who speaks above a whisper gets my blaster barrel across the face."

"Aeona—"

"And the next guy who *argues* with me is gonna get it up his—"

"All right, all right. Shee, relax, huh?" Tripp let himself half slide, half scramble down the hillside toward the cave.

Aeona jammed the electrobinoculars back against her face. She'd relax when she was long gone from this stinking ball of rock.

From behind her came the scrabble of boots on lava

as Tripp worked his way back up the slope. "It was nothin'," he said.

"What kind of nothing?"

Tripp waved a hand disgustedly. "A nothing kind of nothing. Just a couple pings."

Aeona's scowl deepened. "Pings?"

"Yeah—some kind of signal, and an echo, like a transponder response—"

"I *know* what a ping is," she said through her teeth. "Where did the initializer come from?"

Tripp shrugged. "Outside the system, prob'ly. A HoloNet repeater or something."

"And the response came from *here*?"

"Well, yeah. Um . . . how'd you know that?"

She was already backing herself out of her position. She scrambled down the slope. "Up! Everybody up!"

People in the lava-glued survival suits scrambled to their feet from all around the little cave.

"Lock and load, people." Aeona started moving through them toward her scout bike. "I want every speeder, swoop, and skimmer in the air in five. No supplies except weapons, power cells, and medikits. Full alert."

"Alert?" Tripp said as he scrambled after her. "What's going on?"

"You think it's a coincidence that after months, those jammers go down just now? Just in time to let through a transponder ping that's probably coming from some kind of tracker?"

Tripp frowned. "What, it's a trap?"

"Not for us. And we need to make sure we don't step into it." Aeona pulled her blaster and checked its charge, then spun it around her finger and let it slip smoothly back into her holster. For an instant, she smiled. But only for an instant. "We'll wait and watch, but we need to be ready to move."

* * *

GROUP CAPTAIN KLICK STOOD STIFFLY AT ATTENTION, flight helmet gleaming black beneath his black-armored left arm. Oblivious to the pleas and curses, sobs and occasional screams from the captives in the Sorting Center behind him, he faced a huge slab of durasteel that sealed a starfighter-sized archway carved from the wall of this volcanic cavern. Soon enough, the slab would pull aside, and a Pawn would come to beckon, and Klick would be ushered into the Presence of Lord Shadowspawn.

To suffer the consequences of his failure.

Despite the durasteel gray of his little remaining hair, the deeply weathered creases of his face, and the smear of burn scar that rumpled his cheek and swept upward over the remains of his left ear, when he took off that helmet anyone who knew stormtroopers knew they were looking at something special. Klick was one of the original Fetts, a veteran of the Clone Wars from Geonosis to the Jedi Rebellion, and he was proud of it. This was his sole point of vanity; he never minded the slightly silly sound of his call sign, hung on him by a humor-challenged Jedi Padawan some twenty-five years ago. "Klick" was short for "kilometer," a reference to his crèche identifier of TP—Trooper Pilot—1000.

The vast cavern around him had been expanded and shaped from the local meltmassif stone before being fusion-formed into a vault of black glass. Its walls and roof glimmered with cold green highlights, reflected from the gently bobbing flock of repulsor lightglobes that floated ten meters above the polished floor. Scattered across this floor were clots of prisoners, standing or sitting or lounging in as much comfort as could be had on the bare cold floor.

The prisoners were a motley group, from beggars to aristocrats, thieves to Rebel officers. These prisoners were the actual targets of the raids Klick's Defender wings had been conducting throughout the Mid Rim these past months, taking three or four here, a half-dozen there, never so many that the Rebels might suspect. The loot taken on these raids—and the destruction left behind—was no more than camouflage, so that these prisoners would be written off by their families, their friends, and their respective planetary governments as missing and presumed dead in the resulting mass slaughter.

So that these prisoners could be permanently disappeared.

Disappeared here, to Mindor. To the Sorting Center of Lord Shadowspawn.

Behind Klick, four or five of the Pawns drifted among the prisoners, hems of their long robes trailing behind them. Here and there a Pawn might stop, the red-limned shadow of his broad crescent headgear falling across this prisoner or that. These Pawns never spoke, and their expressions never changed—*couldn't* change, as their faces were only holomasks projected by their Crowns—but sometimes a pale hand would extend from a darkly voluminous sleeve. If the prisoner was lucky, a slicing gesture would bring a quick burst of blaster-fire to the back. If the prisoner was less lucky, a long pale finger, laid upon his head, would indicate that this prisoner had been elected to the Pawns.

From the sudden whine of a neural stunner in the cavern behind him, Klick judged that another captive had just been so elected. Sure enough: shortly a pair of Pawns approached, dragging between them an unconscious human youth of fifteen or sixteen Standard years. The slab of durasteel retreated, then slid silently aside, revealing the fusion-formed corridor beyond. Klick remained at attention, without the slightest flicker of expression, as the Pawns dragged the youth past him, through the archway and down the corridor.

He had been waiting, at attention, ever since the Defender wing of his starfighter group had limped home from its disastrous attack on the false *Corellian Queen*. He was fully prepared to wait all day. All the next, too. If necessary, Klick was willing to wait all week.

This was not from fear of Shadowspawn's anger; the Lord of the Shadow Throne was no lunatic like the assassin Vader, to slaughter a loyal subordinate in a fit of pique. What held Klick in place was nothing more nor less than a passionate desire to be worthy of the trust Shadowspawn had placed in him. If doing so would help advance the Great Cause, Klick would stand at attention until he starved to death.

Group Captain Klick had been Squadron Leader Klick nearly a year before, on that black day when Lord Vader's treason, and his cowardly murder of Palpatine the Great, had allowed the Rebel Alliance to escape the trap at the moons of Endor. The destruction of the second Death Star had been nothing compared with the shattering dislocation Imperial forces had suffered at the loss of their beloved Emperor. Without the leadership of the great man, the Imperial military had splintered into competing factions squabbling over whatever scraps of territory could be secured by local Moffs or regional Admiralty commanders. Conflicts had smoldered, and even some skirmishes had flared, Imperial against Imperial.

Then had come Shadowspawn.

No one knew his real name. No one knew from whence he'd come. But it was clear to all who so much as heard his voice that this was no mere Moff, no general or admiral with delusions of Imperial grandeur. To be received into Shadowspawn's presence was as awe-inspiring as standing before the Emperor himself.

When rumor had begun to spark throughout the Imperial regions of a new leader, a man of mystery with the cunning and charisma of a second coming of Palpatine,

Klick had been promoted to wing commander in the service of Admiral Kraven, the self-styled warlord of a Mid Rim stellar cluster, and sent with his squadrons to destroy this upstart. But the upstart in question had received Klick's fighter wing with welcome instead of combat . . . and greeted him with an array of authentic command codes, even *Palpatine's own secret codes* that had been buried in the deep core programming Klick had received in the crèche on Kamino. Shadowspawn claimed to have been handpicked by Palpatine to be his steward, to hold the throne in trust for Palpatine's chosen heir; Palpatine had given these codes to him so that every loyal clone would know Shadowspawn for the galaxy's rightful, if temporary, ruler.

It had been Shadowspawn who had revealed to Klick the tale of Vader's treason, the monster's cowardly murder of his longtime friend and benefactor, a tale so dark and gruesome that even now, Klick shuddered to think of it. Why, Vader would have died years ago, without the caring and generosity of the great man he would eventually assassinate; it was well known among the clones that Darth Vader had been a charity case, his life saved free of any charge at one of Palpatine's great legacies, the Emperor Palpatine Surgical Reconstruction Center on Coruscant. Palpatine's caring and generosity had not only saved Vader's life, but had gifted him with mechanical arms and legs, remaking a helpless cripple into perhaps the most feared and powerful man the galaxy had ever known.

It was all just a small part of the greatest holothriller Klick had ever seen, the one Shadowspawn himself had created and was now circulating among the systems still loyal to the Imperial Dream: *Luke Skywalker and the Jedi's Revenge.*

The holothriller had shown in vivid detail how Vader's madness had grown with his unholy ambition, how the Dark Lord had pretended to play along with Palpatine's quest to rescue the last remaining child of the Jedi hero, Anakin Skywalker, from the evil web of lies in which the Rebels had snared him. How on the day when Luke Skywalker had finally stood before Palpatine on the bridge of the second Death Star, when the Emperor had declared his great love for Skywalker's father— who, as all honest clones knew, had been the Emperor's most beloved protégé until his tragic, untimely death in the Jedi Rebellion—Vader's mind had finally snapped.

It was Vader, as *Luke Skywalker and the Jedi's Revenge* made so painfully clear, who had always secretly dreamed of being Palpatine's successor. It was Vader, in his madness, who had believed *himself* to be Palpatine's beloved protégé; he had even tried to bend young Skywalker's mind to evil, to recruit the virtuous young Jedi in his treasonous plans, but young Skywalker had roundly rejected Vader's insane machinations. And so, on that dark day among the moons of Endor, when Palpatine had revealed to young Skywalker that he, and he alone, the son of Palpatine's beloved companion, the child of the sole Jedi to remain loyal to the Senate and the Chancellor during the Jedi Rebellion, was to be the new Emperor, Vader could no longer control his rage. With a roar of mindless fury, he'd attacked like a blood-mad rancor.

As the innocent young Skywalker had looked on in horror, the black-armored monster had fallen upon the frail old man who had once befriended him. Only after Palpatine had been mortally wounded had young Skywalker snapped from his daze. With righteous fury, he had risen up against the most feared fighter in the galaxy, and had struck down the black-armored assassin, the murderer of his late father's greatest friend. But it was too late to save Palpatine; poor Skywalker could only avenge the great man's death.

Though Klick knew that what he'd seen was only a dramatic reenactment, there was something so *real* about it, so powerful—a truth greater than any mere facts.

It was Luke Skywalker's grief and guilt at his failure to save the Emperor, Shadowspawn had explained, that had driven him back into the grasp of the Rebels. Skywalker believed that he deserved no better than to be just another outlaw among the thieves, pirates, and murderers of the Rebel Alliance.

"And this is what I ask of you, Wing Commander," Lord Shadowspawn had said to Klick on that day. *"That you join me in my quest to fulfill the dying wish of our Beloved Emperor: to heal the broken heart of the son of the last true Jedi hero, and to put Luke Skywalker, Palpatine's chosen heir, in his rightful place as the absolute ruler of our Galactic Empire."*

Klick had been proud to surrender his forces to the great Lord Shadowspawn's epic struggle to bring the shattered galaxy together again; there was no greater honor he could imagine than to lay down his life for Palpatine's chosen heir, and Lord Shadowspawn had rewarded his devotion with promotion and command of his own fighter group. He only hoped that he could somehow survive the coming struggle, that someday he might have the privilege to kneel and pledge his service in person to the newly anointed emperor.

Now, far beyond the archway along the fusion-formed corridor of stone, one of the Pawns paused and turned, as though he had somehow sensed Klick's thought. A pale hand came up and beckoned.

Klick followed them into the Election Center.

This was not Klick's first visit to the Election Center; he knew what to expect. He'd tried to train himself not to look at the Elect. He'd tried to school himself not to hear them. He'd tried to discipline his mind to think of the Elect as the privileged, the chosen, the luckiest of the lucky, yanked from despair into this once-in-a-millennium opportunity to serve the Great Cause.

Tried, and failed.

Every time he entered this place, the Elect were not invisible, nor inaudible, and he'd never be able to think of them as lucky. They were always, and would always be, terrified victims, helplessly screaming or sobbing or pleading for their lives, sentient sacrifices tragically necessary to Shadowspawn's plan for Skywalker's eventual victory.

The Pawns ahead of him dragged the stunned prisoner to a vacant Pawning Table: a slab-like pedestal of stone, molded from the local meltmassif. They let the prisoner slump over its edge as they drew their neural stunners; a short burst from each into the surface of the Pawning Table altered the electrocrystalline structure of the meltmassif, liquefying a coffin-sized area in the smooth stone into a fluid that had the consistency of cold barkmeal. Then the Pawns lifted the prisoner onto the table, pressing his limp body into the liquid stone, which flowed around his limbs until only his head was exposed. They carefully supported his chin as the stone resolidified around him, molding the hardening rock up along his neck and around his jaw.

Then a burst of precisely calibrated radiation flash-burned off all the hair on his head and face, and the Pawns produced a pair of self-cauterizing laser bone saws and began to cut away the top of his skull.

This was not what produced the screaming, sobbing, and pleading that characterized the Pawning process; the Elect were never even awake enough to experience the messy details of having the upper hemispheres of their skulls removed. The screaming, sobbing, and pleading would begin after a particular Elect had awakened, as a series of neural probes selectively stimulated differing nerve clusters of their exposed brains. The anguish, however, was short-lived; soon the neural probes would identify the precise location of, say, the tickle reflex, and the screams would instantly be replaced by giggling. Shortly, stimulation of olfactory neurons would have the giggling Elect asking for a slice of the grilled bantha steak he believed himself to be smelling, and perhaps a mug of that delightfully rich hot chocolate that he was quite certain someone must have been brewing just out of sight.

And at each and every point, from the nerves that registered the color blue to the nerves that controlled the curl of the Elect's toes, the Pawns would place a tiny crystal of meltmassif, the same stone as the Table. The same stone as the entire Election Center, and the vault outside. And after the skull was replaced, these crystals would grow into a gem-like latticework spreading throughout the Elect's brain cavity.

Every Pawn had a head full of diamonds.

Klick did not know what criteria might be used to choose the Elect. Nor did he comprehend the subtle gradations of rank among the Pawns, why and how some seemed to be in charge at some times, and at other times seemed to take the orders of those they had recently commanded. All he knew was that once an Elect had been fitted with his crescent Crown and released as a full Pawn, he was instantly the superior of any trooper or pilot or officer. His slightest gesture was to be obeyed as though it had proceeded from Lord Shadowspawn himself. Very few of the Pawns ever spoke, but some peculiar eloquence in their gestures could make their orders instantly clear to even the dimmest nat-born trooper; Klick suspected it was some arcane use of the Force.

He'd never understood the Force, though he did not doubt its existence; he'd seen the Force used in action by countless Jedi during the Clone Wars. He had no interest in understanding. He'd been bred not for insight, but for obedience. He was content to allow the Force to remain a convenient mystery: one he could use to explain whatever he might find otherwise inexplicable.

Like, for example, how Lord Shadowspawn was able to shape meltmassif seemingly with the power of his will alone. A simple electromagnetic burst was enough to temporarily break down the curious crystalline structure of the rock, but that could not explain how, when Shadowspawn was near and set his will upon it, the meltmassif seemed almost *alive*. Klick had witnessed it more than once: Shadowspawn would stretch forth his hand, and the stone would flow and shape itself into whatever fantastical form might suit the Lord's wildest desire.

Ahead, another Pawn beckoned. This Pawn stood at a blank slate-gray wall of meltmassif, but as Klick marched toward it, the Pawn swept a hand as though to usher him on, and the stone dimpled, drawing away from him in a bubble that became a shaft a few meters long. Klick entered the shaft without hesitation, and didn't even blink as the stone flowed together to seal itself behind him, cutting off all light along with the possibility of retreat. He kept marching through the absolute darkness without breaking stride, trusting that the stone would continue to open before him and close behind.

And if the stone should fail to part before him, should Lord Shadowspawn see fit to entomb him alive as a punishment for his failure, he would stand and wait until his air ran out, and then he would go to sleep forever. No clone spawned in Kaminoan pods and raised in crèche school could even comprehend the concept of claustrophobia, much less suffer from it.

The faintest of breezes stirred his hair, and the sound of his boot heels on the stone took on added resonance, a multiplicity of echoes: though he could not see it, the stone had opened before him into a chamber of perfect night.

"*Hold, Group Captain.*" In the lightless void, Lord Shadowspawn's voice came from every direction and from none at all, as though the darkness itself spoke these words. "*Stand and report.*"

"My lord." Klick inclined his head. "I regret to inform my lord that—"

"*Do not regret, Klick. Only inform.*"

"The ship you ordered us—ah, that we were ordered to strike, my lord, along the Corellian Run. It was a Rebel ambush. The *Corellian Queen* was not even a ship at all, only a shell—a mock-up, really, full of Rebel starfighters. Somehow—" Klick swallowed, hard. His next words would be someone's death sentence. Possibly his own. "Somehow they knew we were coming."

"*Did they?*"

"They must have, my lord. Not only were they lying in wait, they had a new weapon, a torpedo of a type I've never seen, that seemed to be specifically designed to engage our superior Defenders. My starfighters were forced to retreat with almost thirty percent casualties. My lord—" Klick swallowed again. "My lord, there must be a Rebel spy. Here, on Mindor."

"*Must there? Can you conceive no alternate explanation?*"

"I—I can't imagine, my lord."

"*I can. But continue. There is more, is there not?*"

"Yes, my lord. We have detected a signal. Some sort of subspace transponder. We've traced it to the Defenders damaged in the engagement on the Corellian Run. We detected it when—" Klick swallowed hard, as if he was trying to down a mouthful of rocks. "When the subspace jamming system was deactivated."

"*Ah.*"

"It's the work of this Rebel spy, my lord. It *must* be."

"*It was not. The jammers were deactivated by my order.*"

"My lord?" Klick blinked rapidly as he tried to take this in. Would Shadowspawn betray his very own Great Cause? "My lord—I fear those torpedoes were used to plant some sort of *tracking* device—"

"*At last!*"

"My lord?"

"*Klick, you have done well. Very well indeed.*"

"My lord, I believe the Rebels have *found* us! According to the most recent intelligence reports, they have an entire task force on constant ready alert—my lord, a fleet could be on its way here *right now*!"

"*Could be? No. It is.*"

Klick blinked even faster. "Shall I sound general quarters, my lord?"

"*Of course not. We can't have our unexpected guests discover that we've been expecting them, can we? Are we so rude?*"

"I, ah, well—" Klick hoped the question was only rhetorical.

"*Order the Combat Space Patrol to stand down and return to their bases. But they are to stay with their craft and keep their engines hot. Also, order all the gravity crews to stand ready for initiation on my command.*"

"But if they strike while our forces are grounded, our losses—my lord, it could cost us the battle!"

"*We will lose this battle,*" said the voice from the darkness. "*We must. Losing this battle is how we will deliver the Empire to its rightful ruler: Emperor Skywalker!*"

CHAPTER 4

THE LONE PASSENGER SHUTTLE GLEAMED IN TASPAN'S light as it left the atmosphere, slipping neatly through the hurtling asteroids that crowded Mindor's low planetary orbit. As it left LPO, the shuttle traced a long, gracefully curving path, swinging wide to avoid the clouds of radioactive debris that were all that remained of Shadowspawn's sizable force of TIE Defenders.

On the battle bridge of the *Justice*, Lieutenant Tubrimi rolled the vast black orb of his left eye back from his console. "Unarmed shuttle, sir. A single lifesign—human, sir! It's hailing us under terms of the truce." The red-gold streaks in his iris brightened with excitement. "It's Shadowspawn, sir!"

Admiral Kalback shifted forward in his command chair. Nictitating membranes swept his eyes and retreated only halfway—the Mon Calamari version of a satisfied smile. "Accept the hail."

The lieutenant swept his webbed fingers through a complex curve in the air above his console, and the battle bridge's holoprojectors flickered to life.

The image they formed was of a tall human male, standing motionless in robes so long that they draped in folds around his feet. His hands were similarly hidden, folded before him within voluminous sleeves. His face was pale as a corpse's and as expressionless, and his eyes were rimmed in black. He wore some sort of curious headgear: an inverted crescent as broad as his substantial shoulders, which framed his head as though his face were a mountain, looming in silhouette before a cloud-blackened sun half below the horizon.

"Unidentified Rebel command cruiser," the image intoned in a voice black as a subterranean cavern, *"I am Lord Shadowspawn. You have defeated us. I respectfully request permission to board, that I may formally treat for the lives of my men."*

Lieutenant Tubrimi said, "That's all of it," and the image flickered out.

The admiral had never been a particularly demonstrative being, but there was quiet joy in his voice as he turned to the young human who stood beside his chair. "It seems congratulations are in order, General."

The general stood exactly as he had throughout the operation: motionless on the *Justice*'s battle bridge, hands folded behind him, a faint frown painting his brow. Beside him, maglocked to the deck, waiting with electronic patience, stood an R2-droid series model. The general seemed to be listening to some faint and distant sound, far beyond the confines of the ship, and it appeared that he didn't like what he was hearing.

Shadowspawn's voice . . . he couldn't pin it down. There had been something weird about it, some strange resonance, that struck him as both too familiar and just plain *wrong*.

"General?" Admiral Kalback repeated. "My congratulations—"

Luke replied grimly, "Not yet."

The battle had gone like chronowork. The sudden appearance of the Twenty-third Combat Starfighter Wing coming out of hyperspace at the very limit of Mindor's gravity well had apparently caught Shadowspawn's forces entirely by surprise; the Twenty-third's Y-wings

had managed two devastating torpedo runs on the
warlord's base before the first TIE Defenders on combat
patrol had been able to get back to engage the Twenty-
third's X- and B-wings; the Ys managed several more
runs during the ensuing dogfight. The battle at the edge
of Mindor's atmosphere had drawn in the rest of the
combat patrols from across the system, leaving clear
space for all twelve of the Rapid Response Task Force's
capital ships to jump in.

The five Slash-Es had come out of jump in a precise
formation—a regular tetrahedral dipyramid, to be
exact—with the planet of Mindor at its geometric center. Once their gravity-well generators activated, they
bracketed the planet with a mass-shadow more than
seven light-minutes across. But before the generators
were triggered, the other seven ships had jumped in. Six
of these remaining seven were a motley collection of various styles and makes, from a pair of refitted *Acclama-
tor II* assault cruisers to a battered old Techno Union
Bulwark-class battleship, dating from before the Clone
Wars; all they had in common were retrofitted Class 0.6
hyperdrives, multiple-redundancy deflector and particle
shields, and the ability to transport a minimum of three
full squadrons of starfighters apiece. Adding to the un-
gainly, cobbled-together appearance of these ships were
the vast number of pre–Clone Wars Jadthu landers maglocked to their hulls, which not only added their own
very substantial armor as additional protection for the
cruisers, but also gave the four non-atmosphere-capable
ships the capacity to hot-ground a fairly large chunk of
their marine complements in exceedingly short order.

The final ship was the *Justice,* flagship of the task
force: a sleek, graceful Mon Cal cruiser, sister ship to the
legendary *Liberty.* This twelve-hundred-meter work of
art was almost literally the *Liberty*'s sister; constructed
simultaneously, she resembled her famous sibling more

than almost any two ships ever to come out of the fantastical imaginations of Mon Calamari designers. The *Justice* had been intended to complement the *Liberty*'s speed and sheer destructive potential with more powerful shielding, additional docking bays, and vastly expanded troop capacity, because the Mon Calamari designers worked hand-in-glove with their equally imaginative strategists, who knew that while blowing things up was all well and good, wars were actually won by boots on the ground. Lots of them.

Of the eighteen thousand Republic marines deployed with the RRTF, nearly eight thousand were on the *Justice* alone, and the additional hangar bays that made her look, as Luke Skywalker had remarked when he first saw her, "a little bit pregnant," could carry ten full starfighter squadrons as well as a repair-and-refit shop deck more capable than most Republic stardocks.

The cruisers had taken up station in the centers of each face of the dipyramid marked off by the Slash-Es, and deployed two each of their starfighter squadrons. The Slash-Es were able to deploy a squadron apiece. With complete hyperspace interdiction and the sheer volume of firepower available to the cruisers and the twenty squadrons of starfighters, the marauders had been swiftly overwhelmed, and not a single Imperial craft had escaped the perimeter.

By the time the *Justice* had cruised majestically into a geostationary orbit above what clearly seemed to be the marauder base—it being the only installation on the planet defended by massive ground-based turbolaser batteries and eight planetary-defense ion cannons—the marauders' surviving starfighters had retreated to underground hangars.

It was over.

The lone frown among the jubilant bridge crew of the *Justice* belonged to Luke Skywalker. "It's not over."

Admiral Kalback blinked. "It was a brilliant plan—"

"It was an *obvious* plan."

"Yet it went precisely as you devised."

"That's the problem."

"General?"

"When was the last time you heard of a battle that went exactly as planned?"

Kalback's right eye swiveled independently to join his left, and the stately old officer leaned gently toward him. "When was the last time a battle was planned by a Jedi?"

"I couldn't say," Luke murmured. "But I bet it wasn't *this* smooth. And since when does a Lord of the Empire worry about the lives of his men?"

The Admiral flicked his left eye toward his rear and back again: a shrug. "We've cleared local space; his force is confined to the planet, which qualifies this as dirtside operations. That makes it your call, General."

"Then we make the best of bad choices. Tell him to hold station and present his conditions. We can negotiate from here."

"Prepare to transmit," Kalback said.

When Tubrimi signaled his readiness, the admiral rose. "Lord Shadowspawn, I am Admiral Kalback." The depth and dignity of his voice was more than equal to Shadowspawn's. "This is *not* a Rebel cruiser, sir; there is no Rebellion any longer. This ship is the *Justice*, flagship of the New Republic's Rapid Response Task Force. On behalf of the Joint Command, we are prepared to consider your offer of surrender. Hold your position, and transmit when ready."

He signaled to Tubrimi to cut transmission. "Let's give him time to think that over."

"I'm the one who's thinking it over." Luke paced the deck, frowning at the various sensor readouts on the battle bridge. "I think it's a trap."

Kalback's eyes twitched. "A trap? A trap for what? *With* what? We've *crushed* them."

"It's still a trap."

"Is this some Jedi insight? Do you feel it in the Force?"

Luke shook his head. "Artoo, bring up a tactical display."

R2-D2 whistled a cheerful assent and rolled away from Luke's side, extending his datalink toward the nearest port. Lieutenant Tubrimi swung around and waved his webbed hand. "I have it, sir."

"Leave it to Artoo," Luke said. "Mind your station."

"But—with all due respect, sir, even astromechs of substantially more advanced design than that old Artoo unit find our information technology almost imposs . . ." The lieutenant's voice trailed off as the battle bridge's holoprojector array flared to life, filling the room with a schematized holorepresentation of the Taspan.

Luke let himself smile, just a bit. "*That old Artoo unit,* Lieutenant, is not exactly an ordinary astromech. I trust him more than most people I know."

The lieutenant's nictitating membranes slid halfway across his eyes and flittered there for a second or two as he turned back to his console: the Mon Cal equivalent of a sheepish blush. "Yes, ah . . . sorry, sir. It won't happen again, sir."

Luke reached out and laid a hand on the lieutenant's shoulder. "It *should* happen again, Lieutenant. Being a general doesn't make me infallible."

"But, sir—the general is also a *Jedi,* sir."

Luke sighed. "Jedi aren't infallible, either. " He turned once more to Admiral Kalback. "If you were based in this system, how would you have set up your defenses?"

Kalback's eyes rolled to take in the whole cloud-fogged system at a glance, and nodded slowly. "Without capital ships, I suppose I would have based my starfighters in the asteroids."

"Me, too," Luke said. "If I were Shadowspawn, I wouldn't even *have* a base. Hollow out a couple dozen of the bigger asteroids, and they become your carriers and base stations. It wouldn't take much to make them practically invisible. It's the perfect camouflage."

"Then we're lucky you're not Shadowspawn."

"Ben Kenobi used to tell me there's no such thing as luck. Think about it: I'm a brand-new general. A few weeks ago I was just a jumped-up fighter jock. If I could think of it in a couple seconds, how did Shadowspawn miss it when he's had *months*?" Luke paced through the holodisplay and waved a hand at the pinpoints that represented the CC-7700/Es. "Look at those asteroid clouds. How many good places are there to station interdiction ships?"

Kalback responded only with a thoughtful blink.

"So if you knew your enemy had to bring capital ships, and you knew pretty much exactly where those capital ships had to go, what would *you* have done?"

"I'd have filled those points with mines," Kalback said. "And concentrated my starfighters nearby."

"But he set up his base—and his forces—on the planet." Luke nodded at R2-D2. "Artoo, bring it up."

The tiny shining disk of Mindor swelled to engulf and erase the rest of the system. It was an ugly place.

What had once been a lush and beautiful resort world was now mere rockball, battered clean of life by the endless rain of meteorites left over from the Big Crush; the only significant geographic features were the ubiquitous volcanoes that boiled from cracks in the planet's crust. Even the oceans had shriveled to widely scattered toxic sumps, churning at the very bottoms of what had once been the sea floor, and the atmosphere was so charged with vaporized metal and mineral salts that it formed a significant barrier to all forms of real-space communications; Lord Shadowspawn's initial transmission requesting the truce, for example, had been voice-only, with significant static interference.

Even the *Justice*'s powerful sensors could only scan through the murk with difficulty, and at very low resolution. The only way to locate Shadowspawn's base had been visible-light optical sensors, and even now, the task force's best scans could not determine with any certainty how many troops, vehicles, and emplacements might be down there, aside from the major planetary-defense installations visible from orbit.

Luke shook his head, frowning. "He's tied himself down on a planet that has no drinkable water, no food supply, and where the atmosphere's caustic enough to cause long-term lung damage. With the interference from the atmosphere, he can barely even communicate with his fleet. All that base is really good for is something to shoot at."

Kalback's eyes widened even further: a Mon Cal frown. "General, we don't necessarily *have* to honor the truce; after all, this Shadowspawn has not conducted his operations like a soldier, but like a pirate." He swiveled his right eye toward the ground base. "It seems a pity to let such a tempting target go to waste."

"No. If word gets out that that's how we treat surrendering Imperials, *no one* will surrender. This business will get a whole lot bloodier."

"Then how should we proceed?"

"I don't know," Luke said, more grimly than before. "I just don't know."

A chime that sounded like the splash of icy water over river stones caught Lieutenant Tubrimi's attention, and he swung back to his console. "Incoming message from the shuttle, sirs."

Kalback nodded. "Bring it up."

"Um," Luke said, "with your permission, Admiral?"

The admiral gave his assent with a roll of his left eye.

"Lieutenant, set the playback for audio only," Luke ordered. "Artoo, keep the tactical going. Plot the *Justice,* the shuttle, and the shuttle's vector."

"General?" Kalback leaned toward him, chin palps flaring in concern. "Is there a problem?"

"I'm pretty sure there is," Luke said, nodding. "Lieutenant?"

Tubrimi waved a hand. The darker-than-black purr of Shadowspawn's voice seemed to come from everywhere at once while the tactical holodisplay highlighted the relative positions of the *Justice* and the warlord's shuttle.

"How am I to offer surrender, when our eyes have not met? Am I to cast the lives of my men into wind and wave before I have judged the angles of your gaze?" Shadowspawn sounded honestly puzzled, almost plaintive. Luke's frown deepened to a scowl. The warlord was playing on Kalback's cultural inclinations: to his people, the truth of a being's character was expressed through its eyes. *"Pray indulge this one humble request from a defeated foe; do not force me to deliver the lives of my men unto some figment of my hopes for mercy."*

The flare of Kalback's chin palps widened. "General?"

Luke barely heard him. That voice . . .

He recognized the quality now: it was electronically synthesized, modulated deeper, darker, with subtle harmonics that worked on primitive parts of the human brain, commanding instant attention. Demanding respect. Requiring obedience. Inspiring dread.

That was it: Shadowspawn sounded like *Vader.*

The only other time he'd come across a voice that dark, that unsettling, that downright chilling had been another synthesized voice, speaking from a holoprojected silhouette filled with stars—

Could it *be*?

Luke's jaw clenched. "Blackhole."

Kalback swiveled one vast eye toward him. "You say that like a curse."

"It is for me," Luke said grimly. "We've had dealings before. He's an Emperor's Hand. I should say, *was* an Emperor's Hand. I've seen some reports that suggest he might have been director of Imperial Intelligence back around the time of Yavin. I should have pegged him right away—that strange headgear, for one thing—but these raids really aren't his style."

"No?"

"He was more, I don't know, kind of theatrical. He would always appear as a holoprojection of empty space—you know, just an outline filled with distant stars, and—" Luke's eyes went wide. "—and he *never* did his dirty work in person!"

He lurched toward the shifting star that was the tactical display's representation of the shuttle: that shifting star was shifting entirely too fast. "Is this accurate?"

The ensign at the tactical console angled his eyes in a shrug. "Yes, sir. In fact, he's accelerating."

"Project his course."

A cone of blue haze spread forward along the shuttle's vector. "That's assuming constant acceleration—no, wait, he's increasing acceleration. Eight gravities . . . eleven . . ." The cone kept spreading until it enveloped the holodisplayed *Justice*.

"Order marines to the landers, and all hands to environment suits."

Kalback blinked. "General?"

"You, too, Admiral." Luke strode across the deck to a suit locker and starting pulling out flight suits. "Come on," he told a nearby yeoman. "Pass these out. Get going."

Kalback still looked doubtful. "You're expecting a direct attack?"

"Or something like it. Get me firing solutions for fifteen to twenty-five gravities throughout that cone," Luke told the fire control officer. "Lock targeting with all nearside batteries and prepare for torpedo launch."

"General?" The lieutenant twisted toward Luke, blinking in astonishment.

"Belay that!" Kalback sputtered. "That's—that shuttle's *unarmed*!"

"That's an order, Lieutenant." Luke turned crisply to Kalback. "I should say, that's an order, *Admiral*. Excuse me for giving orders to your men on your bridge. Direct your men to follow my command."

"But—but at least we must *warn* him!"

"He'll get the message when his sensors pick up our targeting lock."

"Are we the Empire? Would you destroy an unarmed craft? That's *murder*!"

"Admiral?" The ensign's voice had gone tight as a full dragline. "Countersensor measures and evasive action from the shuttle. Acceleration still increasing."

"No simple shuttle comes with CSM," Luke said. "Admiral, give the order to fire."

"But without weapons—"

"It *is* a weapon." Luke could feel it now. "It's a flying bomb."

"But—but Shadowspawn *himself*—"

"Isn't in there," Luke finished for him. "Look at the evasion pattern—that's an Imperial fighter pilot. A good one, too."

"Admiral—" The ensign's voice was barely more than a strained hiss. "Vector change. Intercept course at twenty-five standard gravities. Five seconds."

"Admiral," Luke said, calm as a stone. "Now."

Kalback's nictitating membranes swept across his

huge eyes, and this time they did not retreat. "May my pod and all its ancestors forgive me," he said. "Fire."

Turbolaser blasts clawed through space. In the bare eyeblink before they would strike the shuttle and obliterate it, the shuttle vanished in a flare of actinic white.

This flare did not expand in a spherical shock front, like an explosion, but instead shaped itself into a single plane, like a planetary ring or a black hole's accretion disk. This plane of white flashed outward at lightspeed and whipped through the *Justice*'s shields without resistance. It also whipped through the *Justice*'s armor, hull, and internal structure.

And the ship just . . . fell apart.

CHASK FRAGAN HAD BARELY BEGUN TO RELAX AFTER the battle; he had just canceled the B-wing's HUD and was settling back in his pilot's couch, allowing a long whistling sigh to escape through the gill slits above his eyes, when Kort Habel fluted an unprintable expletive from the gunner's couch behind him.

"What now?" Chask half rolled toward his ventral side, twisting so that he could see Kort's screens . . . but Kort wasn't looking at his screens. He was looking at a brilliant white star that had suddenly bloomed entirely too close to the coordinates of the *Justice*, five light-seconds away. "Hot staggering glurd! What was *that*?"

"Dunno," Kort answered through clenched masticators. "Nothing on scan—wait, nothing on comm either! Subspace gives back only fuzz." He went grim. "They're jamming us."

"Who is?"

"The comm fairies, chitin-brain. How should I know?"

"Try realspace EM."

"Radio? We're five light-seconds out—"

"Which means that explosion happened what, twelve seconds ago now?"

"Nothing on EM. I mean *nothing*. Just fuzz. Wait, here it comes."

In scattered spits and static-fogged gasps, the real-space comm gave up the news: *Justice* had been hit by an unidentified weapon, and hit hard. Ship damage was so severe that the massive battle cruiser was breaking up in orbit. No estimate of casualties, though its fighter escort reported sighting landing craft and escape pods ejecting from the wreckage; only seconds later, the fighter escort reported engaging a superior enemy force as it swept in to fire on the pods. "They're pounding the wheezing garp out of us!"

"*Who* is?"

"At a guess?" Kort flicked a mandible up and out, toward the tumbling storm of asteroids outside the cockpit—a storm of asteroids that now flared with the plasma signature of dozens—no, *hundreds*—of ion drives firing on full throttle. "Them."

Chask produced a string of expletives even more foul than Kort's as he stabbed at the B-wing's controls, powering up all shields and blasting full power to the engine—and that string of expletives turned out to be his last words. Some invisible force reached through the fighter's shields like they weren't even there, and wrenched his ship in half.

"WE'VE LOST THE FEED, SIR." SECOND LIEUTENANT Horst Devalo, ComOps officer for the *Lancer,* frowned at his console. "*Justice* has gone dark."

Captain Tirossk leaned over Devalo's shoulder to peer curiously at the lieutenant's console. "Their problem or ours?" This was a legitimate question, as the *Lancer* was a retrofitted freightliner over a century old, and was known affectionately by all who served on her as "Old

Cuss'n'Whack," this being descriptive of the first two repair actions traditionally undertaken to address any of her endless minor malfunctions. "Raise the *Paleo* and the *Unsung;* see if they're having the same problem."

The Taspan system was so deep in the Inner Rim that space itself was crowded; there was no safe direct route. The last few legs had to follow a jagged path of short jumps, only a few light-years each, before a ship would have to drop out of hyperspace and change vector. The final chokepoint was here, in interstellar space, less than two light-years out. The reserve force could jump into any of several sets of preprogrammed coordinates at various distances from Taspan and Mindor itself as fast as they could make the run up to lightspeed, the better to apply an extra punch where it would do the most good, whether to press an assault or cover a retreat. They had been monitoring the battle, the victory, and the subsequent abortive negotiation by subspace feed.

"It's *our* problem," Lieutenant Devalo said. "I can't get comm even with the others."

"This useless scow of an excuse for a frigate—" the captain began, but Devalo cut him off.

"It's not the ship, sir." The lieutenant's voice had gone tight. "Subspace interference—they're jamming us, sir!"

"Out here? Can you pinpoint the source?"

"Sensor accuracy degrading . . . fifty percent. Forty. Has to be local, sir: they're blanketing our whole sensor and comm spectrum."

"Battle stations. All engines full," Captain Tirossk ordered, his voice grinding like rusty gears. "Get on realspace to *Paleo* and *Unsung* and tell them to prepare for jump."

"Sir?"

"You heard me. We don't know what's happening and there's only one way to find out."

"Gravity wave!" the NavOps officer sang out. "Multiple point sources—in motion!"

Tirossk had been an officer too long to use an obscenity, but he thought several. "Vectors?"

NavOps read out a string of numbers; the gravitic energy was spread in a hemisphere eclipsing the outbound hyperspace lanes—a hemisphere that continued to expand toward englobement. "Gravity mines," Tirossk rasped. "They're trying to pin us here."

"Imperial starfighters inbound!" the TacOps officer said crisply. "Fourth Squadron reports visual confirmation—TIE Defenders—engaging multiple bogies—"

"Reporting *how*?" Tirossk snapped.

"Realspace EM, sir."

Now Tirossk did swear. Very quietly—not even another Bothan could have heard him. Realspace communications crept along at lightspeed; that meant inbound bogies could be here as soon as, roughly—

Now.

The forward viewports whited out, and the *Lancer* bucked like an angry dewback. The convulsion was violent enough to jar the bridge despite the frigate's anti-acceleration field. Tirossk clutched the back of his command chair and almost dislocated a shoulder keeping himself upright. The forward viewports cleared.

Local space was lousy with TIEs—and bloody well full of intersecting lines of cannon fire and the hurtling stars of proton torpedoes.

"Damage reports!" he snarled. "And get us *moving*. Burn out the engines if you have to. We need hyperspace *now*!"

"But—jump *where*, sir?"

"Those Defenders came from somewhere," Tirossk said. "They'll have left open a route back."

"Sir?"

"Mindor," Tirossk said grimly. "We're going in."

* * *

HALF BLIND, EYES STREAMING FROM THE THICKENING fog of acrid black smoke that filled the *Justice*'s battle bridge, half retching, half deafened by the impact Klaxon and the screech of the overloading atmosphere processors, Luke reached into the Force. Ten meters away, a plexilite retaining box flipped back and the manual trigger for the battle bridge's fire-suppression system clicked over to ACTIVATE.

Jets of icy gas surged up from deck grates and curled themselves around the consoles that still spat sparks and gushed smoke. Luke moved toward the comm console, stumbled on something yielding, and dropped to one knee.

He'd tripped over Kalback. Over his body. Half the Mon Cal admiral's face was crushed; it looked like he had taken a square console corner to the head at some point during the series of impacts that had knocked everyone on the battle bridge off their feet and shaken them around like dice in a cup. Luke lowered his head, laid one gentle hand on the intact side of Kalback's face, and commended his departed spirit to the Force.

In the instant he touched the Force, it gave him back the profound certainty that if he didn't get moving, he'd soon be similarly commending the spirits of everyone on the ship. Including himself. In the Force, the truth was solid as the deck on which he knelt. The *Justice* was doomed.

He made it to the comm console. Lieutenant Tubrimi was still at his post, but he was clutching a bloody shoulder and looked unsteady and shocky. "What—what *was* that?" was all he could say, again and again.

"Lieutenant, put out an all-hands. Marines to the landers. Everybody else to escape pods. We're abandoning ship."

"The—the admiral—he won't—we can't—"

"He's dead, Tubrimi. Pull it together."

"But—but we don't even have *damage reports* yet—"

"Damage reports?" The battle bridge shuddered, and more Klaxons went off. "Feel that?" Luke said. "That was another piece of this ship *exploding*. Get that all-hands out. Then get yourself to a pod, too. That's an order."

"Sir, I—copy that, sir." Tubrimi turned back to his console with a grimly desperate look. "Thank you, sir."

Luke had already moved on. Farther down the deck, R2-D2 was down, whirring and whistling, leaking smoke as he rolled from side to side. Luke reached out through the Force and set the little droid upright. "It's okay, Artoo, I'm here," he said, crouching beside him. "Let's have a look."

R2-D2 whistled plaintively and rolled in a tight circle; one of his locomotor arms was bent and spitting sparks at the joint; the rollerped on that side wasn't functioning at all, just skidding as Artoo dragged it across the deck. "Okay, I see it. Doesn't look serious—you can probably fix it yourself, once we're clear. Come on."

The little astromech tweetered in a more decisive tone.

"Forget it," Luke said. "I'm not leaving you. We'll get out of this together."

"Um, sir?" Tubrimi said with a shaky laugh. "We might not get out of this at all."

Luke rose, and cleared smoke from the air around Tubrimi's console with a gesture. "Show me."

The blurred, hazy readout that ghosted into existence above the console had no good news for them: the *Justice* had already broken up. The three major pieces tumbled helplessly through Mindor's asteroid-filled orbit, each surrounded by swarms of dogfighting X-wings and TIEs. The two larger pieces streamed pinwheel fountains of thruster signatures as marine landers and escape pods streaked away in random directions through the fight. The smaller piece streamed only billows of flash-frozen atmosphere. "That small piece—that's *us*, sir. The bridge section has taken multiple torpedo hits to the pod bays. There, uh, aren't any pods. Not anymore. There aren't any pod bays. There aren't any—"

Luke stopped him with a firm hand on his shoulder. "How many hands trapped with us?"

Tubrimi swallowed hard. "Can't say, sir. Could be several hundred. But they won't be with us for long." His webbed fingers fluttered helplessly at the display. "In no more than five minutes this battle bridge will be the only place with any life support at all. The breakup has wiped out atmosphere processors and antibreach systems throughout the ship—I mean, this part of the ship." He started shaking. "What used to be the ship."

"Hold it together, Lieutenant. I've gotten people out of tighter spots than this." Luke stepped up on the command dais and raised his voice. "All bridge personnel—every one of you—get back to your stations. Secure the wounded and the dead, then strap yourselves in. Except for you," he said to the pilot. "Strap in somewhere else. I'm taking your station."

"You?" The pilot blinked in astonishment. "But sir—Mon Calamari control systems are not designed for human operation—"

"That's my problem." Luke slid into the pilot's couch. "Yours is finding a place to secure yourself. This ride's about to get bumpy."

"Sir?"

"We have crew aboard who are running out of air. So we'll go get them some." Luke pointed to the wide brick-colored curve of Mindor. "There's a whole planet-ful, right next door."

"Sir!" Tubrimi gasped. "We don't have engines—we don't even have *repulsorlifts*. You're not actually *sug-*

gesting we take this—this *fragment* of a ship into atmosphere with nothing but *attitude thrusters*—"

"That's right. I'm not suggesting. I'm ordering. And I'm not just taking us into the atmosphere."

Luke stretched his hands out into the electrostatic control fields above the pilot console and let himself smile, just a bit; for the first time in weeks, he felt like a Jedi again. "I'm going to *land* this thing."

NONE OF THE NEW REPUBLIC FORCES SAW THE FRAGment of the *Justice* dip into the atmosphere; even the kilometers-long stream of flame and smoke trailing off its burning hull attracted no attention at all. The Republic forces were wholly engaged with the more immediate problem of staying alive.

Gravity wells had erupted throughout the system, their mass-shadow thresholds spreading in a 3-D version of the ripples from a handful of pebbles tossed into a still pool. With their subspace comm and sensors jammed, the New Republic ships couldn't even guess how many gravity mines or projectors might be hidden among the trillions of asteroids; the overlapping layers of the interdiction field not only wiped out any hope of hyperspace travel, they also suddenly—and in many cases catastrophically—altered the already-unstable orbits of every object in the system smaller than a medium-sized moon, turning what had been a dangerously crowded system into a nightmare of intersecting storms of rock.

And the hail that streamed from these storms was squadron after squadron of TIE Interceptors.

The Interceptor was not so dominating a weapon as its successor, the Defender. With less armor, less weaponry, and no shields or hyperdrive, they were nonetheless incredibly swift and maneuverable, and could be exceedingly difficult opponents, especially when appearing en masse. Here at Mindor—as the desperately scrambling Republic X- and B-wing pilots discovered, to their dismay—*en masse* translated to (in the words of one flight leader) "*thousands* of the beggars, comin' from everywhere all at frappin' *once!*"

In the swirling chaos of randomly hurtling asteroids, the Interceptors' lack of shields was actually an advantage, as deflectors don't affect material objects; the deflectorless Interceptors had proportionally more engine power for acceleration and to recharge the capacitors for their laser cannons, and there were so many of them that they could swarm the Republic fighters like Pervian blood crows mobbing a wonderhawk and still have plenty left over to strafe the capital ships, which was why nobody was keeping an eye on the optical sensors or monitoring the *Justice*'s EM channel, on which was playing a loop of Luke Skywalker's low, preternaturally calm voice broadcast by an emergency signal buoy orbiting the planet.

"This is New Republic cruiser *Justice*, Luke Skywalker commanding. Admiral Kalback is dead. The ship has broken up, and there are no escape pods remaining. I have taken the helm and will attempt to set down behind the dawn terminator above the north tropic. Begin the search for survivors at the coordinates on the encoded supplementary frequency. Good luck, and may the Force be with you. Skywalker out."

Only the *Lancer,* yanked unexpectedly from hyperspace by the Imperial gravity mines half a light-hour out from Mindor, had the chance to catch the actual landing, such as it was.

Lieutenant Devalo, at ComOps, went ashen as he picked up the broadcast from the signal buoy; when he reported it to Captain Tirossk, the captain's response was to instantly aim the *Lancer*'s most powerful optical scope at the day-night terminator of the distant planet.

The aged ship's sensor suite had just barely managed to focus on an image of a long, long smoke trail, and was tracking it down through the atmosphere when it picked up the fringes of a brilliant white flash, followed by a vast expanding ball of smoke-laced flame.

"Oh," Tirossk said numbly. There was no thought of obscenity now; how he felt could not be expressed in words.

"Was that—" Devalo had to swallow before he could go on. "Was that the *Justice*?"

"I'm afraid it must have been." Tirossk sank into his command chair. "I'm afraid . . ."

"General *Skywalker*'s ship?"

"No one could have survived that," Tirossk said. "We're half a light-hour out. What we just saw, it happened thirty minutes ago."

Devalo couldn't even ask the question, but he didn't have to.

"He died half an hour ago." Tirossk shook his head, blankly astonished at the bleak weight that settled onto him. "Luke Skywalker is dead."

CHAPTER 5

HAN SOLO STRETCHED BACK FAR ENOUGH IN THE CON-
ference room chair that when he laced his fingers together behind his head, he had to jam one knee up under
the table to keep from toppling over. He stared at the
ceiling and wondered, for the three or four hundredth
time that day, if it was possible to die of boredom.

He decided, as he had all the other times, that if such
a thing *were* possible he would have bumped off at least
two days ago. If there was anything in the galaxy he
hated more than sitting around in a room for hours on
end with nothing to do but listen to people yap, it had to
be sitting around in a room for hours with nothing to do
except listen to *Mandalorians* yap.

Man, he hated those guys!

Han was no bigot; despite some unfortunate experi-
ences with a certain Mando bounty hunter—who, if the
Force believed in justice, was still to this very day
screaming as he slowly dissolved in a sarlacc's digestive
juices—he didn't hate Mandalorians in general. He'd
just never met a single one of these stuck-up more-
studly-than-thou self-proclaimed MESFACs (Masters of
Every Single Flippin' Aspect of Combat) who could even
so much as say "Good morning" without making it
sound like he was really saying *It better be a good morning, because if you pull anything, I will without hesita-*

tion jariler *your weak peace-lovin' Corellian butt till you don't even know what galaxy you're in.*

He didn't hate Mandos in general; he only hated the ones he'd actually met.

Further, some screwed-up sense of honor or ethnic pride or something had somehow made these particular Mandalorians unwilling to speak Basic during these talks. Which didn't stop them from yapping, of course. They just yapped in Mando'a, a language that, to Han's more-than-somewhat biased ear, made them sound like a pride of sand panthers trying to cough up hairballs bigger than his head. And this hairball-hacking then had to be dutifully translated into Basic for the convenience of the chief New Republic negotiator by the chief negotiator's high-strung, hypersensitive, relentlessly neurotic protocol droid, who somehow among his six million flippin' forms of communication had never managed to lose that snooty Core Worlds accent that, after hearing it nonstop for a couple of days cooped up in this room with nothing better to do, made Han want to whop him so hard he'd land somewhere back on Tatooine.

The main consideration that stopped him from engaging in catastrophic droid-remodeling was the presence beside him of the New Republic's chief negotiator, who was so breathtakingly beautiful that Han couldn't even glance her way without feeling his heart begin to pound.

She was not only beautiful but brilliant and fiercely courageous, and she had done only one really foolish thing in her life: a couple of years ago, she had let herself fall in love with a dashing-but-impoverished tramp-freighter captain—well, okay, a disreputable smuggler on the run from Imperial authorities and various bounty hunters and crime lords, but who was counting?—and Han could never shake this lurking dread that if he, say, did something nasty to C-3PO, who, after all, usually meant well, Leia might suddenly wake up and realize what an awful mistake she'd made.

Not that he would ever admit this, not even to Chewbacca. Not even to himself, most days—his ego was nigh-invulnerable to self-doubt—but on those rare occasions when he found himself getting irritable and depressed because he was stuck somewhere with way too much time to think and not nearly enough to do, these little whispers would start hissing around the back of his head. He could quiet them only by privately reaffirming his personal blood oath that he would never—never ever *ever*—give the woman he loved a reason to regret falling for him.

Which left him sitting in a conference room in a pressure dome on an unnamed asteroid in some Inner Rim system so obscure he couldn't remember its name, pretending to give a damn while C-3PO translated yet another string of Mandalorian gabble. "The commander repeats that surrender simply is *not* possible, and reiterates that the only peaceful solution to this unfortunate situation is for all Rebel—that is, New Republic, of course; he doesn't seem to understand the distinction, or else is being deliberately obtuse, but no matter—is for all Rebel forces to depart the system forthwith. Of course, this is not his exact phraseology; the literal translation—stripped of vulgarity—is roughly along the lines of *You Rebels stay, everybody dies, you Rebels leave, everybody's happy,* which wholly fails to capture the entirely savage brutality of his vocabulary. Really, Princess, having to process such *coarse language*—my vulgarity-filter capacitors are on the brink of overload!"

Han didn't even entirely understand what the negotiation was all about; he'd missed the battle completely, as he and Leia had been off somewhere on the far side of nowhere, hammering out the details of bringing into the New Republic a minor star cluster inhabited mainly by hairy spider-looking critters who had thoroughly creeped him out, not least because these, unlike most of the arachnoid races, had very humanoid-looking faces, including mouthfuls of gleaming white, entirely human-looking teeth.

Anyway, by the time he'd brought Leia here at the urgent summons of the local system authority, the Imperial forces had been thoroughly defeated and scattered to the stars—all except five or six hundred Mandalorian mercenaries, who were dug in around several trineutronium power plants on the system's main inhabited world; the Mandos had proclaimed themselves ready and willing to detonate these installations at the first touchdown of a Republic ship, which would sterilize the planet and kill all three and a half billion people who lived there.

They'd taken the world hostage.

Han had been able to gather, through the endless hours of tense negotiations, that the final order from the fleeing Imperial commander had been for the Mandos to deny the planet to Republic forces "by any and all necessary means." The Mando commander had interpreted that to mean "Even if you have to kill *everybody,* including yourselves." But the New Republic wasn't about to give back a system that was not only rich in natural resources and manufacturing capacity but had also, in a system-wide referendum, voted *overwhelmingly* in favor of Republic membership, with something like ninety-seven percent recommending union. Han privately hoped that the three percent diehard ImpSymps all lived right next door to one of those trineutronium plants.

Anyway, the negotiation had disintegrated into a standoff: Leia's rationality and persuasive powers matched against the rock-ribbed *Mandalorians Never Surrender* nuttiness of the mercenary commander. It had gotten to the point that Han was actually looking forward to Lando's arrival.

This was surprising not because of anything to do with Lando himself, whom Han, despite their long and often unhappy history together, actually *liked*—well, most of the time—but rather with what Lando was bringing to this table. Well, less *what* than *who*.

Lando Calrissian, unlike his old buddy Han, had hung on to his general's commission. He was currently the director of Special Operations, a fancy-sounding title that apparently involved, today, being a highly decorated chauffeur. He was on his way back from Mandalorian Space, where he had gone to corral the one guy in the galaxy Lando claimed could change the alleged minds of these commandos: the Big Boss of the Mandalorian Protectors and self-styled Lord Mandalore, Fenn Shysa himself.

Or, as Han usually thought of him, Fenn You-So-Much-as-*Look*-at-Leia-That-Way-One-More-Time-and-I-Swear-I'm-Gonna-Pop-Your-Mando-Skull-Like-a-Bladdergrape Shysa.

Shysa and his men had given up the mercenary life, and he'd organized his cadre into the kernel of the Protectors—kind of civic-minded volunteer police and freelance do-gooders, more or less. Which meant that Shysa, on top of his born-and-bred MESFAC more-studly-than-thou thing, had piled more-honorable-than-thou, more-self-sacrificing-than-thou, and more-all-around-good-guy-than-thou.

If Han were inclined to be entirely honest about such things—which he was not, on principle—he might have admitted that his problem with the Protector commandant had more to do with a sneaking suspicion that Fenn might also be better-looking-than-thou, and with how much attention this particular Hero of Mandalore paid to Leia. And how much Leia seemed to enjoy it.

This time, though, Han was actually grudgingly willing to let Shysa have the pleasure of spending time in a room with Leia—a *conference* room, with Han and a few dozen officers as chaperones—as long as it got this situation resolved. He figured this proved he'd grown as a person. A little. Maybe.

Just how questionable that growth might be was amply demonstrated when Leia turned to him, put a hand on his arm to draw him close, and leaned toward him to whisper in his ear; he actually more than half expected that she was about to tell him how much she was looking forward to seeing Shysa again.

Instead, she muttered in a voice stretched thin with tension, "Han, Luke's in trouble."

The front legs of Han's chair bumped back down to the floor. "What?"

Leia gave her head that little shake, one Han knew so well, barely more than a lip-compressed shiver that signaled *I don't know why, but I don't like this at all.* "It's a—feeling. He might—"

"Hey, I worry about him too, but—" Han laid a comforting hand on her shoulder. "He can take care of himself, you know? The stuff he can do . . ."

His voice trailed off as he felt the knots of tension in her shoulder; instead of him giving her comfort, she was giving him dread.

A dimple appeared at the corner of her mouth that told Han she was biting the inside of her lower lip. "It's not just the Mindor raid. I think—I think there's something . . . *wrong* there. Something bad."

"Something he can't handle? I mean, we're talking about *Luke,* here—Luke I-Must-Face-Vader-and-Palpatine-Alone *Skywalker,* y'know?" Han thought it was a pretty good line, but it sounded hollow, even to him. He forged on. "How much trouble can he really be in?"

"I—I don't *know,* Han!" The twist of uncertainty at

the corners of her eyes brought a similar twist to Han's heart. "If I *knew,* I wouldn't even have mentioned it—or else we'd be on our way already."

"Excuse me, please—I beg your pardon most awfully, Princess—" C-3PO leaned in between them. "Though my vocabulary filter and voice-stress analysis subprogram suggest that your conversation is very likely private, the commander is becoming restive, and is requesting a translation. Not very respectfully, I might add."

"Ask him if he needs you to translate *this*—" Han began, but the gesture he'd been referring to was interrupted by Leia's astonishingly strong grip on his arm.

"Han, can you just—just find out? Try the comm center. The RRTF will be in subspace contact. Just—make sure he's all right. And tell him to be careful." Her urgent whisper dropped to a barely audible hush. "Tell him I have a bad feeling about this."

HAN TROTTED THROUGH THE HUGE ROCK-DOMED docking bay, buckling his blaster belt and tying down his holster as he went. He threaded through deck gangs busily shifting fighters and shuttles into parking slips, sneezing at the thick petrochemical fumes belched out by overstressed dry-tugs. When he reached the *Falcon,* the shadow of her starboard mandible was littered with a bewildering array of components in various states of disrepair and disassembly, most of which—to his sadly all-too-experienced eye—appeared to belong to the control assembly of her starboard deflector unit. The party responsible for this wanton destruction of property was currently standing down to his knees in the proximal access hatch—all that could be seen of him was a pair of vast russet-shagged feet on top of a coffin-sized toolbox that rested on a rusty, battered scrap of scaffolding that looked like it had once been some kind of picnic table, while the rest of his vast hairy body was jammed way up into the innards of Han's ship.

"Chewie—hey, *Chewie*!"

The feet gave back no reaction, which was no surprise. The growl of dry-tug engines and the electronically amplified orders bawled by the deck bosses were so loud Han could barely even hear himself. He swept up a nearby gauss wrench and whanged the *Falcon*'s hull hard enough to leave a bright new scar. From deep within the access hatch came a thump Han could feel though the hull—Chewbacca's head was fully hard enough to dent durasteel—and a brief but heartfelt snarl of Wookiee expletive, which would be enough to erode the confidence of almost any human being in the galaxy. Almost. "Get the ship zipped and clipped," Han said. "I'll start the launch sequence. Skids up in ten."

Chewie howled a protest. Han said, "Well, if we could land somewhere for more than twenty minutes before you start taking the ship apart, we wouldn't *have* this—"

Chewbacca's reply of "*Geeroargh hroo owwwweragh!*" translated, roughly, as *If I missed any chances to take the ship apart, we wouldn't have a ship at all,* which was so patently true that even Han couldn't argue, so he changed the subject. "Lando's escort drops skids in about twelve minutes. The *Falcon* needs to be ready to go when Traffic Control drops the particle shields so we can slip out."

Chewie's massive brows pulled together, and he grumbled a wary interrogative.

"No, no, no, nothing like that. Nobody's after us."

"*Garouf?*"

"It's—an errand, that's all. We need to, uh, drop in on Luke. Pay him a little visit. A, ah, social call."

"*Rhouergh hweroo snngh.*"

"What's the matter? Don't you want to see Luke? What, you don't like him anymore?"

"*Lowerough. Lowerough garoohnnn?*"

"No, she's not coming."

"*Garouf?*"

"Because I *said* so. Am I still the captain around here?"

"*Hnerouggr fnerrolleroo!*" Chewbacca's voice rose, as did one vast finger that waggled in Han's face. "*Sscheroll ghureeohh—*"

"All right, all *right,* keep it down, huh?" Han took a quick glance around to make sure nobody was close enough to overhear on the noisy deck. "I was just up at ComOps. Luke's whole task force has gone dark—they haven't gotten a peep out of him since insertion—and his reserves went dark about ten minutes ago." His face darkened. "And Leia's got a feeling he's in trouble."

Chewie began to grumble another question, but Han cut him off. "I don't *know* what we can do about it. Maybe nothing. But at least we can find out what's going on. I can't—Chewie, you know me. You understand. I can't just *leave* him out there . . ."

"*Ghn lowerough?*"

"No, she asked me to try to contact him. She doesn't know we're actually going. And she's not *gonna* know. There is no way I'm gonna let her come along."

"*Howergh?*"

"Because . . ." Han made a face. "Because I have a bad feeling about this, too," he said, and vanished up the boarding ramp.

LANDO CALRISSIAN WALKED DOWN THE RAMP OF HIS personal command shuttle looking every centimeter the general he was, from the millimetrically level brim of his gleaming cap to the subtly iridescent uppers of his similarly gleaming boots. The elegantly close-fitting jumpsuit he wore was also subtly iridescent, so that its powder-blue sheen could pick up complementary highlights from whatever environment he might find himself in—because a gentleman and an officer must never, ever clash—and it fit as if it had been designed specifically for him, which, of course, it had. He'd designed it himself.

Thrown over one shoulder he carried his custom belt-length uniform jacket—jet black, naturally, because black goes with everything—which he'd commissioned after being reliably informed that Ackbar and Republic Command would absolutely draw the line at an opera cape. At his side walked Fenn Shysa, wearing only his usual battered flight gear—which, Lando had to admit, suited him rather well.

When Lando had come into the shuttle's cabin for the first time wearing these dress blues, Shysa had snorted openly. "Don't recall ever seeing a holo of Madine in an outfit like *that*."

"That's because Crix can't pull it off," Lando had replied with a shrug, admiring the jacket's cut in a full-length mirror. "He carries a bit much in the middle, know what I mean?"

"And you're wonderin' why Mandalorian mercenaries don't seem to respect you."

Lando grinned. "I like being underestimated."

"I'm thinkin' it's mostly that you like your fancy clothes."

"If looking good ever becomes a crime, Fenn my friend, I'm ready to do life."

Shysa marched through the busy docking bay with his usual straight-ahead military stride. Lando lagged a bit, nodding to this tech and that deckhand, greeting most of them by name, introducing himself to those he didn't know. The same uncanny knack of memory that let him mentally track the tactics and tells of thousands of gamblers across the galaxy also helped him recall the names of anyone he'd ever met—often the names of their children and details of their homeworlds, too. It was more than just a trick, though; he genuinely liked people, and this had made him almost ridiculously popular with the rank and file of the RDF. But it could slow him down when he had to move through a crowd, which was why he was a bit late to catch what Leia was saying to Fenn as he came up, something about C-3PO waiting in the conference room with full briefing and status report.

Something had brought an entirely lovely blush to Leia's cheeks, which Lando automatically assumed must be the result of some clumsily flattering compliment from Shysa. Since to be outsmoothed by a gruff-mannered fighter jock would never be part of Lando's life plan, he stepped up and bowed over Leia's hand. "Princess, I apologize in advance for my inadequate words," he said, "because as usual, your beauty leaves me entirely speechless."

"Stow it." Leia reclaimed her hand with a brisk yank; that high color in her cheeks was apparently not due so much to pleasure as to, say, rage. "Answer a question instead."

Lando blinked. "Princess?"

"Why is it," she said through clenched teeth, "that the only man I know under the age of sixty who is capable of even *pretending* to be a grown-up is my own *brother*?"

Before Lando could begin to stammer out anything resembling an answer, she swept off along the corridor, stalking toward the docking bay in a stiff-backed march that reminded him uncomfortably of a Socorran granite-hawk's threat display.

Fenn leaned toward him. "What's with *her*?"

"She does seem a bit wrought up."

"I thought she's a diplomat—isn't she supposed to be more, I dunno, kinda self-possessed?"

"She is. She was once interrogated by Darth Vader himself and never so much as blinked. Look up *unflappable* on the HoloNet, you'll find her profile."

"She's sure flappin' some right now."

"I'd say so."

"So what is it that can get a girl like her so spittin' mad and all?"

"It's not a what, it's a who," Lando said with a smile of fond remembrance. "In her defense, he could make a Jedi Master throw a full-scale hissy fit."

Shysa nodded. "You must be talkin' about Solo."

LEIA BROKE INTO A TROT AS SHE ENTERED THE DOCKING bay cavern, but stopped short when she registered the absence of a familiar silhouette that should have been in the repair bay beyond the lines of shuttles and fighters. She pushed her way through the deck gangs to the place where the *Falcon* had been docked. There was nothing to be seen there except some grease and coolant stains, a few scraps of hull plating and random electronic components, and one lone gauss wrench with a dented head. Setting her jaw, she swept the gauss wrench up and weighed it in her hand. But then she lowered her arm and just gazed balefully out into the dark of space beyond the docking bay's particle shield.

She should never have sent Han in the first place. She should have made *him* stew in that stifling conference room listening to C-3PO struggle to find polite translations of that Mandalorian's sneers. He hadn't been gone ten minutes when she'd realized what a mistake she'd made. And why.

It was because she didn't take herself seriously enough.

Even after all these months, she couldn't make herself entirely believe that actual Jedi blood ran in her veins—not only Jedi blood, but the blood of arguably the most powerful Jedi in history. She had never entirely gotten her mind around the truth that her instincts and intuitions and premonitions were much more than psychological phenomena: that they were, really and truly, the whispers of the Force itself. She had sent Han because, deep down, she'd really believed that he'd just run on up to the communications center and check on the real-time subspace status reports coming from Luke's task force, and when he found out that all was well, he'd just run on back and tell her so. With maybe a bit of teasing about *some static today on the Feminine Intuition Channel, huh?*

Coming to grips with their Jedi heritage must have been easier for Luke; growing up on the Outer Rim, he'd barely even known what a Jedi was. Leia, on the other hand, had been raised in a household that was steeped in reverence for the Jedi Order and everything it had stood for. The man she still thought of as her father— Bail, the Prince Consort—had had an inexhaustible fund of tales of the Jedi, not just from the Clone Wars but from the whole history of the Republic. He had never spoken of any Jedi with less than absolute respect for the way they had devoted their lives wholly to the cause of peace and justice, sacrificing everything in the tragic Clone Wars.

Was it any wonder that she couldn't quite believe it? That one of those legendary heroes had been Anakin Skywalker, her real father . . . and that this legendary hero had somehow been transformed into the most ruthless, homicidal, and terrifying enforcer of the Empire's tyranny . . . and that the eager puppy of a Tatooine farm boy who had burst into her cell on the Death Star to rescue her—without the faintest ghost of a plan beyond a naive faith in the essential justness of the universe—was her twin, who now expected her to follow in his, and their father's, footsteps . . .

It was all just too preposterous. She might, just barely, be able to believe it could possibly have happened . . . to somebody else.

Right up until something equally preposterous would happen. Like sitting in a bleak conference room on an airless asteroid and suddenly knowing, just flat *knowing,* that her brother—thousands of light-years away— was so deep in danger that even he didn't have a chance of surviving on his own.

But then she'd still had to hack through the thickets of *Oh, I'm just being silly* second thoughts; what finally cleared her mind and righted her course was the added premonition, after some fifteen minutes spent fitfully waiting for his return, that now *Han* was also in danger. Even then, after she'd become alarmed enough to mutter a lame excuse to the Mandalorians and leave the room, she'd had to go all the way up to the communications center to confirm in person what was going on. When she found out that the RRTF's subspace real-time reports had suddenly gone dark—and that Han had been up here some fifteen minutes earlier and had gotten the same information—she had turned straight for the docking bay cavern, because she knew Han would jump out of here just as fast as he could get the *Falcon*'s engines hot.

She also knew why: Han could no more leave a friend in danger than he could jump to lightspeed by flapping his arms. And she knew that he'd leave without telling her he was going, because he knew she was, in this respect, no different than he was, and he still had this profoundly silly masculine notion that he could somehow keep her from danger just by leaving her behind. Just how profoundly silly this masculine notion was she planned to demonstrate graphically as soon as she caught up with him. Maybe she'd draw him a picture. On his skull. With the gauss wrench.

But how could she catch him?

She looked around the docking bay, but in the chaos of hustling crew and tugs and the clouds hissing out from gas exchangers and the space dust billowing away from hulls hooked up to electrostatic reversers, there were no answers to be found. She thought, *What would Luke do?* . . . and when she closed her eyes and took a deep breath or two, she decided that right now she should be going *that* way . . .

She drifted aimlessly through the docking bay cavern for a few minutes, bemusedly waiting for another feeling to strike her; she was so focused on her inner feelings that it took her a second or two to register that the handsome profile of that tall pilot up ahead, the one chatting with the deck crew men who were cleating down his B-wing, belonged to a friend of hers.

"Tycho!" She waved and headed over to him. "Tycho, I am *so* glad to see you!"

Tycho Celchu greeted her with a bemused look of his own. "Princess? Aren't you supposed to be in the negotiations?"

"Forget the negotiations," she said. "I need a ride. It's a diplomatic emergency."

Tycho frowned. "Um . . ."

"I'm a rated gunner on that thing," she said, nodding toward the B-wing. "I need you to get it space-ready as fast as possible."

His frown deepened. "Princess, you're a civilian—"

"And my mother was your queen." Trading on her family's station always left a sickly weight in the pit of her stomach, but this was an emergency. "You've been Alderaanian a lot longer than you've been an officer. Will you do this for me, or should I ask somebody else?"

"Ask somebody what?" Wedge Antilles had come up beside her. "Hi, Princess. How go the negotiations?"

"Wedge, hi." Leia winced—another friend she'd have

to lie to. "Uh . . . something's come up. I need to borrow Tycho and his B-wing. Maybe for just a few hours."

"If it were up to me . . ." Wedge spread his hands apologetically. "But Lando—that is, General Calrissian— he's a real nice guy, y'know, easygoing and relaxed when he's out of uniform. But the first time you violate his orders, you find out he's got no sense of humor at *all*."

She looked from one to the other. Why would the Force have sent her in this direction in the first place if there were no chance she could—

What would Luke do?

She took a deep breath, shut her eyes, and sighed it out again. When she opened her eyes, she could now see the two men before her clearly. Tycho had been only a vehicle for her, Wedge only a roadblock . . . but now they were men, good men, friends who honestly cared about her obvious distress. They deserved better than to be conned into helping her.

Slowly, clearly, simply, she said, "Luke's in danger."

Wedge and Tycho exchanged an unreadable glance. Wedge said, "What kind of danger?"

She couldn't keep a hint of quaver out of her voice. "The fatal kind."

Tycho looked at Wedge. Wedge's mouth compressed and he stared down at the deck. Not for long—less than a second—and then he huffed a sigh, and gave a decisive nod. Tycho wheeled and sprinted away.

Leia watched as the Alderaanian raced headlong through the chaos in the docking bay cavern. "Where's he going?"

Wedge was already jogging toward his own X-wing. "To round up the rest of the Rogues," he called back over his shoulder. "Fifteen minutes."

* * *

LANDO SAT IN THE CONFERENCE CHAIR HAN HAD ONLY recently vacated. He'd stopped listening to Fenn Shysa argue with the mercenary commander about thirty seconds after he'd finished the introductions; Lando had enough Mando'a to get along in conversation or fleece an unwary Mandalorian over a sabacc table, but he'd seen in those first thirty seconds that the commander wasn't buying what Fenn was selling—a combination of "Lord Mandalore Commands You" and an appeal to civic responsibility and Defend Our Honor sentimentality. Lando probably should have mentioned to Fenn before they'd gone in that those kinds of arguments worked only on people who already believed in that stuff, and people who believed in that stuff didn't often end up spilling blood for Imperial credits.

Like most fundamentally decent men, Fenn seemed to believe that down deep, nearly everybody else was fundamentally decent, too. He seemed to think that because he had once been a mercenary, other mercenaries were just like him: a cynical shell over a core of natural nobility. But Fenn had never been exactly your factory-issue mercenary.

Lando, on the other hand, was a gambler. A successful gambler. Like all successful gamblers, he knew that "natural nobility" was more rare than a flawless Corusca gem, and that over the long run, you never lost by assuming that everyone you met was driven by a combination of greed, fear, and stupidity.

After half an hour, he'd found himself wondering how Han had managed to sit through two days of this without taking his own life. After an hour, it became clear to him that neither Han nor Leia was going to be returning to the conference room anytime soon. Nearly another hour had passed before the ensign he'd sent looking for Leia had returned to the conference room door with a look on his face that indicated either failure or chronic illness.

Lando leaned forward to speak softly in Fenn's ear while the opposing commander was making yet another long, insultingly skeptical-sounding speech. "I have to step out for a minute or two. Cover for me, huh?"

Fenn nodded without hesitation. He must not have been really listening either. "Don't blame you," he said from the side of his mouth. "Are you as sick of this fella as I am?"

"I never get sick of people," Lando said, smiling. "I'll be right back."

Out in the corridor, the ensign looked like he was wishing he could be just about anywhere else. "She was last seen, General, getting into Lieutenant Celchu's B-wing."

"Really." Lando was still smiling. He'd been a gambler too long to give anything away. "And where was the lieutenant last seen?"

"Well, I—I mean, General, *you* would know . . . wouldn't you?"

Lando's smile went wider. "Pretend I don't."

"Rogue Squadron lifted off over an hour ago, sir—traffic control says they were on one of your, ah, *special* missions, sir . . ."

"One of *my* special missions?"

"Yes, sir. Commander Antilles gave the verification code."

"Did he, now?"

"Yes, sir. Is—is there, uh, a *problem*, sir?"

"Why would there be a problem?"

"Well—the Princess had just been up to ComOps, sir. She was asking about General Solo."

"Of course she was."

"And General Solo had been there just a few minutes earlier. He was asking about General Skywalker."

"And what did General Skywalker have to say?"

"Oh, uh, well—nothing, sir. I mean, he's out of contact—the whole RRTF has gone dark."

"Has it? Well, well."

"Yes, sir. And, um, there is this, as well, sir." The ensign held out a datareader. "It's a transcript of an automated burst-transmission that is being fed into the HoloNet over and over again, at five-minute intervals. The transmissions began less than a minute after the RRTF went dark."

Lando weighed the reader in his hand. "Summarize it for me, will you?"

"Well—it claims to be from Lord Shadowspawn, sir. ComOps hasn't verified authenticity yet, but—"

"But you thought I might want to know about it. Because you think it might have something to do with our missing princess and her two favorite generals."

"In the transmission, sir, Lord Shadowspawn claims to have captured the entire task force—and he says he will kill them all in three Standard days unless the Republic agrees to an immediate cease-fire . . . and acknowledges his claim on the Imperial Throne."

"Really. Hm. Well, well again."

"But like I said—" The ensign licked nervous sweat from his upper lip. "We don't know if—ComOps hasn't verified its authenticity—even if it really is from Shadowspawn, we have no way of knowing if any of it is true—"

"Sure we do. It's all true," Lando said. "Luke's already there. Han and Leia are on their way. Not to mention Rogue Squadron."

"Sir? I don't understand."

"That's because you're new around here, son."

"Sir?"

"Forward your personnel file to my exec. I can use a man like you."

The ensign's mouth dropped open. "Sir—? I don't—I mean, I *failed*—"

"When you submit your file, put a note in there that I'm promoting you to lieutenant j.g."

The ensign's eyes went as wide and slack as his mouth "Sir—?"

"You've just saved a general from being bored to death. If I thought I could get away with it, I'd give you a medal, too." He left the ensign gaping in the hallway.

Inside the conference room, Lando nodded a grin at Shysa and kicked his empty chair out of the way. "Let me handle this."

He slipped around the corner of the table, to the mercenaries' side. He sat on the edge and grinned down at the astonished commander. "Okay. Negotiation's over. You win."

Shysa frowned. "They do?"

The commander blinked. "We do?"

"Sure. I'll put it in writing. No Republic forces will land on, permanently orbit, or otherwise occupy this world or this system while you live to serve the Empire. Satisfied?"

"Well, I—ah, I suppose, I mean—well, yes."

"Great!" Lando's grin got wider. "Now what?"

"Now?" The commander blinked again. He was still so astonished he entirely forgot he was supposedly refusing to speak Basic. "What do you mean?"

"I mean you've *won*. Your victory is complete. What now?"

"Well, we—I suppose, I mean—"

"How are you planning to get paid?"

"Paid?"

"I have to tell you, our sensors aren't picking up any sign of Imperial ships dropping out of hyperspace to, y'know, jettison bags of cash or anything."

The commander's face clouded over. "I see what you mean."

"Strikes me," Lando said carelessly, examining his flawless manicure, "that failure to deliver payment qualifies as a breach of contract, doesn't it? Not to mention scampering off and leaving you all here to die. Forget that part. I guess they figured that with you all dead, they'd never *have* to pay. And if you live, well, you're trapped on a planet deep in Republic space. How are you supposed to collect?"

The commander scowled. "You're trying to trick me."

"Not at all." Lando winked at him. "I'm trying to *hire* you."

The commander looked thoughtful.

"Might you and your men be interested in, ah, a *new* position? Working for people who give a damn whether you live or die? Who will actually—believe it or not—*pay* you?"

The commander's scowl got deeper and deeper the longer he thought it over; after what seemed like a long, long time, he turned that scowl on Lando.

The commander said, "In advance?"

CHAPTER 6

"WHAT DO YOU MEAN, LUKE SKYWALKER IS DEAD?"

Lord Shadowspawn's holoprojected image was only a half meter tall, but something in his posture, or his inhumanly corpse-pale face, or the glittering malice that dripped from every word, made the nervous wing commander, Norris Prang, feel even smaller than that. He felt roughly the size of a Kashyyyk mouse-spider, and he had a feeling that Lord Shadowspawn was about to come down on him like a Wookiee's heel.

He swallowed hard and snugged his gleaming black flight-trooper helmet more tightly into his uncomfortably damp armpit. One good thing about this black armor—the sweat didn't show much, even when it leaked through the wicking fabric joints and trickled down his chestpiece, which it had started to do right about the same time Lord Shadowspawn had started to smile.

Had Shadowspawn's teeth *always* been so large? And so white . . . and kind of *pointy*-looking?

He couldn't remember. In fact, now that he thought of it, he couldn't remember ever having seen Shadowspawn smile. Until now. Which could not bode well for his future.

Maybe this was why his commanding officer, Group Captain Klick, had insisted that he report this personally. "I had, uh, thought, my lord, that my lord might find this to be *good* news."

"*You thought?*"

"The, uh, death of Luke Skywalker," the wing commander struggled on gamely, "will be a substantial blow to the Rebels—"

"*It would be a substantially greater blow to me. Tell me again. Slowly.*"

"The gravity slice worked as well as can be expected, given that the Rebels fired first," Prang said.

"*They have been known to do so.*"

"While the Rebel flagship was not entirely destroyed, the g-slice did manage to cut it into three pieces, of which the two largest are currently derelict in orbit. The smallest section included the bridge, which retained some manu—"

"*Wing Commander.*"

Prang felt himself swallow again. Involuntarily. "Yes, my lord?"

"*Speak to me of how you plan to capture Luke Skywalker.*"

"Plan to—? My lord, the only evidence we have of his presence is a single unencrypted EM transmission, which could easily have been some kind of a trick."

"*A trick? Luke Skywalker doesn't use tricks. The only evidence we need is that someone landed a third of a Mon Calamari starship using nothing but attitude thrusters. That's a Skywalker at work.*"

"My lord, the bridge section exploded on impact."

Shadowspawn's interstellar-black eyes narrowed dangerously.

"*If Luke Skywalker had perished, I would have felt it in the D . . . in the Force. Find him, Wing Commander. Find him and bring him to me. Alive. No harm must come to him, do you understand? Do this as though your own life depends on it.*"

The wing commander threw his hand up in an enthu-
siastic salute. "It will be done, my Lord."

LUKE TOILED UP THE OUTER SLOPE OF THE CRATER LEFT
by the final destruction of the *Justice:* a ring of half-
fused volcanic rock thrown up five meters above a hillside that was itself piled and fused rock. In fact, from
here it looked like the whole *planet* was nothing but
fused and blasted rock; the only colors were the dull
reds and shabby blues, rot-green and vomit-yellow of
exposed minerals, and the iridescent metallic smears left
by meteorites from the daily rock storms.

At the lip, he lay flat and slowly, cautiously, lifted the
rad sensor above the rim. He used his artificial hand.
The scant bacta he and the crew had been able to salvage from the wreck wasn't sufficient to treat the casualties they already had; no sense adding to the burden by
getting himself rad-burned.

At the base of the ring below him, R2 bounced from
side to side, whistling a caution. "I know," Luke said,
squinting up at the rad sensor. "But I have to confirm destruction before we abandon this position—we can't afford to let these guys get their hands on next-generation
Mon Cal tech."

R2's answer sounded vaguely scolding, and Luke let
himself smile. "Once you get that rollerped back in
working order, you can do these jobs again. Till then,
though—"

This time, R2's *terrooweepeepeep* came out distinctly
defensive.

"If you worried as much about yourself as you do
about me, we wouldn't be having this conversation.
Honestly, I think you spend too much time with Threepio."

The rad sensor flickered blue, then red, then blue
again; radiation levels were low enough that Luke de-

cided he could risk a peek. The interior of the crater was only about fifteen meters deep at its lowest point, though it was several hundred meters in diameter; the sponginess of the volcanic rock appeared to have absorbed a lot of the blast. As for the *Justice* itself, Luke could see that Mon Calamari scuttling charges were as efficient as everything else they made: he could spot no remaining piece of the ship bigger than his doubled fists. He would have taken a longer look, but the smothering-hot wind was whipping streamers of dust into his face.

He ducked back below the rim, fighting the urge to wipe his eyes until he could produce enough tears to wash out the sand; lacking bacta, a scratched cornea would be no picnic, either. He took a couple of seconds to retie the scrap of battle-dress blouse that he wore across his face. He held his breath till he got the rag in place, and tight. Breathing that dust was even less fun than getting it in his eyes. But keeping out the dust was only a partial solution; the atmosphere itself was mildly caustic. He'd been dirtside barely a Standard hour before a rasp had begun to scrape inside his throat with every breath.

Terroo-weet-weet-weet-weet-weet!

R2's insistent warning brought Luke's head around. "What is it?"

The astromech's holoprojector lit up trails of blue-tinged fire streaked toward the schematized curve of a planetary surface. Luke bared his teeth and turned toward the south, where the lightening-orange sky already blazed with an incoming meteorite storm.

"Great." He pulled out his comlink and twisted it to the *Justice*'s command channel. "Tubrimi, come in. Tubrimi, do you read?"

A burst of static was his only reply. Mindor's heavily ionized, metal-oxide-charged atmosphere made communications difficult at best; the power of a starship's comm suite was required to broadcast an EM message more than a kilometer or two, especially during a dust storm, since the dust itself was mostly metal oxides, as well: remnants of meteorites and the barren rock they'd struck. He could actually see the caves where the crew had taken shelter, a couple of kilometers away through the rolling hills, but his comlink just didn't have the juice to punch through. "Artoo! Tightbeam an alert to Tubrimi and Sthonnart! Tell them to break up the perimeter and retreat into the caves—"

Luke frowned. In the Force, a sudden surge of emotion . . .

Panic. Terror. Shock and rage—and there, at the crew's caves, two kilometers away: flares of scarlet, flashes of actinic white . . .

Blasterfire. Thermal detonators.

Battle.

Terroo-oo-weet?

"Don't wait for confirmation. Just get under cover," Luke said, leaping from the crater's rim. "I'll tell them myself."

He drew his lightsaber as he ran.

LIEUTENANT TUBRIMI CRUMPLED THE TRANSCRIPT OF the decrypted burst signal in his good hand as he stood up. "All right, you heard the orders," he said to the pair of ensigns managing the comm gear, his great black eyes swirling straight forward for emphasis. "Get everything packed up and moved into the caves on the double! Everything out of sight until we get a command-coded recall beacon."

Every step jabbed a lance through his broken shoulder, despite the emergency foam-cast a marine corpsman had sprayed on. Maybe later, there might be some bacta left after the wounded had been stabilized. "Major," he called as he approached the cave mouth. "General Sky-walker's orders are to set up a—"

He stopped, and his voice trailed away. The cave was empty.

The corpsmen were gone. Even the wounded had just . . . vanished, leaving behind only a litter of emergency blankets, water packs, and used bacta patches. Tubrimi gaped. "Major Sthonnart? Hey, what's going on? Are you in there?"

From behind him, all at once: blasterfire on full auto. The ear-shattering blasts of thermal dets. Shouted orders, and the cut-short screams of wounded marines. He whirled back to where the ensigns had been taking down the comm dish unit. They were gone, both of them; the comm dish lay on its side, rocking in the gritty breeze. *"Hey—"*

He scrambled over a fold of ground just in time to see one of the ensigns—on his back, eyes wide and staring—*sink* into the solid stone beneath him as though the volcanic rock were only thick oil. He leapt for the ensign's hand, but before he could get there the ensign had sunk from view—and the rock that closed over where he had gone was solid and cool. As Tubrimi stood up again, looking around wildly for any sign of the hundreds of sailors and marines, something touched his ankle, and darkness exploded across his brain.

LUKE WATCHED THE BATTLE END WHILE HE WAS ON HIS way. Using the Force to leap from rock to rock so swiftly he practically flew also relieved him of the need to watch his footing. He covered the two kilometers in about two minutes.

It didn't end like an ordinary battle. It just stopped. No carting-away of prisoners. No evacuation of wounded.

Nothing at all.

There were no bodies outside the caves. There were no bodies inside the caves. No sailors. No marines. No astromechs or medical droids. The only sound was the hush of sand stirring in the breeze, and the clicks of cooling stone. The air in the caves reeked of the ozone from recent blasterfire, and pockets of slag still glowed yellow where thermal dets had gone off against the rock. Luke left his blaster in its holster, and clipped his lightsaber back onto his belt. He felt no threat here.

The cave floor was littered with emergency blankets and used bacta packets, ration bars and water jugs, even a few of the DH-17 carbines favored by the marines. Luke drifted through the caves, eyes half-closed, brushing the rock with his fingertips. He felt fading resonances of the same emotions he had sensed, more distantly, from the base of the crater's rim. But these were only echoes in the Force.

Somehow, in the process of leading the entire task force into a trap, he had also managed to misplace several hundred people. Captured? Not by Imperials, that was for sure. Killed? Disintegrated, leaving not even dust behind? It didn't seem possible.

It *wasn't* possible.

He wasn't even upset, not really; the magnitude of everything that had happened was too vast, far beyond any emotional response he could imagine. He was numb. Stunned, he supposed.

He sagged, leaning into the rock wall, and let his head hang. "Ben?" he said, softly, sadly, without hope. "Ben, can you hear me? What *should* I have done? Master Yoda? What was I supposed to *do*?" In the rustle and hush of the sandy breeze, he heard no answer.

All he knew was that this was all wrong.

He slid down and sat, his back against the stone. He let his head roll back and squeezed his eyes shut. Suddenly he felt like *everything* was all wrong.

He'd made wrong choices every day of his life. In his mind's eye floated everyone who'd died because of him. Everyone who'd been hurt. From Mindor to Endor, back to Yavin—back to the corpses that had lain, still smoking, in the ruined doorway of the Lars moisture farm. *I guess I sort of thought everything was over. I got my happy ending. I thought I did. I mean, didn't I do everything you asked me to? Master Yoda, you wanted to break the rule of the Sith. And they're gone. Ben, you asked me to destroy Darth Vader. I did that, too. Father—even you, Father. You told me that together we would throw down the Emperor. And we did. Now it's over. But it's not the end. It's never the end.*

The cave boomed and shivered as the rock storm arrived like an artillery barrage. Luke just sat, head down, letting dust and grit trickle inside the back of his collar as meteorites pounded the hills.

I guess I was still kind of hoping there might be a Happily Ever After in there somewhere. Not even for me. I was ready to die. I still am. It's everybody else. It's like everything we went through, it was for nothing. We're still fighting. We'll always be fighting. It's like I didn't actually save anybody.

Gone is the past, he remembered Master Yoda saying once. *Imaginary is the future. Always now, even eternity will be.* Which Luke had always interpreted as *Don't worry about what's already done, and don't worry about what you'll do later. Do something* now.

Which would be fine advice, if he had the faintest clue what that *something* should be. Maybe if he'd had more experience as a general, he'd know if he should search for his missing men, or return to the crash site and wait for pickup, or try to find some way to signal the task force spaceside. *I never should have taken this job. I just don't know what a general would be doing right now. All I know is what a Jedi . . .*

Then his head came up. *I do know what a Jedi would be doing—and it isn't sitting around feeling sorry for himself, for starters.*

Especially, now that he thought of it, because the ground had stopped shuddering and the thunder of the storm outside had changed to the thunder of multiple sonic booms. He got up and walked outside.

The sky was full of TIE fighters whipping through a trans-sonic search grid.

Luke unclipped his lightsaber and thumbed the activator. The blade of brilliant green snarled and spat as its plasma consumed airborne grit. When a TIE fighter swung down through a barrel roll for a closer look, Luke smiled and beckoned with his blade like a ground crewman directing them in for a landing.

Then he put away the lightsaber, lowered himself into a cross-legged meditation posture on the warm rock, and folded his arms to wait.

He waited while the TIE fighters circled his position. He waited while the atmospheric gunships arrived and landed a few hundred meters away. He waited while hundreds of black-armored stormtroopers poured out of the gunships, assembled in ranks, and advanced on him in a broad arc, blasters leveled. He waited while a trooper with a group captain's flash on his chest stepped cautiously forward and called, "General Skywalker!"

Luke rose.

The assembled stormtroopers tensed. Several hundred blaster carbines snapped to shoulder-ready.

The group captain called again. "General Skywalker! *Are you Luke Skywalker?*"

"If it's not too much of a cliché, take me to your leader." Luke held out his lightsaber, inert, on his open palm, and smiled. "If it *is* too much of a cliché, take me anyway."

*   *   *

R2-D2 HAD PASSED THE ROCK STORM IN A SNUG LITTLE lava cave near the rim of the crater, unconcernedly repairing his rollerped's damaged arm. When the meteorite strikes got powerful enough to interfere with the repairs—a few of the ground shocks bounced the little droid around his lava cave like a Touranian jumping-stone in a bumble-dice cup—R2 just drilled four of his auxiliary manipulators into the sides of the cave to anchor himself in place and went on. With his enormous array of onboard tools, a good-enough repair was simple, though R2 did file a memo in his maintenance archive to have the arm replaced the next time he could find his way into a fully outfitted service center.

Soon the rock storm's thunder had faded, and R2's auditory sensors registered the characteristic shriek of air whistling through the accumulator panels of TIE fighters—always heard when TIEs were used in-atmosphere. R2's onboard threat-assessment algorithm estimated the shrieks to be coming from several kilometers overhead, which meant that a quick peek outside carried an acceptably low level of risk. First came an extensible minidish, with which R2 made a quick scan of sensor channels; discovering no droid-sensitive scans in progress, the little astromech extended his now-functional locomotor arms, deanchored his manipulators, and whirred up to the surface.

"*There* you are, my little beauty!" The shout registered in R2's auditory sensors as a series of sonic impulses whose wave characteristics corresponded to the natural vocal production of a human male speaking Basic with a distinctively Inner Rim accent; R2 instantly filed a copy in his medium-term audio log, because he knew from long experience that C-3P0 derived a great deal of pleasure-analogue from analyzing distinctive vowel/consonant interactions to deduce the planet of origin—and region of that planet—not only of the speaker in question, but also of the speaker's parents, childhood companions, teachers, and, if applicable, mate or mates. R2 himself was confident—over seventy-three percent probability—that this accent would turn out to be native to Mindor, but he was content to leave such final determinations to the expert. After all, every droid has to be good at *something* . . . and C-3PO had a long history of unpleasantly human-like insistence on his innate superiority in such matters, so R2 also filed a memo to pretend complete ignorance, which he estimated might prevent as much as thirty-seven minutes of pointless bickering.

R2's threat-assessment algorithm also registered the origination point of the shout—some eighty-seven degrees from planetary north, at a range of less than three meters—and so when the shouter grabbed the little droid, R2's antitamper capacitors were already fully charged. "Aeona! I've got him! I've got hi*youerghh* . . ." was the new shout, the *youerghh* being the shouter's response to receiving a burst of static discharge that hurled him back a meter or so and left him twitching on the lava, sparks still spitting from half-charred gloves.

"Boakie!" a different human male, though with a similar accent, shouted. "That little grubber killed *Boakie*! Give me that ion blaster—"

"*Cancel* that!" This voice, by contrast, was clearly the product of a human *female,* who, based on the harmonic overtones of authority, was equally clearly accustomed to instant obedience. "Stow the blaster, Tripp."

"But—but it killed Boakie—"

"He's not dead. He's just learning about keeping his hands to himself. Now stow that blaster before I take it away and feed it to you."

"But I was only—"

"Tripp."

"All right, Aeona. I mean, jeesh, you can't fault a guy for getting—"

"Sure I can. Now back off. I want to talk to this thing."

There was motion among the rocks. To R2's optical array, it looked like the lava itself had come to life and was closing in. This being new to R2's long, long data chain of filed experience, the little droid dutifully recorded the lava's approach.

R2 also subjected this recording to real-time multispectrum analysis and discovered, through a combination of thermal and bioelectric field output, that what appeared to be living rock was instead nineteen human beings who were *wearing* rocks—the humans appeared to have constructed a rough analogue of Imperial stormtrooper armor out of chunks of lava attached somehow to the ragged remnants of survival suits. Which was a particularly compelling example, R2 observed in a note appended to the file, of the endless human inventiveness with camouflage.

"Hey, little guy," the authoritative woman said, approaching R2 with open, empty hands, crouching a little, as though the droid might be a nervous Shistavanen cub. "What are you doing all alone, way out here? Waiting for somebody?"

"Waiting for a junk dealer, I bet," the one called Tripp said. "Can you believe how *old* that thing is? If it ain't defective, who'd leave it out here? I say we blast it and break it up for parts."

"What counts around here is what *I* say," the woman growled, then put on that same gentle, friendly tone as she turned back to R2. "Don't mind him."

"But—but listen, Aeona, seriously. Our last three astromechs are barely functional—and they're *all* newer than this one. We really need those parts!"

The woman's face shifted into an expression that

R2's optical-analysis algorithm couldn't parse, which triggered his threat-assessment system to initiate a measured response: R2 decided that a prudent course would be to warn these humans of the possible consequences of aggressive action.

A quick scan of his data archives brought up a recording of the rescue of Han Solo on Tatooine: the chaotic battle above the Pit of Carkoon aboard the sail barge of Jabba the Hutt. A bit of judicious editing—to intersplice a more recent recording—replaced Gamorrean guards and other servitors of the Hutt crime lord with human beings in armor improvised of broken lava, and replaced the deck of the Hutt's caravel with the devastated landscape of Mindor. This process took only .78 seconds, and when it was complete, R2 initiated its holoprojector array to display its handiwork: a miniature Luke Skywalker wielding a lightsaber of shining green, who leapt and spun and somersaulted among images of R2's captors, cutting them down on every side.

"What is *that* supposed to be?" Tripp said. "Is that little grubber *threatening* us?"

"Shut up." The woman—Aeona—dropped to one knee and leaned in to get a better look at R2's holodisplay, and for a moment her face softened, her eyes went wide, and her voice went hushed with awe. "That's a Jedi . . ."

"You don't really *believe* that thing, do you?" Tripp shook his head, one hand on the DEMP blaster. "The Empire wiped out the Jedi before I was born."

"Not before *I* was born." The woman stared at Luke's image. "This little fella belongs to a Jedi. That's who he's waiting for. I'm thinking maybe we should wait with him—I'd really like to meet this Jedi, when he finally shows up. We could use his help."

"What if whoever shows up turns out *not* to be a Jedi?"

She stood, and shook off that gentle expression like a bad dream. "Then we take their ship and leave 'em to the Melters." She shrugged. "Saves having to kill them ourselves."

THE GUNSHIP SET DOWN ON A BROAD LANDING FIELD IN the shadow of turbolaser towers. One of the black-armored stormtroopers gestured with his blaster rifle. "Out."

Luke looked at the towers, at the hundreds of gunships in neatly ordered ranks, up at the mouths of caverns high above on the curve of the volcanic dome, in and out of which flew clouds of TIE fighters.

They sure didn't seem worried about him getting a look at their defenses. No surprise there; he didn't figure they had any plans to ever let him go.

A whole platoon of stormtroopers in gleaming black armor surrounded him, marching with weapons ready. The two behind him had blaster carbines aimed at the middle of his back, and fingers on their triggers. Their sergeant marched ahead. Behind them all, at a vantage that kept them all in view together, walked what Luke had come to assume was some kind of political officer.

Rather than armor, this individual wore dark, vaguely Vaderish clothing and a cape, and a curious hat, or headgear—a jet-black version of the odd half-moon hat that the putative Lord Shadowspawn had worn in the holoprojections. This individual had the pale, frozen face and jet-black eyes of Shadowspawn, as well—exactly, in fact. Luke might have assumed that this individual was in fact Shadowspawn himself, were it not that the drape of the jet-black cape clearly showed that the body beneath was female—and a short, fairly plump female at that.

She carried his lightsaber, and she stank of the dark side.

She'd been on the troop carrier that had brought him here from the caves. She never spoke, but her slightest gesture was enough to make a trooper snap to his duty with a will. Here in the installation, among the hundreds, maybe thousands of troopers, he had seen some dozens of these headgear types. They all had the same face—had to be some sort of holomask—and all of them seemed to get the same deference from the black stormtroopers. And there didn't seem to be any Imperial regulars here at all, just the black stormtroopers and these dark-side Moon Hats.

And the Moon Hats all had this same dark-side stink: an aura of *wrongness* so palpable that Luke could close his eyes and target them by the revulsion they inspired.

The base's defenses weren't impressive, just five ion-turbo surface-to-orbit dual cannons and a double ring of turbolaser batteries that appeared to be calibrated for surface work—antiarmor and the like. Of course, those were only the fixed defenses; what sorts of mobile fighting craft the warlord might possess was impossible to guess, because the base itself appeared to have been hollowed out of the interior of a volcanic dome more than five kilometers across. Luke figured that with a little crowding, he could have fit most of the RRTF inside there and had room to spare—especially since there was no way to know how deep some of those vast steam-billowing caverns might prove to be.

And there was a single emplacement of some kind at the uppermost curve of the volcanic dome, in the middle of the ring of surface-to-orbit cannons. It appeared to be covered in some kind of heavily armored shell. He turned to one of the stormtroopers who marched at his side and pointed up at it. "Tell me what that is."

He felt a pulse from the Force, and he looked over his shoulder in time to see the Moon Hat touch fingertips to her lips, then flatten her hand, palm down. One of the troopers behind him jabbed Luke in the kidney with the muzzle of his carbine. Hard. "You heard her."

"I did?"

"No talking. We know what Jedi can do."

Luke shrugged and kept walking, a little stiffly until the knot in his back eased. "Please don't hit me."

This earned him a carbine stock across the back of his head hard enough to buckle his knees. "Didn't you *hear* me?"

Luke straightened again and shook the stars out of his head. He paused long enough to look over his shoulder. "I heard you. But I don't see any particular reason to obey you."

"Obey this."

The Force whispered a warning, and Luke whirled in time to catch the oncoming butt of the blaster carbine in the palm of his flesh hand and hold it fast. "I said please."

The astonished stormtrooper tried to yank his carbine free, but instead Luke tightened his grip and let the Force add strength to his arm; a twist of the wrist shattered the carbine's stock to plastite splinters. The other stormtrooper swore and triggered an autoburst from his carbine. Luke's other hand, the prosthetic hand that had replaced the one his father had taken, came up in an arc that precisely followed the motions of the carbine's muzzle and caught all five bolts squarely in its palm.

"Please don't shoot me, either." He turned the palm upward in a friendly shrug and let the astonished troopers stare at the only effect of the Force-blunted blaster-fire: a faint curl of steam that trailed upward from his unmarked palm. "Let's try to end the day with nobody else dying, shall we?"

The stormtrooper sneered, "Tell that to Lord Shadowspawn."

"I plan to," Luke said. "That's why I'm here."

CHAPTER 7

HAN SOLO WAS STRONGLY OF THE OPINION THAT SPACE battles, despite how much fun certain demented thrill-monkeys—say, any member of Rogue Squadron—liked to claim they can be, ranked somewhere below being kissed by a Traptoforian razor slug, and only a whisker above being dropped headfirst into a barrel of bantha poop. He'd been in this one for less than five minutes, and so far it had done nothing to change his opinion.

It wasn't like he hadn't been expecting trouble. He'd been expecting trouble ever since he'd ditched those Mando negotiations. That expectation of trouble had become absolute certainty when he and Chewie had hit the jump point three light-years from Mindor and been yanked out of hyperspace and ambushed by a couple dozen TIE Defenders, which hadn't been an actual problem because he was not, despite Leia's occasional insistence, an idiot. He'd preset the final leg in the *Falcon*'s navicomputer, so they had been in and out of the jump point before those astonished Imps could so much as shout "Emperor's black bones!" or whatever stupid pretend curse they liked to shout when caught with their armored pants around their armored ankles.

If he hadn't been so worried about Luke, he might even have stuck around and taught a few of them the value of *real* cursing, Corellian-style—Corellian curses being a synergistic blend of vulgarity, obscenity, and outright blasphemy that were the only things really worth saying when one was in the middle of being blown to monatomic dust.

Also, the navicomputer preset should have dropped them out of hyperspace about twenty light-minutes from Mindor, which would, in theory, have given him and Chewie plenty of time to get a solid read on the situation with the *Falcon*'s medium-range sensors before deciding whether to go on in or head back out, because Han—recent military service notwithstanding—still tried, at least in spirit, to adhere to the principles outlined in the Combat Litany of the Smuggler's Creed:

Never fight when you can bluff.
Never bluff when you can run.
Never run when you can sneak.
If no one knows you're there, you win.

This was the theory, anyway. The distinction between theory and reality was announced by the mass-proximity Klaxon in the *Falcon*'s cockpit, which unleashed an ear-shattering blast that was underlined by the *Falcon* being unceremoniously dumped back into realspace in the middle of a battle between three Corellian frigates, half a dozen fighter wings, and a giant cloud of TIE Interceptors that was, unbelievably, taking place in the middle of an even-more-giant meteor storm.

THE X-WING PILOT AND HIS WINGMAN WERE LINING UP desperate deflection shots at an oncoming formation of six TIE Interceptors when an ancient, battered YT-1300 freighter suddenly arrived in the middle of their dogfight, blocking those last-ditch shots.

The wingman's demand to know what a saucer-shaped relic from Old Republic days was doing in the middle of a space battle quickly turned into a gasp of awe as the battered hulk slewed into an astonishingly precise skew-flip that turned its sublights into weapons to blast a pair of Interceptors enough off-course that they slammed into a nearby asteroid. At that point, the relic in question hurtled headlong at the remaining four of the TIE flight—who were boxed together by the maze of asteroids—barrel-rolling through a storm of laserfire while unleashing a salvo of concussion missiles with either astonishing accuracy or even more astonishing luck, so that after a single pass the freighter streaked away, hurtling off through the maze of asteroids after having dusted six Interceptors in under five seconds.

Inside the freighter's cockpit, Han didn't have a chance to celebrate his victory. Bleeding from a minor scalp wound he'd collected off the front viewport strut owing to not being fully strapped into his pilot's couch, he was busy yanking the control yoke this way and that, thumbing fire-control switches wholly at random, and ducking and throwing his weight as though he could bodily increase the ship's maneuverability to help dodge the meteors that kept denting his hull. All the while he kept screaming at the top of his lungs things like "Chewie, we *need* those *deflectors*! We really, really *do*!" and "Is that *smoke*? Why am I *smelling smoke*?" From the forward service access came half-panicked yowls of frustration and apology: in the haste of their sudden takeoff, the problem in the balky forward deflector-array control assembly had failed to get entirely repaired, which could be a seriously fatal problem in the middle of a couple of hundred enemy starfighters, a number of which were now apparently *right on his tail.* But he ignored Chewie's yowls, because on top of everything else he was dealing with, something was entirely screwed up with local space: the *Falcon*'s navi-computer couldn't make any kind of sense out of the trajectories of all the different rocks swirling around, and the ship was yawing and starting to tumble in a way he hadn't experienced since his legendary race through the Kessel Run, where tidal effects from the local black holes had—

"Hey . . ." Han straightened up, his face suddenly clearing. It *was* like Kessel—*exactly* like Kessel! He checked a sensor; sure enough, the asteroids were clustered around a powerful mass well, almost certainly produced by a gravity mine or projector somewhere in the middle. "That's *it*! Chewie, forget the deflectors! Give me particle shields forward! *Now!*"

Chewbacca replied with a series of growling snorts and hoots that translated, roughly, as *You'd better not be thinking what I know you're thinking!*

Han grinned, remembering a vaguely similar situation some years before. He gave the same answer now. "They'd be crazy to follow us, wouldn't they?"

Without waiting for the shields or even an acknowledgment from Chewbacca, Han slewed the *Falcon* through a radically tightening arc that set it rocketing full-speed into the thickest part of the asteroid field. The particle shields flared to spectacular life; radiation scatter from their disintegration of dust and the smaller rocks on the cloud made the *Falcon* look like it was flying within a shell of fireworks.

And he reflected, briefly, that those demented Rogue Squadron thrill-monkeys might actually be right. Once in a while.

To the pilots of the TIE Interceptors in pursuit of the *Falcon,* the ship simply vanished. The asteroid field was dense and unpredictable; so much of the pilots' attention had to be concentrated on staying out of the way of hurtling rocks that they were forced to rely more and more on their sensor locks as the *Falcon* pulled away, and so when the ship suddenly disappeared from their sensors, they assumed—correctly—that Han had pulled the old smuggler's trick of powering down his sublight engines and his weapons systems once he was deep within the cloud of metallic asteroids.

Which was a tricky place to go, as the gravity-well projector in the center had perturbed the entire cloud, sending asteroids in unpredictable directions. However, having their prey powered down and weaponless removed a great deal of the danger involved in hunting it. This prey would be in more danger from the asteroids than they were, being a bigger target and unable to maneuver without revealing its position—so a six-TIE flight spread out into a search matrix and began to methodically sweep the entire cloud.

Han, though, had learned as a cadet that even while flying through a large asteroid field crowded with pretty substantial rocks moving in more-or-less random directions, there were a couple of factors he could count on to keep his ship relatively safe. One was that a rock going in a particular direction would continue to go roughly in that same direction, unless it actually ran into something or was acted upon by an external force. Even collisions had a predictable result; postimpact trajectories of colliding objects could be reliably projected by any standard nav program, being a rough resultant of the vectors and respective kinetic energies of the objects in question. As for the TIE pilots, the only external force that concerned them was the grav projector, whose effect on the local rocks was also well within the capacities of their navicomputers to predict.

Which was why it came as a substantial surprise to the flight leader when an asteroid roughly the size of a speeder bike suddenly made a sharp forty-five-degree turn as though it had bounced off an invisible paatchi ball and slammed through his port engine, his hull, and his cockpit before continuing out the other side, taking his head with it.

Another of the flight suffered a similar fate before the

remaining TIE pilots made visual contact with the *Millennium Falcon,* which was zipping in rings around them without, apparently, using its drives at all. Meanwhile, asteroids seemed to actively *avoid* it, leaping aside from its path—and ending up, with improbable frequency, in new trajectories that proved catastrophic to the TIEs.

The last that was heard from any of these unfortunate pilots was a panicky final transmission: *"It's some kind of bloody Jedi! I swear to you, he's throwing rocks at us! I don't know how—with his mind, or some—"* The transmission ended in a crash that sounded very like a ton or so of asteroid crushing a titanium hull. Which, in fact, it was.

SO LONG AS IT HAS SUFFICIENT MASS AGAINST WHICH TO push, the repulsorlift is the most efficient transportation device ever devised: it uses virtually no energy, produces no emissions and virtually no radiation signature—not even waste heat—so it is detectable only by gravitic sensor. Repulsorlifts were so widespread that nearly everyone in the galaxy simply took them for granted, using them in everything from Star Destroyers to swoop boards. TIE Interceptors, though, were carrier-based craft, designed to operate in space well beyond the kind of planetary masses that made repulsorlifts work. TIEs had no need of repulsorlifts, and Imperial ship designers, with typically unimaginative thrift, simply left them out. For the same reason, the sensors aboard these fighters were calibrated to detect the field signatures of sublight engines and charged weapons arrays, not the gravitic-pulse output of repulsorlifts . . . which weren't really useful in starfighter combat anyway; they were just not powerful enough to provide the near-instantaneous accelerations necessary for modern dog-fighting.

Republic starfighters, on the other hand, were designed to operate independently of capital ships, and were regularly used for certain atmospheric applications where silent fuel efficiency was more important than raw speed. And one of the two relatively little-known features of the repulsorlifts was that the device functioned not only in planetary gravity wells, but in *any* gravity well—even the mass-shadows projected by gravity mines and interdiction ships.

The other little-known feature of the repulsorlift was that it did operate with reassuring respect for the laws of motion. It moved a ship because it was shoving against the gravitational field of the planet; the ship moved because the planet wouldn't. If, on the other hand, one directed one's repulsorlift toward a mass significantly smaller than that of one's ship—like, say, a metric ton of asteroid—it was the mass that moved. Often very, very swiftly indeed. Some pilots had come to refer to this maneuver as the Solo Slide.

Not because Han Solo invented it—the trick was far older than he was—but because no one in the galaxy had ever done it better.

As soon as his mastery of the Solo Slide had bought the *Falcon* a few seconds' breather, Han called to Chewie to join him in the cockpit. The Wookiee slid smoothly into the copilot's chair, strapped himself in, and observed succinctly, *"Baroough wonnngar row-oo-wargh."*

"Couldn't have said it better myself." Han spun the dial on the comm unit. "Still jamming subspace; going to realspace. Republic frigates, this is the *Millennium Falcon*. Do you copy? Repeat: do you *copy?*" he said, louder, as though shouting might help.

The reply came through, crackling with static. "Millennium Falcon, *this is the RDFS* Lancer. *We copy. Confirm receipt of following message.*"

Han shot a frown at Chewie, shrugged, and replied, "Go ahead."

"*Message reads: Where's my eight thousand credits, you thieving pirate?*"

Han grinned. "Message confirmed. Reply: Regards to Captain Tirossk. How about I offer one dusted grav projector on account?"

Chewbacca gave him a look. "*Hoowerghrff?*"

Han shrugged. "Who *else* do I owe that much money to?"

"*Freghrr. Khooherm. Flighwarr—*"

"Yeah, yeah, all right, drop it."

The comm crackled. "*Solo—Tirossk here. If we both get out of this alive, my friend, we'll call it even, yes?*"

Han winced. No Bothan would make that kind of offer if he thought there was any chance it might actually happen. "Maybe you better fill me in."

The situation played out like an extended good-news-bad-news joke. The good news was that Shadowspawn didn't have enough Interceptors to defend all his gravity-well projectors. The bad news was that this was because there were *thousands* of them, scattered throughout the system-wide debris field. Good news: the projectors, lacking the engines of capital ships to power them, seemed to depend on asteroid-based generators and a system of capacitors that—in the best estimate the *Lancer*'s computer could make—would be able to power them for only about four Standard days. The bad news: these thousands of new gravity wells had destabilized the entire system, sending vast clouds of asteroids spiraling inward to the star, with the first impacts to begin in less than *two* Standard days. The good news: most of the asteroids were small enough to simply burn up in the star's corona. The bad news: that was only *most* of them; some of the larger asteroids were capable, on impact, of triggering flare-like stellar eruptions that would put out enough hard radiation to sterilize the entire system, including every single ship—Republic, Imperial, and otherwise—and every single life-form of any variety on the surface of Mindor. More bad news: each gravity projector the task force managed to destroy would actually *speed up* the infall of the asteroids, because the outer gravity wells actually slowed the decay of the inner asteroids' orbits by partially balancing the star's gravitation. And to counter that bad news, there was no good news. None at all. Everyone was going to die.

Everyone.

"I don't buy it," Han said. "I don't buy it for a tenth of a Standard second. No Imp commander would throw away all these men and all this equipment just to take out a few Republic ships. They can't *afford* to. There's a way out. There's gotta be a way out. We'll cut our way in and link up with the task force; once we get Luke's boys behind us—"

"There's more," Tirossk said. *"The* Justice *broke up in orbit. General Skywalker tried to land part of what was left. There was . . . an explosion."*

Han stopped listening after that, amid vivid visions of putting his DL-44 against the forehead of a certain septic-soaked warlord with a made-up darksider name.

Chewbacca threw one arm over his face, leaned his elbow against the overhead console, and moaned. Han swallowed the knot in his throat—which didn't make it go away, just added a few new ones in his stomach—and forced a smile onto his face. "Look on the bright side, Chewie."

"Browwergh."

"Sure there is," he said. "At least we managed to avoid dragging Leia down with us. She's safe. That counts for something."

The *Falcon*'s comm crackled. *"You do know this is an open channel, don't you, Slick?"*

Han gaped. Chewbacca moaned again.

"While General Solo spits out his foot," Leia went on, *"will somebody kindly cover Rogue Squadron so we can take out that grav projector?"*

"Leia—Leia, Luke is—" Han choked, and had to cough his voice clear. "Luke is—"

"Nonsense."

"You—you *said* he was in trouble—"

"And he still is." Even through the static on the comm, he could hear that her conviction was absolute. *"Han, do you copy? He's still in trouble."*

Han found himself grinning. "That's the best news I've heard all day."

ONE LAST ROUNDING OF A TUNNEL'S CURVE, DEEP WITHIN the volcanic dome, brought to sight an archway that glowed with a pulsing red-tinged light. The stormtroopers prodded Luke onward, out onto a tiny arc of ledge high above a vast lake of molten lava.

Behind him in the mouth of the tunnel, the Moon Hat sank to her knees.

Lord Shadowspawn's throne room had been cut from the living rock: an immense vault whose ceiling and walls vanished into a shroud of sulfurous gases. The vault's only light came from a river of white-hot lava that fell from the mists above into the lake of fire below, its killing heat restrained by force screens. From the ledge, a long, narrow rock bridge led to a platform of black granite cantilevered out above the lake. The uppermost point of the platform had been carved and polished into a gleaming black throne the size of an Imperial shuttle, positioned so that the long form of Lord Shadowspawn, lounging within it, was shadowed by the lava fall behind and the pool below into a pall of scarlet gloom.

Luke stopped. This place could have been lifted intact from the climax of *Han Solo and the Pirates of Kessel:* it was so holothriller theatrical that it was almost funny . . . but Luke didn't feel like laughing. In the Force, this place read like a bomb wrapped as a birthday present.

Like a Sith Lord disguised as a kid's party clown.

Was he supposed to be impressed? Or was he supposed to dismiss all this as some kind of demented practical joke? He shot a disbelieving glance over his shoulder at his stormtrooper escort.

They stood in a shallow arc, carbines leveled at him; the Moon Hat, still on her knees, had inclined her head, his lightsaber balanced on her outstretched palms like an offering.

Luke got it: this wasn't about *him* at all. This show was for *them.*

Looked like it was working, too.

What exactly was Blackhole up to? And was this really Blackhole at all? On Vorzyd V, Blackhole had appeared only as a holoprojection—but the figure of Lord Shadowspawn on the Shadow Throne was no projection. Luke could feel, in the Force, a dark malice of wholly human origin—glittering malevolence and nastily sniggering glee—and it came from the man before him.

The Force smoked with threat. Luke felt some danger here darker than mere death.

"Luke Skywalker." Lord Shadowspawn's voice boomed through the cavern, probably using concealed speakers. *"Tremble before me!"*

"I think you have me confused with some other Luke Skywalker."

"*Kneel, Skywalker! Pledge yourself to me, and I will spare your life, and the lives of your crew.*"

Luke said nothing. The shape of Lord Shadowspawn shifted and lengthened, rising from the throne. That odd headgear of his seemed to glow with a light that cast no illumination on his expressionless face. His robes shimmered crimson as though drenched in blood, and he wore around his waist a broad belt from which hung a scabbarded sword. "*Bring him to me!*"

"Don't bother," Luke said. "I can manage on my own."

He walked out onto the long, narrow bridge of rock, using his slow progress to breathe himself deeply into Force awareness. He could feel the trap now.

As he neared the end of the bridge, Shadowspawn raised a fist as though to hurl thunderbolts. "*You are beaten, Skywalker!*"

"Don't bet your life on it."

Shadowspawn's fist hung in the air as if he'd forgotten he'd raised it. "*I have done what the vain, arrogant Emperor and his pathetic hound Vader never could! I have defeated Luke Skywalker!*"

"Not yet," Luke said. "Or if it makes you feel better, I can say 'Do not underestimate my power.' "

"*I hold your fleet in the palm of my hand—my gravity weapons will destroy this entire system. Not one ship will escape!*"

"That's a problem," Luke admitted. "But that means none of *your* ships will escape, either. Which is why I came to see you. Don't you think that together we might find some, well, less-*lethal* solution?"

"*You came here,*" Shadowspawn intoned, "*to kill me.*"

Luke spread his hands. "I told your troopers outside that I'm hoping to end the day with nobody else dying."

"*In this—*" Shadowspawn finally lowered his fist and

rested it on the hilt of his scabbarded sword. "—*you are doomed to disappointment.*"

"You don't want to do that."

"*Your Jedi tricks mean nothing to me!*"

"No—no, I mean it." Luke frowned. "You really *don't* want to do that. I can feel that you don't."

He stepped closer and lowered his voice. "Blackhole—that is you, isn't it? What's going on? Why the playacting?" He glanced around—in the Force, he could feel eyes upon him, many eyes, more than the company of stormtroopers on the ledge behind him. "Are you *recording* this?"

"*Fool!*" Shadowspawn thundered as he drew forth his sword. "*Kneel, or die!*"

The blade was huge, a hand wide and half again longer than Luke's lightsaber, and it appeared to have been cut from faceted crystal, like a single vast diamond. As Shadowspawn pulled it free from the scabbard, it kindled with a scarlet glare, as though it had gathered to itself the light of the lava pool below. It was, Luke mused, the same color as Vader's. Was that why this all felt, well, *staged*?

But staged or not, there was a limit to how far Luke was willing to play along.

"Listen to me, Blackhole or Shadowspawn or whoever you are," he said quietly. "I'm a Jedi, but I never had time for all the training some of the old Jedi were supposed to get. I've heard they tried to end conflicts without violence . . . but that's something I'm still learning. Do you understand? If you attack me, I will hurt you. If hurting you isn't enough, I will kill you."

"*You think you can defeat me? Fool! This blade is the product of untold millennia of Sith alchemy! Against such power, your Jedi toy is but a broken reed!*"

"Sith alchemy?" Luke squinted at him. "Are you kidding?"

"Come, Skywalker! Summon your blade and fight! Destroy me, and my men will instead serve you!"

Luke blinked. "What?"

"Legions of Shadow! Hear the word of your Lord!" Shadowspawn lifted his blade above his head, and the cavern shivered with the power of his voice. *"If this Jedi pup can defeat the Lord of the Shadow Throne, you will be his! Obey his every word as you would my own! Thus is the command of Shadowspawn!"*

"Really?" Luke frowned. "So if I beat you . . ."

"My legions are bred to absolute obedience. They will obey my command until their deaths, or my own . . . when they will serve the command of Luke Skywalker, instead."

And from the Force, Luke got the distinct feeling that Shadowspawn was actually, inexplicably, telling the truth.

Luke extended his right hand. From far back in the cavern, on the ledge at the tunnel's mouth, green fire crackled and spat from his lightsaber as it wrenched itself from the Moon Hat's grip and rose into the air. It whirled and spun and soared through the gloom until it smacked precisely into the palm of his outstretched hand. He shifted his weight and settled his shoulders.

"All right, then," he sighed. "Take your best shot."

CHAPTER 8

HAN MADE A FACE AND TRIED TO SWALLOW THE TASTE of the wind, bitter and stinging even through his filter mask. "Wasn't Mindar supposed to be some kind of resort planet, or something?" He kicked loose cinder away from the foot of the *Falcon*'s cargo ramp and surveyed the blasted landscape of rock and sand that was the last known position of the *Justice*. "This place would depress a Tusken."

From topside, Chewie registered a gruff *Earough*.

"Oh, sure, Mindor, whatever," Han said. "Who cares, anyway? If I want to call it Mindar, who's gonna argue? You? How about you, Princess?"

Leia didn't answer. She was moving slowly, as if she was feeling her way, as she followed a zigzag path up the slope of half-fused lava around the crater, which still emitted a better-than-fair amount of hard radiation.

Han sighed as he walked to the forward access ladder and clambered up onto the *Falcon*'s dorsal hull to join Chewbacca; he'd had to go forward to avoid the back-jets of the *Falcon*'s sublight engines, which he'd decided to leave hot in case they needed to make a sudden exit. Up on the portside forward mandible, Chewbacca was grumbling mournfully as he sprayed the ship's innumerable meteor punctures with patchplast. "How long till we're space-ready?"

"Garhowerarr haroo!"

"Is it *my* fault they decided to have their battle in the middle of an asteroid field?"

"Meroowargh harrwharrrhf."

"You do *not* do all the shipwork! Haven't I been sweeping out the holds ever since we landed? A lot of that dust is radioactive, too." Before Chewie could reply, Han turned and waved at Leia. "Getting anything?" he called.

"He was here!" she replied, her voice muffled by her own filter mask. "I mean, I *think* he was here. I'm pretty sure—well, *mostly* sure . . ."

"Got any, y'know, *feelings* about which way he went?" Han didn't really care what the answer was, so long as it was in the general direction of food. And drink.

He'd been planning to restock the *Falcon*'s galley back at the asteroid base, but that had been one more thing forgotten during their hasty exit. And back during the negotiations, Leia had sternly informed him that it would be a serious breach of Mandalorian diplomatic etiquette to break his fast while the central issues were still unresolved, which meant that it had been more than a day since Han had had anything more substantial to eat than the remnants he'd been able to scavenge from the *Falcon*'s deep freeze, namely some reconstituted pukkha broth and stewed stickli root. Not his favorites, to say the least, which was why they'd still been in the freezer after roughly five years.

And he'd forced those down *before* Rogue Squadron had joined the *Falcon* and they'd all set out on what turned out to be basically a running battle as they cut their way through the maze of grav projectors and swarms of TIE Interceptors to get here. They came in by microjumping on a jagged course toward the planet; each time a gravity station yanked them out of hyperspace, there'd be another battle in yet another asteroid cluster, which gave them an advantage over their usually surprised enemies, because the X-wings all carried standard repulsorlifts and thus could not only maneuver undetectably through the rock fields, but could also use the Solo Slide.

When Han had outlined the plan, Wedge had said, "You want us to take on Interceptors using nothing but *repulsorlifts?*"

"Sure," Han had replied. "How much training you think those eyeball-jockeys get in repulsorlift combat?"

"Couldn't guess," Wedge had said. "But I sure know how much training we *don't* have . . ."

"Then I guess we better hope their learning curve's steeper than yours is, huh?"

And it had been—so much so, in fact, that even Han Solo had once or twice found himself shaking his head and giving a low whistle. Those Rogue pilots were *good*. Maybe as good as he was. Almost. Not that he'd ever say so out loud.

The battle—really, succession of battles—had seemed to go on for a year or two. And they'd still be up there, too, if Chewie hadn't had a sudden brainstorm and realized that if Han could bring the *Falcon* close enough at the proper vector, they could take out a grav projector just by lobbing a couple of thermal detonators out the trash ejector: the projector's own gravity well would suck the dets straight in for a direct hit.

On the downside, the *Lancer*'s navicomputer now estimated that the stellar flares would begin in less than twelve hours. The upside, Han figured, was that the radiation would kill him before he actually starved to death.

"Leia?" he called again. "Anything?"

"I—I'm not sure," she called back. "Maybe—no—I think . . ."

"Well, you better make up your mind, sister! If the Imps decide to fly atmo patrols, this might get a little hot. Hotter."

Han was trusting mainly in the thick dust that swirled on the winds to keep the *Falcon* concealed from orbital scans; Rogue Squadron was off somewhere, trying to clear a route out through the maze of gravity wells that still sealed the system. He wished them all the luck in the galaxy—he was planning to need that hypothetical route as soon as they found Luke—but he also wished they were hanging around to fly cover for his uncomfortably exposed butt.

"I think—" Leia straightened, staring past the *Falcon*. "I think we should probably go *that* way."

"Why that way?"

"So all those people with blasters coming out of the rocks over there," she said, raising her hands, "don't decide to shoot us."

Han turned, very slowly, keeping his hand well clear of his blaster. The crater's rim had suddenly sprouted a couple of dozen people wearing patchwork armor that looked like it might have been cobbled together from the local lava. Nearly all these Lava Gear types had shoulder arms of some variety, from Imperial DC-17s to one guy who actually had an antique Dubloviann flame rifle, and they were pointing these weapons in Han's general direction as they came forward.

Chewie grumbled and started to rise, but Han said softly, barely moving his lips, "Stay low. When the shooting starts, roll off the hull. Once you're inside, open up with the belly gun."

"*Garooargh.*"

"Forget it. I can take cover behind the sensor-dish mount. You won't fit."

"*Hermmmingarouf roog nerhowargh.*"

Han squinted at them as they picked their way toward

the ship. Chewie was right: they were military. Some kind of military—deserters, mercenaries, something. They came on in skirmish lines, covering each other. "We've handled pros before," he muttered. "Get ready to move."

He walked forward to the sensor dish and rested his right hand on its rim, angling his body to make himself look like he was leaning on it even though in fact he was perfectly balanced and that hand could go from the dish's rim to the butt of his DL-44 faster than any of them could blink.

"Got anything to eat?" he asked the Lava Gears.

A red-haired woman stepped to the front of the bunch. She was the only Lava Gear type not holding a weapon, though Han's practiced eye instantly noted that the grip of the KYD in her tie-down thigh holster had a worn-shiny look that signified a whole lot of regular use. "Who are you, and what's your business here?" she demanded.

"Oh, sorry—are these your rocks? We're just borrowing them to rest my ship on. I promise they'll still be here when we go."

"Hey, that was funny. Do a lot of people tell you you're funny?"

"Only ones with a sense of humor." He also noted that she carried her weight forward, evenly balanced over the balls of her feet, and that while her left hand was thumb-hooked to her belt buckle, her right hand dangled bonelessly alongside that well-used blaster: a gunfighter's stance. Also, against his will, he found himself thinking that she was dangerously good-looking. *No redheads,* he reminded himself. He'd had enough of that kind of trouble to last him two or three lifetimes. *Besides, my dance card's full. For the rest of my life, if I'm lucky.*

"Let's try a riddle," he said in a friendly way. "What

does the captain of a ship armed with a pair of quad laser turrets say to people stupid enough to point blasters at him?"

"Let me guess," the woman said. "How about: 'Please don't shoot my girlfriend'?"

Han looked over his shoulder. Five more of them stood in an arc back there, covering Leia. He said, "Maybe we got off on the wrong foot."

"Oh?" Her smile didn't look amused. "Is that the answer to your riddle?"

"Yeah," he said. "I guess it is. Look, I don't know what you want with us—I don't even know whose side you're on."

"We're on our own side."

"So you're what, local?"

"Local enough."

"I take it you're not fans of the Empire, huh?" It was a fair guess, given the state of their gear and their hodge-podge of mismatched weapons.

"Not so much."

"Well, us either. Neither. Whatever. We're just looking for a friend."

"Huh. Us, too. How's that for a coincidence?" The woman's head canted just a bit. "This friend you're looking for wouldn't happen to be a Jedi, would he?"

Han blinked. "What do you know about Jedi?"

Her eyes went wide. "*Cover!*" she shouted, as she and the others scattered and dove to the ground—which promptly erupted in flame and molten rock under a barrage of laserfire from above and behind him.

Han looked up. Down from the clouds swooped dozens of TIEs looping in for strafing runs.

"Oh, come *on*!" he said. "Before I even get *dinner*?"

SHADOWSPAWN BROUGHT THAT SCARLET-SHINING CRYS-tal sword whistling down at Luke's head with all the subtlety and grace of a spice miner swinging a sonic hammer. Luke met the strike easily, almost without effort. A blinding flare of green and scarlet energy flashed when the blades met, and the air stank of ozone.

And about a decimeter of the end of Shadowspawn's crystal blade, still shimmering with that bloodshine glow, clattered faintly as it fell to the stone at Luke's feet. "Sith alchemy, huh?"

Shadowspawn snarled and chopped at him. Luke took half a step to one side, and the blade missed him by a hair and drove into the stone beside his boot. Shadowspawn yanked it free and hacked again, and again Luke shifted his weight just enough to avoid the strike. The warlord came at him, crystal blade trailing fire as he whirled it into another thundering overhead chop.

Luke circled, still not striking back; he couldn't figure out what to make of Shadowspawn's style. The warlord fought like someone who'd heard of swordplay but had never actually seen it done. Luke would have found Shadowspawn's clumsiness kind of funny, had he not been able to feel the gathering threat in the Force. The danger still grew; its shadow darkened his future.

But it didn't have anything to do with this silly man swinging his silly sword. With his strange name . . .

Wait, Luke thought. *That strange name . . . Shadowspawn. Lord Shadowspawn . . .*

He reached into the Force and opened his perception. Waves of darkness beat against his consciousness, a tidal surge of fear and malice . . . but the deeper he let that surge enter, the more certain he became.

This was a put-up job.

Lord Shadowspawn . . . His eyes widened. He got it now, as clearly as if the Force itself had whispered in his ear. Not Lord Spawn-of-the-Shadow. Not at all.

It wasn't a name. It was a pun. *Lord Shadow's Pawn.*

The crystal sword came down again, and this time Luke didn't dodge.

The blade froze in the air, its edge a finger's breadth from Luke's forehead.

Luke smiled and leaned just far enough around the blade to deliver a single, very precise punch. Not to the jaw, or the temple; this was not a conventional knock-out. Luke's fist landed exactly at the point the Force had chosen for him—on Shadowspawn's forehead, just above his right eye—and in the fraction of a second that Shadowspawn's head snapped back and upset his balance, Luke reached out and snatched the Moon Hat right off his head. Luke had to put some real muscle into the yank; it came free only with a wet ripping sound as if he might be tearing flesh away with it.

And the great Lord Shadowspawn collapsed like a holomonster on an overloaded dejarik board.

The corpse-looking Shadowface holomask must have been projected by the headgear itself; for an instant, before it flickered and died, it looked like Luke was holding Shadowspawn's whole head in his hand. The Moon Hat was curiously heavy—more than two kilos—and appeared on first look to be a structure of carbonite frozen over and around a complex array of some kind of mineral crystal, almost like that weird sword . . . crystals that extended downward into spiky filaments that were damp . . . with *blood* . . .

And the man who lay crumpled at his feet didn't look like Shadowspawn at all anymore: his shaven head was streaked with blood that still leaked from the hundreds of tiny puncture wounds left by the crystal filaments inside the Moon Hat. Behind the blood, his skin was dark as stimcaf, and when he lifted his face, his eyes were a wholly extraordinary shade of vivid blue. "Kill me," he croaked. "Skywalker, you have to *kill* me . . ."

"You don't need to be killed," Luke said. "You need to be rescued."

"Too late . . . too *late* for that . . ." He spoke with an accent Luke hadn't heard before, and his voice bore not the slightest resemblance to the faux-Vader rumble of Shadowspawn. "Kill me, and kill yourself . . . if you don't, you'll *become* me . . ."

"You wouldn't be the first guy to be wrong about what I'm going to become." Luke dropped to one knee beside him. "Who are you?"

"Call me . . . Nick. I thought you . . ." He coughed weakly, and forced an unsteady smile. "Are you related to *Anakin* Skywalker? He'd have . . . smoked me without a second thought."

"Yeah, well," Luke said with a slightly unsteady smile of his own, "I'm not the man he was."

"Too bad . . . could use a guy like him right about now . . ."

"But all we've got is us. Can you get up?"

"Sure, kid, sure. Someday." He twisted his head to look back down along the rock bridge to the tunnel's mouth, where the clustered stormtroopers still stood with their blasters slung. "They're not shooting. Why aren't they shooting?"

Luke squinted at them consideringly for a moment, then shrugged. "Maybe it's because I won."

"What?"

"How much do you remember? You ordered them to serve me, if I defeated you."

"Oh, I remember . . . 's just that—" He shook his head. "Wasn't . . . exactly *me*."

"I figured that out," Luke said dryly. "But if we're lucky, *they* haven't." He stood, and pointed the blade of his lightsaber at the two closest troopers. "You and you—come out here and assist this man. That's an order."

Without even an instant's hesitation or so much as an exchange of glances, the two troopers shouldered their weapons and marched out onto the rock bridge. Luke murmured, "It *can't* be this easy . . ."

"Got that right," the erstwhile Lord Shadowspawn— Nick—said. "Listen—that headgear. You gotta understand. It's a device—a machine—Sith alchemy—"

"There really is such a thing as *Sith alchemy*? That wasn't part of the act?"

"Look at my head, Skywalker. That blood look like an act to you?" He shut his eyes and gathered strength with a deep breath. "There are . . . crystals implanted in my brain. That headgear concentrates the Dark—what you call the Force—so that Cronal . . . Blackhole . . . can use me like a puppet. He can see through my eyes, hear with my ears . . . the more Force-touch you have, the more he can do with you. That's why he made me into Shadowspawn . . ."

Luke blinked. "Those other officers—the Moon Hats—"

"They're none of them exactly volunteers," Nick said. "Minor-league Force-sensitives. That's what the raids have really been after. He kidnaps them, puts them through the surgery, slaps the headgear on 'em, and then they not only become his puppets but also his eyes and ears. And hands. And mouth."

"They're all *innocent*?"

"Most are. Some are like me." Nick tilted his head. "It's been a while since I was innocent of anything."

"I'm not sure what you mean by that."

"After five years of war, you're still not sure? Maybe you haven't been paying attention." He waved a hand. "Forget it. Blackhole and me—we tangled while he was . . . uh, *recruiting* . . . out in the Outer Rim. I chased him till he caught me."

"*You* chased *him*?"

"Him and others. Got my own reasons . . . to hate dark siders." He waved a trembling hand. "Everybody . . . needs a *hobby*, kid . . ."

Luke smiled, a little sadly. "No one calls me *kid* anymore."

"Hey, sorry . . ."

Luke nodded. "Me, too."

Nick wheezed, "Get up . . . on the throne."

"What?"

"*Do* it! Right now!"

Luke put his hand on the arm of the Shadow Throne. It was smooth and cool as polished glass. "Why?"

"The throne's . . . obsidian. This other rock, it's all meltmassif. Like the bridge."

"So what?"

"So *that*." Where he pointed—just ahead of the approaching stormtroopers—the rock bridge had suddenly and inexplicably thinned, as though it were putty or soft clay, pinched by the fingers of an invisible giant. The stormtroopers hesitated . . . and the rock bridge parted, its ends recoiling from each other like severed strands of wander-kelp, and the far side, where the stormtroopers now stood uncertainly, literally yanked itself out from under them. They clutched desperately at the retreating stone; one fell, flailing helplessly in the smoky red-washed gloom, until he vanished in a splash of sudden flame at the surface of the lake of fire below. The other found a grip and clung, dangling over the molten lava, but only for an instant: a blue-sparking energy discharge of some sort flicked across the surface of the stone and the trooper's hands sprang open.

This one didn't flail as he fell. He just dropped, already unconscious or dead.

The rest of the troopers and the Moon Hat woman on the ledge at the tunnel's mouth also collapsed as if shot by a bank of stunners . . . and the ledge sagged beneath them, spreading like hot khaddi-nut butter until their unconscious bodies slid off and tumbled the fifty meters down to fiery death.

Then the stone that had been ledge flowed *back upward* until it had sealed off the tunnel's mouth.

"So much for the witnesses . . ." Nick said.

Luke felt a sudden surge of danger sense that gave him half a second's warning; he tangled a fist in "Shadowspawn" 's robe and let the Force lend wings to his heels and might to his arm as he leapt upward from the rock onto the polished obsidian throne just as that same electric crackle played over the stone on which he'd just been standing. "Okay, we're up. Now what?"

"Can you use the Force to get us out of here somehow?"

"I don't think so," Luke said grimly. "But if he wants us dead, all he has to do is turn off the repulsorlift that's holding up this throne. Or drop the heat screens."

"He won't. That's what I've been trying to tell you," Nick said. "He doesn't want to kill you. He wants to *be* you."

Before Luke could ask him what that was supposed to mean, the rock into which the throne had been set suddenly shifted and flowed and stretched into a vast hand holding them in its palm. Huge fingers of stone, each three times as long as Luke was tall, closed over them. Luke brought up his lightsaber instinctively and slashed one finger off at the knuckle . . . but the rock-finger simply fell beside him and melted and flowed around his feet, instantly hardening to lock him in place.

The cavern boomed with mocking laughter from those concealed speakers.

"I believe the appropriate word here," said the amplified fake-Vader voice, *"is CUT!"*

Then a burst of blue energy blasted up Luke's legs and ripped away his consciousness.

CHAPTER 9

HAN'S MENTAL CATALOGUE OF PREFERENCES WAS AS agile as any other part of him; a couple of squadrons of TIE fighters coming straight at his nose transformed, in the blink of an eye, the top of his list from "At least I'll roast before I starve" to "I don't want to die on an empty stomach!"

He whirled and sprinted aft. *"Chewie! Go go go GO!"* he shouted, heedless of the fact that the Wookiee had already scrambled to the rim and thrown himself off the hull.

Han sprinted headlong as laser blasts splashed around him. Splatters of molten titanium that once had been the *Falcon*'s armor burned holes in his pants and shirt, and even as he tripped over an EVA grip and belly flopped headfirst off the hull, some coolly disconnected part of his brain filed the datum that the laser bolts looked about ten times the width they normally would, and they weren't actually penetrating the *Falcon*'s dorsal armor. Something in the metals-charged atmosphere must screw up laser collimation, that cool part of his brain decided, while the rest of his brain was more concerned with trying for a diver's tuck-and-roll to keep his headfirst trajectory from resulting in a headfirst impact on the cinders around the boarding ramp.

While the result was not entirely graceful—he landed

on his rear end with a thump—it was close enough for his purposes, so that when Leia sprinted up to him he was able to shove himself to his feet. "Go on!" he gasped. "I'm right behind you!"

"Any landing you can walk away from, eh, Slick?" she said as she passed him and disappeared up the boarding ramp.

"Got *that* right." He staggered up the ramp and hit the autocycle to close it behind him. "Leia! Bottom turret! Chewie, take top! I'm driving!"

He scrambled forward. Chewbacca's feet were just disappearing up the upper turret access; Wookiees could climb faster than most species could run. Leia paused before clambering down into the lower turret. "You okay? Really?"

"Mostly," Han said. "Considering I landed on my brain."

"As long as there's no permanent damage." Leia flashed a grin and gave his injured anatomy a quick pat as he squeezed by. "It's your best feature—and that's saying a *lot*."

"You're adorable," he said. "Now let's go shoot some bad guys, huh?"

The ship rocked with more cannon blasts, which were answered by an ear-shattering Wookiee war cry and the deep-throated *thoom-thoom-thoom-thoom* of the top-side quad turret. Han finally reached the cockpit and threw himself into the pilot's couch. While he stabbed buttons and flicked switches, he whispered a quick *"Thankyouverymuch!"* to whatever part of the Force might be looking after fools, scoundrels, and reformed smugglers, grateful that the Empire had never thought to arm their TIE Interceptors with missiles or torps, especially since—as a searing red FAILURE indicator informed him when he tried to fire up the active defenses—the atmosphere seemed to have a similar effect on deflectors and particle shields.

Which meant, on balance, that the most effective weapons in this particular engagement just happened to be loaded in the *Falcon*'s forward missile array. Han muttered, "That works for me," yanked back on the control yoke, and punched the sublights. The *Falcon* leapt straight up as if it had been drop-kicked by the entire planet.

The ship spun skyward through a hailstorm of cannon fire. Inboard comm crackled. *"I can't hurt them,"* Leia said, her voice tight and calm with concentration. *"My shots glance off the collector panels. Is something wrong with the guns?"*

"No, something's wrong with the atmosphere! Don't complain, it's keeping us alive right now!" Han shouted back. "Their forward viewports aren't armored—aim for the eyeball and shoot 'em in the face when they swing in on attack runs!"

He twisted the ship through a half loop that sent it straight for a new line of TIEs as they dropped through the cloud deck in that follow-the-leader formation they favored for air-to-ground work. "Speaking of eyeballs," he muttered under his breath, and thumbed the missile release without bothering to engage the targeting computer; at this range he didn't need a missile lock. Twin contrails painted parallel lines from the *Falcon* to the lead TIE in less than a heartbeat. In the next heartbeat, the TIE had blossomed into an expanding sphere of flame and debris—which touched off the following TIE, and the one after that, while the rest of the flight broke formation and spiraled into strafing runs.

"Hey, they're going after the Mindorese!" Han crowed as he spun the ship into an escape vector. "Blow 'em a kiss for luck, kids—we're out of here!"

"Han," Leia began, and he clenched his teeth. He recognized the tone, and he knew what was coming next.

"Don't tell me," he said. "We have to go back."

"They'll be slaughtered!" she said. *"And Han—they know something about Luke!"*

"Oh, sure," he muttered through his teeth. She *would* bring Luke into this. "But when your bleeding heart gets us all killed, don't come crying to me . . ."

He pulled the *Falcon* into a looping evasion curve, and this time he did engage the targeting computer— which promptly informed him, in no uncertain terms, that the *Falcon* was out of missiles. *"Now* you tell me."

Han keyed the comm. "Rogue Leader, Rogue Leader. Wedge, you out there? If you're in the area, we could use a little cover right about now!"

The speakers crackled. Faintly, through the bursts of static: *"Negative on the cover,* Falcon. *Do you read? Negative cover! We are buried—there's more TIEs than rocks out here! Do you read?"*

"Loud and too damn clear," Han muttered. "Can you pry open a window for us?"

"No joy starside, Falcon. *Do not attempt! Hostiles have you under the blanket. Find a hole and pull it in after you. We'll be back as soon as we round up some friendlies."*

"Negative that. Stick to Leia's plan; we'll make our own way. We'll find Luke and meet you on the far side of the jump point."

"Copy that. Clear skies, Falcon."

"See you soon, Wedge."

"Copy, Han. Take care of the pretty lady."

"I always do," Han said, and only after a second or two did it strike him that Wedge had been talking about Leia, not the *Falcon.* "Uh, yeah, her too," he muttered, and keyed the inboard comm. "All right, kids, we have to do this the hard way. Belt up—this ride's about to get bumpy!"

The targeting computer shrilled an alert: MISSILE LOCK DETECTED.

"*Missile* lock? They don't even *have*—" But even as he was arguing with the computer, Han had kicked the *Falcon* into a high-g sideslip, and before he could finish the sentence a pair of concussion missiles screamed past so close the cockpit rattled. "Who's shooting at us *now*?"

"*Incoming!*" Leia sang out over the sudden thunder of the quad turrets.

"I *saw* them alrea—oh." Han stared out through the forward viewport at a swarm of missiles that looped toward them from the general direction of a giant wall of billowing dust, which had been kicked up by a skirmish line of four or five dozen heavy assault gunships that skimmed the hills a few kilometers away, angling for envelopment. "You have *got* to be *kidding* me!"

"*Arroowerrhowoo!*"

"Sure, laugh it up," Han snarled as he yanked the *Falcon* back into an intercept course with the strafing TIEs. Trust a Wookiee to find this *funny*. "Chewie, target the fighters! We need to break their formation. Princess—hey, wait . . ."

From down among the rocks at the crater's rim, at every impact point of every laser bolt from every one of the strafing TIEs, rose a billow of reddish-black cloud: dust and smoke, thick enough to completely shroud the ground beneath.

Han found himself grinning. "Princess! Aim for the *ground*!"

"*What?*"

"Just *do it*! Angle the turret forward and hold down the triggers!"

"*You're the captain, Captain.*" He could hear in her voice her skeptical shrug, but an instant later she opened up the belly quad and hosed the lava ahead with a non-stop stream of laserfire.

And even as Han kicked the *Falcon* into a dive that speared straight into the billowing wall of red-black dust kicked up by Leia's laser blasts, he was contemplating, with mild astonishment, that for very possibly the first time in her life, Leia had just done as she was told without a word of argument. Must be the captain thing. Why hadn't he thought of that before? His mouth quirked upward in a slight, lopsided smile.

He was still smiling when the *Falcon* roared up from the cloud into open sky and was instantly clipped across its starboard mandible by the collector panel of a TIE Interceptor whose astonished pilot never even had a chance to blink before his starfighter was transformed by the impact into a flaming ball of wreckage tumbling toward the all-too-close lava below.

The glancing impact knocked the *Falcon* into a flipping whirl like a cred chip spinning on a sabacc table that sprayed the surrounding area with molten chunks of titanium from the gash in its armor plating. The TIE fighter collector's leading edge missed the front view-panel of the *Falcon*'s cockpit by roughly the diameter of a Wookiee's nose hair. Han was too busy saying *Whoa!* and being generally astonished to find himself still alive while trying to wrestle the *Falcon* back under control to even distantly worry about the *other* TIEs streaking toward him, not to mention the concussion missiles that looped toward them indiscriminately, having lost their targeting locks when the *Falcon* had disappeared into the cloud of metallic fog.

The *Falcon*'s spin, though, brought the intersecting contrails of the oncoming missiles through Han's visual arc just in time for him to wrench the yoke and stand the *Falcon* on its tail, side-on to the missiles, for one flash of a ghost of a second . . . just long enough for the lead missiles to whip past so close that he would later swear he could *smell* them before they continued down into the murk in pursuit of the largest energy signature their targeting sensors had found to relock on: the exploding TIE Interceptor. The following missiles had already located the ion signatures of the other TIEs, since the atmosphere apparently also presented enough EM interference to screw up the missiles' reception of IFF transponder signals. While the TIE pilots struggled with that problem, Han was able to bring the *Falcon* back under control and angle it toward the folds of lava where the Mindorese had taken cover.

Over their position, he kicked the *Falcon* onto its side and circled them at high speed, while both Chewie and Leia fired their quads at full power into the ground, raising a huge cylindrical cloud of blasted-up rock and metal that Han figured would cloak them from the oncoming gunships for at least a minute or so; then he set down in the clear middle and dropped the *Falcon*'s boarding ramp as he activated the exterior loudspeakers. *"Okay, let's go! Mount up—we're at B minus thirty, and B stands for Bagload of Bad Guys!"*

The Mindorese scrambled for the boarding ramp, some of them limping, some carrying or dragging wounded comrades. The redhead paused just long enough to send a sardonic grin toward the cockpit and follow it with a blown kiss that somehow managed to look grateful and sarcastic at the same time.

Han canceled the loudspeakers and keyed the turret comm. "Chewie. Leia." Even though the Mindorese couldn't possibly overhear, he kept his voice low, just above a whisper. "Secure the turret access bulkheads, and don't come out till I tell you."

Those bulkheads would stand up to anything short of a mining charge.

Chewie growled assent, but Leia said, "*Han—these aren't enemies. I can* feel—"

"I believe you," Han said. "Do it anyway."

"*Han—*"

"*Leia!*"

"All right. I'll stay put."

"And get ready to shoot, huh?" Without waiting for her answer, Han keyed the comm channel for the *Falcon*'s cargo hold. "Hey down there! You people inside? We're out of time!"

"*We're in! Are we taking off sometime today?*" Had to be the redhead. "*Is this a ship or an artillery target?*"

"Little bit of both," Han muttered as he kicked power into the thrusters and swung the mandibles toward vertical.

The *Falcon* broke clear of the dust and smoke cloud. "Here they come!"

The Interceptors hadn't gone anywhere in the meantime; immediately the battered freighter bounced and shuddered under the impact of multiple cannon hits, and Han spotted the flight of heavy assault gunships circling into formation for a new attack run. "I hope somebody's got a good idea, here!"

"*Hrowwwroor!*"

"Of *course* keep shooting!" Han replied. "I said a *good* idea!"

The intercom crackled with the redhead's voice again. "*Seventy-seven points off true north, and punch it!*"

Han scanned the horizon from north to east: desert, featureless but for low rolling hills. "There's nothing *there*!"

"*If you want, we can argue about it while the Imps blast your ship to scrap.*"

"Or maybe we could mount you on the hull and use your nerve for armor plate," Han muttered, but he kicked the underjets and fired the thrusters. Six Interceptors hurtled past, and Han pumped the missile trigger by instinct, snarling to himself *That's it, knucklehead, waste your time firing dry tubes.* The TIEs weren't his main problem anyway; the big issue was the flight of heavy assault gunships skimming the ground straight toward them . . . from east by northeast. "Do you know you're sending us *straight for them?*"

"Hey, sorry. You feel safer here?"

"You and me, we're just never gonna get along."

"Stop it, you'll make me cry. Get the TIEs in a tail chase so—"

"—they'll be in the gunships' line of fire, and the gunships in theirs." Han was already doing so, swinging high to place the *Falcon* squarely between the enemies behind and those in front. The TIEs' cannons would do even less to the distant gunships than they were doing to the *Falcon,* but the gunships had to hold fire on their missiles, and Han was starting to let himself believe that he just might get the *Falcon* clear. "This isn't exactly my first scrape, y'know."

"Could've fooled me. How we doin' up there?"

"Not bad," Han admitted—then changed his mind as another salvo from the TIEs rocked the ship. Hard. "But they're *gaining* on us—pretty soon they'll be close enough that those cannons will start doing real damage. And the gunships are wheeling to join up on the tail chase when we pass them in about five seconds, at which point we're pretty well f—"

"Pull up!"

"What?"

"Climb, dammit! Full power!"

"You can't even *see* out there!"

"I know this planet like your rear knows your pants, flyboy. Climb or die."

"You want to come up here and drive? No, forget I asked."

Han gritted his teeth and hauled back on the control yoke. The *Falcon* lurched and bucked and whipped for the sky fast enough to overload its inertial compensators; acceleration squashed him into the pilot's couch and pinned him there, and he caught himself indulging an uncharitable fantasy that one particular Mindorese had failed to secure herself and had fallen and broken something.

Preferably her mouth.

The pursuing TIEs climbed with them, spreading wide to open a window for the gunships, which obliged by launching a spray of concussion missiles. The *Falcon*'s missile-lock alert blared. Han cursed under his breath as he forced the yoke forward and twisted it to yank the ship into a looping spiral. Just then the whole sky flashed scarlet and the whole ship *thoommed* with magnetic resonance harmonics that sounded, to Han's all-too-experienced ear, like a near-miss by a really, really big turbolaser blast. "Where the hell did *that* come from?"

Leia's voice, from the ventral turret: *"Quarter-roll to your left and you'll see it."*

Han kicked the ship through the quarter roll, got a look at what Leia was talking about, and started swearing. He kept on swearing for some considerable time, even while wrenching the ship through ridiculously violent evasive maneuvers as the whole sky kept flaring around them and the ship rang with a near-continuous *whang-ng-ng-ng* like a Ruurian beating a dinner gong with all fourteen hands.

The sudden climb he'd undertaken on the redhead's advice had cleared them over the horizon of a vast rounded mountain that bulged up into the orange sky, like some kind of young volcanic dome that hadn't yet blown its crater, and the whole blasted place was studded with rings of huge turbolaser towers, which were powerful enough that the interference from Mindor's atmosphere had no effect except to spread the blasts wide enough to vaporize his entire ship, instead of just blowing holes in it.

"Oh, brilliant. Oh, this is just *great*," Han shouted into the intercom. "You sent us straight for their main *base*!"

"Quit whining. Those turbo batteries'll keep the TIEs off our tail, and probably dust some of the missiles, too."

She was right, which only made Han hate her even more. No one that annoying had any business being right about *anything*.

"There should be three parallel box canyons about five klicks off your left front. See them?"

"Yeah." Three long gouges in Mindor's crust, shallow at this end and deepening as they extended off to planetary east until they came to sudden ends—looked like maybe three pretty good-sized chunks of meteorite had come in at the same time a few years back. "Now what?"

"Hug the deck straight in to the right-hand canyon. Once we're below ground level, there are side canyons and caverns and all kinds of places to hide. Blast some rocks, kick up some dust, and you won't have any trouble losing these guys. There's too many places to look, and they've got bigger problems than us."

Han gave a slow nod as he nosed the *Falcon* into a screaming dive toward the canyons through the storm of intersecting cannon and turbolaser fire. "Not bad," he admitted grudgingly. "You do seem to know your way around."

"What do you think kept us all alive out here? Good looks?"

"Nah," Han said. "I figured it was your winning personality."

* * *

A HUNDRED-SOME PLANETARY DIAMETERS FROM MIN-dor, the Slash-Es were moving.

Asteroid clusters had been drifting toward them, accelerating as they came, following lines of gravitic interaction between the Slash-Es' gravity-well projectors and the thousands of gravity stations scattered through the asteroids. This effect had been clearly visible on the heads-up displays of the *Lancer*'s starfighter pickets, which was what had sparked the idea in Captain Tirossk, who, as the senior commander still active in the theater, was now unexpectedly in command of the entire RRTF.

As he explained it to Wedge and Tycho in encrypted transmissions, the combined effects of the inbound asteroid clusters and the gravity wells would produce semicoherent planetoids. With seat-of-the-pants reckoning, Wedge and Tycho had guesstimated that a dozen of these planetoids, moving in the proper orbits, would be enough to clear a brief hyperspace window that might allow some of the task force to escape. The *Lancer*'s navigational computer had put the minimum number at close to eighteen hours . . . and the window would open only briefly and unpredictably several times until it finally stabilized, if all went well, in about twenty hours.

However, all was not going well. Very little was going well.

Asteroid impacts on Taspan's stellar sphere had already begun, owing to the ongoing perturbation of the asteroids' unstable orbits, and radiation levels were rising. The Imp officers directing the TIE fighter wings had known what was up the instant they detected the Slash-Es moving out of planetary interdiction configuration—and they had a seemingly limitless supply of Interceptors piloted by an equally seemingly limitless supply of suicidal psychopaths, which meant that the Slash-Es were doing their best to perform this delicate and intricate set of maneuvers while plowing through clouds of enemy fighters that swirled and spat plasma blasts as if somebody had armed a swarm of Gamorrean thunder wasps with laser cannons.

For the original model of CC-7700s, this would have been a suicide mission, and a brief one at that. The Slash-E series, however, was clad in the latest carbon-nanofilament armor to supplement their six shield generators; they had eight quad turrets each, and their power output had been upgraded to nearly the level of a Clone Wars–era turbolaser. Further improvements included a pair, dorsal and ventral, of 360-degree proton torpedo turrets and a staggering number of anti-starfighter cluster bombs—essentially shaped charges set into the hull that would explode outward into clouds of bomblets when they sensed the approach of enemy fighters—all of which meant that the only way TIE fighters could have a serious shot at taking out a Slash-E was to swarm it in enough numbers to overload its defenses so that a few could slip in for full-speed headers. But even a direct impact wouldn't generate enough kinetic energy to take out a CNF-armored frigate unless the TIE was traveling at very close to its maximum realspace velocity.

Making sure no TIE reached that cataclysmic velocity on an intercept course with one of the Slash-Es was the job of the X-wing pilots.

Though the RRTF fighters were outnumbered hundreds to one by the TIEs, they had a few advantages that shaved the odds a bit. First, the Imperial forces could not make a full-commitment assault, because that would have required pulling fighters from all over the system, which would have exposed their gravity stations to the RRTF's capital ships. Second, the Interceptors had to focus all their firepower on the Slash-Es to have any hope of taking them out; they had very little to spare for dogfighting. Third, despite being at a substantial disadvantage in speed and maneuverability versus the Interceptors, the X-wing—the Incom T-65 Space Superiority Starfighter—had one key feature no TIE fighter could match.

It was *rugged.*

This went deeper than the combat defenses loaded onto this model; it was a feature of quality construction and attention to detail, and it meant that the X-wing could survive certain physical stresses that would rip the collector panels off a TIE. Like, for example, the extreme tidal stress created by a *very* close pass through a *very* steep gravity well.

Which was why each new wave of Interceptors found itself under fire from flights of X-wings whipping out from around the gravity-station planetoids a great deal faster than X-wings were supposed to be able to whip. Rogue Squadron had the point, and their path between the planetoids became a looping chain of gravity-assisted slingshots that could, with no more than a twitch of the controls, send them toward whichever one or two or three of the five Slash-Es the Imps had decided to concentrate on.

Even with all these advantages, the overwhelming odds took their toll. Some X-wings were lost to friendly fire, as they were traveling too fast for the Slash-E gunners— or even their own superb reflexes—to react as they swept through the quad turrets' fields of fire. Some were lost to simple collisions, flying at near-relativistic speeds through very, very crowded space. Almost half of the Twenty-third's Green Squadron was taken out by a mass of asteroids that didn't cohere into a planetoid as quickly as the navicomps had predicted.

They didn't have anything like a count on the enemy fighters they'd destroyed; the TIEs just kept coming.

"These guys never stop!" Wes Janson groaned through his teeth during the far side of his twentieth or thirtieth bruising way-too-tight slingshot. "It's like all these beggars *want* to die!"

"They're already dead," Hobbie said from two hundred meters off Janson's starboard wing. *"Think about it, Janson—no shields. No hyperdrive. They can't hide and they can't run. All they've got is the chance to take us all with 'em."*

That stopped Janson cold. For a moment, he had no words at all. Then he set his jaw and rolled his starfighter starboard.

"I've got it!" he said, pointing his X-wing toward a TIE flight and holding down his triggers. "I know exactly what we need."

"Yeah?" Hobbie said. *"What's that?"*

"A miracle."

"Seal that chatter!" Wedge snapped from the point. *"And check your midrange scans."*

When Janson did, he discovered that a brand-spanking-new Mon Cal–designed Republic battle cruiser had just dropped out of hyperspace through that half-opened mass-shadow window, and was currently disgorging what appeared to be a full starfighter wing.

"Hot staggering—" For the second time in a few moments, Janson found himself entirely at a loss for words. "Where in eight Stalbringion hells did *that* come from?"

The comm crackled with the voice of the current director of Special Operations, General Lando Calrissian. *"Did somebody order a miracle?"*

THE CAVERN HAN HAD BEEN DIRECTED TO BY THE RED-head was roomy, looked acceptably dry in the bleached glare from the *Falcon*'s exterior lights, and was deep enough within a mountain that Han didn't have to worry about being detected. That didn't stop him from worrying, though.

First, he didn't like having a hold full of armed strangers, no matter how much they might hate the Empire. Second, this mountain looked *way* too much like a dormant volcano. And third . . . well, he just didn't much like parking in caves. Call him superstitious. Somehow landing his ship inside a big hole in a rock never seemed to work out that well.

On the other hand, the Mindorese might have brought along something to eat.

He keyed the intercom. "Okay, everybody. Looks like we're clear. You in the hold? No offense, but pile your blasters and other weapons in the number-six hopper, will you? It's not that I don't trust you, it's just that I don't trust you."

The comm responded with the sound of the redhead's voice. *"What about that Jedi? Where's he?"*

"That's what we wanted to ask *you.*"

"Like that, is it? Well, I'll tell you what—we'll down weapons and have our Jedi chat if you can help us out with bandages and bacta. I've got a lot of wounded in here."

"Fair enough. I'll be with you in a nanosec."

When he reached the forward cargo hold, the place looked like a field hospital way too close to the front lines. On the losing side. People sat or lay sprawled every which way, some wrapping their own bandages, some twisting or moaning softly, others just staring blankly at the bulkheads as if they couldn't believe they were actually alive. Leia and Chewie were already hard at work treating the wounded. Han hurried over to Leia's side. "Hey, hey, hey, take it easy with the bacta, huh?"

"Han, he's hurt."

"Sure, I know. But he's not *dying,* is he? Do you know how much that stuff *costs?*"

A woman's voice came from behind his left shoulder. "You can bill me."

Han rounded on her, then stopped, making a face. "Oh, it's you."

"Yeah, it's me," the good-looking redhead said, and offered him a lopsided smile that made her, if anything, even *better*-looking. She stuck out her hand. "Aeona Cantor. You the pilot of this scow?"

"I'm the *captain* of this scow," Han corrected her, but then grinned and took her offered hand. Her hand was warm, and harder than it looked. He just didn't have it in him to bicker right now. Besides, Leia would probably think he was flirting. "Han Solo."

Her eyes widened. "For real? *The* Han Solo?"

He started to flush. "The only one I know."

"Wow." She looked impressed. "I mean, the Han Solo who supposedly outdrew Gallandro in a fair fight?"

"Well, y'know . . ." His face was getting full-on hot all of a sudden. "It wasn't exactly a fair fight—and I didn't exactly out*draw* him. You shouldn't believe everything you see on the HoloNet."

"I don't," she said. "I always figured you shot him in the back."

"Hey, now—"

"That your weapon? BlasTech, huh? Kinda old-fashioned, isn't it?"

Han dropped his hand to the blaster's grip and fiddled with it as though uncertain. "Uh, well . . ."

"I favor the Twenty-one myself." She nodded toward the number-six cargo hopper, where a weathered but exceedingly well-cared-for blaster belt lay on top. From the holster projected a custom KYD grip that showed an equal amount of wear, and even more care. "Go ahead," she said. "Feel free. Here—"

She reached over and pulled her blaster from its holster using only two fingers, nice and slow, plenty slowly enough that Han didn't feel like he needed to shoot her, then spun it around her finger and offered it to him butt-first. "Give it a feel. Combat-action tournament model. Trigger-pull's smooth as bantha butter, and you can shoot the eyestalks off a terramoth at seventy-five meters."

Han took the weapon and weighed it in his hand. It was a nice piece, he had to admit. Beautifully balanced, and he said so.

She grinned. "Knew you'd like it." She nodded toward his holstered blaster. "D'you mind?"

Han shrugged and passed it over.

She squinted into the DL-44's optical electrosight and whistled. "Nice. Modified for speed-draw, right?" She spun it around her finger. "Little barrel-heavy, though, huh? Wait, what's this custom work here?"

She took a close look at the gas chamber and collimator. "Oh, I get it—enhanced output. What does it generate, double power?" She gave him another look and that lopsided grin. "Don't you know that's illegal?"

He felt himself flushing again. "Okay, give it back."

"Nah. I like yours better."

Han blinked. "What?"

"You can have mine. Fair trade. Even counting the custom work, mine's worth double this old relic. Call it even, huh?" She turned and walked toward a knot of her men. "Hey, Tripp, check this out—I just traded for *Han Solo*'s blaster! Can you believe it?"

Han was the one who couldn't believe it. "Now, hold on a minute—"

"Han—" Leia caught his arm. "Look over there—isn't that *Artoo*?"

Sure enough, against the far curve of wall a couple of the Mindorese were trying to install a restraining bolt on a blue-domed 4-series astromech that looked suspiciously familiar. Leia moved toward them. "You—you there, where did you get that droid?"

"We found it abandoned. It's salvage," one of them snapped back.

"Salvage? *Excuse* me?" Leia drew herself up in a way Han recognized all too well, so it was his turn to catch her arm.

"Play it smooth, Princess," he said softly from one side of his mouth while the rest of it gave the Mindorese a reassuringly stupid smile. "Low and slow. I don't trust these jokers."

"Han, I told you, these aren't the enemy—"

"And they aren't old friends, either." He caught Chewie's eye, over where the Wookiee was spraying foamcast around a Mindorese's injured ankle, and rolled his eyes with a slight sideways nod toward the number-six hopper. Before he turned back to his task, Chewie let one eyelid droop into half a wink. "Listen, how hurt are these guys, really?" Han asked Leia. "How long before we can dump them and get on our way?"

"Well . . ." Leia tilted her head, considering. "They're not as bad as you'd expect. Mostly superficial burns—it looks like that crude armor they make out of lava isn't so crude after all."

Han nodded grimly. "So: head shots."

"Han—"

"See what they're up to with Artoo," he said. He looked down with distaste at the KYD-21 in his hand, then jammed it into his holster.

Leia nodded. "Maybe I can help you with your salvage," she said in a friendly way as she came up to the men tinkering with R2's restraining bolt. Without waiting for a reply, she reached over and put her hand on the bolt—and on his hand, where he held it—and gave him a maybe overly warm smile. He flushed, just a bit, and smiled back.

"Uh, better be careful, lady," he said. "This little grubber may look harmless enough, but it can deliver a *nasty* shock—"

"Oh, nonsense," Leia said briskly as she deactivated the bolt with a decisive twist. "This droid's been with my family a long time. Artoo, power up. What happened to Luke?"

R2-D2 whistled an affirmative, and his dome swiveled to angle his onboard holoprojector toward the floor. It flickered to life—but the image was of Aeona Cantor. "No," Leia said. "We know about her. Where's *Luke*?"

The little droid whistled again, more insistently, and again showed Aeona.

"Artoo—"

"No, let him run it," Han said, instinctively lowering his hand to his blaster—and then grimacing at the unfamiliar feel of the KYD's grip. "I want to see this."

A recorded voice came from R2-D2's speaker. *"What if whoever shows up isn't a Jedi?"*

The Aeona-image answered, *"Then we take their ship and leave 'em to the Melters. Saves having to kill them ourselves."*

Han snarled something that would have been a curse if it had come out in words as he whirled, drew the KYD, and squeezed the trigger just as the emitter centered on Aeona's forehead.

It made a dry click.

"Say, you *are* fast." She grinned at him. "Sorry about the blaster—somebody must have pulled the power cell. So I guess it wasn't exactly a fair trade after all, huh?"

She drew his beloved BlasTech and leveled it at Han's face. "This next trade won't be exactly fair either," she said. "Because I also really like your ship."

CHAPTER 10

DEEP IN DARKNESS, LINGERING IN THE SHADOW CAST BY the holoeditor's imaging screen that was the chamber's only light, an old, old man practiced his Luke Skywalker impression.

"Listen to me, Blackhole or Shadowspawn or whoever you are," he murmured, forcing his leathery mouth to shape the rounded vowels and mushy consonants of Skywalker's barbarous Outer Rim accent. "I'm a Jedi, but I never had time for all the training some of the old Jedi were supposed to get . . . No, no no. Not *geht.* Almost *git*—really, barely a vowel at all. G't."

The old, old man sighed. To spend the balance of a human lifetime pretending to be a half-educated rube . . . ultimately, the reward would be worth the sacrifice, of course, and no one would ever know his private humiliation, but still . . .

Perhaps after a decade or two ruling the reborn Empire, he could allow himself to slowly "pick up" a properly civilized mode of speech, but until then he'd have to keep up the pretense. Perhaps the only thing that could undermine his ultimate victory would be to have these Rebel scum notice that their pet Jedi had suddenly begun talking as if he'd been educated on Coruscant by way of Dromund Kaas.

A desiccated finger stretched forth to key the holoeditor and run the recording back two minutes, so that he could study again every slightest detail of Skywalker's bearing, his walk, his gestures, the angle of his head, every faintest twitch of his eyebrows. This was critical to the old, old man's plans; these few recordings, taken from the holocameras embedded in the stygium armor of his black stormtroopers, and from the concealed recorders in the Cavern of the Shadow Throne, were all he had with which to study the *real* Luke Skywalker.

Yes, there were all those numberless holothrillers—and studying them had been a useful preparation, especially in creating the theatrical Shadowspawn persona and devising the stage dressings of the Shadow Throne—but the computer-generated Farmboy Hero depicted by these holothrillers would convince none but the ignorantly credulous fans who devoured such preposterously contrived tripe.

When Luke Skywalker emerged from the Battle of Mindor, no one must even suspect that this legendary Jedi hero was only a shell: a living, breathing life-support system for the mind of this old, old man.

This old, old man who once had been known to a select few as Lord Cronal, director of Imperial Intelligence . . . and to many, many unfortunate enemies of the Empire as Blackhole, the Emperor's Hand . . . and who would, after today, be known to the entire galaxy as Luke, the First Skywalker Emperor.

CRONAL'S RISE TO POWER HAD STARTED WITH A VISION: a vision of the Dark.

More than a vision, in fact; more than a simple prophecy, or precognition. To the Nightsisters of Dathomir, it was the Heartshadow. Other Force users had other names for it.

But Cronal called it simply *Darksight.*

Deep in the area ignorantly described by the Old Republic, and later the Empire, as the "Unknown Regions," there was a vast cloud of dust and rock and interstellar gas that pulsed with a bloody and forbidding scarlet glow as it radiated away the energy of twelve stellar clusters within. This was the Perann Nebula; the twelve clusters that it surrounded were known collectively as the Nihil Retreat. The absolute rulers of the Nihil Retreat, dreaded masters of dark magicks beyond the grasp of even the Sith, were the Sorcerers of Rhand.

The Sorcerers of Rhand were the only family Cronal would ever know. The Rhandites had plucked him from the arms of the nameless woman who had borne him, and had forged him as a weapon is forged, awakening his insight, refining his will, opening his mind to the One Truth:

Only power is real, and the only real power is the power to destroy. Existence is fleeting. Destruction is eternal.

Every child was born waiting for death. Civilizations fell, and their very ashes were swallowed by time. The stars themselves burned out. Destruction, on the other hand . . .

Destruction was the will of the universe.

Some called it entropy, and tried to quantify and constrain it with the laws of thermodynamics. Some expressed it with a simple poetic declarative: *Things fall apart.* Some even tried to dismiss it with a joke: *Anything that can go wrong will.* But it was not a joke, or poetry; it was not science, nor was it subject to any law.

It was the Way of the Dark.

Destruction was easy . . . and *permanent*. When a being was killed, everything he or she would have ever done or possessed, seen or felt, was murdered. And that murder made a *permanent change in the structure of the universe*—it emptied the universe of an entire life, and left behind only a void.

That void was the foundation of truth.

That was why the Jedi and the Sith would remain for-ever locked in their pointless battle: because all their philosophy of light versus dark, of service versus mas-tery, was as meaningless as the whistle of wind through desert rocks. Service and mastery were equally futile, even illusory, in the face of the One Truth. All the end-less Jedi vs. Sith nattering of "the dark side of the Force" blinded them one and all to the bare reality that there was nothing *but* the Dark.

The Dark was not a side of the Force, and it was no mere portion of reality. It *was* reality. The Sorcerers of Rhand had never spoken of the Force, and Cronal was to this day unsure whether they would have had any un-derstanding of how the Force was viewed and spoken of in the rest of the galaxy. To the Rhandites, it was only *the Dark,* and the only pertinent feature of the Dark was that it would respond to the will of a properly trained being, so long as that being's will was in line with the Way of the Dark.

It was the Dark that set world against world, nation against nation, sibling against sibling, child against par-ent. It was the Dark that brought pestilence and starva-tion, hatred and war. The Dark was the hidden energy of the cosmos itself: that which pressed galaxy away from galaxy, star away from star until finally each and every world would fade within its own private black hole, moving too swiftly from its neighbors for their light to overtake it.

This was why Cronal had chosen the code name *Blackhole*: because he had willed himself to become an event horizon of the Dark.

And of all the powers the Dark granted its adepts, the greatest was Darksight. It was Darksight that had led Cronal far from the Nihil Retreat, beyond the Perann Nebula and out of the Unknown Regions altogether, in search of the truth of his visions. It was Darksight that had led him to Dromund Kaas, where he had easily infiltrated and come to dominate that pack of pathetic, self-deluded fools who styled themselves Prophets of the Dark Side.

Imagine, to waste one's brief foray in life, the fleeting bright instant between the infinite dark before and the eternal dark beyond, in mere *study*—in trying to learn to use the "dark side of the Force" to merely predict the future.

With Darksight, Cronal could *create* the future.

He was familiar, in concept, with the pale shadow-imitation of Darksight that had supposedly been employed by some exceptional Jedi and certain among the Sith—the pathetic conjuror's trick they called *battle meditation*. Through massive concentration and expenditure of energy, they claimed to subtly influence the course of a single combat, or, for the most powerful among them, an engagement of greater forces, like armies in collision or fleet-to-fleet battles. They claimed that their simplistic Force-powered *visualization* of a desired outcome would subtly shift probabilities and grant them luck, that it would inspire their allies and demoralize their enemies. Of course, these claims could never be proven, or disproven; any charlatan might simply take credit for any random victory, or ascribe a defeat to the will of the Force—or a supposedly more powerful Force-user practicing his or her own "battle meditation" in service to the opposite side . . .

Battle meditation. Idiots.

Anyone trained by the Rhandites could have told them: any and all battles, all wars, the very concept of *battle* itself, served but a single end. Their only function was destruction. Only by setting one's will upon pure destruction could victory be achieved.

When your will was fixed steadily upon the Way of

the Dark, the Dark itself became your partner in all that you did.

Cronal was living proof of this truth. It was Cronal's Darksight that had attracted the attention of Palpatine and brought Vader to Dromund Kaas; even Kadann, the fool who pretended to be the Supreme Prophet of the Dark Side, never suspected how entirely his order served not some fantasy of Sith power, but the Dark itself . . . because Cronal had made it so. Palpatine had plucked Cronal from the Prophets and set him apart from even the other elite Emperor's Hands, for Palpatine had been swift to recognize that his was a gift that transcended mere prophecy. Any fool with a trace of ability could see echoes of the future—Palpatine himself was rather good at it—but Cronal's ability transcended mere prophecy as hyperdrive transcends the wings of a shadowmoth.

Palpatine had been impressed with the "accuracy" of Cronal's "predictions" . . . yet not even the great Darth Sidious had ever suspected that Cronal's predictions were accurate not because Cronal had seen the future, but because he had *chosen* that future.

That *exact* future.

He had decided, and his choice had molded all of history to his will.

That was the power of Darksight: to search among all the possible futures for the one that best suited your own desire and the Way of the Dark . . . and then to map each step that must be taken to bring you to that future, and bring that future to you.

But to make it happen, you had to bind your desire to the Dark, and dream only of destruction.

Palpatine had been a fool. He had thought he could make the Dark serve him, instead of the opposite. In the days of the Old Republic, before he had revealed his Sith identity, Palpatine literally *could not fail*. Every blind flailing gesture of every Jedi who'd set himself against him had turned to his advantage, and even the sheerest accidents of fortune had served his goal . . . because that goal had been the destruction of the Jedi Order, and the death of the Republic. He'd served the Dark unknowingly, all the while believing that the Dark was only a means to an end, a tool to help him destroy his enemies and clear his path to absolute power.

What he'd never understood was that destruction *was* his power.

As soon as he'd turned his will to rulership, to building instead of destroying, he had forsaken the Way of the Dark . . . and everything had begun to go wrong for him. Where before he could not fail, now he'd had no chance of succeeding, because when you turn your back on the Dark, the Dark turns its back on you.

Only days after the Battle of Yavin, Cronal had cast his mind deep into the void, seeking the future of the young Rebel pilot who had destroyed the Death Star, and had found him as an older, more seasoned man, dressed in dark robes—and bearing a lightsaber.

Kneeling before the Emperor, to swear his allegiance to the dark side.

My fate . . . will be the same as my father's.

Which was when Cronal finally understood who Darth Vader was, and saw the terrible flaw that would bring the Order of the Sith to its ultimate destruction. A destruction that Cronal not only was determined to survive, but was certain he could transform into an eternal victory for the Dark.

And, not incidentally, eternal life for himself.

Near to eternal, anyway; as long as a single living thing struggled and suffered and fed the Dark with killing and dying, Cronal would be here. His ultimate sacrifice to the Dark would be the survival of his consciousness until the heat death of the Universe . . . when he would be joined forever with the final oblivion of all that had ever been. All that will ever be.

He would be the last.

Slowly, subtly, through the months and years from Yavin to Endor, Cronal had served his vision. A delicate balance had had to be meticulously maintained, to navigate the intricacies of the relationship between Palpatine and Vader . . . to inculcate a rivalry with the half-mechanical terror that Palpatine had elevated to the rank of Lord of the Sith. For all his undoubted physical power, Vader had never been more than a blunt instrument, with no real understanding of the truth of the Dark, nor of the uses of real power. He had been, all in all, only a thug with a lightsaber . . . and, as it proved, a weakhearted, emotionally crippled, impulsively treasonous thug at that.

Though Vader could never have been Cronal's equal in coursing the mazy paths of dark power, it had served Cronal's purpose to pretend jealousy—even to appear to fail, more than once, and to openly bridle under Vader's supposed authority, so that Palpatine had begun to suspect that Cronal might deliberately sabotage the monster's operations. Thus it was that he had persuaded Palpatine—subtly, oh-so-delicately, so that the Emperor believed to the day of his death that it had all been his own idea—that Cronal could better serve the Empire from afar, away from Coruscant, away from the prying optical receptors of Vader's ridiculous helmet. Away from the entirely too-keen vision, both physical and mystic, of Palpatine himself.

Out among the forgotten fringes of the galaxy, Cronal had appeared to merely bide his time, running minor operations through his private networks of agents, while in truth he had devoted his life to searching out forgotten lore of the ancient Sith and other supposed masters of the Dark. If they had done so much damage even with their limited understanding of the Dark, how much greater destruction might be wrought by one who knew all their secrets, and also knew the One Truth?

He traveled in secret, deep into the Unknown Regions, following his Darksight vision to worlds so ancient that even legend had no memory of them. Among the drifting moon trees that flowered in the interstellar space of the Gunninga Gap, he was able to discover and assemble scraps of the Taurannik Codex, which had been destroyed in the Muurshantre Extinction a hundred millennia before; arcane hints in that forbidden tome led him to the Valtaullu Rift and the shattered asteroid belt that once had been the planet-sized Temple of Korman Lao, the Lord Ravager of the long-vanished race of demon-worshipping reptoids known as the Kanzer Exiles. The lore in the Temple fragments gave him the knowledge he needed to capture the corrupt spirit essence of Dathka Graush, to rip it free from its resting place in Korriban's Valley of Golg, to eventually extract and consume even the most secret lore of Sith alchemy that the ancient tyrant had carried to his grave.

And that ancient Sith alchemy had given him the knowledge to forge a device to control the living crystal that formed the structure of Mindorese meltmassif . . .

Because the Emperor had once confided in him that the transference of the spirit to another was a pathway to the ultimate goal of a Sith: to cheat death. Of course, he had been thinking of clones, but Cronal's plans were more ambitious; if such a feat was possible, he determined that he would perform it—and not to a mere clone body, either. After all, his own body had never been strong, and his service to the Dark had eaten away what little strength he'd had until he could no longer stand—until he could no longer feed himself, or even breathe without the life-support functions built into his gravity chair. Why should he settle for exchanging his flawed and failing body for another of the same model, every bit as certain to fail?

No. His devotion to the Way of the Dark had shown him a path to power greater than Palpatine could have ever dreamed: to transfer his consciousness permanently into a body that was young, that was healthy and handsome in a way Cronal had never been. A body more powerful in the Force than Vader, potentially more powerful even than Palpatine. The body of a true hero, beloved by all right-thinking citizens in the galaxy as the very symbol of truth and justice . . .

He would not simply turn Luke Skywalker to the service of the Dark. Why should he? Luke Skywalker served the Dark already, without ever guessing; he had powers of destruction that humbled even the Death Star.

No: Cronal would *become* Luke Skywalker, and serve the Dark *himself*.

RECLINING IN HIS LIFE-SUPPORT CHAMBER, CRONAL shut down the holoeditor. He had enough material already to persuasively make the case to the Republic as to why the stormtroopers would release him, even serve him, once he had become Skywalker. This was why his top commanders were all clones; he was counting on their conditioned obedience to even the most outrageous orders. Then the galaxy-wide release of his own little reality holodrama would make him—that is, Luke—even more famous, even more beloved, as the hero who had stood alone against the mad warlord Shadowspawn and single-handedly ended his reign of terror . . .

He actually found himself getting a bit giddy. He cackled softly as he indulged a fleeting fantasy of allowing Skywalker to awaken in the Election Center, so that Cronal could spend his last moments in this decaying body gloating, and boasting, and explaining to Skywalker every last detail of his fiendish plan.

That *would* be in character, wouldn't it?

It's what "Shadowspawn" would do, at any rate . . . but, sadly, it was not to be. However amusing it might have been, the risk was too great. Darksight, however powerful, was not perfect.

There was, after all, that slight issue about his puppet Shadowspawn surviving the climax of Cronal's little holothriller. That punch to the forehead . . . it was all *wrong*. The final blow should have been delivered with the blade of Skywalker's lightsaber. *That* was how Cronal had planned it. How he had *seen* it.

The lesson was clear: something could still go wrong. No more time would he waste in rehearsal. He must finish this. Now.

He closed his eyes and drove his mind into the Dark.

First he set his will upon the hairline web of meltmassif he'd grown within his own body: an ultrafine network that replicated his nervous system like a shadow cast in mineral crystals. Then he reached forth his hand in the darkness of his life-support shell and stroked the control that would lower the Sunset Crown from its compartment behind his headrest. Once the Sunset Crown was in place upon his head, he no longer had need of controls. He had no need of hands, or mouth, or eyes.

The Sunset Crown was his great achievement, the device that had been the object of his long quest into the depths of Sith alchemy; it was a transmitter, a transformer, that worked via the Force instead of electromagnetism. It converted his disciplined will into a signal that could interact directly with the unique electrochemical structure of meltmassif . . . and with the alien beings who used meltmassif as an anchor, a physical form to localize their energy-based consciousness, even as a human nervous system anchored and localized the energy-based consciousness called the human mind.

He had used this device to create the Pawns, those mind-locked technozombies who had become Cronal's eyes and mouths and hands; the Pawns were not only a conduit for his orders, but a necessary stepping-stone on his path toward self-transformation. Each Pawn had been chosen because he or she could touch the Dark—what the ignorant Jedi and the deluded Sith called being "Force-sensitive"—and because their wills could be utterly controlled by his own, through the Sunset Crown's influence over the crystals of meltmassif seeded within their skulls. On his command, their wills would align with his own and provide the added boost to his own Dark-touch necessary to make the transfer of his consciousness permanent.

When his mind awakened the power of the Sunset Crown, it sent his consciousness outward, an expanding sphere of will. When it touched the crystals in the meltmassif that lined every tunnel, every chamber, every nook and cranny of his entire vast base, the crystals resonated with the frequency of his desire, like a sounding board the size of the surrounding volcanic dome. He *became* the base, and the base became him; all within the base registered in the part of his brain that had once only registered his kinesthetic sense of his body position.

Throughout the base, his thirty-nine most Force-powerful Pawns instantly dropped what they were doing and converged on the Election Center, where Luke Skywalker already lay embedded in the hardened stone of the primary Pawning Table, his lightsaber buried in the rock beside him.

The fortieth, and most powerful, Pawn was already there: his puppet Shadowspawn, having unexpectedly survived the climax of Cronal's little holothriller, had been delivered to the same chamber. When this was all over, Cronal intended to discover exactly why the dead-man interlock in "Shadowspawn"'s Crown had failed to activate, but until then, there was no reason to simply discard him; he had a great deal of Force potential—worth ten of the others—and so Cronal had simply directed that "Shadowspawn" 's Crown be recovered and replaced. Adding him to the Pawns for the focusing would substantially accelerate both the neurocrystalline interpenetration and the consciousness transfer itself.

Unlike what occurred during the standard Pawning process that Cronal had painstakingly developed, Skywalker had not had his hair flash-burned away, had not had his skull opened and crystals implanted in his brain. No neurosurgery, not for Skywalker, nothing that might leave a suspicion-arousing scar.

He lay wholly within the meltmassif, buried alive with not even a breathing tube. Well, semi-alive: in full thanatizine II suspension, he had at least another hour before he would next need to take a breath. Before that breath would come, the combined power and perception Cronal channeled through the Pawns would have induced the meltmassif surrounding Skywalker's body to pierce his skin with invisibly fine needles of living crystal . . . they would enter through every pore, through his mouth and his nose, his ears, his tongue . . . and with the arcane powers he had ripped from the spirit of the ancient King of the Sith, Cronal would shape those crystals within Skywalker's body as he had shaped the ones in his own: into a webwork mirror of the young Jedi's nervous system.

Then Cronal would simply close his eyes and pour forth his consciousness like water into a waiting jug. With a twist of will—for thanatizine II only affected the organic body and would have no effect upon the crystalline neuroweb—he would liquefy the meltmassif of the Pawning Table and arise, quite literally, a new man. When he opened his eyes again, those eyes would be blue.

And he would extend his hand, and the Force would answer his call, bringing Skywalker's lightsaber—no, *Cronal's* lightsaber—up from the same meltmassif, because what was a Jedi without the Jedi weapon?

And should anything go wrong, well . . .

Should anything *at all* go wrong, the last living Jedi— the last being in the galaxy that Cronal would ever have any reason to fear—was already buried alive; all that Cronal might need to change in that description would be the word *alive*.

CHAPTER 11

LANDO STOOD AT THE FORWARD VIEWSCREENS OF THE *Remember Alderaan*'s bridge, watching as the battle cruiser's A-wing squadrons mopped up the last of the marauding interceptors that had been attacking the Slash-Es. He nodded—the Mandalorians were proving to be every bit as good as their reputation claimed—and turned to the *Remember Alderaan*'s commander. "Well done, Captain," he said. "Recall all fighters and initiate search and rescue. And see to it that when Lord Mandalore lands, he receives my compliments and gratitude, as well as my urgent request for the honor of his company at his earliest convenience."

The captain nodded. "As the general orders."

Lando turned to the ComOps officer. "Get me a secure channel with Commander Antilles of Rogue Squadron."

"Um, subspace is heavily jammed, General—"

"Okay," Lando said with an agreeable smile that somehow didn't look the slightest bit friendly. "Now that we've got that straightened out, get me a secure channel with Captain Antilles."

The ComOps officer swallowed and turned back to his console. "Yes, sir."

"And when you get that channel," Lando said crisply,

coming to a snap decision, "tell him I'm waiting for him in the Deck Seven fighter bay."

"Sir."

"Tell him that I've *been* waiting. Remind him that I don't *like* waiting. And let Lord Mandalore know where we are." He spun and headed for the turbolift. He jabbed a finger at C-3PO, who had been inconspicuously eavesdropping by an engineering console. "You. With me."

"Me? Really? But, but, General Calrissian—"

"Now," Lando said as he passed.

"That's a bit brusque, isn't it?" C-3PO nonetheless shuffled into the turbolift after him. "Please, General Calrissian, you do seem, if you don't mind my mentioning, just the slightest bit *agitated*—"

"I can't imagine why." Lando stabbed the turbolift's destination panel and the door cycled shut.

The turbolift had barely hummed into motion when the whole compartment seemed to lurch a meter or two to one side, hard enough that Lando had to clutch at C-3PO—who had his peds, as he preferred when on a moving surface, maglocked to the deck—to keep his feet. "What was *that*? It felt like an impact—but an impact big enough to shift the whole ship like that should have pretty much *vaporized* us."

"I'm sure I couldn't say, General, but—"

"It was a rhetorical question, Threepio." Lando dusted himself off and grimaced when he discovered a tiny spot of machine oil on one cuff. "You're not expected to answer."

"Oh, yes—I entirely understand. I, myself, am programmed with a number of conversational null-content phrases, used only for emphasis or—"

"Okay, okay." Lando fished out his comlink and brought it to his mouth. "Calrissian here. What just happened?"

"Unknown, General. We're looking into it."

C-3PO was still nattering on. "I misunderstood your rhetorical intent, General, because I *can* acquire that information for you."

Lando lowered the comlink. "You can?"

"Oh, certainly. The ship will know."

"It will?"

"Of course, General. Mon Calamari designs are *quite* intelligent—much more capable than any organic brain." C-3PO emitted a brief burst of static that sounded remarkably like an apologetic cough. "No offense intended, of course . . ."

"Of course." Lando nodded at the turbolift's comm panel. "Please."

The protocol droid stepped over to the comm panel and his vocabulator emitted a high-pitched whine nestled in white noise. The comm panel gave back a noise that to Lando's ears sounded indistinguishable from the first.

"What?" C-3PO's hand came up to his vocabulator slot. "Ooh, that's *awful*! Oh, my goodness!"

"What did it say?" Lando said. "What was that jolt?"

"The jolt? I don't know."

"Then what's the problem?"

"The ship made an *improper suggestion*," C-3PO said primly.

Lando blinked. "Are you kidding?"

"If only I were," the droid sighed. He leaned close to whisper in Lando's ear. "She's a *terrible* flirt," he confided. "You *know* how sailors can be . . ."

"I sure do." Lando was, after all, Lando. "Flirt back."

"General, really!"

"You want a girl to tell you secrets, you better be ready to at least nuzzle her ear."

"Well, I *never*!"

"I know—but you should."

C-3PO was still sputtering static when the turbolift doors hissed open on Deck Seven. Lando strode off toward the fighter bays without looking back.

Mon Calamari fighter bays were as beautifully functional as any other feature of their ships. Fighters entered the bay in a smoothly continuous stream, assisted by force-shield-reinforced capture netting that also gathered each one up and delivered it, as appropriate, either to its designated berth or to the huge transfer field that would carry a badly damaged craft to the battle cruiser's onboard repair bay. There was virtually none of the barely controlled chaos that characterized fighter bays on more conventional warships; even the roar of the entering fighters' engines was muted by phased-array sonic dampers.

Nestled among the ranks of A-wings were, unexpectedly, an X-wing fighter and a B-wing bomber—and standing stiffly at attention in front of them stood Commander Wedge Antilles and First Lieutenant Tycho Celchu.

"*You* got here fast," Lando said as he received their salutes.

"Yes, sir." Wedge, still at attention, sounded not the slightest bit like an insubordinate troublemaker who was roughly one atomic diameter short of demotion and serious brig time. "I did happen to recall that the general hates to be kept waiting, General. Sir."

"Don't think you're gonna smooth your way out of *this* one, Wedge—" Another shift-shock rocked the whole ship sideways and knocked Lando off-balance again; this time he had to steady himself against Wedge's shoulder, which was nearly as hard as C-3PO's. "*Damn* it! What *is* that?"

"The ship informs me," C-3PO reported calmly as he came up behind, "that it was gravity shear of unknown origin, interfering with the ship's engines as well as its artificial gravity and inertial compensators, not to mention placing *substantial* physical stress on its structure—oh, oh my. Oh, *my*. That's *terribly* dangerous, isn't it?"

"I'd say so," Wedge said.

"But I'm not *ready* for demolition!"

Wedge went on as if the droid hadn't spoken. "We call 'em gravity bombs, sir. Point-source grav projectors, going faster than an A-wing on a header into a black hole. They're ballistic—no drive signature, so you can't detect them until you're already inside their radius of effect. Dangerous enough by themselves—something like them was loaded onto the fake shuttle that took out the *Justice*—but the worst part is that they play merry hell with the gravity stations Shadowspawn scattered throughout the asteroids. There's not a navicomputer in the fleet that can predict the orbit of practically anything in the whole system—that's why we've got the Slash-Es sweeping the fields; we're trying to pry open a jump window before the star goes supercritical."

"I get it." Lando discovered that he was more interested in the tactical problem this presented than in punishing Rogue Squadron. Especially since it looked like he'd need them. "How's it going?"

"Could be better," Wedge said. "We have the planetoids aimed to keep the process self-sustaining, but we've still got who knows how many TIEs out there hitting us whenever we make a move. Our best estimate has periodic windows starting to open within eighteen to twenty hours."

"That's not too bad."

"It'd be better if the star wasn't gonna start massively flaring in less than three—and we can't tell exactly when, and we don't know how massively, there's no way to reliably predict—and those gravity bombs could still screw it all up."

"Those gravity bombs," Lando said slowly. "They have to be coming from somewhere. Otherwise they'd have all burned out or crashed into something by now, right?"

Tycho nodded. "General Solo did say he'd spotted a major installation planetside, sir. In the mouth of a volcano, I think; it was just about the last communication we had from him and Princess Leia before we lost contact."

"Han and Leia are out of contact planetside?" Lando shook his head disbelievingly. "What are they doing *there*?"

"Um . . . they went to rescue General Skywalker. Sir."

"And what is *Luke*—ahhh, never mind. I don't want to know."

"Master Luke is in danger?" C-3PO sounded horrified. "Oh, General Calrissian, you can't just *leave* him— what about *Artoo*?"

"Nobody's leaving anybody," Lando said. "We're getting scan-bounce from the atmosphere: heavy metals and an intense magfield. What do you have on it?"

Wedge shrugged. "It's breathable enough, if you don't mind coughing. But it's so charged that nothing we've got will penetrate very well—you want to really see what's there, the only way is to go down and have a look."

"If our scans won't get through it, it'll block just about *any* kind of radiation, right?"

"Well, yeah, but—" Wedge's frown deepened. "General Calrissian, I have to tell you I don't much like the direction this conversation's going. We don't really know their defenses—General, we don't even know how many *troops* they have!"

"Good."

"*Good?*"

"Like an old friend of mine says sometimes . . ." Lando grinned fiercely. "Never tell me the odds."

HAN SOLO HAD NEVER BEEN MUCH IN FAVOR OF STARing into the business end of a blaster's emitter. Staring into the emitter of his own blaster was no improvement at all. Doing it while he was standing in the cargo hold of his own ship . . .

He decided not to think about it. Getting crazy wasn't going to help the situation any.

"Okay," he said, letting her KYD dangle from his finger through its trigger guard. He threw a *Get behind me!* glance over his shoulder at Leia, because a whole bunch of the Mindorese in the cargo hold had suddenly produced a whole bunch of hold-out blasters from cavities in their Lava Gear armor. Chewbacca was still on one knee between the two wounded men he'd been treating, but those massive Wookiee hands were becoming massive Wookiee fists, while his massive Wookiee snarl was peeling back around his massive Wookiee fangs, and Han said, "Easy—*easy,* Chewie. No need for the hard way. We're gonna do this the *easy* way, you follow?"

Chewie slowly relaxed and lowered his head, but not until Han saw the gleam of agreement in one bright blue eye.

"On the floor." Aeona Cantor braced her other hand on her gun wrist to steady Han's DL-44 straight at his nose. "Now."

Han sighed. "You picked a lousy time to pirate my ship, lady."

She shrugged at him. "Is there ever a *good* time?"

"What do you think you're gonna *do* with it?" Han gave her a pitying look. "Where do you think you're gonna go? Shadowspawn's got this whole system so loaded with gravity stations that it'll take you two days to make jump."

"Didn't I tell you to get on the floor?"

"Listen to me." Han took a step toward her. "Those asteroids are about to start *falling into the star*. Take this ship out of atmosphere and we'll all *roast*."

"Not your problem." She leveled the BlasTech at Han's right eye. "Your problem is getting on the floor before I blow your brains all over Princess Kissy-Face."

"Princess *excuse me*?" Leia snapped with that instantly dangerous tone Han knew so well. He put out one arm to hold her back but she ducked under it without breaking stride. "You want to put down the blaster and say that *again*?"

"What *is* it with you people?" Aeona said. "Get on the floor! Now!"

"I have a better idea." Han hooked his thumbs behind his belt. "How about instead you give me back my blaster while my partner demonstrates what we mean by the *easy way*?"

Chewbacca's demonstration was straightforward. Vast hairy hands shot out, seized the throats of the two irregulars on the deck in front of him, and knocked their heads together briskly, which made a sound very like a very large hollow tok nut landing on a very large hard rock. The two men sagged. Chewbacca didn't. Instead he simply stood, holding his victims so that they dangled from his fists in front of him and made a pretty efficient shield.

"They're still alive, so far. That's what *easy way* translates to in Shyriiwook," Han informed Aeona helpfully. "And before you get any ideas about trick shots, you should know he gets a little excited when people start shooting—and then people's heads tend to pop right off their necks. Makes a heckuva mess. Now, you want to hand over my blaster, or should we start a pickup game of borgleball with your friends' skulls?"

The blaster in her hand had never wavered. "Maybe I'll just shoot *you,* instead."

Han shrugged. "Knock yourself out."

She yanked the trigger, and its dry click elicited from her an incomprehensible snarl that Han confidently interpreted as some sort of obscenity. He turned over his left hand to reveal the BlasTech's power cell that he'd kept tucked in his palm. "Think I'm gonna hand over a charged weapon? To *you?*"

Her next comprehensible utterance was a shrill shriek of *"Take them!"* as she hurled Han's blaster at his head and charged with her hands outstretched as if she wanted to rip his face off with her fingers.

Han snagged his blaster neatly out the air, thumbed open the charge compartment, and had the power cell back in place before she made three steps, though this was due less to superb reflexes on his part than to the fact that by the time Aeona had taken her second step, Leia had jumped forward and kicked the other woman's legs out from under her, dropping her in a face-first flatcake, then jumped on her back and pounded her head into the deck.

About this time, a preposterous number of blaster bolts began zinging through the cargo hold more or less at random, as pretty much all the irregulars with the little hold-out blasters had opened up at once, filling the air with a lethal red storm of plasma packets.

The main reason these bolts flew at random—instead of, say, detonating inside the flesh of Han, Leia, and Chewbacca—was that the Wookiee, with his customarily unsubtle approach to combat, had simply hurled both unconscious men bodily into the mass, then charged in himself right behind them, on the personal conviction, acquired over years in Han Solo's company, that when you're caught unarmed in a firefight, the safest place to be is right in the middle of the bad guys.

This was only partially because they couldn't fire on him without risking shooting their friends. Mainly, it was because—as the Mindorese discovered, to their considerable dismay—once one gets within reach, there is no such thing as an unarmed Wookiee.

Han got his blaster primed and snapped off a burst at a couple of Mindorese who'd had the bright idea to aim high, thinking to blast Chewie over their friends' heads. One ducked and darted away, but the other caught Han's bolt square in his chest; the blast of the impact sent him toppling backward, but the spreading cloud of reddish-black smoke coming from his armor reminded Han of what Leia had said about that flippin' Lava Gear armor of theirs.

Now that he'd thought of it, the air in the hold was getting distinctly thick with smoke and dust, stinging his eyes and rasping his throat as Mindorese armor absorbed ricochets from bulkheads and deck and ceiling, which reminded him of which three people in that hold *weren't* wearing tough armor made of the local lava. An estimate of how long his, Leia's, and Chewie's luck could conceivably last before one of those stray bolts blew off an irreplaceable piece or two of their respective anatomies made the decision for him in an instant.

He whirled and put a blaster bolt into the cargo-ramp release. The panel exploded into sparks and smoke and the ramp began to descend. Leia was still kneeling on Aeona's back with a fist tangled in her long red hair, holding her to the deck.

"Hey!" Han leapt over and grabbed her shoulder. He had to shout over the blasterfire and the ear-shattering whoops of Chewbacca's war howl. "Playtime's over! We gotta go!"

Leia looked up at him with a fierce grin, sparkling eyes, and high color blazing on her cheeks, and Han thought again, for the tenth or hundredth—maybe thousandth—time, that the Princess of Alderaan really was never more beautiful than when she was knocking the Sithspit out of somebody.

She leapt to her feet. "Where's Artoo? We can't leave him!"

"I'll get the droid! Just go!"

"One second—"

She dropped back to one knee and snatched Aeona's KYD-21 from the deck where Han had let it fall. Han covered her with a barrage of marginally aimed fire, blasting more and more armor smoke off every irregular he could spot in the thickening haze, while she rifled the semiconscious woman's pockets and came up with the KYD's power cell. "My turn!"

From one knee, she started snapping off shots into the fringes of the melee, in the middle of which a joyously berserk Wookiee was now swinging a Mindorese by the ankles, using him as a human club to batter others in all directions. "Go get Chewie!"

Han flashed her a grateful glance and charged into the thick of the fight. Leia started backing down the open ramp, still firing. Han lowered his shoulder and just dewbacked his way in, shoving and kicking and smacking a couple of guys with his blaster until he was close enough to Chewbacca that he had to duck to keep the Wookiee from flattening him with his club of unconscious Mindorese. He caught Chewie's arm, and the battle-maddened Wookiee roared and tried to backhand Han away. Han didn't take it personally; he just hung on and rode Chewie's arm while he shouted, "Chewie, it's *me*! Code Black, Chewie—you understand? *Code Black!*"

Chewbacca blinked down at him, and Han watched

comprehension snap into those blue eyes. The next flick of those eyes instantly took in the situation, which had actually gotten *worse* as Chewbacca had battered down man after man; the more Mindorese who went down, the less there were to get in each other's way—and now a couple of Big Brains among them had remembered the pile of weapons in the number-six hopper and were in the process of digging out blaster carbines, which meant that this situation, already ugly as a drunken monkey-lizard, was about to escalate all the way to Naked Gamorrean.

"*Harrraroufgh!*" Chewie said, and Han let go of his arm. The Wookiee hoisted the unconscious Mindorese over his head and hurled him into the two guys over by the hopper, then howled to Han his complete agreement with the idea of Code Blacking out of there while they still could. He whipped one vast hairy arm around Han's waist, yanked him off the ground, and charged for the ramp as if Han were a borgleball and Chewbacca was running him in for the game-winning goal.

"Artoo!" Han shouted, still firing back past the Wookiee's shoulder. "Where's that flippin' *droid*?"

An instant later, Han spotted the astromech, standing at the ramp-release panel Han had blasted, a manipulator arm and a data socket both shoved into the sparks and smoke sputtering out from the shattered electronics. "Hey, *Stubby*!" Han yelled. "Now is *not* the time for *field repairs*!"

R2-D2's tootled reply sounded distinctly sarcastic, and when Chewie carried Han past to the ramp, the little droid retracted his tools and whirred along behind just as fast as his locomotor treads would carry him. Leia knelt at the base of the ramp, pouring fire up into the hold without bothering to aim, trusting that the ricochets would cause enough havoc to keep Mindorese heads down.

"Drop me and go get Artoo!" Han shouted, and Chewbacca complied with such unexpected alacrity that Han landed hard on that already-bruised portion of his anatomy. He scrambled to Leia's side, adding his blasterfire to hers as Chewbacca sprang back up the ramp far enough to seize the droid. R2 squealed as Chewie lifted him; then the Wookiee spun and raced back down for the cavern through a buzzing hailstorm of energy bolts—some of which were now the thick, stretching smears of rifle blasts.

"Fall back!" Han told Leia. "Follow Chewie—I'll hold 'em here!" *Not for long,* he thought, but he might be able to buy her a chance to get away.

"I'm not leaving you!" Leia said, still firing. "We go together or not at all!"

"Oh, for the love of—what happened to *You're the captain, Captain?*"

"Things change," Leia said, just before a random bolt clipped her shoulder and knocked her spinning to the cavern floor, which decided the issue, because Han leapt to her side, swept her up in his arms, and—despite her irritable insistence that "I'm *fine,* Han! It's barely even a scratch!"—carried her at a dead run toward the mouth of the tunnel where Chewbacca and R2-D2 stood waiting.

"What's the *matter* with you idiots?" Han cried at them. "*Keep running!*"

Chewie replied with a gruff "*Hrrowrrh,*" which was when Han realized the droid had extended his little parabolic antenna through a hatch in his dome and was now chirruping something that sounded less like his usual attempts at human communication, and more like the feedback from a high-speed electronic encryption protocol. Han skidded to a stop and looked over his shoulder.

Instead of what he expected to see—a flood of heavily

armed irregulars streaming down the cargo ramp with rifles blazing—he found instead a narrowing aperture leaking smoke, artificial light, and the occasional badly aimed blaster bolt as the cargo ramp swung closed and latched itself in place.

Han blinked down at R2-D2. "Did *you* do that?"

The astromech rocked on his locomotors. *Bee-woop!*

"Not bad, Stubby—can you shut down the engines? Lock out the controls? Anything?"

Tyreepeep loo toooeee wrp! was the droid's replay, which Han took to mean something along the lines of *Maybe if you'd given me a chance to work it a little . . .*

"Han?" Leia said. "Han, it'll be all right. We'll get the *Falcon* back."

He didn't hear her. He couldn't hear her. He could only stand with her in his arms and watch.

Watch as somebody got the *Falcon*'s repulsorlifts engaged and lit the sublight thrusters. Watch as his ship slowly lifted from the cavern floor and rotated toward the way out. Watch as a flare from the sublights kicked his ship from the cavern.

Watch as his departing ship ripped open his chest, snatched out his heart, and took it along.

He set Leia on her feet. She stayed close against his chest and slid one arm up around his neck. "Han?"

He didn't react. He only stood staring at the cavern's empty mouth.

Chewbacca stepped over and draped a hand over Leia's shoulder. *"Rowowr,"* he said softly. She nodded and let Han go, then followed Chewie and R2-D2 a little way off into the tunnel.

Han stood there for a long time, with an icy fist clenched inside his chest where his heart should be.

Finally, he took one deep breath and released a long, long sigh.

"Well, *that* could have gone better," he said, and turned to follow his friends.

STARFIGHTERS FILLED SPACE AROUND THE *REMEMBER Alderaan*, streaking and looping and whirling so fast that in visible light they became mere smears of motion; even the cruiser's sensor suite could distinguish friend from foe only belatedly, and by ratios of probability rather than certainty. The battle seemed to intensify by an order of magnitude with every light-second closer to the planet the cruiser moved.

Lando stood at the bridge's forward viewscreens, hands folded behind him, his face entirely blank, expressionless—only the quick flicker of his eyes from starfighters to cruisers and back again betrayed the level of his concentration. Fenn Shysa had been pacing the deck behind him, faster and faster, becoming more and more agitated as starfighter after starfighter exploded, so many now that hurtling debris from their destructions had overloaded the *Alderaan*'s particle shields and now rattled the hull and starred cracks into the transparisteel viewports.

Finally Shysa couldn't take it anymore. "Lando— General Calrissian—we can't just *stand* here!"

"I'm standing," Lando said. "You're pacing."

"I have to scramble my men. We should be *out* there!"

"You can join the battle if you feel that's best; I'm the last man in the galaxy who'd presume to give orders to Lord Mandalore. But the commandos aren't your men. Not right now, anyway. They work for *me*."

"But—but—" At a loss for words, Shysa could only wave expressively at the battle outside. "We're cut off already—they're gonna pin us against the *planet*—"

Lando turned to him with, astonishingly, a broad *smile* on his face. "You think?"

"General!" the ComOps officer interrupted, staring into his screen. "We have visual verification—a substantial mass of asteroids inbound for the star. Coronal entry in . . . three minutes, sir!"

Lando nodded. "Flare activity?"

"Already begun, sir—sensor analysis indicates that we're about twelve minutes away from a spike in intensity high enough to take down every deflector shield in the system. Then we'll have maybe an hour, probably less, before we're all cooked . . ."

"Okay, you heard the man," Lando said generally. "Send out an all-ships: disengage and make for Mindor's nightside, then launch escape pods. Tell the Rogues to take two more squadrons and cover the pods—"

"Lando, you *have* to commit my men! It'll be a *slaughter.*"

"No, it won't."

"Three squadrons'll never cover that many pods, and these marauders don't take prisoners!"

"Doesn't matter," Lando said crisply. "Let 'em blow up the pods. It'll keep them busy."

"What?"

"All we're launching is *pods,* get it? *Empty* pods." Lando shook his head. "Think I'm about to set up my forces halfway around the planet from the bad guys? Not *this* general, my friend."

"Then—" Fenn stared out through the forward screens, suddenly thoughtful. "Yeah, I get it: from nightside, you have the planet as a shield against the stellar flares . . . then we come in low-level, through the atmosphere . . . but if you're planning to bring capital ships close to that volcano base of theirs, first you've got to take out their ground-based artillery—turbolasers, ion cannons . . . and *especially* that gravity gun. How do you figure on doing *that*?"

"Might be a problem." Lando was *still* smiling. "You wouldn't happen to know where I could lay my hands on, say, five or six hundred Mandalorian supercommandos, would you?"

Fenn blinked, blinked again, and then discovered that he was starting to smile, too.

CHAPTER 12

THOUGH HE WAS FAR FROM CONSCIOUS, LUKE KNEW something was wrong.

He felt . . . cold.

Unbelievably cold. He'd been cold before—a couple years earlier, on Hoth, he'd come within a shaved centimeter of freezing to death before Han had found him—but this was different. That cold had been a creeping numbness, and weakness, and a growing inability to force his hypothermic muscles to move. This cold, though, froze him without the comfort of numbness. Tiny razor-edged crystals of ice—colder than ice, so cold they burned, cold as liquid air—grew inward through his skin at every pore, becoming hairlines of freeze that crept along his nerves.

And with the cold came silence.

Physical silence, deeper than a living creature can truly experience: not just the absence of external sound, but the absence of all concept of sound. No whisper of breath, no hush of blood coursing through arteries, no faintest beat of his heart. Not even the vaguest sensation of vibration, or pressure, or friction on his skin.

But the cold and the silence went deeper than the merely physical. They were in his dreams.

These dreams were glacially slow, actionless, featureless hours of empty staring into empty space, hours becoming years that stretched into numberless millennia, as one by one the stars went out. He could do nothing, for there was nothing to do.

Except watch the stars die.

And in their place was left *nothing*. Not even absence. Only him.

Floating. Empty of everything. Without thought, without sensation. Forever.

Almost.

His first thought in a million years trickled into his brain over the course of decades. *Sleep. This is the end of everything. Nothing left but sleep.*

The second thought, by contrast, followed instantly upon the second. *Wait . . . somebody else is thinking with my mind.*

Which meant he wasn't alone at the end of the universe.

Even in frozen dreams of eternity, the Force was strong with him. He opened himself to the Sleep Thought and drew it into the center of his being, where with the Force to guide and sustain him, he could examine the thought, turn it this way and that like an unfamiliar stone.

It had *weight*, this thought, and texture: like a hunk of volcanic basalt around a uranium core, it was unreasonably dense, and its surface was pebbled, as though it had once been soft and sticky and somebody had rolled it across a field of fine gravel. As he let the Force take his perception into greater and greater focus and detail, he came to understand that each of these pebbles was a *person*—human or near-human, every single one, bound into an aggregate matrix of frozen stone.

As the Force took him deeper, he came to understand that this stone he held was also holding him; even as he turned it in his hand, it also surrounded and enclosed him—that it was a prison for every one of these pebble-lives, and that these imprisoned lives were also imprisoning *him*.

He was the stone himself, he discovered: the very matrix of dark frozen stone that bound them all. He trapped them and they trapped him, and neither could let go. They were bound together by the very structure of the universe.

Frozen by the Dark.

And here was another strangeness: Since when did he think of the structure of the universe as capital-D Dark? Even if there might be some trace of truth in that bleak perception, when had he become the kind of man who would surrender to it? If the Dark wanted to drag him into eternal emptiness, it was going to have to fight him for every millimeter.

He started looking for the way out. Which was also, due to the curious paradox inherent in his Force perception, the way *in*.

The imaginary thought-stone in his imaginary hand was a metaphor, he understood—even as was the frozen stone he had become—but it was also real on a level deeper than nonimaginary eyes could ever see. He *was* the stone . . . and so he did not need to reach out to touch the lives represented by the pebbles. He was touching them already.

He only had to pay attention.

But each life-pebble on which he focused gave back no hint of light. No perception even of the human being it represented, only a featureless nonreflective surface like a smoothed and rounded spheroid of powdered graphite. Each one he touched gave back no hope, no purpose, no dream of escape, but instead drew these out from his frozen heart, swallowed them whole, and fed them to the Dark.

And the Dark gave up no trace of evidence that they had ever existed.

All he got from the pebbles was gentle wordless urging to let himself sleep. *Struggle is futile. The Dark swallows everything in the end.* All his hopes, all his fears, every heroic dream and every tragic reality. Every single distant descendant of everyone who had ever heard of him. All would be gone, leaving not even an echo to hint that they had ever existed. The only answer was sleep. Eternal sleep.

Sleep.

Luke thought, *Never.*

He had an intuition that was half memory, half guess, and maybe altogether a hint from the Force, because when he again turned that imaginary stone in his imaginary hand, one of those imaginary pebbles of powdered graphite had a crack in it that wasn't imaginary at all.

And through that crack, tiny beyond tiny, nanometrically infinitesimal, so small that if it hadn't been imaginary, Luke couldn't have seen it even with the most advanced instruments in the galaxy, shone the very faintest conceivable glimmer . . .

Of light.

With the Force to guide him, he focused his perception into a similarly nanometric filament. And through that tiny crack of light within the imaginary stone, Luke found the universe.

FOCUSING HIS WHOLE SELF INTO HIS FORCE PERCEPTION with all his power and every scrap of the mental discipline that Ben and Master Yoda had pounded into him, Luke could send enough of himself along that filament of light that he could see again—dimly, distantly, through waves of bizarre distortion—and what he saw was sleeves.

Voluminous sleeves, draped together as though concealing folded hands . . . and beyond them, a floor of smooth stone, illuminated by cold, flickering blues, like the light cast by the screen of a holoplayer. He tried to lift his head, to get a look around, but the view didn't change, and he realized that the eyes through which he saw were not his.

With that realization, other perceptions began to flower within his consciousness. He became aware that the floor at which his borrowed eyes were staring was *connected* with him somehow . . . that it was not ordinary stone at all, but a curious semicolloidal structure of crystal . . . that it was, inexplicably, somehow *alive*.

That when he set his mind to it, he could feel the life, like a subsonic hum can raise a tingle on the skin. But it wasn't on his skin that he felt it, it was *inside his head* . . . and he felt it because he had crystals of that semicolloidal somehow-living stone *growing* inside his *brain* . . .

No—

Not *his* brain.

The crystals grew within the other brain, the one connected to the eyes he was borrowing from outside the universe. This became another subject of contemplation, like his imaginary stone, because like that imaginary stone he was both inside this borrowed brain and outside it, pushing in while looking out. And when he touched those crystals with his attention, he could hear—no, *feel*—the whisper of despair that had murmured to him at the end of the universe.

Sleep. Struggle is futile. All things end. Existence is an illusion. Only the Dark is real.

He could feel now that the whisper came from outside this borrowed brain, even as his own perception did, and that the crystals somehow picked up this whisper and amplified it, adding this brain's limited Force power to its own, the same as it had done with the other hundreds of brains that Luke could now feel were all linked into this bizarre system.

There was somebody out there.

Luke thought, *Blackhole.*

And with that thought, he could feel the malignancy that fed this field of Dark: the ancient wheezing cripple entombed within his life-support capsule, who poured his bleak malice through a body-wide webwork of this selfsame crystal . . .

Just like the one growing within Luke's own body.

And with that understanding came power: he set his will upon the web of crystal within his body and allowed the Force to give power to his desire; now he was able to clearly perceive the link between his crystals and those within this borrowed brain. Then, when he willed the head to raise, it did, and when he willed the eyes to take in the room, he saw a stone cavern, dimly lit by waves of blue energy discharge that crawled along the stone walls and ceiling like living things—the same crackling discharge Luke had seen in the Cavern of the Shadow Throne—though this energy did no harm to the people gathered here.

The cavern was filled with Moon Hats.

Each and every one among them stood motionless with head lowered, hands folded invisibly within the drape of their sleeves. Each and every one among them faced a large stone pedestal that stood empty in the center of the room. The pedestal was of a single piece with the floor, but not as though it had been carved from it; it looked as if it had grown there, like a tumor. It was about a meter and a half high, and its flat top was roughly the same size and shape as a comfortable single bed. From time to time, with a kind of regularized increase of frequency like the tide coming in, the electric discharge from the walls and ceiling would pause, and shiver in place as though captured between electrodes; then with a painfully bright flash, they would converge upon the stone pedestal and vanish into its surface.

Luke understood. *That's me,* he thought. *That's where I am. Buried alive in solid rock.*

This didn't particularly bother him; after spending eternity at the end of the universe, mere death didn't mean much at all. Death was better than what Blackhole was trying to do to him. With him.

As him.

He didn't know if he could save himself, but he might be able to help these people. That would have to be enough.

Luke reached out through the crystals with the Force . . . and found nothing beyond this one lone brain to grasp. Though he could feel them clearly, though he could listen to the whisper of the crystals in their heads, he could find no surface on those crystals that his will could grasp. Exactly like his dream: these were the pebbles of featureless graphite. Nothing there but the Dark.

This one alone had that fissure of light . . .

In the distant reaches of his memory, he found a lesson of Yoda's, from one long solstice night, deep in the jungle near Dagobah's equator. *When to the Force you truly give yourself, all you do expresses the truth of who you are,* Yoda had said, leaning forward so that the knattik-root campfire painted blue shadows within the deep creases of his ancient face. *Then through you the Force will flow, and guide your hand it will, until the greatest good might come of your smallest gesture.*

He'd never really understood that lesson. He'd only tried to live according to the principle . . . but now there was an image slowly breaching the surface of his consciousness. An image of his own hand, delivering a punch.

Just to the right of center, on the forehead of "Lord Shadowspawn." Which had been precisely the impact required to crack the crystalline matrix inside his brain.

A simple act of mercy, born of no other desire than to

end a conflict without taking a life, now had become his own lifeline, by which he could draw himself back from the eternal nothing at the end of the universe.

He could *feel* his connection now, could sense the control he might exert through this connection; a simple twist of will would seize this body and make it act at his command—he could even, he sensed, send his power with the Force through this body to serve his desire. He could make this man his puppet, and forge his own escape.

Or . . .

He could abandon his fear, and express the truth of who he was.

For Luke Skywalker, this was not even a choice. Instead of a command, he sent through the link a friendly suggestion.

Hey, Nick, he sent. *Why don't you wake up?*

THE FIRST INKLING CRONAL GOT THAT SOMETHING WAS going terribly wrong came in the form of an alarm Klaxon blaring inside his life-support chamber. The Klaxon shattered his concentration and jerked him back into his own body; for a long moment that seemed to stretch on toward forever, his desiccated flesh could only shudder and twitch while he struggled to catch his breath. Finally he could move his hand to silence the Klaxon, push the Sunset Crown up from his head to its resting place behind his couch, and answer the urgent hail incoming from Group Captain Klick.

He was so rattled by the sudden interruption that he very nearly forgot to restrict his transmission to synthesized audio-only. At the last instant he keyed the proper code, and then had to take several more deep breaths to steady himself again. To let his pet clone commander see, instead of the robust and masterful Lord Shadowspawn, the sunken creases of his ancient face, his slack bloodless lips peeling back from his prominent yellowed teeth, the few tangled wisps of hair that straggled across his wrinkled scalp, to let him hear Cronal's own weak and wheezing voice—this could have caused considerable difficulty, if not outright disaster.

"Group Captain," he croaked, his thin wheeze crackling with strain. "Was my order unclear? No interruptions!"

The group captain, of course, could hear only the computer's synthesized version of Shadowspawn's sepulchral basso. *"My lord, the Rebels are attacking!"*

"How do a few fighter squadrons constitute an emergency so dire that you would defy my direct order? Destroy them, and don't bother me again."

"More than fighters, my lord. A battle cruiser of Mon Calamari design has initiated orbital bombardment, targeting our ground emplacements, primarily our ion-turbo cannons. We believe it's in preparation for a surface assault."

"A Mon Calamari battle cruiser? Impossible. Their sole Mon Cal was destroyed by our gravity slice."

"Yes, my lord—but this is a new *one!"*

"Impossible," Cronal repeated. "No new cruiser could have entered the system so soon—our gravity stations should keep them at least a light-hour away!"

"My lord, the Rebels have opened a temporary jump window."

"Imposs—" Cronal bit his tongue; clearly none of this was impossible at all. Those bloody Rebels—may the Dark swallow every miserable one!

The group captain went on at some length, describing the battle near the Rebel interdiction ships. Cronal listened in growing disbelief. "Why was I not *informed*?"

"My lord, your order—"

"Call out every squadron—throw in every reserve! Get every single fighting craft in action *now*, if you have to draft deckhands to fly them! I want those Rebels so busy they don't even have time to watch the star flares that will kill them, do you understand?"

"Yes, my lord."

"And detail a company of your best commandos to the Election Center entry; they are to hold that door at all costs. No matter what happens with the battle, no Rebel can be allowed to interrupt what happens within, do you understand? See to it personally."

"Yes, my lord. I will take personal command. No enemy will breach the Election Center while one trooper lives, my lord!"

"Let it be so," Cronal snapped. "You have complete authority to command this situation, Group Captain— do not disturb me again!"

"It will be done, my lord."

Cronal stabbed the cutoff. His joints creaked as he tried to find a comfortable position on the life-support chamber's couch. So close . . . he was so *close* . . . a few minutes more was all he needed to give himself youth, and strength, a Jedi's power and the name and face of a hero . . .

He yanked the Sunset Crown back into place upon his head and closed his eyes.

He sucked in a breath as deep as his withered lungs could hold, then sighed it out as slowly as his hammering heart would permit. He did the same again, and again, until gradually his heart began to slow, and his head began to clear, and he could once again drive his will into the Dark.

There he found, winking like glitterflies on a moonless night, the warm comfort of his Pawns, like little bits of himself scattered out into the Dark to point his way. He focused his mind and stabbed downward to a deeper level of concentration, where he could grasp every one of those little bits of himself and squeeze until he was

wholly inside them. Then the slow cycle of breath . . .
until each and every Pawn inhaled when he inhaled . . .
sighed when he sighed . . . until their very hearts beat in
synchrony with his own . . .

All but one.

SOMEBODY HAD SWITCHED ON THE LIGHTS INSIDE
Nick's head.

He jerked awake, blinking. His eyes wouldn't focus.
"Man . . . I have been having the *weirdest* dream . . ."

He tried to rub his eyes, but his hands were tangled in
something . . . what was this, sleeves? Since when did he
wear pajamas? Especially pajamas made out of brocade
so thick he could have used it as a survival tent on a
Karthrexian glacier . . . And his head hurt, too, and his
neck was stiff, because his head had gained a couple of
dozen kilos—must have been some serious party, to
leave him with *this* bad a hangover—and when he did finally free his hands and rub his eyes and massage his vision back into something resembling working order, he
took in his surroundings . . . and blinked some more.

He was standing in a stone chamber along with about
forty other people who were all wearing funny hats and
robes just like his, who all stood motionless and silent in
a crowd around a big stone pedestal with heads lowered
and hands folded inside their sleeves, and he said, "Oh,
okay. *That* explains it."

It hadn't been a dream.

Okay, sure, a nightmare, maybe—but he was wide
awake now and the nightmare was still going on, which
meant it was as real as the deep ache in his feet, not to
mention his back and his neck. How long had he been
standing like this, anyway? Plus there was this knuckle-
sized knot of a bruise over his right eye . . .

Oh, he thought. *Oh yeah, I remember.*

For a long, long moment, he didn't move.

He couldn't guess exactly how long he'd have to make his moves from the first instant he attracted Blackhole's attention, but he had a pretty good idea what the old ruskakk's reaction was gonna be: the walls and floor and ceiling of this whole chamber were made of melt-massif.

This was always the problem with Jedi, Nick decided. Whenever there were Jedi around, you ended up in some kind of trouble that nobody in the galaxy could possibly survive. Not even the Jedi himself. And this time, it wasn't even about dying. It was about getting stuck as Blackhole's sock puppet for the rest of his natural life. So what was he supposed to do?

On the other hand, doing nothing sure wouldn't make anything better. He could feel Blackhole inside his head—a cold slimy goo like the trail left behind by a Xerthian hound-slug on a damp autumn day—and he could feel, too, that Blackhole could snatch back control of Nick's arms and legs and brain anytime he felt like it; the only reason Nick had any self-awareness at all was that Blackhole's whole attention was focused on the kid inside the stone slab.

Overall, it looked like both of them were pretty well fragged. *But, y'know,* he reminded himself, *that kid is supposed to be a Skywalker.* Nick had never been super-stitious, but there was something about that name. It seemed to carry the promise, or at least the possibility, that the day might be saved in some incomprehensibly improbable fashion. Even if the situation was so clearly hopeless that only a lunatic would even try.

And so he yanked off his Crown.

It hurt. A lot. And it made this damp juicy *ripping* sound, very much how Nick imagined the sound of someone ripping his scalp in half like cheap broadcloth.

"Okay: *owww!*" He threw the Crown on the floor. "That's *it,*" he declared as blood began to trickle into his eyes. "Nobody's putting that thing back on me, because that was the *last* time I want to take it *off*."

"No . . ." Cronal moaned in the darkness. "It's not *possible* . . . not *now*, not when I'm so *close!*"

He stabbed savagely at the comm panel in front of his couch. "Klick! Are you in position?"

"My lord Shadowspawn!" the Group Captain exclaimed. *"We're on our way!"*

Cronal ground out words between ragged yellow stumps of teeth. "When you get there, secure and seal the door. If anyone tries to come out, kill them."

He reached up to adjust the Sunset Crown upon his wrinkled scalp. As for the inside of the Election Center, he could handle that himself.

Nick gave his robes a quick pat down, hoping he might find a liquefier belted to his waist or something—somebody around here must have one, to have softened the meltmassif to get Skywalker into it in the first place—but he came up blank, of course, because nothing was ever that easy. Not for him. Nick was absolutely certain that on the day of his birth the Force had looked down upon his life, smiled, and cheerfully made an obscene gesture. Or something.

He scanned the room. Thirty-some mostly identical Pawns. Who had the liquefier? Was he supposed to search every single one of them? On the other hand, it occurred to him that the charge emitted by a liquefier was very similar to that of a blaster on stun . . .

He gazed down thoughtfully at his Crown, suddenly reflecting that it might turn out to be useful after all. He picked it up and went to the door.

"Guard!" he barked in his resonant Shadowspawn voice, lifting the Crown over his head. When one of the troopers outside opened the door, Nick hit him with it.

Hard.

The impact buckled the stormtrooper's knees, and Nick—mindful both of the stormtrooper's helmet and of his homeworld's ancient adage that "anything worth hitting is worth hitting twice"—smacked him again, harder, which laid the stormtrooper facedown and twitching.

The other door guard cursed and brought his carbine around to open fire with impressive speed—but a couple of kilos of carbonite made an even better shield than it did a club. Nick shoved the Crown right into the carbine's muzzle and put his shoulder into it, which knocked the trooper backward off-balance; before the trooper could bring his carbine back in line, Nick had the first guard's carbine in his own hands . . . and stormtrooper armor, it seemed, was not quite as sturdy as carbonite when it came to absorbing blaster bolts.

Beyond the door, he found a long, down-sloping corridor that looked like it had been melted through shimmery black stone. He had time to mutter, "So on top of everything else, I don't even know where I fraggin' *am*," before a door at the far end of the corridor opened to reveal a squad of stormtroopers, most likely wondering what all the shooting was about.

"This just keeps getting better and better." Nick dragged the unconscious trooper inside and blasted the door panel, which exploded in a shower of sparks. The door slid shut, and Nick could only hope it might slow the oncoming troopers for a few seconds. It would have to be enough.

But when he looked up at the Pawns, all the Pawns were looking back at him.

He thought, *Oh, this can't be good.*

The Pawns in front of him bunched together, blocking his shot at Skywalker's pedestal tomb, while the others spread out and began to circle toward him, arms outstretched, without making a sound—and though Nick knew it was because most of them couldn't actually talk, it was still excessively creepy. He bared his teeth and thumbed the carbine over to full auto.

And hesitated.

He had this instant, extraordinarily vivid vision of trying to explain to the sadly patient face of Luke Skywalker—the man who had spared Nick's life a couple hours earlier based on nothing more than a pun and a vague intuition that he might be innocent—how *I just blew away thirty-some innocent men and women so I could dig you out of there,* because he had an overpowering intuition of his own: if Luke Skywalker thought he might save thirty innocent lives by sacrificing his own, he wouldn't hesitate. Ten innocent lives.

One.

"Or, hell, one not-so-innocent life," Nick muttered. "Like mine."

He flipped the carbine's power setting to stun. "I hate Jedi. Hate 'em. Really, really, really. Hate."

He had no way to know how a stun blast would affect someone when channeled by the neural network of the Pawn Crowns directly into their unprotected brains, but he was pretty sure it wouldn't be good, and the only thing he was looking forward to less than explaining to Skywalker how he'd killed all these people because he was a bloodthirsty son of a ruskakk was explaining how he'd killed them all because he was too stupid to pour water out of a boot. Fortunately, he didn't have to stun them to stop them.

He only had to stun the floor.

He opened fire on the ground in front of the feet of the oncoming Pawns, and around each shot, a meter or two of the meltmassif that layered the chamber's floor instantly liquefied to roughly the viscosity of warm toknut butter. Pawns went down in heaps. Nick turned his fire on the floor between himself and the Pawns blocking the pedestal tomb, and they slipped and fell into a pile of their own, struggling and pawing at each other helplessly.

Not bad, he thought. *Maybe not up there with slipping on a raballa peel, but still pretty funny.* Now if he only had a *real* liquefier he could have rehardened the stone, which would have been even better. Loads of comic possibility. Though they were still struggling to rise and kind of climbing over each other, and if a few of them actually reached hard floor that would bring a sudden end to the chuckles. "And now, for my *next* trick . . ."

He flipped open the downed trooper's medpac and loaded an ampoule of vivatherin into the chromostring canister. Then with the chromo in one hand and the carbine in the other, he took a three-step running start, jumped over the gooey floor, and landed on the chest of the nearest downed Pawn. He skidded and slipped and almost went down as the Pawn gasped and clutched at his ankle, but he kicked his way free and lurched forward, stepping on stomachs and legs and probably a head or two until he could claw his way to the pedestal and clamber up on top. As the Pawns tried to pull themselves up after him, he aimed the carbine between his feet and held down the trigger.

The pedestal collapsed into a spreading pile of slimy goo, and Nick found himself sitting on Luke Skywalker's chest. Without pausing to consider how ridiculous they both must look, Nick triggered the chromostring canister against Luke's neck. Given the chromostring's ability to enhance systemic absorption of the vivatherin, Nick figured Skywalker would be jumping back to life any second now, which wouldn't be a second too soon, because the pedestal's collapse left Nick and Luke down on the floor with the goo-covered piles of

Pawns, who were now climbing over each other to claw at Nick's ankles and knees and pull him down and drag themselves up him like slashrats chewing down a turk-root trunk, ripping away his robes and gouging at his skin, and they were pushing him deeper and deeper into the muck, which was starting to flow up over his ears and into his eyes, and the more he struggled the more they piled onto him, until he heard what was, for a man in the midst of getting ripped to shreds by a pack of dark-sider-controlled zombies, the sweetest sound in the history of the galaxy:

spssshmmmm

The hum got louder, and took on a strange *whop-whop-whop* rhythm like some kind of mechanical toy, a kid's gyrothopter or something. The Pawns stopped clawing at him and started falling limp, and Nick began to wonder if maybe he'd underestimated Skywalker's own bloodthirstiness until he was able to push himself up to a sitting position and get a look at what Skywalker was actually doing.

Make that: what Skywalker's *lightsaber* was actually doing.

It whirled through the air with no hand to guide it, spinning very much like the blades of a toy gyrothopter after all, and as it passed any Pawn it would dip and cant for a shaved second, just long enough to strike, and another Pawn would fall limp. Though they weren't even injured.

Because the blade struck only each Pawn's Crown.

A quick slash or two and a Crown would fall in smoking pieces, which folded each and every Pawn like a losing sabacc hand. Nick twisted to look at Skywalker.

"Shh." Luke sat just behind him, eyes closed in a frown of concentration, right hand lifted, palm outward. He was coated head-to-toe with a black oily sheen of liquefied meltmassif. "This isn't as easy as it looks."

The shining emerald blade whirled through a last few revolutions; the last couple of Crowns fell to pieces, the last couple of Pawns collapsed, and the lightsaber flipped back to Luke's hand before its blade shrank away.

Luke opened his eyes. "All right," he said. "What do we still need?"

"Um, it's not like we're out of trouble right now—"

"You mean the stormtroopers outside the door?" Luke hefted his lightsaber. "I'm sure we can figure something out."

"No, actually, I was talking about being lost somewhere inside an active volcano, and—"

"We're not lost."

"We're not?"

"No."

"Um, okay." From past experience, Nick could assume that when a Jedi said something straight out and simple like that, he could usually be taken at his word. "The other problem is that this whole place is lined with meltmassif—remember what happened over at the Shadow Throne? Any second now, Blackhole's gonna shock the snot out of all of us, and—"

"He won't."

"What makes you—"

"Nick," Luke said, "you worry too much."

He closed his eyes again, and the slimy black meltmassif goo began to flow across his body . . . but instead of dripping down, it flowed *forward,* thickening across Luke's chest, then it separated itself from him altogether, pooling into a floating sphere like mercury in free fall. Thinning tendrils flowed into the sphere from Luke's pants, and sleeves, and from the ends of his hair, as well as away from the floor around his legs, so that in only a moment, he could stand on dry, bare floor, and his clothes and face and hair were all entirely clean, and the ball of liquid meltmassif hovering in front of him was the size of his doubled fists.

"Blackhole's 'treatment' has had some side effects he probably didn't plan on," Luke said.

"I'm guessing. Can you, like, make it into stuff and make it shock people and everything, like he does?"

Luke shook his head. "I don't think he actually *does* that stuff either—it's more like he's controlling something that does it, if you get what I'm saying."

"Sounds like his style; doing it himself would be too much like work." Nick nodded at the fallen Pawns. "What about these types?"

Luke frowned around the room at them. Not one had moved. Not one had made a sound. He lifted a hand as if he were reaching for a handful of air. He took a deep breath, and his eyes drifted shut. He looked like something was hurting. His head, maybe.

Maybe his heart.

"Nick . . ." Luke said, barely above a whisper. "Nick, they're dead. They're all dead."

Nick felt like something had stabbed him.

"They're dead," Luke repeated numbly. "And I killed them."

CRONAL LET HIS CONSCIOUSNESS SLIP ASIDE FROM THE fading sparks of his fallen Pawns—they had outlived their usefulness anyway. He let his mind slide back down into the harmonics of the crystalline web along his nerves, until once again he could touch the structure of the meltmassif that lined the entire interior of his volcanic dome, and brought his mind into resonance with the alien slave minds who controlled the rock. He could sense their baffled frustration and pain as they tried to extend themselves into the liquefied meltmassif in Skywalker's chamber, and he could feel the countervailing pressure of Skywalker's Force-empowered will.

The Jedi had somehow learned to manipulate melt-massif using only the Force!

This did not dismay Cronal, however; on the contrary, it instantly transformed his frustration and doubt into unalloyed delight. A *wonderful* talent! It meant that once Cronal took over Skywalker's body, he'd no longer have need of the Sunset Crown.

With Skywalker's body—and his unparalleled connection to the Force—to complement Cronal's unparalleled knowledge of Sith alchemy and the unique properties of meltmassif, he would indeed rule the galaxy.

He could, should he choose, *become* the galaxy.

Every living thing would answer to his will . . .

All that remained was to permanently impose his will upon Skywalker, though the boy had shown an astonishing gift for defying anyone's plans for him—even plans enforced by the incalculable power of Cronal's Darksight. That pesky Jedi training of his!

Cronal reached out through Darksight, his anger mounting, searching for release . . . and found the last thing he would have expected: another presence, one very near. Very near and very powerful. And yet, he could feel, comparatively untrained.

He frowned. How had it never occurred to him that Skywalker might not be an only child . . . ?

LUKE STOOD FROZEN, UNABLE TO MOVE, UNABLE TO think, before the litter of dead Pawns—dead men and women, *innocent* men and women, dead by his hand. His mind spun with endless splintering echoes of his exchange with Nick on the Shadow Throne.

They're all innocent?

Most of them. Some of 'em are like me—it's been a while since I was innocent of anything.

Nick knelt beside one, a middle-aged woman, and

probed her neck with his fingertips for any hint of a pulse. He sighed and lowered his head. "I remember— there's something grown into us. Our skulls. The Pawns' skulls. An antitamper feature for the crystals and the crowns . . ."

"A deadman interlock," Luke murmured.

Nick looked up, his mouth going slack. He lifted a hand to the bruise that swelled on his forehead above his right eye. "That punch . . ."

Luke nodded distantly. "Must have damaged the interlock, or you would have died right there on the throne."

Nick's eyes widened. "And if I had, how would you have gotten yourself—"

"I wouldn't have," Luke said. "That punch saved both our lives."

"Then I guess we're both lucky you're such a nice guy."

"Maybe we are," Luke murmured. He looked down at the dead. "But it didn't help *them* any."

"Skywalker—Luke—this is *not* your fault. You didn't bring them here. You didn't open their skulls and stick stuff in their brains—you did everything anyone could."

"Yeah," Luke said. His voice came out thin and dry as moondust. "I'll be sure and explain that to their families."

"*Blackhole* killed these people. He killed them when he stuck those crystals in their heads."

"And I pitched in and helped him do it."

"This is a *war*, Luke. Innocent people get killed."

"Maybe so," Luke said softly. "But they're not supposed to be killed by Jedi . . ."

Nick stood. "Come on, kid, snap out of it. Like an old friend of mine used to say, the difference between fighting a war and shoveling grasser poop is that in a war, even the guy in charge gets his hands dirty."

Luke looked at him and Nick sighed. "Ah, sorry. Another old friend of mine used to say my mouth's stuck in hyperdrive. He was a Jedi, too."

"You knew Old Republic Jedi?"

"Met a few. Only really knew one. Dead now, of course."

"Of course."

"Way I heard it, Vader killed him personally."

Luke let his eyes close. "Vader? You're sure?"

"Had to be. Nobody but Vader would have had a chance."

Luke only nodded. Maybe he was getting used to revelations like that. Or maybe it was that he felt like he was still in that stone tomb, hanging in the darkness at the end of the universe . . . He hadn't escaped it at all. He'd just turned it inside out.

That darkness—that Darkness—lived *inside* him now.

He'd clawed his way back to the dream-world of light . . . but look at what he'd done. All this death. All these lives wasted. It didn't matter whose fault it was. Not at all. It wasn't anyone's fault. Everything that lived struggled, and suffered for a brief interval, scrambling in pain and terror to stave off the inevitable tumble back down into the Dark.

And all that suffering, all that struggle . . . all for nothing.

These weren't the only wasted lives. *Everybody's* life was a waste.

What did it matter if you succeeded beyond your wildest hopes, or if your dreams were shattered and ground to dust? Win or lose, all your triumphs and joys, regrets and fears and disappointments, all ended as a fading echo trapped within a mound of dead meat.

Blame it on the Force.

Why should there be life at all? Why did life have to be nothing more than a thin film of pond scum drifting on an infinite dead sea? Better to have never lived at all than to exist for only a brief moment of struggle and suffering, deluded by the illusion of light.

Better to have never lived at all . . .

"Hey! Skywalker! You with me? Is anybody in there?"

"Yes—yes," Luke said. He gave himself a little shake and brought up a hand to rub his eyes. "Yes, sorry. I was just . . . thinking, I guess."

"Thinking? You were *gone*, kid. Your lights were on but there was nobody home. It was scary."

"Yes," Luke said. "For me, too."

CHAPTER 13

NIGHT WAS FALLING ACROSS THE SHADOW REALM.

At the center of the system, clouds of asteroids spiraled in toward Taspan's photosphere. The interaction of the gravity stations and Taspan's own gravity gave them a kind of order: as they fell inward, tumbling toward the fusion-powered furnace of the star's surface, the clouds elongated, and curved, and melded from individual clouds to an array of twisting streams like the stripes on a candy sparklemint stick.

Smaller rocks vaporized in Taspan's corona and chromosphere; larger asteroids ignited on the way down, becoming streaks of fire whose photosphere impacts created splash rings as wide as a major planetoid and hundreds of kilometers tall, as well as central rebound spikes that actually ejected stellar material beyond the critical point where the star's gravity and magnetic field could contain it, unleashing huge bursts of *very* hard radiation—which was exciting enough in itself, because it managed to knock down deflector shields throughout the system.

The only shields these bursts *didn't* knock down were those of the starfighters making atmospheric attack runs on Lord Shadowspawn's volcano base—these shields weren't knocked down because interference from the atmosphere prevented them from being raised in the first place—and those of the Slash-Es and the other Republic cruisers huddling into the radiation-shadow cast by Mindor itself.

And night was falling.

As Mindor turned its face from Taspan, out of the blood-colored west came waves of Republic starfighters. They hurled themselves at the dome's defenses with reckless abandon, their half-useless laser cannon battering the heavy armor of turbolaser towers. The towers, mounted on gimbals the size of spacecraft, tracked the streaking fighters, their massive guns pumping out so much plasma so fast that they superheated the nearby air into a titanic updraft, blasting a vast rolling mushroom cloud of corrosive sand and dust and smoke from the dome to the stratosphere.

Down through that cloud came wave after wave of TIEs.

There were so many that the atmosphere's effect on their cannons was irrelevant; they could destroy whole flights of X-wings by simply being airborne *obstacles*— their presence over the dome forced the Republic pilots to break formation and reduce their speed to avoid midair collisions . . . and the slightest reduction in speed could be fatal. Turbolaser drive technology had advanced in the years since the destruction of the first Death Star; these were far faster on traverse, and included range-sensitive trajectory-projection software that automatically timed their fire to intercept any starfighter unwary enough to go in a relatively straight line for more than a second at a time.

And against an unshielded X-wing, even a glancing hit from a tower-mounted turbolaser left nothing but an expanding globe of plasma.

Still the X-wings came on, in wave after wave, pilots giving their lives to shield flights of B-wing bombers that swooped in for torpedo runs. The B-wings weren't after the towers; they focused their fire on six heavily armored domes atop the highest curve of the volcano.

These domes were closed up tight, relying on their multiple-meters-thick ceramofused armor to absorb the shattering blasts of proton torpedoes and detonite-tipped missiles, which it did very well indeed. "We're barely even leaving dents!" a B-wing pilot shouted over the comm.

"Shut up and keep shooting," his squad leader ordered.

"But we can't hurt them as long as those armor domes are closed!"

"The point is, as long as we make 'em keep *those armor domes closed, they can't hurt* us!"

Inside those armored domes were the base's planetary defense weapons. The five smaller domes that surrounded the vast central dome contained dual-mounted ground-to-orbit ion-turbo cannons: the twin mounted barrels would fire on a precisely timed interval, ensuring that a strike from the ion cannon to disable a capital ship's shields and electronics would be followed instantly by a disintegrating blast from the turbolaser. Those were deadly enough in themselves, but the central dome housed a weapon against which no ship of the line could defend: the gravity gun.

And once night fell across the battle, every Republic capital ship in the system—clustered in the planetary shadow, to shield them from the ejecta bursts—would be in its field of fire.

This was not their only problem.

Troubling as the stellar ejecta bursts were, they were only the result of ordinary asteroid clusters infalling through Taspan's corona, chromosphere, and photosphere. When those asteroid clusters included one or more of the thousands of gravity stations, the effect was substantially more spectacular.

The unnaturally steep gravity gradient of the infalling projectors drew stellar tide surges—bulging mounds that swelled like blisters on the surface of the star—and the warping of the local magnetic fields triggered titanic stellar flares bigger around than entire planets, great fountains of thermonuclear flame blasting hundreds of thousands of kilometers up from the surface, racing along beneath the inward spiral of the projectors like unimaginably huge space slugs made of fire.

Before they engulfed each one and slowly subsided back to Taspan's surface, these fountains also blasted jets of gamma radiation that swept through the system like searchlights of destruction, melting larger asteroids to slag and disintegrating the smaller ones outright. One of these jets brushed the curve of Mindor's atmosphere, a mere glancing blow as the jet swung across the system's plane of the ecliptic.

This glancing blow was enough to set a couple of cubic kilometers of the atmosphere on fire.

This had an effect like a slow-motion fusion blast, as the powerful thermal updraft sucked huge quantities of dust up into the firestorm, where the dust ignited in turn, becoming an expanding ringwall of flame that swept across Mindor's shattered landscape toward the battle that raged around the volcanic dome.

Sensors at the base, as well as those mounted on the Republic capital ships, were easily able to predict the path and eventual progress of the firestorm; while it would blow itself out short of becoming a planet-wide conflagration, before doing so it would roll right over Shadowspawn's base like a line of thunderheads whose clouds were toxic smoke and whose rain was fire.

This would be fatal for troops caught in the open, but more pertinently, it would force starfighters on both sides to withdraw or ground themselves; between the natural sensor interference of the atmosphere itself and the thick clouds of fiery smoke, any who sought to continue the fight would be flying entirely blind.

It would also, as was pointed out to Lando Calrissian by Fenn Shysa, force the domes to remain closed over the surface-to-orbit weapons, as well as temporarily overload the heat exchangers that cooled the turbolasers in the rings of towers. "And if you don't mind me bringin' it up, General," Shysa had gone on, "maybe the only tactical error this Shadowspawn character has made so far is that he's clustered all his planetary defense weapons together, right on top of that big hill."

Lando had nodded. "Easier to defend."

"That they are," Shysa had agreed. "Even if it's not *them* defending 'em, you follow?"

Lando had considered this for a moment. Only a moment; he had never been slow to jump on an opponent's weakness. "Fenn, my friend," he'd said slowly, "have I told you today how much I admire the way you think?"

When those smoke-thunderheads rolled over the dome, fire was not their only rain. Screened by the advancing flame front, three Republic capital ships came in low and slow, feeling their way through the atmosphere. The capital ships did not fire on the domes; through the hurricane of dust, smoke, and flame within the firestorm, even the considerable power of their weapons would have taken some time to breach the armor—time they simply did not have.

Two of them scattered a downpour of landers filled with Republic marines into the ring of ion-turbo emplacements. The third of the capital ships was the *Remember Alderaan*. Its landers dropped into place around the gravity gun.

For a moment, all of the battle was contained by the raging firestorm. Starfighters could not fly, overheated turbolaser towers could not fire, armored domes could not be opened, and no ground forces could leave either the landers or Imperial bunkers.

But the storm didn't last long; in minutes, the tons of dust and sand and gravel it sucked up into itself reached the tipping point beyond which the debris no longer added to the conflagration but began to smother it. As the storm shrank, the three Republic battlecruisers withdrew behind its retreating face.

Seconds later—while the rock and sand still glowed scarlet with heat—turbolasers began to cough plasma blasts at incoming starfighters. Concealed blast doors swung open across the summit and disgorged streams of armored stormtroopers and files of rumbling hover-tanks. Republic landers opened fire with their antipersonnel turrets, and their own troop ramps swung down to make a path for charging marines, and the Battle of Mindor was now joined on the ground. Face-to-face. Blaster-to-blaster.

Knife-to-knife.

WHEN GROUP CAPTAIN KLICK AND HIS COMPANY OF elite commandos had opened the wide arching doorway to the Sorting Center, the place had been in chaos. The bombardment on the surface above sent shock waves through the stone that made the floors shudder and shift continuously like a long, low-level groundquake, and filled the air with a just-above-subsonic rumble like a nonstop roll of thunder; the prisoners, panicked at the rain of dust and chunks of stone from the vault ceiling overhead, rushed the doorway en masse. Klick's men had driven them back; stun blasts dropped the leading ranks, and full-power blasterfire over their heads sent the others cringing toward the far walls. Klick had kicked his way through the twitching bodies, raised his E-11, and triggered another burst over the heads of the cowering prisoners.

"Down! Facedown! On the floor! Now!" He turned to the trooper beside him. "Sergeant, take Second Platoon and shoot any prisoner still on his, her, or its feet five seconds from now. The rest of you, on me."

He led them trotting through the black-gleaming fusion-formed cavern to the Election Center's door.

"Fourth Platoon: front and center." He stepped to one side. "Seal this door! No one in, no one out. First Platoon: firing position in support of Four. The rest of you, prepare to repel assault."

A couple of troopers from Fourth Platoon deployed their foamplas canisters. Engineered for a quick-and-dirty seal for envirosuit ruptures or minor hull punctures, foamplast would expand to fill any and all available space around its application point, then harden almost instantly. A thin bead around the edges of the door sealed it permanently in place, and not a moment too soon—only seconds after the foamplast had set, Klick heard the whine of the door's servos as someone tried to open it from the far side.

"Back!" he snapped. "Company: form up and prime weapons! Prepare to fire on my order!"

For a long, long second the only sound in the Sorting Center was the rustle and snap of blasters being readied and the clacking of the nearest troopers dropping prone, those behind to one knee, and the rear taking firing stances with carbines at their shoulders. Klick himself stepped away from the door; the only way to open a foamplast-sealed door was a breaching charge.

Seconds ticked past with no explosion, and just when Klick began to wonder if he'd imagined the servo whine, a spot high on the right-hand side of the door glowed red and brightened almost instantly to white before it burst and vaporized around a bar of green plasma.

All right, two ways through a foamplast-sealed door, Klick amended silently. *Breaching charge, and lightsaber.*

A *green* lightsaber . . . !

Klick had a terrible premonition. "Hold fire," he warned. "Anybody shoots before my order, I'll kill him myself."

The bar of green plasma cut a ragged oval through the door. When the cut was finished and the oval slab of durasteel fell through a shower of sparks to clang on the fusion-formed stone, Klick did not give the order to fire. He did not give any order at all. He simply stood, staring, awestruck beyond words.

Standing in the doorway were only two men. One was a tallish wiry man with dark skin, and blood trickling sluggishly down his shaven scalp, dressed in Pawn robes and holding an E-11 dangling by its shoulder strap. The other, smaller man was dressed in a sodden and filthy Rebel Alliance flight suit, and his damply tousled hair of radiation-bleached blond stuck in tangles to a tanned face whose features, Klick ever-so-slowly realized, had the exact contours of his very fondest dream . . .

Klick's mouth went dry and his legs went numb and he could barely force the words through his slack lips. "Emperor *Skywalker* . . ."

He dropped to one knee, undogged his helmet, yanked it off, and inclined his head in reverence. "Down weapons! Down weapons! Buckets off and kneel to your Emperor!" he cried. "Your pardon, my lord, I did not know you!"

REPUBLIC MARINES FEVERISHLY TRIED TO DIG IN AROUND the ion-turbo emplacements while they poured fire into the advancing stormtroopers. Their armored landers added antipersonnel punch with turret-mounted Soro-Suub clusterfrag launchers; the whole curve of the base's summit sparkled with thousands of tiny detonations, each of which scattered high-velocity flechettes, though most of them only clattered off the rocks in a rushing roar like a Chadian monsoon.

The stormtroopers advanced at a run behind the cover of heavily shielded hovertanks. The tanks' forward cannon arrays pounded away at the landers and blasted marines to bloody bits, and their drivers ran them right up against the landers' skirt armor. From there the stormtroopers could charge into hand-to-hand—but when they did, the stormtroopers discovered to their considerable dismay that Republic marines, unlike many other enemies, didn't seem at all intimidated by the stormtroopers' vibroknucklers, and that the marines favored, for close combat, 18 cm aKraB clip-point vibrodaggers that could cut Mark III armor like rendered gorgan blubber.

Around the dome that housed the gravity gun, twelve landers from the *Remember Alderaan* had come down in a double ring: four close in around the emplacement with the other eight encircling them. The inner four were too close to the emplacement's infantry bunkers for artillery or tank fire—so close that the landers' own antipersonnel turrets could not depress their aim to ground level; all they could do was chip away at the upper curves of the bunkers and the gravity gun's dome. Black-armored stormtroopers came swarming out from the bunkers like ravenous carrion beetles, using the inner landers themselves as cover from the fire of the surrounding eight while they went to work on the hulls with fusion torches and shaped-blast breaching charges. If any of the stormtroopers found it odd that these twelve landers, unlike the ones around the ion-turbo emplacements, remained tightly sealed instead of disgorging their own swarms of marines, none of them remarked on it.

The explanation for this unusual tactic was discovered by one particular stormtrooper officer, who led one of the strike teams that blasted their way into one of the landers and found no Republic forces at all—only a remote computer link jacked into the pilot's station, and another jacked into the fire-control board. The lander was not, however, actually empty. It was packed, wall to wall and floor to ceiling, with detonite fused to motion detectors.

It was the last thing the officer saw—the simultaneous explosions of all four landers vaporized not only him and his strike team, but also all of the hundreds of stormtroopers nearby, as well as buckling the blast doors of the infantry bunkers.

Though most of the force of the explosions was directed inward toward the bunkers and the gravity gun, the residual blast was enough to rock the other eight landers and to shove several of them skidding a few meters. Before they even came back to rest, their gang ramps had flipped down to unleash a different kind of infantry.

These troops did not shout or howl; they did not charge with blasters roaring. Instead they deployed with silent efficiency, leapfrogging from cover to cover toward the bunkers.

Another black-armored officer got a glimpse of them through his bunker's damaged blast doors as they came on, and he muttered a curse that the oncoming infantry would have recognized—even though they would have sneered at the officer's Core Worlds accent—as being a debased hand-me-down dilution of their native tongue. "Fall back!" he shouted. "Barricade the corridors! Hold the corners and crossways!"

Because the last thing this officer wanted to do was waste his men by going head-to-head against Mandalorians.

* * *

THE CAVERNS THROUGH WHICH HAN, LEIA, AND CHEW-bacca walked—and R2-D2 rolled—had shrunk to a series of mazy tunnelways. In the light of R2's extensible torch, the stone looked black but was also semitranslucent, showing gleams of internal crystalline structure like Harterran moonstone.

Han walked between R2 and Chewie, head down, silent. He couldn't stop thinking about Mindorese running wild all over the *Falcon*. And who was flying her right now? Whose grubby hands were all over his controls? *"Growr,"* Chewie agreed softly, seeing Han's anger. But then he lifted a hand to gesture ahead and said, *"Herroowarr hunnoo."*

Han frowned and continued along the tunnel. Leia had been walking briskly since they'd entered the tunnels; she'd given up trying to talk to him after a couple of minutes and now was so far ahead that all he could see of her was the distant swing of her glow rod. He nodded. "I think she's mad at me. You think she's mad at me?"

"Meroo hooerrree."

"It's not my fault." Han scowled. It seemed like he said that too often. "It's *not* my fault—I *warned* her, didn't I? Didn't I warn her that we'd be sorry for rescuing those scumballs?"

Teeeooorr weep? R2's whistle came out dry and somewhat ironic, and Han had a pretty good idea what he meant.

"Not sorry about finding *you*. That's not what I meant," he said. "Man . . . she's really upset, huh?"

"Rowroo," Chewbacca said thoughtfully.

"Really?" Han brightened a little. "You think?"

Chewie grumbled a bit more, waving Han on. Han chewed a corner of his lip, staring ahead at the swing of Leia's glow rod, and came to a decision. "Maybe you're right. Stay here with the droid."

R2 put in, *weep weep teeerrr.*

"You, too? Look, it's my problem, let me handle it, huh?" Han started walking faster. Pretty soon he was trotting. "Princess! Hey, Princess, wait up, huh?"

She didn't even look back. He broke into a run, and when he caught up he fell into step beside her. "Leia, wait. I need to check your shoulder."

"No time."

Han frowned. "You say that like you know where we're going."

"I do. Sort of." She pointed the glow rod into the darkness ahead. "That way."

Han squinted. All he saw was darkness. "What's that way?"

"Luke."

"Luke? Are you kid—uh, I mean, you're sure? How can you be sure?"

She didn't even look at him. "I'm sure."

"Oh. Oh, yeah, I guess you are." Han stopped for a deep breath, then had to hustle to catch up with her again. "Y'know, Leia, this Force stuff, it's—y'know, it's one thing to see Luke do it but—"

"But *what*?" Now she did stop, and she did look at him, and from the flash her eyes picked up off the glow rod he kind of wished he'd been smart enough, about fifteen seconds ago, to bite his tongue in half.

"It's just that you—y'know, you and I—"

"I'm sorry I make you *uncomfortable*, General Solo," she said tartly. "I suppose you'd be better off with someone like—"

"Well, fuse my bus-bars," Han said. "Chewie was right: you *are* jealous."

"*What*? What did that mountain of mange say about me? I'll hold him down and shave his—"

"Easy, easy, come on, Leia—"

"I'm not jealous, I'm *angry*. She took you completely off-guard."

Han flinched. "Not *completely*—"

"You think she would have caught you flat-footed if she wasn't good-looking?"

"Maybe not," Han allowed through the beginning of a slow grin. "But I *am* pretty sure that if she wasn't good-looking, you wouldn't have hit her so hard."

"Hope I broke her nose," Leia muttered darkly, then suddenly answered his grin and added a little chuckle. " 'Fuse my bus-bars'? Really?"

Han shrugged, feeling himself start to blush. Again. "Just an expression I'm trying out. When I get too old to be dashing, I'll have to be colorful."

"You're already colorful," she said. "And you'll always be dashing."

"Aw, you take the fun out of everything."

A burst of static from his comlink made them both jump. *"Han! What the hell are you doing?"*

Han fished out his comlink. "Lando? I'm standing in a cave, knucklehead. What the hell are *you* doing? Why are you even in this *system*?"

"Han, that was Hobbie you just clipped! He's going down—again! Cease fire and get the hell out of my battle!"

"That was Hobbie I just *what*?"

"Han, if you don't stand down, we'll have to take you down!"

Han started to run, not going anywhere but he just had to *move*, shouting into the comlink. "Oh, no—oh, no no no, you don't *understand*! That's not us in there—"

"Great! Rogue Leader—light 'er up!"

"Don't do it! Wedge, *don't*! Don't you dare shoot down my ship!"

"Don't you mean my ship?" Lando said. *"Should*

*have known it wasn't you—flies like a bantha in a tar
pit—you fly more like a constipated nerf with a broken
leg—"*

"Lando, I'm serious—put one scratch on the *Falcon*
and I'll—"

"Never find it under all the dents," Lando finished
for him. *"Wedge—see if you can take out just the
thrusters."*

"Lando—Wedge—" Han grimaced in frustration and
turned back to Leia, who had stopped a few meters behind him and now stood motionless, frowning in concentration. "Come *on*, Princess!"

She shook her head. "Something's wrong here . . ."

"Oh, you think? Is it the lost-inside-a-volcano thing?
Or the losing-the-*Falcon*-and-it's-about-to-be-shot-down
thing? Or maybe it's the we've-just-managed-to-lead-all-
our-friends-along-with-half-the-Alliance-into-a-giant-
death-trap thing?"

"Not so much," she said. "It's more the we've-been-
running-in-the-dark-through-a-cave-and-we-haven't-
fallen-down-a-hole thing."

"What?"

"Artoo," she called back along the tunnel, "do an en-
vironmental scan and analysis—I think these caves
aren't natural. Something *made* this—"

Han looked around and froze in place. "You mean,"
he said slowly, "some kind of rock-looking critters that
can, like, melt themselves out of the walls and floors and
stuff?"

"I don't know, maybe—" She stopped and looked
back at Han, who was surrounded by rock-looking critters that appeared to have melted themselves out of the
walls and floor.

"Good call," Han said, and then the floor opened beneath him and he dropped out of sight.

"Han!" Leia sprang toward him, but the stone of the

tunnel had gone soft and gooey, and an instant later it parted beneath her feet and she fell into darkness.

THE STORMTROOPER OFFICER WHO KNELT ON THE SHINing black stone of the cavern's floor stammered out his unlikely story without even rising from one knee; Luke didn't bother to listen. He barely heard anything after the group captain had started babbling about how powerful a masterpiece he'd found *Luke Skywalker and the Jedi's Revenge* to be. Another blasted fan of that blasted show . . .

Who'd have thought so much damage could be done by one stupid story?

"This was the objective of his entire Great Cause!" the group captain exclaimed. "To rescue you from the evil Rebellion and restore you to your rightful throne!"

"Not exactly *me*," Luke muttered.

"My lord Emperor?"

"Forget it." Luke looked around at the dozens of prisoners prone on the cavern floor. "Who are these people?"

"No one of consequence, my lord—Rebel captives, bound for the slave pits. Don't concern yourself."

"Slave pits?" That was all he needed: more innocent lives that he would fail to save. "How many slaves do you have here?"

"Too many, my lord. Possibly several thousand. Even on starvation rations we can barely keep them fed. And the water situation—"

Luke held up a hand. "I get it." He turned a grim glance on Nick, who only shrugged.

"Don't look at *me*," Nick said. "*I'm* not the Emperor."

Darkness closed like a fist around Luke's heart.

He stood in the doorway, staring. A vast cavern of gleaming black, which seemed to be filled with stormtroopers in armor that matched the stone, all kneeling to him with heads uncovered. Hundreds upon hundreds of other people, regular people, whose only crime was that they'd lived in places Blackhole had targeted, now lying facedown on the smooth cold stone with their hands behind their heads, afraid to even lift their faces to look upon him.

"I'm the *Emperor* . . ." he said dully.

And what was wrong with it? Had this not been, after all, his father's plan for him?

Vader's plan.

Maybe Vader had understood fully a truth that Anakin Skywalker had only glimpsed: that all striving comes to nothing in the end. That the only answer was to take what you could get. To rule at ease. To enjoy whatever fragmentary instants of pleasure one's brief life might offer.

What difference did it make? Heroes, villains, kings, and peasants, all went to the same final Dark. Why *struggle*?

He didn't have an answer. He *remembered* answers— answers he'd gotten from Ben, from Yoda, even from Uncle Owen and Aunt Beru, empty talk of duty and tradition, of honor and love—but none of them had understood. Not really.

Or maybe they had.

Because what was that talk of duty and honor and love, really? Wasn't it just their way of controlling him?

"My lord Emperor? Are you unwell?"

Luke shook himself. He took a deep breath and looked at Nick. "Happened again?"

Nick nodded. "You just . . . went away."

Luke again lifted a hand to rub his eyes. Now his hand was shaking. "He . . . did something to me, Nick. I don't—I can't *fight* it . . ."

"*Who* did something to you?" The stormtrooper officer was on his feet, and his face flushed red to the roots of his graying hair. "Name this traitor, and my men will *destroy* him!"

Nick turned to Luke with lifted brows and a sudden sparkle in his eyes; Luke turned his hand outward in a no-arguments, don't-even-say-it gesture. "No," Luke said. "No destroying *anybody*. There's been too much destroying."

Another round of distant blasts sent a shiver of shock wave through the cavern. Nick rolled his eyes toward the vault's ceiling. "Yeah, no kidding. And these guys can help us stop it."

"No."

"Skywalker, think about it—" Nick began.

"I can't," Luke said. "I *can't* think about it. That's what you don't understand. Thinking about it will . . . send me away again. Back into the . . ."

His voice trailed off. He couldn't make himself talk about the Dark. Talking about it would break the surface film of light that was all that stood between him and the unbearable truth—it would rupture the illusion that was the only thing keeping him going right now. "I have to—I have to pretend to trust what I've always known. I have to act like I believe it's all still true. That they weren't all *lying* to me. That I wasn't just kidding myself, do you get it?"

"Uh, no. Not really." Nick's vivid blue eyes shaded gray with growing concern. "Not really at all."

"Then just take my word for it." Luke looked at the group captain. *All you have to do is pretend,* he told himself. *Do what you would have done back when you believed lives were worth saving. Maybe if you pretend long enough, you can fall back into that dream of light . . .* "Okay," he said. "Okay. New orders. You and your men—" He waved vaguely toward the prisoners. "I want you to take care of them."

"Yes, my lord." The group captain turned to the troopers who stood guard over the prone captives and raised his hand. "Second Platoon! You heard the emperor. Prepare to fire on my order!"

"No!" Luke said hastily. "No, that's not a euphemism. It's a direct order. I want you to *care for* them. Tend their wounds. Get them food and water. Keep them *safe*, do you understand?"

The expression on the group captain's face showed clearly that he *didn't* understand, but nonetheless he saluted. "Yes, my lord!"

"And . . . and send your men—not just these guys, but all the men you command—send them to do the same for the slaves. All the slaves."

"You would have my pilots *withdraw* from the *battle*?"

"It's not a battle, it's a mistake," Luke said. "A misunderstanding."

"My lord?"

"Never mind. Round up all slaves. Protect them. As soon as you have them organized and secure, turn them and yourselves over to the Republic—what you call Rebel—forces. You will cooperate in every way with the Republic military, up to and including assisting them in battle."

"My lord Emperor?" The group captain looked appalled. "You would have us give aid and comfort to the *enemy*?"

"No," Luke said. "They're not your enemy. Not anymore. Do you understand? From this point forward, you and your men are to consider yourselves part of the Republic military. Do not fail me, Group Captain."

"My lord Emperor!" The group captain's eyes glazed, but the discipline of obedience was absolute. "My lord, we will *not* fail!"

"Very well," Luke said. "You have your orders."

The group captain saluted again and executed a precise about-face before replacing his helmet. He strode off, barking orders punctuated by crisp hand gestures, and his men snapped to without hesitation.

Luke just stood and watched. He couldn't think of a reason to move.

"Okay, sure, Skywalker, I get it," Nick said. "But what now?"

"I don't know."

"What do you mean, you don't *know*? What's the matter with you?"

Luke shook his head numbly. "It's like . . . it's like I'm still inside the stone, Nick. Except the stone's inside me."

"Oh, *that* makes sense."

"*Sense* has nothing to do with it. It just *is*."

"This is what you were talking about, right? What did that ruskakk do to you?"

"He infected me," Luke said listlessly.

"Infected—? With some kind of disease or something? A parasite? What?"

"Worse," Luke said. "He infected me with the truth."

"Huh?"

"That it's all a joke. Not even a funny one. A pointless, stupid waste. A spark of suffering extinguished to eternal nothingness."

He could see that Nick didn't understand. That really, he *couldn't* understand. How could he? And how could Luke explain? What words could he use to share the Dark? What words could illustrate the hideous illusions that came from being raised by loving parents who seemed to really believe in the ideals of the Old Republic, who'd acted like they'd honestly thought that the Jedi had been real heroes, instead of hidebound, ruthless enforcers of the will of the Republic's rulers. How could he explain the pointless cruelty of the universe—where you had to just stand with your arms restrained by stormtroopers and watch as the Death Star destroyed your homeworld for no real reason at all . . .

Wait, Luke thought. His breath went short. "Oh, no," he said out loud. "Oh, no, no, *no* . . . this can't be happening!"

That flash he'd just had wasn't a memory.

It was a *vision.* Of the future.

"What?" Nick said. "Skywalker, talk to me!"

Luke shook himself as if throwing off a dream. "It's not *me* inside the stone," he said. "It's not me hanging in the Dark at the end of the Universe. It's her. It's going to be *her.*"

"Her who?"

"Leia," Luke said. "My sister."

"You have a *sister?*"

Luke nodded. "And Blackhole's found her."

R2-D2 FELL THROUGH DARKNESS.

Fell was not entirely the right word for what had transpired since the stone beneath his treads had suddenly melted away and dropped him and Chewbacca through the tunnel's floor. It was more akin to some sort of bizarre carnival ride, with sudden stops and sideways slippages and all manner of other contortions of downward progress that R2's internal vocabulation data simply did not have words for.

For that matter, *darkness* wasn't entirely accurate either. While a human eye would see nothing but featureless black, for R2, it wasn't dark at all; his internal sensors could register a substantial span of the electromagnetic spectrum, several hundred thousand times wider than the tiny human range they referred to as "visual light." The entire downward fall/slide/lurch/bump/twist/jolt process was alive with all manner of electromagnetic radiation; of particular interest to R2 were the intermittent flickers of a magnetic field signature that was very similar in frequency to that emitted by the nervous systems of many oxygen-breathing organics.

It looked like the rock was *thinking*.

Not only that, it looked like the rock was thinking with a number of distinct minds, which seemed to have some sort of self-reinforcing phase relationship, analogous to the process in social insects by which discussion leads to consensus.

Which was a development that R2 would have liked to investigate more thoroughly, but he was currently preoccupied by constantly recalibrating his internal gyromagnetic stabilizer to keep himself from landing, when he did eventually land, on his damaged locomotor arm; this ongoing recalibration—owing to the bewildering unpredictability of the shifting magnetic fields—took up most of R2's processing capacity.

Another slide, two bounces, and one last tumble brought R2 to a brief halt, as he fetched up against Chewbacca's short ribs hard enough to make the Wookiee grunt and wheeze for breath; then the stone opened beneath them for a final time and dropped them another three point six meters, which left the two of them unceremoniously deposited on the smooth stone floor of yet another cavern.

R2 activated a pair of manipulators to shove himself off Chewbacca—which elicited a groan of protest from the half-stunned Wookiee—and righted himself on the cavern floor. There was human-visible light in this cavern, though the light source swung so violently from side to side and up and down that shadows whirled and blended and parted again so swiftly that R2's photoreceptor lens couldn't parse the scene; he cycled back to his previous EM sensor band and began to make sense of the situation.

The human-visible light source was revealed to be

none other than the glow rod, which was being wielded as an improvised club by Han Solo to swat at a mass of vaguely humanoid shapes while he shouted, "Back off! I'll bash any one of you who takes one more step! Back *off*!"

R2 assumed that Captain Solo was either highly agitated or speaking in the confusing idiomatic human code that C-3PO referred to as *metaphor,* because it was certainly clear—to R2's sensors, at any rate—that these humanoid shapes to which he spoke did not actually have legs, much less feet, and thus were already certain, regardless of threat or instruction, never to *take one more step*. It was also entirely clear to R2 that these humanoid shapes were not, in fact, creatures at all, at least not as his programing generally understood the term.

These shapes were only nominally humanoid, in the sense of being generally upright and having a vaguely head-shaped knob on top, as well as a pair—several had more—of arms; these shapes grew upward from the very stone of the cavern itself, more like animated stalagmites than actual living things, but they moved as though directed by some type of consciousness, and they clearly exhibited that peculiar electromagnetic field signature R2 had noted during his precipitous descent. A quick scan of his data files for any reference to this type of apparently mineral life-form came up blank . . . except for one provisional reference that he had preserved in his short-term cache because he had no internal referent to guide him in choosing where to file it.

It was the recording of Aeona Cantor, when her companion had asked what they should do "if whoever shows up *isn't* a Jedi":

Then we take their stuff and leave 'em to the Melters.

R2 found this to be a satisfactory correlation, and he consequently created a new file tagged with the keywords MINDOR, MINERAL LIFE-FORM (MOTILE), and MELTERS.

This entire process, from Han Solo's shout to R2-D2's filing decision, took only .674 of a standard second, which left R2 plenty of time for a full systems self-check and operational verification while Chewbacca was still rolling to his feet and drawing breath for a Wookiee war whoop.

Chewbacca's war cry was followed by a headlong charge against the Melters—that these were the "Melters" in question seemed undeniable—that crowded in upon Han Solo and Princess Leia. There was an astonished howl of pain when flesh-and-bone Wookiee fist met stone Melter "head." This was followed by a blue-crackling energy discharge—which R2 noted was analogous in wavelength and intensity to a charge from a blaster on its maximum stun setting—from the Melter in question. Chewie howled again and went staggering back until he bumped into another Melter and an additional energy discharge cut short the howl and folded the now-unconscious Wookiee like a retracting manipulator.

R2 continued to watch with detached interest as Han Solo shouted *"Chewie!"* and threw himself against the mass of Melters, whose response was several bursts of that same energy that almost instantly dropped Han Solo twitching on the ground beside his copilot. However, the collapse of Han Solo apparently triggered a similar human emotional response from Princess Leia, who shouted to Han and leapt toward the Melters—and in the .384 seconds she was actually in the air, R2 called up an array of highly specialized subprocessors that had been originally installed as a customized aftermarket modification by the Royal Engineers of Naboo and later extensively refitted and programmed with a very specific set of behaviors by a particularly gifted tinkerer, who'd had, in his day, a justified reputation as the finest self-taught improvisational engineer the galaxy had ever produced: Anakin Skywalker.

Turbojacks deployed powerfully from the bottoms of R2's locomotors, kicking him through the air directly into the mass of Melters. His antitamper field sizzled to life with an unusually loud discharge crackle; based on the extraordinary drain on his internal power supply, R2 was able to calculate that the antitamper field was currently operating at triple strength, which was actually beyond its theoretical limit, owing to potentially lethal effects. R2 also noted that when a nearby Melter reached for him with a stone pseudo-arm, the touch of his triple-strength antitamper field instantly liquefied the electrocrystalline structure of the Melter's stone body . . . as well as those of the four Melters nearest to it.

With a fierce *Thooperoo HEEE!*, which was his closest approximation of a Wookiee war whoop, R2-D2 waded into the Melters, sparking them to slag on every side. As long as he had a single remaining erg in his energy supply, he would allow no harm to come to Princess Leia.

He did, however, note one particular flaw in this determination, which was that his level of energy output had already outstripped the self-regeneration capacity of his energy supply, and so that *single remaining erg* situation was, as C-3PO might say, no mere metaphor. And the walls and floor just kept on humping into lumps that would become new Melters.

For a brief flicker of a millisecond, R2-D2 experienced a power spike in a tiny audio loop in one specific memory core: he heard C-3PO's voice exclaim *We're doomed.*

CHAPTER 14

NICK TROTTED ALONG THE CURVING CAVERNWAY AFTER Luke, his breath going short. How was it that every time he met a Jedi, the guy turned out to be some kind of nikkle nut? Skywalker had gone from brown dwarf to nova just like flipping a switch. Now Nick could barely keep up with him. "Take it easy, huh? Unless you want me to just, y'know, wait for you here. Which would be fine. Between you and me, I could use a nap."

"No time." Skywalker kept going. "You said Black-hole needs somebody who can use the Force. My twin sister's just as strong as I am—but she doesn't have my training. Once he gets his paws on her . . ."

Now he did stop, and turned back to Nick, and the bleak fury in his eyes brought a sudden twist of fear to Nick's gut. "I won't let that happen," Luke said grimly. "That's all. I won't. No matter what I have to do."

"Uh—"

But Luke had already turned and was jogging away.

"Shee, kid. Two minutes ago, things were going pretty good and I could barely get you to *talk*. Now everything's going wrong, and you're making the jump to lightspeed without bothering to board a ship!"

"Yeah, funny how that works," Luke said. "I guess I can handle things going wrong in the world. I'm used to it. I can do something about it. It's when things go wrong in *here*—" He rapped the side of his head with his knuckles as if he were knocking to get in. "—that's where the problem is."

"The crystals."

"I don't know. All I know is that it makes me want to die. No. Not die. Just . . . *stop*."

"You know what makes me want to just stop?" Nick said. "Running. Especially running in ten kilos of floor-length fraggin' *robe*."

"You want to stay here? Go ahead. I'm sure Blackhole will be happy to make you another crown."

"Are you this nice to everybody, or am I just special?" Nick sighed and kept on going after him. His time as Shadowspawn was hazy, but not so hazy he couldn't figure out which way they were going. "Um, Skywalker? This is *not* the way out of here."

Luke didn't even slow down. "That's because we're not leaving. I came here to put a stop to all this, even before I knew what was going on. Now that I know, I'm not going anywhere till it's over."

"Over how?"

"However."

"I guess you must be a real Skywalker after all," Nick said, wheezing a little as he caught up. "This is just the kind of stunt Anakin would have pulled. But I didn't know he had kids."

"Neither did he," Luke said grimly. "You knew my father?"

"Knew of him, more like. Met him a few times. He debriefed me once, after an op. So you really are his son, huh?"

"Is that so hard to believe?"

It wasn't easy to shrug while running in robes, but Nick managed. "He was tall."

"I'm told I favor my mother," Luke said dryly, and for

a second Nick thought he was going to smile. But only for a second. "You knew my father in the Clone Wars?"

"Kid, in the Clone Wars, *everybody* knew him. He was the greatest hero in the galaxy. When he died, it was like the end of the universe." Nick's gut twisted again at the memory. "It bloody well *was* the end of the Republic."

Luke stopped. He looked like something hurt. "When he . . . died?"

Nick came to a halt gratefully, bending over with hands on his knees while he tried to catch his breath. "Way I heard it, he was the last Jedi standing in the Temple Massacre—when Vader's Five Hundred First went in and killed all the Padawans."

"What?"

"That's where your father was killed: defending children in the Jedi Temple. He was not only the best of the Jedi, he was the last. Nobody ever told you the story?"

Luke's eyes were closed against some inexpressible pain. "That's . . . not the way I heard it."

"Well, y'know, I wasn't there, but—"

"And *I* am the last of the Jedi. I was trained by Ben Kenobi."

Nick's jaw dropped. "You mean *Obi-Wan*? I thought that was, y'know, just more holothriller gunk. Kenobi's *alive*?"

"No," Luke said softly. "Who *are* you?"

"Me? Nobody. Nobody special," Nick said. "I was an officer in the GAR—the old Grand Army of the Republic—but I didn't get along real well with the new management, know what I mean?"

"An officer?" Luke frowned. "Special enough. The Alliance could have used you. The New Republic still can. What have you been doing for the past twenty-five years?"

"Hiding from Vader, mostly. He's the management I didn't get along with."

"You can stop hiding. Vader's dead."

"What, just like in the show? *That's* good news."

"If you say so. The Emperor died the same day."

Nick tapped his head and grimaced. "I haven't exactly been keeping up with the news. Did you kill him?"

"What? No. No, I didn't kill either of them."

"Not exactly like in *Luke Skywalker and the Jedi's Revenge*, huh?"

"No," Luke said, even more softly. "Not like that at all. But they *are* dead. That part's true." He lifted his head as if he was listening to something Nick couldn't hear. An instant later, a new round of shock waves rattled the cavernway. "When this is over, you and I need to sit down together for a long, long talk."

Nick's breathing had barely started to ease. "I'm ready to sit down *now*."

"When this is over," Luke repeated. "For now, we run."

"I was afraid you were gonna say that . . ." But Nick was already talking to Skywalker's retreating back. He wheezed a sigh, hiked up his robe, and went after him. He could hear, coming from up ahead now, the thunder-roll of explosions that were shaking the whole mountain. "Where are we going in such a hurry?"

"I'll show you."

They rounded another curve and ahead, the tunnel ended in a narrow ledge. Above the ledge was night, and stars, and streaks of X-wings hurtling down for strafing runs. Below the ledge was a long, long drop down the inner bowl of a huge, ancient caldera that was studded with impact craters and lit by the burning remains of crashed starfighters from both sides. The far rim had crumbled, and much of it still glowed dully with residual heat from the explosions that had shattered it; through the gaps Nick could see, far down the curve of the volcanic dome, turbolaser towers swiveling and pumping gouts of disintegrating energy into the sky.

"Uh," he said, hanging back from the edge. "Maybe I'll just wait up here."

"Maybe you won't."

"Have I mentioned that I've got, y'know, a minor issue about heights?"

"I'm sorry about that," Luke said seriously. "But you're coming along. I have a feeling I'll need you."

"But listen—you're going after your sister, right? Who's going after *Cronal*? Somebody's gonna have to take him out."

"And you're volunteering to play assassin?"

Nick cocked his head. "The crystals in my head . . . I can *feel* him, sort of. I can find him. I can take him out."

"I believe you. But no. That's final."

"It may be the only way to save your sister. Not to mention you."

Luke sighed. "And what happens if he gets to her before you get to him? What happens if she doesn't have somebody like you around to break her out of the treatment, the way you saved me?"

"Then we'll just have to—" The look on Luke's face stopped Nick cold. "Uh. Yeah, I can see your problem with that. I guess I'd better be extra fast."

"*I* guess you'd better do what you're told."

"Hey, news flash, General Skywalker—I'm not one of your soldiers."

"Hey, news flash, *Lord Shadowspawn,*" Luke said, a faint smile on his lips but only bleak darkness in his eyes. "You're a prisoner of war."

"Aw—aw, c'mon, you're not serious—"

"You said you knew Jedi," Luke said. "Ever win an argument with one?"

Nick sighed. "Where to?"

"There." Luke pointed down into the caldera. "Right there."

Nick squinted. It looked like featureless rock scattered with wreckage. "What's the big deal about *right there*?"

"That," Luke said with quiet certainty, "is where the *Millennium Falcon* is about to crash."

"What? The *Millennium Falcon*? Like in *Han Solo in the Lair of the Space Slugs*?"

"Sort of."

"You're not kidding? I thought—y'know, I thought that Han Solo was, y'know, a fictional character. That those stories are just, well, *stories*."

Luke closed his eyes and extended a hand. His voice took on a distant, distinctly hollow tone. "They *are* just stories. But Han's real, and as for the *Falcon*—look up."

Nick did. A rising shriek of something large and not so aerodynamic flying very, very fast gave him a half second's warning before a huge dark shape roared *way* too close overhead—an oblate disk with the forward cargo mandibles of a Corellian light freighter—that wasn't really flying so much as it was, well, hurtling, flipping end over end through the air like a deformed coin tossed by a hand the size of this mountain. On fire and out of control, it tumbled toward the crater's floor and certain destruction.

"Oh," Nick said. "Awwww—I would have liked to meet him—I love that show . . ."

"Shh." Luke's forehead squeezed into a frown of concentration, and the fingers on his extended hand spread as his breathing deepened. "This isn't my best trick."

His fingers twitched as if he were tripping an invisible switch—and out on the dark spinning disk of the freighter, automated attitude thrusters blasted to life, dorsal on the mandibles, ventral to aft above the engines, slowing the ship's tumble. Nick heard the sudden shriek of overpowered repulsorlifts, and the forward attitude jets swiveled to add their thrust, and the freighter slammed into the ground, which must have been some kind of cinder pit, because the front mandibles drove in almost to the cockpit at a sixty-degree angle . . . and stuck fast.

And the ship just stayed there. It didn't fall over. It didn't blow up. It didn't do anything that any reasonable person would expect a ship to do after a full-on crash.

Nick stared at it with his mouth open. Some few seconds later, he realized he hadn't been breathing. "Did you . . . I mean, did I just see . . . ?" he gasped. "Did you just now *catch that ship*?"

Luke opened his eyes. "Not exactly."

"And that's not your best trick?" Nick shook his head, blinking. "What *is* your best trick?"

"I hope you never find out," Luke said. "Come on."

LEIA HAD KNOWN THEY WERE IN DESPERATE DANGER even before the floor had melted away beneath her feet. Chewbacca's sudden reappearance in the cavern they'd fallen into had given her an instant's hope—but only an instant's, as the Wookiee was almost immediately felled by these rock creatures and now lay twitching on the ground, smoke curling from his singed fur. Then one of them had flowed around Han's ankle and shocked him with some kind of energy discharge that had made all his hair stand on end, spitting sparks and smoke, before he collapsed in turn. Another woman might have lost heart then; or when all the rock creatures seemed to turn and converge on her together; or when, just as she was leaping for Han, one of the rock creatures flowed over the glow rod and the cavern plunged into impenetrable darkness . . . but Leia wasn't the type to lose heart.

Something about being in trouble this deep made her calm and focused. And determined.

Even in the darkness she seemed to somehow just know where Han was—and where the rock creatures *weren't*. Her hand found the top of Han's boot, and she latched on to drag him back—and her efforts were rewarded with an ear-shattering electronically fierce *Thooperoo HEEE!* as R2 launched himself through the air, so haloed in sparks from his overdriven antitamper field that he lit up the cavern like flares of summer lightning.

Seeing the rock creatures melt to slag at his touch gave her an inspiration. "Artoo! The hold-out!"

The astromech's dome spun and a concealed hatch popped open, releasing a spring-loaded ejector that had been, less than a year before, engineered to deliver a lightsaber to Luke Skywalker's hand. What shot forth from it now was no lightsaber, though, but instead a SoroSuub ELG-5C hold-out blaster.

The compact pistol flipped through the air, and Leia lost sight of it in the uncertain light—but she put out her hand anyway, and somehow wasn't even surprised when the blaster smacked neatly into her palm. She swung the hold-out through a quick arc, firing as fast as she could squeeze the trigger. The stun blasts triggered more discharges from the rock creatures as they sagged and liquefied; the walls around her crawled and crackled with blue fire.

"Artoo! Grab Chewie and get behind me!"

The droid chirped an affirmative and shut down his antitamper field before he extended a pair of manipulators to grip the unconscious Wookiee by the bandolier. Leia covered them, driving back the rock creatures with a barrage of stun blasts. The servos in R2's locomotors whined in protest as he dragged Chewbacca past Leia. "And see if you can wake him up!"

Keeping up the fire with one hand, she used the other to shake Han. When that didn't work, she gave him a couple of sharp smacks across his face, which elicited only a thin groan. Finally she grabbed one of his ear-lobes and pinched it as hard as she could, digging her thumbnail in deep enough to sit him bolt upright with a wide-eyed howl of protest.

"Ow-wow-ow-okay-I'm-awake-*lay-off-the-EAR*, huh?" Han scrambled to his feet, then half sagged again, dizzily clutching his head. "Woo. What hit me?"

Leia was still firing as she backed up. "What do you *think*? What am I *shooting* at?"

"Good question." Han blinked, trying make his eyes focus through the flashes and flickers of stun blasts and energy crackles. "What are those things?"

"Unfriendly," Leia said tightly while she blasted another.

"Yeah, sure, make fun of the woozy guy." He clutched at his hip, but his hand found only an empty holster. "Um, you wouldn't happen to have seen my blaster lying around anywhere, would you?"

"I'd help you hunt for it, but I'm a little—" She laid down a line of fire that slagged three or four more. "—*busy* right now, okay? Keep backing up."

"They're not behind us?"

"Not yet."

Han squinted. "How do you know?"

"You want to go look? I *know*."

"Right, right, I get it." Han waved to R2. "Hey, Stubby! A little light, huh?"

R2-D2's holoprojector swiveled and flared to life, emitting a wide cone of brilliant white light. Han peered into the advancing ranks of the rock creatures that just kept slithering forward—and kept regrowing up from the sludge Leia had melted them into—and tried to keep the desperation out of his voice. "No hint from the Force? A clue? Anything?"

"Just stay back and let me save your life again, will you?" But even as she spoke, her series of stun blasts wholly liquefied a couple of them, and there in the thin puddle of rock gruel Han spotted a blessedly familiar silhouette.

"Now, *that's* more like it!" He pounced on it and fished his DL-44 out of the muck, giving it a good shake to clear the works before the stone could reharden. His first shot sent a puff of vaporized rock curling out from the DL's emitter, but after that it seemed to work just fine.

"I'll take over here!" he told Leia, stepping up with a wide-dispersal rebound shot off the wall that spread to take out three of the creatures at once. "See what you can do to get Chewie on his feet—these power cells won't last forever!"

When Leia turned to comply, Chewbacca was already sitting up and dazedly struggling to rise; he was urgently groaning something that Leia's still-limited knowledge of Shyriiwook couldn't follow. "What's he saying? Is that 'Code Black'? What's *Code Black* mean?"

"It means *Drop everything and run like hell*," Han said.

Leia looked back over her shoulder at the massed rock creatures that still kept pressing forward no matter how many Han blasted. "He always *was* the brains of this operation."

"I was thinking the same thing." Han had to leap back and dodge, ducking toward her as the rock creatures started to flow out of the walls to either side of him. "Go! Chewie, get the droid! I'm right behind you!"

Chewbacca swept R2 up in his massive hairy arms and shambled off unsteadily, though his gait was strengthening with every step. R2 kept his holoprojector aimed at the ceiling to provide as much light as possible. Leia pelted along after them, throwing glances back to make sure Han was still right behind her, which he was, running hard, firing at random back over his shoulder.

The rock creatures came after them in a swelling wave of stone.

They ran.

Han drew even with her, puffing. "Got any idea . . . where we're going?"

"Sure." Leia's breath had gone short, too. "Away from *them*."

"I mean . . . do you have a *feeling* . . . what might be up ahead?"

"You went pretty fast . . . from *it's one thing to see Luke do it* to *Use the Force, Leia,* didn't you?" She tried for her usual crisply tart tone, but the wheeze of her breath only made her sound tired.

"My line of work . . . you gotta be a . . . flexible thinker."

"Just keep running. Follow . . . *him*." She waved a hand toward Chewbacca, who pounded along the cavernway ahead of them. "Don't know what's ahead," she said. "Not escaping . . . know that much."

"The Force . . . tell you that?"

"Uh-uh. The tunnel." She waved her blaster toward the floor. "Slanting *down* . . ."

"Oh . . . that *can't* be good . . ."

"Look," she gasped. "I can . . . slow 'em down. You go on . . . I'll catch up—"

"Not a . . . not a *chance*. You're just saying that . . . as an *excuse* for a *breather*," Han insisted between wheezes. "If anybody's gonna take a break . . . it's *me*."

She gave him a fond sidelong smile. "On three?"

"Huh." He grinned back at her. "How about . . . on *one*?"

"Good plan." Just ahead, the tunnel opened out into

a cavern; Chewie and R2 were already inside. There was no way to tell how big the cavern might be, but she knew that the only thing keeping them going this far had been that the rock creatures had had to bunch together inside the tunnel to come at them; in a more open area, they wouldn't have a chance. Just as she and Han reached the tunnel's mouth, she sucked in as deep a breath as her starved lungs would hold. "One!"

Shoulder-to-shoulder, they skidded to a stop and wheeled, triggering a storm of stun blasts back along the cavernway. The front ranks of the rock creatures sagged, and melted . . .

And the ones behind them stopped.

"Hey . . . hey, how about that?" Han sagged forward, hands to his bent knees, doubled over and panting. "Maybe they've . . . had enough. You think?"

"I . . . doubt it."

"Maybe they're as tired of chasing us . . . as we are of running . . ."

Chewbacca howled something incomprehensible. R2 twittered. Neither of them sounded happy. Leia turned, and the rest of her breath left her in a smothered version of one of Han's Corellian curses. "Or maybe," she said, "they stopped because we ran exactly where they wanted us to go."

The cavern was full of bodies.

Dead bodies.

Dozens, maybe hundreds of bodies, half-sunk into the stone—as though it had been liquid and hardened around them. Up to their waists or chests in the floor, pushed into the walls so that only a face or a back of the head was clear. Some of the bodies—human ones—wore what looked like stormtrooper armor, except that it was black as the stone around them. Some—fresher ones, some human, some Mon Calamari, who looked like

they might only be sleeping—wore New Republic flight
suits.

"For the record?" Han sounded a little shaky. "*This* is
why I didn't want you to come along."

AN ENDLESS SWARM OF TIE FIGHTERS SWIRLED AROUND
the *Remember Alderaan* and the other capital ships of
the Republic that were huddled together in Mindor's
radiation-shadow. Republic firecontrol tracked the
fighters desperately to lock in missiles, and gunners
poured turbolaser bolts through the vacuum, but the
nimble starfighters were almost impossible to hit, and
the only TIEs that got close enough to trigger the *Remember Alderaan*'s antifighter cluster munitions were
the ones streaking in for full-speed physical intercepts.

Suicide crashes.

Even a lightly built TIE fighter generated a titanic
amount of kinetic energy when traveling at the high end
of its sublight velocity; the particle shields of the capital
ships couldn't dissipate it fast enough. A couple of suiciders were enough to trigger a momentary partial shield
failure, and if another TIE timed it just right to slip into
the gap, the impact could rip through whole decks.

The *Remember Alderaan* rocked and shuddered
under its third such impact; clouds of gas and crystal-
lized water vapor billowed out from three enormous
rents in its hull. Like all battle cruisers, the *Alderaan* was
designed to suck up an astonishing amount of damage
and go on fighting, but when Lando got the preliminary
damage and casualty report on this latest blast, even
his legendary unquenchable optimism was pretty well
quenched. Over a thousand crew members wounded or
missing; a third of his turbolasers out of commission;
and one main engine was overheating and would either
shut down or melt down sometime in the next three or
four minutes.

Lando leaned on the comm board on the *Alderaan*'s bridge. "Where the hell is our *fighter escort*?" he snarled. "Somebody has to stop these guys!"

But he knew the answer: the task force's fighters were overcommitted in support of the ground action against the STOEs—the surface-to-orbit emplacements. He didn't even have enough to adequately cover his marines, let alone defend his fleet.

"General Calrissian! General, can someone give me a hand?" C-3PO, knocked off his feet by the impact, had somehow gotten himself wedged under the security console. "Oh, what a terrible *dent* I'm going to have!"

Lando waved a hand and ordered, "Somebody pick up that droid!" because otherwise the blasted thing would just lie there and complain until somebody snapped and blew his gold-plated head off. He turned to his executive officer, a Glassferran, whose three expressionless eyes were fixed on three different tactical holodisplays. "Close the fleet up, Kartill," he said. "We need to bring the ships together. As close as possible—seal the gaps in our antifighter coverage."

"We're practically kissing each other's shields as it is," Kartill replied. "And—begging the general's pardon—being that close together is about to be a serious problem, once those STOEs swing over the horizon."

"Don't remind me." He turned to the officer at the communications board. "Anything from Shysa?"

"Report coming in now, sir. I'll put it on speaker."

The crisp sizzle of blasterfire was the only thing that came clearly over the comm channel; everything else was half-buried in static. Lando leaned over the board and tried to keep smiling. "Shysa! Calrissian. I need good news, Fenn! We're only eight minutes off that gravity gun's firing window, and I've got a whole lot of ships with their bellies hanging out up here!"

C-3PO had reached his feet and now shuffled toward Lando. "General Calrissian—"

"Later. Fenn, do you read?"

The comm crackled with more blasterfire and a louder burst of static that might have been a proton grenade. *"We're making progress, but it's room-to-room! These black-armor types are dug in and they don't seem to believe in runnin' away."*

"Do they believe in *dying*?"

"Oh, that they have a talent for. Problem is, they keep tryin' to take our boys with 'em when they go!"

"Keep on it, Fenn. I'll see if I can organize some help."

"Anything you can do will be welcome."

"General Calrissian, please!" C-3PO hovered at Lando's shoulder, and he sounded even more agitated than usual. "You might be interested—"

"I said *later.*" Lando pointed at the communications officer. "Open the dedicated channel to Captain Antilles in Rogue One."

The officer nodded. "Ten seconds, sir."

Lando turned to C-3PO. "Okay. Ten seconds. What's so interesting?"

"Well, you *may* find it interesting; I can't know for certain," the droid replied defensively. "But interesting or not, it's unquestionably *significant*. In my opinion, that is."

"Your *opinion*?"

"General? Captain Antilles," the officer said.

"Please, General Calrissian, my opinion, on this matter, is *most* reliable!"

"Lost your chance." Lando turned back to the comm board. "Wedge. Change of plans. Pull the Rogues off the turbo towers. The Mandos are having trouble securing the gravity gun. If that dome opens up, I want more ordnance going in than coming out, do you read?"

"*Copy that, but I'm down three birds. Got a squadron or two you can spare?*"

"Don't make jokes, Wedge. Just get there. A lot of lives are depending on you."

"*We're used to it, sir.*"

"That's why I wouldn't give the job to anybody else. Clear skies, Wedge."

"*See you on the far side, General. Rogue Leader out.*"

"But—but General *Calrissian*—"

"Not *now,* Threepio!" Lando clenched his jaw. He'd had a feeling all along that it might come to this. "Kartill, alert the fleet. We're going atmospheric."

All three of the exec's eyes blinked at once. "Sir?"

"You heard me. Dirtside. Everybody. It's the only way. If we're still in orbit ten minutes from now, those STOEs will cut us to pieces."

"Land? Land *where,* sir?"

"We'll worry about that after we're out of their fire window, yes?"

"Yes, sir."

"General—General, *please*!"

"Keep bothering me, Threepio, and I swear I'll hit you so hard you'll think you're a *garbage* loader."

"But, General, I thought you wanted to find Captain Solo!"

"What?" Lando turned and stared at the skinny protocol droid. "You know something about Han?"

"Possibly. In your brief communication with him—"

"Yeah, that *was* weird, wasn't it? We can barely reach our own ships once they're in that atmosphere, but we could pick up Han's comlink, and he said he was in some kind of cave—"

"Yes, General. Yes, that's it precisely. During that communication, I detected a subtle modulation in the carrier wave. Sort of a background noise, one might say."

"What kind of background noise?"

"It appears to be a retrograde ortho-dialect of Surmo-Clarithian electrospeech interspersed with a creole of the Black Dwarf variant of Imperial digital encryption and a Neimoidian trade cipher—fascinating, really, especially in the structural vocabulation—"

"Threepio."

"Oh, yes. Of course. Essentially, something was speaking on the comm wave. Or rather, the comm signal was picking up something's speech."

"Another comm signal?"

"Oh, no no no, nothing so sophisticated. It's simply a language—electrospeech is a type of direct energy modulation used by a variety of life-forms; to date, I believe the total known to science numbers over—"

"Forget that. This electrospeech—you understand it?"

The droid drew himself up proudly. "I *am* fluent in over six million forms of—"

"I don't need a list. What'd it *say*?"

"Well—translated as best I can, you understand, their accent is perfectly barbarous—they were about to take a pair of humans captive, and will deliver them to the crypt chamber."

Lando shook his head. "What crypt chamber? And who's taking who captive?"

"I'm sure I cannot say who the captors might be; the language would be appropriate for any number of energy-based life-forms."

"Then why are you wasting my time with this?"

"Oh, well, it's because these two captives were apparently accompanied by a Wookiee."

"A *Wookiee*?"

"It *does* seem an unlikely coincidence. And they also mention a droid—hmm, parsing . . . half human size, round as a pillar spine, rotating dome—Artoo! Oh,

General Calrissian, we must *do* something! They have *Artoo*!"

"All right, all right, slow down." If whoever this was had R2-D2, they might even have Luke—or at least know what happened to him. That's what Lando told himself, anyway; somehow it made him feel better to have at least a theoretically valid argument of military necessity for the rescue mission he was already pretty sure he was going to order anyway. "How did that signal punch through in the first place?"

"That's exactly the point, General. I suspect that the natural frequency of this particular energy-based lifeform confines it to a certain variety of electromagnetically active rock—this would be this life-form's natural environment, as it were—and while this rock may very well interfere with an ordinary comm signal, its conductive properties should actually enable it to resonate with and *reinforce* a properly modulated—"

"I get it. Can you reproduce this modulation? Can you run it through the ship's comm?"

"Well—in all modesty, perhaps Artoo would be more—"

Lando gritted his teeth against an almost overpowering urge to twist C-3PO's head off. *"Can you do it?"*

"I *am* fluent in over—"

"Don't tell me." Lando pointed at the comm board. "Tell the ship."

LUKE SCRAMBLED THROUGH THE DEEP CINDERS WITH Nick close behind. Taspan had sunk below the horizon; the only light came from the burning wreckage scattered across the floor of the crater, and from the occasional flashes and flares of the battle that raged above.

The cinder crunched and gave way almost like fine sand beneath every step, making the going slow and hard. The crater was also littered with bigger chunks—

masses of hardened lava and rocky ejecta, most of which were a featureless, nonreflective black, which made them very hard to see; even Luke only discovered the medium-sized ones by painfully whacking one with his shins. He would have gone more cautiously, but the first time an ion panel blown off a TIE came whistling down and shattered into shrapnel a couple of dozen meters away, he gave up the idea of slow and careful.

They ran hard. At least when Luke caught his foot on a chunk and fell, he could use the Force to flip himself in the air and hit the ground running. Nick didn't have that option, but somehow he managed to reach the relative shelter beneath the slant of the *Falcon*'s hull only a few steps behind Luke, even though he was limping, both hands were bleeding, and he had a nasty-looking scrape on his forehead.

The *Falcon* loomed over them, blacking out the stars. Its attitude thrusters flared and sprayed jets of gas in a seemingly random sequence—trying to rock itself free—and the whine of its repulsorlifts scaled up from merely annoying to a shriek that was making Luke's teeth ache.

Nick scowled up at the ship's dark silhouette. "What do we do, knock?"

"No comlink." Luke held one hand pressed against his ear. "We have to get their attention somehow."

"Where's the hatch?"

"Up there." Luke gestured vaguely overhead; the belly hatch was high up the underside, out of reach. "Maybe we can climb."

"No problem. I grew up in a jungle. I can climb *anything*."

"Not yet. Something's wrong."

"Other than their landing? Shee, in the holoshows, Solo's supposed to be such a hot pilot . . ."

Luke frowned. "I feel . . . fear and anger. Aggression.

Danger. Han's my best friend—why would his ship feel *hostile*?"

"Dunno." Nick looked around and spotted a slow swing of motion in the darkness above. "Think it might be because that quad turret's tracking us?"

The Force stabbed Luke with an instant overpowering *Move-or-die;* in less than an eyeflick his foot lashed out to slam Nick back deeper under the hull and he sprang into the air, back-flipping away. The night ripped open with the *choomchoomchoomchoom* of high-cyclic cannon fire, burning the air into long streaks of brilliant yellow that lit up the cinder pit like noon on Tatooine, and blowing gouts of white-molten rock in all directions.

The turret tracked Luke, chopping red-hot .craters toward him like the footprints of an invisible fire god. He landed and sprang again on a different vector, and by the time the turret followed that leap he was off again on another that took him behind a boulder the size of an adolescent bantha. He pressed his back against it while the turret blasted away at its other side, and from the amount of smoke going up and debris raining down, he was pretty sure that turret's gunner, whoever he was, figured the easiest way to get him would be to just blast the rock to pieces.

He rolled across to the opposite edge and risked a quick glance. Looked like Nick wasn't kidding about being able to climb anything; he was clambering up the overhanging slant of the hull faster than a hungry mynock. "Nick! Get off of there!"

Nick reached the gimbal cowling of the quad turret. With Nick hanging half across the transparisteel viewport, the gunner quit blasting; Luke could see him inside, shouting *Get your fraggin' grass off my turret,* or something along those lines.

"Nuts to that," Nick called back. "He can't shoot me

here! Toss me your lightsaber and I'll shut this ruskakk down with one swipe!"

"*No,* Nick! Jump! The *Falcon*'s equipped with a—"

A burst of blue-white energy crackled over the freighter's hull; the discharge threw Nick tumbling from the turret to the ground, where he landed on his back with an authoritative *whump.*

"—antipersonnel field projector," Luke finished belatedly.

The gunner opened up again. Luke extended his hand and summoned the Force; a sharp shove sent Nick skidding, and Luke decided he'd had just about enough of being shot at for one night. He took a deep breath and sent his mind into the Force.

The *Falcon* loomed large in his perception, as did the thirty or so desperate people he now felt were inside. He shut them out of his consciousness and focused on the ship itself. There—he felt the circuit he was looking for . . . and he even felt the echo of Leia's hand upon it! She had touched this only hours earlier. Maybe even less . . .

But this was a distraction—even more distracting than the shuddering of the boulder as cannon blasts chewed away at its opposite side. The mere awareness of Leia's recent presence was enough to flood his mind with all manner of fears and hopes that dimmed his perception until he could banish them and focus once more. A few more deep breaths tuned his mind like a targeting laser, and he recovered his hold on the circuit. A slight nudge in the Force, and he felt the circuit trip.

The quad turret went dark, and its guns fell silent. The turret autorotated to face forward between the freighter's mandibles.

Luke could feel the gunner's confusion and rising panic; he figured he had at least five seconds before the gunner figured out that the turret drivers had been reset and locked into their forward-fire default position.

Five seconds was more than he needed.

He stood up and raised his hand. High up the underside of the ship's slant, the belly hatch fell open, spilling light in a stretching rectangle up the night-shadowed hull. One Force-powered leap carried him over the smoking boulder to Nick's side.

"I'm all right . . ." Nick wheezed weakly. "Just need a minute to . . . catch my breath. Or maybe a week. Or two."

Luke knotted his left fist in the front of Nick's Shadowspawn robe, gathered the Force around them both, and leapt straight up, over the edge of the freighter's belly ramp—which, due to the angle at which the ship was stuck, was more like a slide—and skidded down it into the *Falcon*'s main cargo hold.

Which was full of men and women in curiously constructed armor that looked like it had been made out of lava, nearly all of whom were pointing blaster rifles at him.

For an instant, the only sound was the rattle and snap of rifle stocks being snugged against armored shoulders; in the next instant, the only sound was the lethal hum of a green lightsaber blade held forward at guard.

"Don't shoot," Luke said softly. "I've killed too many people already today."

"Weapons down!" The speaker was a hard-looking woman with red hair, sporting a swelling bruise around her left eye. She stood with her left thumb hooked behind her blaster belt while her right hand dangled free and loose near the butt of a slim blaster in a quick-draw rig. "It's the *Jedi*! He's here to help!"

"Yes," Luke said. "I am the Jedi. And I hope I can help." That was true on enough different levels to make his stomach hurt—but on the other hand, this was the second time in a row that someone had decided not to mess with him based on who they assumed he was, which was a trend he hoped to encourage. "Where's Han?"

"Han who?" Her right hand came up, but it came up empty. "Listen, we need you—we need your help. Shadowspawn's got my—"

"No he doesn't," Nick wheezed from behind Luke.

"Nick?" Her eyes sparked and her voice had gone soft and breathless, and Luke could only wonder how he'd thought she was hard-looking; when she gazed past him at Nick, she looked like a Tatooine teenager on the way to her own star-seventeen dance at the Anchorhead community center. She brushed past Luke as if he weren't even there and threw her arms around him. "Nick! I can't *believe* it!"

"Hey, kid. Did you miss me?"

"Did I *miss* you?" She pulled his face down to hers and planted a kiss on his lips that would have opened the eyes of a dead man.

Luke cleared his throat. "I take it you two know each other?"

"Nick—" Her eyes were still shining when she came up for air, and her cheeks were wet, too. "You're all right? How did you escape? What are you doing running around with a Jedi?"

"All right? Mostly." Nick rubbed at the dried blood that crusted his shaven scalp and grimaced. "The running-with-Jedi business, well, we sort of rescued each other. As for escaping . . . um, you *have* noticed that the ship we're on is stuck nose-first in the ground in the middle of a giant pitched battle, haven't you?"

"Doesn't matter," she said, stroking his face. "We've *got* you—that's all that matters."

Nick lifted his own hand to tenderly touch her black eye. "Still haven't learned to duck, huh?"

"You oughta see the other—uh, guy." She grinned at him. "Now all we have to do is find a place to hole up until the flares subside, and we can shake this rockball's dust off our boots forever."

"Um . . ." Luke said quietly. "No."

She looked at him. "What?"

"We're going back for Han."

"Again: Han who?"

"Don't." Luke nodded generally around at the scorch marks and blaster scars that marred the hold's interior walls, floor, and ceiling. "Are you going to tell me this is all from a *slight weapons malfunction?*"

Nick turned. "She's not a pirate."

"Is there another word for it?"

"Hey, this tub was abandoned when we found it—" the woman said.

"Try to remember who you're lying to." Luke sighed. "I know you didn't kill them. That's why I haven't hurt any of you yet. But this has been a really, really hard day for me, and my patience is wearing thin."

"Hey, c'mon, Skywalker, take it easy," Nick said. "I'm sure there's a perfectly innocent explanation."

"And I'll be happy to hear it. Just as soon as we get Han and Chewie and Leia back on board this ship.

"Skywalker?" one of the others chimed in. "Any relation to the guy from *The Jedi's Revenge?*"

"*No,*" Luke said with maybe a touch more emphasis than was absolutely necessary. "No relation at all."

He looked back at the redhead. "Where did you leave them?"

She opened her mouth, but before she could speak Luke raised a hand. "Think before you talk," he said. "I won't ask you again."

She closed her mouth. She looked up at Nick, then back at Luke. "Uhh, okay," she said slowly. "Look, can we make a deal?"

"Sure," Luke said. "This deal: You tell me everything I want to know, and do exactly as I say. In exchange, I'll try to forget that you stole my best friend's ship and abandoned him and my sister to die."

"Your *sister*? Your sister is Princess Kissy-Face?"

"My sister *is* a princess. Princess Leia Organa of Alderaan," Luke said evenly. "And if you called her *Princess Kissy-Face* in person, I can guess who gave you that shiner."

Nick rubbed his eyes. "Aeona . . . you didn't really pirate this ship, did you?"

"Well, what would *you* have done, if it was *me* in the meathooks of that ratbag?"

"Something worse, probably. But you're not gonna win this argument, and there's no time to try. The bad guys know we're here, and they're coming after us."

Luke said, "You're sure?"

Nick flashed him a grim look and tapped the thin scar that stretched around his head from temple to temple.

"So? We should be safe enough as long as we don't try to move," Aeona said. "Who's gonna waste their time blasting a crashed ship?"

"Wait five seconds and you can ask 'em."

Nick barely had time to get the words out before the first explosion ripped away the *Falcon*'s belly ramp and blasted a gout of flaming slag into the cargo hold that set the whole place on fire.

IN THE DEEP SHADOWS OF THE CAVERN FILLED WITH half-buried dead people, away from R2's light, Han gathered Leia into his arms. "Leia, I just—I'm sorry things went this way. I just wish you and I had more time. Together."

She smiled up at him and touched his face. "I know."

"How is it we only kiss when we're about to get killed?"

"Just lucky, I guess." She kissed him, briefly, glancingly, but even that slight contact brought a hot flush of bittersweet regret for all the kisses he was pretty sure they'd never get the chance to share.

"Aroo-oo-ergh! Herowwwougrr."

"What?" Han pulled away from her. "Are you sure?"

Chewbacca was kneeling alongside a young Mon Calamari who was buried to his armpits. *"Herowwwougrr!"*

Leia frowned. "What's he saying?"

Han was already rushing to his copilot's side. He reached down and pressed his fingertips to the Mon Cal's face just above his left eye, checking for his sinus pulse. It was there: thin and thready but maintaining the typical syncopated three-beat rhythm. "He's right!"

"About what?"

"This one's still *alive*," Han said wonderingly. "Looks like some more of them might be, too. Out cold, but breathing."

"What's that insignia?" Leia joined him at the Mon Cal's side. "Artoo, aim the light over here." When he did, her eyes widened and she pointed at the posting flash next to the rank cartridge on the Mon Cal's battledress blouse. "Han—isn't that the *Justice*? The ship Luke was on?"

Han was already up looking at the others. It was a backward progression: the captives became less and less healthy-looking as he went deeper into the cavern. In addition to the Republic soldiers, there were a number of guys in the Lava Gear armor of the Mindorese, but most of them were stormtroopers, and nearly all of them were dead. "It's like those critters stuck them in here and just . . . *forgot* about them."

Chewie grumbled. Han nodded. "Yeah, not my favorite way to go, either."

R2 gave out a warning whistle that brought Han back

to his feet. He drew his blaster. "That sounds like bad news."

"Bad enough," Leia said as she produced the hold-out. In the faint light that spilled out into the tunnel, she could see wave after wave of the rock creatures crowding toward the cavern. "Time to fight."

Han turned, blaster ready. "I don't think we're getting out of this one."

"Trust in the Force, Han."

"You trust the Force," he said. "I'll trust my blaster."

Leia frowned down at the hold-out's power indicator. "The Force never runs out of ammo."

"No? Then how come it's not shooting?"

"What happened to *never tell me the odds*?"

"That's for when there *are* odds. When you fall off a cliff, what are the odds you'll hit the ground?"

"Depends," she said. "How close are you and the *Falcon*?"

"Very funny."

Han's comlink crackled. He grabbed it and shouted, "Yeah, come in! Come in! We're in a little *trouble* here. Do you copy? *Do you copy?*" but the comlink replied only with a burst of static.

He shook it one more time, then made a face and jammed it back in his pocket. "Had me going there for a second. Come on. If we can hold the doorway, we'll slow 'em down, anyway."

But as they moved toward the cavern's mouth, the creatures started melting out of the walls.

IN THE DEEP GLOOM OF HIS LIFE-SUPPORT CHAMBER, Cronal withdrew his consciousness from the realm of Darksight, and found himself well pleased. Anyone unfamiliar with the true power of Darksight might have been astonished to find that Skywalker indeed had a sibling who had never trained as a Jedi; this hypothetical *anyone* would no doubt have been amazed to discover that this sibling had—seemingly of her own accord—presented herself precisely where Cronal needed her to be exactly *when* he needed her to be there. For Cronal, this was only what he had learned to expect. Left to its own devices, the galaxy and everything in it—from the stars themselves to the tiniest virus—served the Dark.

At least up until some blasted meddler started tricking around with the Force, upsetting the natural order of things.

This was the real problem with Jedi: the Force. Their whole *concept* of the Force. Always prattling about *life* and *light* and *justice,* as if those silly words actually *meant* something. He would have found those Jedi fools entirely humorous were it not for their inexplicable ability to occasionally actually interfere with the Way of the Dark.

Palpatine had done a fair job of thinning the Force-user herd, and Skywalker himself had nearly finished the job when he'd tricked Vader and the Emperor into killing each other—because, after all, the Sith could be as troublesome as Jedi if they set their minds to it. And then that Skywalker boy himself had already been more trouble than he was worth.

This problem, however, was on the verge of solving itself, as all such problems were wont to do, when one truly adhered to the Way. He didn't need the Skywalker Jedi anymore; his sister would be an even better fit—not only had she no actual Force skills to defend her from his dominance, she also had *tremendous* political potential. Hero of Endor? Sole survivor of the last royal family of Alderaan?

The only difficulty he had left was to retrieve the Skywalker girl from the wild Melters and get her Darkening under way, which task was decidedly complicated by the fact that all his best Pawns were lying dead on the floor of the Election Center. Yet even this difficulty turned out to be another example of how the Dark anticipated and provided for the every need of its most assiduous servant.

He still had the prototype, the test subject upon whom he had experimented to perfect the Darkening process. This subject hadn't been entirely analogous to Skywalker—his connection to the Force, though astonishingly powerful, was innately of a far darker shade than the boy's, not to mention that he had never received Jedi training. Or any training, really, which was probably why Cronal had failed to anticipate just how large an obstacle Skywalker's training would prove to be. He was, however, enormous and physically powerful, and his very arteries pulsed with a certain innate ferocity that Cronal found more than a bit intoxicating. And with the shadow nerve network of meltmassif lacing his body, he had a connection to the fundamental power of the Dark that rivaled Cronal's own.

The initial test subject had had a number of limitations, though; he was twice Skywalker's age, and instead of a hero to the entire Rebel Alliance and now the New Republic, he'd been a hunted fugitive for longer than the boy had been alive, with a substantial bounty on his head that still stood. He was also more than a bit distinctive-looking, being over two meters tall and built like a rancor, not to mention having teeth filed sharp as a sabercat's. He also, owing to some kind of structural brain abnormality that Cronal had been unable to repair, entirely lacked the power of human speech.

All of which made him a less-than-ideal body for Cronal to spend the next few decades inhabiting, and so Cronal had never taken the final step of permanent consciousness transfer . . . which only made this particular test subject all the more ideal for this particular task: a remote body, through which he could exert the whole of his powers, without risk to himself.

After all, when one needed a job done *properly* . . .

And so Cronal closed his eyes and brought the Sunset Crown down from its resting place onto his hairless scalp. When he opened his eyes again, the eyes he opened were not his.

They were the eyes of Kar Vastor.

CHAPTER 15

LUKE HIT THE DECK ROLLING. HIS FLIGHT SUIT WAS flame-retardant, but that wouldn't stop the molten cinder and white-hot shards of the *Falcon*'s armor that the explosion had blown in through the hatch from burning right through it. Rolling might not have done him much good either, except that the *Falcon*'s automated fire suppressors were squirting supercooled extinguishing foam all over the cargo hold. Luke got himself good and coated with the gunk, then struggled up to his hands and knees.

Nick and Aeona and most of the others were similarly down and rolling, but a few just stood and screamed as they burned. Luke stretched out into the Force and flattened every one of them with a single hard shove, which might not have been necessary since the ongoing explosions were bouncing the ship around enough that nobody would have been on their feet much longer anyway, but Luke wasn't about to leave that to chance.

He kicked off the wall and slid through the cascading foam over to Nick and Aeona, shouting above the blasts and screams. "Get your people secured and ready to move, and have them seal that ramp door! You'll find three or four HatchPatch units in the rear storage compartment. Any questions?"

"Yeah—who put *you* in charge?" Aeona snapped.

"You did, sweetheart," Nick said. "When you marooned his sister and his best friend. Suck it up and do what you're told."

Her eyes flashed like a blaster charging to overload. "You are gonna be in *so* much trouble . . ."

"If we live through this, you can spank me."

"Don't think I won't."

"Get yourself to the cockpit," Luke told her. "Activate as many thrusters as you can bring online, and on my order fire them full ahead."

"Ahead? That'll only drive us *deeper* into the ground!"

"Someday, girl," Nick said, "you and I are gonna have a talk about arguing with Jedi. He's got a plan." He turned to Luke. "Tell me you've got a plan."

"More or less." Luke got up—with a little help from the Force to keep his balance in the soapy, slippery extinguishing foam—and started trotting aft.

"That's not the most reassuring thing you could have said. Where are you going?"

"Quad turret," Luke said without slowing.

"Skywalker, give me the other one, " Nick said.

Luke stopped and looked back. "Can you shoot?"

Nick made it to his feet. "I can clip the wings of a Perthrillian nightwasp at a thousand meters and never wake it up."

"That's not really an answer."

"Hey, the guys in there right now couldn't even hit *me*."

"Good point. Come on."

When they got to the access junction, both turrets were empty. "Looks like they bailed."

Luke moved into one of the turrets and nodded out the transparisteel at the carpet of fire that was the cinder pit. "Do you blame them?"

Nick only shrugged as he belted himself in. "It's not

the worst idea these guys have had today," he called back.

Luke got himself buckled, as well. With a flick of the Force, he reinitialized the circuit that had deactivated the ventral turret. "Nice friends you have."

"She's not a bad person," Nick insisted as he twisted the control yoke back and forth, checking the turret's servo response. "She just doesn't have a lot of patience for the little things."

"Little things like laws and justice and other people's lives?" The turret's tactical screen lit up with unfriendlies. "Here they come!"

Nick hauled on the control yoke and triggered the guns even before the turret swung into line, stitching a curving stream of cannon bolts up the inner wall of the caldera just as a flight of a dozen or so TIEs whipped over the rim and streaked down on strafing runs. The lead TIE flew right into Nick's fire and its cockpit viewscreen shattered; it plowed straight on down into the cinder pit at full speed and exploded, but the rest of his shots glanced off armor and collector panels. "This is gonna be a problem," Nick said through his teeth. "Got one, though."

Luke was holding down the triggers in his own turret. "It wasn't starfighters that set this whole crater on fire. Watch out for bombers."

"Copy that."

TIEs swooped down upon them and cannon blasts rocked the ship; Nick caught another one right in the eyeball, then one more. He let out a whoop. "That's three! How many you drop so far, Skywalker?"

"None," Luke said tightly.

"What, I'm outshooting *you*?" Nick poured enough fire into another TIE's collector panel that it lost control and crashed into its wingman. "Shee, they don't make Jedi like they used to."

"Nick, be quiet."

"Hey, I'm not gloating—well, maybe a little—"

"I know. I need to concentrate."

"On what?" Nick twisted around so he could look up at Skywalker and out through the dorsal turret, which was when he understood why Skywalker hadn't shot down any ships. He wasn't shooting at the ships. Nick also understood why it was that no missiles or bombs or cannons were blasting the *Falcon* to tiny bits.

Because that's what Skywalker had been shooting: the missiles and bombs and cannon fire raining down from the swarm of enemy ships.

"Oh," Nick said softly. He went back to shooting. But he couldn't stop looking at the flames licking upward from the burning cinder pit, and he couldn't help noticing that while Skywalker's blasts were intercepting the cannon bolts and missiles that would actually *hit* the *Falcon,* all the near-misses were splashing so much molten rock around that it'd probably be melting through the ship's hull armor any second now anyway. Just as he realized this, the turret's tactical screen showed blips for *six* TIE bombers inbound, and when he pointed all this out to Skywalker, the young Jedi's only response was to key the cockpit channel on the intercom. "Hey—" He glanced over at Nick. "What's her name again?"

"Aeona."

"Aeona, this is Luke. I hope you got some thrusters hot."

"We're a long way off full power—"

"We'll take what we've got. Full ahead. Angle the attitude jets for extra boost."

"Skywalker?" Nick said. "You just ordered her to bury this ship in a river of *molten* fraggin' *lava.*"

"Yes. Reset your turret to default position and fire on my order."

"Um, you *do* know that *default* is *forward*? Which is *down*." Desperation sharpened his voice. "You *do* know that's the *opposite* of *up,* which is where the bad guys are *coming from*?"

"Nick," Luke said, "you're arguing with a Jedi again."

Nick's response was a snarl of frustration that contained, as its only intelligible words, *nikkle-nut Jedi ruskakk* as he jabbed toggles on the turret's fire-control board.

Luke no longer looked at his own tactical screen. He didn't even glance outside the turret. He didn't need to see outside; he was paying attention to inside.

Inside his head. Inside the Force.

He felt the *Falcon*'s quad turrets swing into line; he felt the TIE bombers whip down over the rim of the caldera, and he felt them release unguided proton bombs in a mechanically precise sequence; he felt the arc of the falling bombs, and he felt their impact points, and he felt how their blast radii would overlap precisely at the *Falcon*'s position and crush the ship like a discarded ration pack.

He said, "Nick. Now."

The quads opened up at full power, blasting chains of laser bolts straight down into the lake of fire between the ship's forward mandibles. The impact area flashed to superheated plasma that shot gouts of burning rock up over the *Falcon*'s hull armor. At the same instant, the port dorsal attitude thrusters fired in tandem with the starboard ventrals, exerting a powerful rotational force that, as the quads continued to vaporize and liquefy the cinder in which the mandibles were buried, was literally *screwing* the ship into the ground.

"You think this is *helping*?" Nick yelped.

"Shh. This isn't my best trick, either."

Luke focused on nothing until he could feel everything. Nick's chatter, his own fatigue, the battle outside, and the doom lowering upon Leia all flowed into him and out again like water, leaving no trace behind. He let himself become clear as a crystal bell, so that he could chime with one pure note.

That note was a tiny twist of intention that the Force channeled high into the atmosphere to gently—*very* gently—nudge the falling proton bombs. This very gentle nudge altered their trajectories by no more than a degree or two apiece, giving each a bit of an outward curve, so that instead of landing in a precise ring one hundred meters in diameter with the *Falcon* at its centerpoint, they landed in an equally precise ring *four* hundred meters in diameter, which meant that their overlapping blast radii did not so much crumple the ship as give it a very, very firm squeeze, much like how one might squeeze a rakmelon pip between one's fingers. And very much like this metaphoric rakmelon pip, the *Falcon* squirted free with considerable force.

Straight down.

That should have presented a greater problem, but the explosion of the proton bombs further weakened what turned out to be the cracked and fragile upper shell of a vast volcanic bubble that formed the floor of the cinder pit; the shock waves from the bombs, combined with the cannon fire from the *Falcon*'s turrets and the corkscrewing motion of its downward pressure, shattered the rocky shell so that the ship broke through and plummeted down a rugged natural vent that was several hundred meters deep, falling through a rain of boulders, jagged rock shards, and burning cinder while it bounced and clanged off rocks on either side.

Nick's comment of *"Whoa-aye-yi-yi-yiiii . . ."* trailed off to silence when he ran out of breath. Luke was clambering out of his turret. "Aeona! Autosequence the attitude jets and engage the repulsorlifts!"

"Oh, you think?"

Luke braced himself in the access hatch as the *Falcon* jerked itself level. The repulsorlift engines screamed. The ship slammed into the pile of rubble at the bottom of the vent with much clanging and screeching of tortured metal, and finally sat, while rocks and cinder and unidentified debris clattered down on top of it.

Nick blinked at the pile of rubble on which his turret currently rested. "Okay, *that* was original. You know if she'd been half a second slower with the repulsorlifts, you'd have been scraping what was left of me out of here with a spatula." He leaned forward to peer up through the dorsal turret at the tiny ragged disk of firelight and blaster flashes that was the hole through which they'd fallen. "And you did this on *purpose*?"

"Sort of. I knew we had to get underground; I just wasn't sure how we'd do it. Nice of the bad guys to help us out, huh?"

"Remind me to send 'em a thank-you card."

Luke fished out a comlink as he headed forward. "Aeona, cut the thrusters and cycle all power to the repulsorlifts. I'm on my way."

"On your way where?" Nick asked.

"Somebody has to fly this bucket."

"*Fly* it? Down *here*?"

"Yes. And from what I've seen of your girlfriend's piloting skills, she's not my first choice."

"You sure *you* can do it?"

"There's only one man alive who can fly this ship better than I can."

"Then maybe we should get *him*."

"That's exactly my plan. Take the dorsal turret and mind your tactical screens."

"Huh? What for?"

"TIE fighters."

Nick craned his neck. Down through that tiny-looking

opening far, far above came a stream of starfighters. "Ohhh, *great*. What's gonna stop them from blowing us to atoms while you get this crate up and moving?"

Luke grinned at him, but that grin didn't look so much happy as it looked like a predator's fang display. "You are," he said, and ran for the cockpit.

HAN AND LEIA STOOD BACK-TO-BACK IN THE MIDDLE OF a tightening ring of rock creatures, sweeping their blasters through short arcs to spread the stun charges around, but each blast bought them only a few seconds, and neither had more than a handful of shots remaining. Chewbacca lay unconscious, half-buried in rehardened stone, and R2-D2 lay on his side, photoprojector dark, smoke trailing up from his burnt-out capacitors. The only light in the cavern came from the crackling energy that played over the creatures as they pushed closer and closer.

"This is a *stupid* way to die!" Han snarled, slagging another couple of them with a single shot. "We don't know what these things are, we don't know what they're *doing* here, we don't even know why they're *mad* at us!"

"They're not mad," Leia said breathlessly as she fired again, and once more. "I can feel it. They don't even want to hurt us. Not really. They only want to bury us in the rock and go about their business."

"What—we just show up in the wrong place at the wrong time and we're gonna *die* for it?"

"Han—" Leia triggered her hold-out and got not even a glow from the muzzle. "Han, I'm out."

"All right, all right," Han said through his teeth; his DL's grip alert had been tingling for the last four or five shots, which meant he had only a handful left, even at this half-power setting. He threw his arm around Leia's shoulders and started backing up, throwing a shot or two behind to start a gap in the ring of creatures. "Stick close. Maybe we can work over to some of their current guests. Maybe somebody's got a charged blaster tucked away somewhere we can get at it—"

"Somebody's coming," Leia said. "Han—somebody's *out* there! Coming for us!"

"Is it Luke? Please say it's Luke." He silently swore that if she said yes, he would never, ever make another joke about the Force, or Jedi, or lightsabers, or really, anything else. For the rest of his life. Or longer, if necessary.

Over by the cavern mouth, rock creatures suddenly collapsed into puddles of liquid stone.

Leia said, her voice hushed, "It's not Luke."

The collapse spread like a slow-motion shock wave; creature after creature simply melted away, their electric crackles fading to silence; as the last of them fell, their light winked out, leaving the cavern in a darkness beyond darkness. Darkness like being blind.

Darkness as if the existence of light had been only a dream.

In that absolute night, something growled.

"What the hell was *that*?" Han asked. It had sounded like a Corellian sand panther warning off an intruder in its den.

"It says," Leia said, low, "*The dark is your refuge. Enter the dark as a weary traveler enters sleep.*"

"What's *that* supposed to mean? And since when do you speak . . . whatever that is?"

"I don't. I just . . . *understand* him somehow."

More growls, moving now; Han tracked the sound with the emitter of his DL-44. "What's he saying now?"

Her arms tightened around his chest. "He says he can smell your fear."

"Yeah? Smell *this*." Han popped off another stun blast. In the instant of glare, he saw it. Him. A dark shape, bigger than the sand panther he sounded like, darting along the wall. Han fired again, and again, but his shots splashed harmlessly on the stone; this guy— this thing, whatever—moved too fast for Han to even get a clear look at it. He set his jaw and very lightly flicked the DL's trigger twice, then again, then twice more, without ever pulling it past the break, so that it made a succession of dry clicks. He let a muffled curse escape through his teeth.

The growling became a deep, dry chuckle that he didn't need Leia to translate.

"You think that's funny? Turn on a light and I'll show you something funny!"

"Han, don't antagonize him!" Leia whispered.

"Why not? You think anything I do is gonna make this *worse*?"

"Yes," she said. "I think he's here for me. I think if you can keep your mouth shut, he might let you live."

There came another deep, half-growled chuckle that didn't need translating, and from off to Han's left, a faint glow began, greenish and cold. In the featureless dark, he couldn't tell how big it might be, or how far away, but the glow spread slowly, growing into an amorphous patch of light, and in the middle of that light there was a darkness, a shadow, in the shape of a man's splayed hand. The glow spidered outward around the hand, sending forth filaments that themselves spread like ice crystals forming on the inside of a window, limning the silhouette of a huge, powerful man, crouching on the floor like a katarn preparing to spring. The glow came from some kind of luminescent lichen that seemed to grow outward from the man's hand; the bigger it got, the faster it spread, until in one final rush it coated the entire floor and walls of the cavern and grew together across the ceiling.

Han's mouth was dry as sand, and he had to cough his throat clear. "Did—did *he* do that?"

"I think so," Leia whispered hoarsely.

The man stood. Han tried to swallow his mouthful of imaginary sand and adjusted his grip on his blaster. This guy was *huge*.

He was almost as tall as Chewbacca, and twice as broad across his bare chest and shoulders. He wore spacer's pants, stretched drumhead tight across thighs as big around as Han's waist. His skin was dark as timmo-sun, his hairless scalp shone as if it had been polished, and when he smiled, his teeth looked jagged and sharp enough to make a Barabel jealous.

The huge dark man spread his hands wide and welcoming. He wasn't so much growling now as making a kind of whirring sound, like a cloud of flying insects.

"He says *Here's your light. What now? Will you shoot me with your empty blaster?*"

Han said, "You mean *this* empty blaster?" and shot him.

The stun blast burst across the huge man's chest, and he swayed but didn't fall, so Han shot him again. And once more for good measure, because it was his last shot and he didn't have anything better to do with it.

"Guess you never heard of the Smuggler's Click, huh?" Han smiled at him. "Sure did *sound* like I was trying to fire an empty blaster, didn't it?"

Han stopped smiling when he realized the huge man was smiling back.

The stun blasts didn't seem to have affected him at all—though Han discovered to his astonishment that the man was standing ankle-deep in a puddle of liquefied stone.

Before Han could make sense of what he saw, the man had leapt across the floor and seized Han by the throat with one enormous hand and lifted him effortlessly into the air. Han smacked him across the face with his empty blaster hard enough to lay open one cheek to the bone, but the huge man didn't seem to notice; he only cupped Han's chin with his other hand and began to push his head back, and back, while pulling with the hand that wrapped Han's neck and growling.

Cartilage crackled and something popped in his cervical vertebrae, and the only sound Han could make was a thin gargling rasp. He was starting to seriously wonder if maybe Leia'd had the right idea with her *don't antagonize him* thing, until she shouted something that sounded, blurred and vague through the roaring in his ears, like *Stop! If he dies so do I!,* which Han thought was a pretty darn silly threat to make, since both of them dying appeared to be the point of this whole exercise—but to his foggily half-conscious astonishment, the pressure on his neck slackened and the roar in his ears faded as blood began to circulate again.

"Let him go." Leia stood with the empty hold-out's emitter jammed up under her own chin and her finger on the trigger. "I mean it."

The huge hand opened, and Han sagged to the floor, gasping. The man stood with hands once again open and spread. Leia said, "Now back away from him. Slowly."

The huge man took a step back, but only one.

"Keep going."

The man dropped to one knee and slowly lowered his right hand to the floor, and in the instant his palm touched the luminescent lichen, the entire cavern went dark.

Han felt an inhumanly swift *rush* pass by him; he kicked blindly in the darkness but missed. All he could do was croak, "Leia, look out!"

"Han—" Whatever she'd hoped to say was smothered to snorts and gasping; then there were only muffled sounds of struggle. Han scrambled to his feet in the darkness and lunged toward the noise. Something hit him across the legs and he fell—

And the floor he fell on *splashed*.

This can't be good, he thought. He managed to make it to his hands and knees . . . and the gooey floor hardened again, becoming stone that clamped solid around feet, calves, knees, and hands, and over his wrists to halfway up his forearms. "Let me go! Let me go, you *freak*! Don't touch her. *Don't you dare touch her! Leia!*"

The darkness gave back only empty echoes.

He knelt there, panting in pain and desperation. He tried to yank his hands free. He tried until his elbows creaked and his arms cramped. He couldn't even wiggle his fingers. His toes he could wiggle—inside his boots—but his legs were entombed even more securely than his hands.

There was nothing he could do. Nothing at all.

And Leia was in the hands of the giant. Who was he? Han couldn't guess. He couldn't make any of this make sense.

And he was probably going to die without ever figuring it out.

Trust in the Force, she'd said. Well, if the Force had any plans to give him the occasional hand, he couldn't think of a better time than right now.

"So?" he said out loud. "You there? Can you spare a little luck for your last Jedi's best friend?"

From his vest pocket came a burst of static, and then a voice. *"Han? Han, do you read? Han, come in! It's Luke!"*

Which would have been a real stroke of luck, practically an outright miracle, the kind of thing that would have made him a believer forever . . . if it weren't for the fact that both his hands were encased in stone, so there was no way to fish the comlink out of his pocket and respond.

Han decided that the Force, if it actually did exist and work the way Luke and Leia always claimed it did, had a really, really nasty sense of humor.

THE *FALCON* ROCKETED THROUGH THE MAZE OF CAVerns at incredible speed—speed that to Nick felt even faster owing to the tightening ridges of rock that threatened to take his head off, if not the entire turret, and the jagged outcroppings the ship had to dodge, and the constant bang and groan and screech of metal slamming into or rasping over stone—and behind it, the smaller, more nimble TIEs just kept coming. Only the twists and turns of the cavern maze sheltered them from the TIEs' cannon fire; through the rare straightaways where the starfighters might have a shot, Nick pounded fire back into them from the dorsal turret. At close range and with no room to maneuver, no chance to even change the angle of their approach, TIE after TIE got an eyeballful of laser bolts and crashed or exploded.

His line about the Perthrillian nightwasp's wings had been a boast—but it hadn't been an *empty* boast.

Nick just kept shooting and tried not to think about the blur of rocky walls whipping past his turret so close that if he could open a window he could touch them . . . at the risk of having his arm torn off. "I hope you know where you're going!"

"Just feeling my way." Skywalker sounded almost cheerful. *"How are we doing back there?"*

Nick scowled at the twists and turns and sideways openings that so swiftly receded into the absolute darkness behind. "We're in pretty good shape as long as they don't come up with a way to shoot around corners!"

Then out of the darkness a matched pair of shining blue-white globes of energy swung into view and streaked straight toward him. "Spoke too soon." He hauled on the turret yoke and tried to bring his guns to bear on those hurtling globes as they whipped through high-g pursuit arcs. "Torpedoes inbound. Looks like those bombers have caught up with us."

"Target the torps."

"Way ahead of you," he said through his teeth as his line of laser bolts intersected the flight path of the nearer torpedo, but the other one shot through the blast and kept on coming. Nick, cursing the turret's glacial traverse—"I'd be better off throwing *rocks*!"—finally brought the guns into line and intercepted the torpedo only a couple of dozen meters short of the *Falcon*'s sublights. "That was too close! Can you route control of the other turret through this one?"

"The other turret's busy right now," Skywalker said, as the ventral quad opened up and cannon bolts shot through the darkness to blast a narrow opening ahead.

The *Falcon* hit the not-quite-big-enough gap with the velocity of a point-blank bowcaster bolt. With a grinding *whannng!* and an impact that just about bounced Nick's head through the transparisteel, the ship crashed through. *"That was a little tight. I think we lost something."*

"Looks like the sensor dish," Nick said, watching it tumble past him and vanish into the darkness behind.

"Oh, great. Han's still teasing Lando about losing his last dish inside the second Death Star. I'll never hear the end of this."

"You'll never hear the *start* of it if we don't get out of here!" Nick said as four more hurtling blue stars swung into view, far back but coming on so fast they swelled from pinpricks to borgleballs in no more time than it took him to mutter, *"Four?* How am I supposed to take out *four*?"

He trained the quad cannons on the roof of the cavern

just behind the ship and held down the triggers, filling the tunnel behind with clouds of smoke and dust—which weren't any impediment for the oncoming torpedoes—as well as a whole lot of chunks of falling rock. Which were.

The first torpedo clipped a falling boulder and glanced upward into the ceiling; its explosion brought down a curtain of cave-in that caught the other three torps in quick succession, close enough behind that the ship's exterior floodlamps clearly illuminated the wall of tumbled and jumped stone that sealed the tunnel from top to bottom.

"Good luck finding a way to get bombers around *that*," he muttered, feeling really pretty pleased with himself, until he realized he could *still* see the cave-in. That it wasn't getting any farther away. "Hey, why are we stopped?"

"*Look forward.*"

Nick swiveled the turret. He said, "Oh."

They'd run out of tunnel. Ahead was only a blank wall of stone. And behind, he'd just managed take the only way out and seal it up tighter than a Hrthgingian firegem vault.

"Um . . ." he said slowly. "Don't back up."

In the cockpit, Luke stared at the stone ahead in grim frustration. He'd been *sure* they were going the right way. Sure in the way he felt sure when the Force was telling him just how sure he should really feel. "I don't get it," he said, shaking his head. He turned to Aeona, who was strapped into the copilot couch. "This is wrong. This shouldn't be here."

"Don't waste time worrying about what *should* be. Worry about what *is*."

Luke decided not to tell her she sounded like Yoda.

She looked drawn, and there was a haunted edge in her voice. "Worry about finding a way *out* of here."

He gave her a sympathetic look. "Claustrophobic?"

"Just a little," she said with a reluctant nod. "But enough."

"Me, too. Especially today. Don't worry. The first thing you do when you're lost is stop somewhere and ask for directions." He keyed the comm system and entered Leia's comlink code. "Leia? Leia, please respond. It's Luke."

No response. Not even static. "Leia, come in."

"You can forget about that," Aeona said. She waved a hand at the rock wall outside. "See the opalescence in that black stone, how it kind of shimmers? Looks like this whole cavern runs through a vein of meltmassif—that's a kind of rock that—"

"I know what it is." Luke flexed his hands; he could feel that shadowy echo of his nervous system—those tiny thin hairlines of crystal that spread throughout his body. "What's it got to do with communications?"

"It blocks comm frequencies," she said. "You'd need the comm suite of a capital ship to even have a chance of punching through."

"Oh, is that all?" Luke found himself wearing a half smile very much like the one he imagined he'd be seeing on Han's face right about now. He began toggling switches and striking keys. "Give me a minute, here."

"I'm telling you it won't help."

"This ship was the personal vehicle of a commanding general in the Alliance of Free Planets." He completed the sequence, and a hatch opened in the rear bulkhead to display an enormous state-of-the-art comm unit. "He resigned his commission, but Han's just not the type to give back upgrades, you know? This unit can punch a signal all the way to the galactic rim. It'll draw most of the power from the reactor core, but we're not going anywhere anyway." He looked up at the comm unit. "Leia? Are you there?"

Still no response. Luke frowned and clicked over to Han's setting. "Han? Han, do you read? Han, come in! It's Luke!"

The comm channel sputtered. *"General Skywalker! We heard you're in a bit of trouble."*

Luke frowned. "Lando? What are *you* doing in this system?"

"Asking myself that same question about sixty times an hour. What's your position?"

"I'm not sure. Underground somewhere. I'm trying to find Leia—I could feel her in the Force near here, but I can't anymore."

"We lost contact with Han and Leia only a few minutes ago. Han said something about being in a cave. That's why we're monitoring his comlink setting. Listen, you're not the only ones in trouble here. We could lose the whole task force."

"We'll lose more than that," Luke muttered.

"Sorry? Didn't copy that. Can you repeat?"

"No. Never mind."

"Luke, I'm doing the best I can, but we really need you in this fight. How soon can you resume command?"

"I—can't. It'll take too long to explain. You run the battle, Lando. You're a better general than I'll ever be, anyway."

"Couldn't prove it by today. Keep me apprised; you just say the word and command is yours. Listen, there's someone here who wants to speak with you."

"Oh, oh, Master Luke! Oh, thank goodness you're all right!"

"All right is a bit of an overstatement," Luke said. "But it's good to hear your voice, Threepio."

"Oh, Master Luke, I'm most concerned! The Princess and Captain Solo are in terrible danger—and so are you!"

"I know," Luke said. "But how do *you* know?"

"*I have been monitoring the communications of their attackers—despite their perfectly barbarous diction. I am fluent in over—*"

"You've told me before. What attackers? Where are they?"

"*Please hurry, Master Luke—Artoo may have already been destroyed!*"

"Threepio, tell me where they are!"

"*Quite nearby, actually—no more than fifteen meters away, directly outward along the planetary radius.*"

"They're right *above* us?"

"*Oh, yes. Their attackers have located you precisely—they've been discussing whether to, ah—the phrase translates roughly as imprison, or sequester, but it's clearly some form of attack—whether to attack you now, or if they should pursue the Half-One, whoever that may be.*"

Luke was no longer listening; he frowned dubiously up at the ceiling of smooth black stone above the cockpit. "Fifteen meters—that's an awful lot of rock to cut through, even with a lightsaber."

"That's not ordinary rock," Aeona said. "It's melt-massif."

"I don't know what that means."

"Then your friends are lucky I'm around, because I *do*. Which is something I hope you'll explain to them when we find them, because I have a feeling they might be a little cranky with me."

She reached over to the antipersonnel system and triggered the hull chargers. "Take it up," she said. "Nice and slow."

"Oh," Luke said, understanding as the stun charge crackled over the *Falcon*'s skin. "I would have figured that out. Eventually."

"Sure, I know," she said sympathetically. "You've had kind of a tough day."

"That's one way to put it." The ship rose to touch the meltmassif overhead. The stone instantly liquefied, sluicing down over the hull armor to pool in the small closed-off section of tunnel below. "How long does this stuff take to reharden?"

"I'm not sure. Why?"

"TIE fighters don't have antipersonnel systems, and laser cannons can't be set for stun."

She nodded thoughtfully. "So we don't have to worry a lot about unwelcome company. How much farther?"

Luke searched the Force. "Right . . . about . . . here."

The *Falcon* breached the surface of the now-liquid stone like an Aquarian demonsquid hunting a leaping gnooroop. Rivers of meltmassif drained off the hull, as well as off and around a filthy human who clung fiercely to the only part of the ship that wasn't sparking with several thousand volts of stun charge: the cockpit window.

Luke . . . Though inaudible, the words were clear on Han's lips. *He took her, Luke. She's gone.*

CRONAL PAUSED IN THE ARCHWAY OF THE CAVERN OF the Shadow Throne. His Throne still hovered on its platform of meltmassif, all dark and sinister in the bloody glow of the lava-fall behind it. Looking upon the cavern through Kar Vastor's eyes, he felt a bit melancholy; it truly was a pity that his magnificently staged reality holodrama would never reach the broad audience it deserved.

But such were the vicissitudes of life and art; rather than mourning his spoiled masterpiece, he resolved to focus entirely upon the truly important task of permanently securing a new and healthy body. Not to mention killing everyone who might know, or even suspect, that this young and lovely girl was in fact an old and ugly man.

He shifted the unconscious Skywalker girl from the massive shoulder of his stolen body and set her gently down.

He could not help taking a moment to contemplate her, as she lay upon the stone, lovely and graceful even in unconsciousness. He could not help recalling how he had watched her, through his years in Imperial Intelligence; he'd monitored her anti-Imperial activities for a considerable span prior to her open break and alleged treason at the time of the Alderaan affair. *Young Senator Organa,* he mused. *Princess Leia* Skywalker, *hiding in plain sight for all those years. Who'd have thought it?*

She was a superior choice to her brother in almost every way. After all, she was no Jedi; in her body, no one would expect him to go gallivanting across the galaxy, risking his life to save strangers. No, after the traumatic experience of surviving the Imperial trap that had taken the lives of her brother, her raffish paramour, and so many of her friends and allies, she would reluctantly retire from her life of adventure and devote herself full-time to politics.

She was *perfect.*

He closed his eyes and let his mind slip partially back into the ancient decrepit body that lay in its life-support chamber. From within that skull, he could send forth his mind into the rock from which the cavern had been shaped, and seize once more the wills of the creatures that used it as their physical forms.

The bridge that had connected the cavern's ledge to the Throne grew once more, carrying the Skywalker girl and Kar Vastor's bulk out to the platform of the Shadow Throne before once more shrinking away. The stone of the platform itself rippled and spread and curved upward to entomb the unconscious girl and the immobile man in a seamless rocky shell that hovered far out above the lake of molten lava.

Cronal decided that this should very likely be sufficient to prevent unwelcome interruption.

Now all that remained was to ensure that his new body would not be consumed in the stellar conflagration that was already beginning. A palsied hand groped through the darkness to the chamber's voice modulator, which would transform his creaky wheeze into Shadowspawn's liquid basso, then he keyed a preset secure comm channel.

"Yes, my lord? Is it time?"

"It is," Cronal said simply. "Engage."

Then again he closed his eyes and returned his consciousness to the Vastor body. He didn't bother to open that stolen body's stolen eyes, for within the tomb of stone was only darkness. He had no need for eyes.

He tuned his stolen brain to the proper frequency for control and *pushed,* and the stone of their tomb responded. Ultrafine hairlines of crystal began to thread themselves in through the Skywalker girl's pores, and in with the crystals came the full power of his will.

Sleep. This is the end of everything. Nothing left but sleep.

Sleep forever.

AS SOON AS THE CAVERN FLOOR HAD REHARDENED enough to support the *Falcon*'s weight, Luke set her down and lowered the freight lift in the engineering bay. He unstrapped himself from the pilot's couch and got up. "Come with me."

Aeona stared out through the cockpit's transparisteel. "I—can't. I can't go out there."

"Yes, you can."

"No—no, I mean it, Jedi. You don't know what this place is."

"Then tell me."

"It's a Melter crypt." She wiped the back of her hand

across her mouth. "Melters are—I don't know what they are. You heard your friend on the comm. The *attackers* he was talking about, they have to be Melters. They . . . just come out of the walls. Or up from the ground. Anywhere there's meltmassif. If they touch you it's like a stun blast. Then they carry you to a crypt and stick you into the rock."

She looked at Luke with haunted eyes. "And they *leave you there.*"

Luke nodded out toward the people partially entombed around the walls and in the floor. "So I see."

"I've been marooned on this planet for *weeks*, trying to get Nick back. That's why I'm hooked up with the Mindorese. They needed a leader. I needed troops. But the Melters . . ." She shook her head. "They'd hit us without any warning at all. Sometimes we could hold 'em off long enough to get away . . . sometimes people got left behind. We found a few. A couple were even still alive. But they were never the same. Not after their time in the dark."

"I can imagine."

"Can you imagine being *trapped* like that? Alone in the dark? Darker than dark. Darker than empty space."

"Yes," Luke said. "I can."

"That's how I got a little claustrophobic, you know? There's *nothing* darker than the inside of a cave."

Luke could have told her different. "If you say so."

"So you understand why I can't go out into a Melter crypt."

"I understand why you don't want to. But you're going anyway."

"What, you're going to make me?"

Luke tilted his head. "It's the only way I can think of to stop Han from killing you on sight."

Her hand drifted near her tied-down holster. "I'm not so easy to kill."

"You don't understand. Han's my best friend." Luke said gently. "If one of you has to die, it'll be you."

Aeona said, "Uh."

"I want you to be absolutely clear on this. There should be no doubt in your mind. None at all."

"No," she said. "I read you. I do."

"Then let's go."

They took the main corridor aft, avoiding the cargo holds that were still filled with Aeona's troopers. When they got to the engineering bay, Luke motioned to Aeona to wait at the hatch while he went in. Han, arms and legs caked with shards of hardened meltmassif, was already standing on the freight lift, jittering with impatience. "Luke! Come on, we have to go! We have to go after her. Bring me up!"

Luke sighed. "You didn't see who was with me in the cockpit."

"There was somebody with you? How did you get the *Falcon* back from those pirates? Please tell me you killed them all. Especially that redheaded piece of—"

"Not exactly." He beckoned to Aeona. "She's here to apologize."

Her face darkened. *"Apologize?"* she snapped. "You didn't say anything about—"

"I'm saying it now."

Han jumped back, his hand full of blaster and his face full of murder. "You! You stole my *ship*!"

She ducked and took cover on the far side of the hatchway. "Brought it back, didn't I?"

"Han. Put your blaster away." Maybe being a general for a few months was paying off; Luke's tone of authority stopped Han cold. "I mean it."

"Ah, whatever," Han said with a disgusted shrug. He spun the blaster around his finger. "It's empty anyway."

Luke nodded. "Aeona?"

She reluctantly came back through the hatch. "Uh, hey, Solo. Sorry. Really."

"Sorry?" Han flushed. *"Sorry?"*

"Hey, what do you want from me? He said apologize. I'm apologizing."

"Aeona," Luke said quietly. "Tell him why you did it."

"Huh? What does that have to do with anything?"

"It might make a difference. To him."

She sighed. "I needed your ship, Solo. My—uh, there's this guy, and we're kind of together—"

Han's eyes narrowed, and his lips compressed. "You're in love with this guy, and he's in trouble."

"Actually, he's in your quad turret."

Han waved this off. "But you're in love with him."

She looked away. "I figured this assault would be my only chance to get him back alive. I couldn't even make a try without a ship, and I just didn't have time to play nice about it, okay?"

"You could have *asked,*" Han growled.

"And if you said no, we'd still have had to fight you— and fight you without having the drop on you. Which, from what I've heard about you, isn't exactly a good idea."

Han's flush deepened. "Well . . ."

"Easier to get forgiveness than permission, right? Isn't that how *you* do it when someone you love is in danger? I seem to recall a couple stories . . ."

"All right, all right," he said. "Drop it."

"I'm not asking you two to like each other," Luke said. "But you have to at least *tolerate* each other. Any problems between you will have to wait until we all live through this. Understood?"

"Wow," Han said. "Who put *you* in charge?"

Aeona snorted. "I asked him the same thing."

"Let me put it another way," Luke said patiently.

"Every second I have to waste worrying if you two will shoot each other is another second we're *not* using to rescue Leia and get us all off this planet and out of this system before the whole thing burns."

He jumped down to the lift platform. "Aeona, muster your Mindorese and start helping the survivors. Han, you look after Chewie. Make sure he doesn't kill anybody when he wakes up, huh?"

"Yeah, he's grumpy in the morning," Han said. "What are you gonna do now?"

"Me?"

Luke stared down at his left hand, the flesh one. He flexed it into a fist and straightened it again, feeling the unfamiliar energy that trickled through the crystalline shadow web that mirrored his nerves. He closed his eyes for a moment and breathed himself into a deeper, more intimate connection with the Force; with the Force to guide him, he touched the shadow web with his mind and bent it to his will. When he opened his eyes again, his hand had sprouted a thin thatch of glistening black crystal threads, finer than human hair.

Han flinched and made a face. "What is *that*?"

Luke moved off the freight lift and knelt, lowering his palm to the floor. "That," he said, "is how I'm going to talk with the Melters."

MAKING CONTACT WITH THE MELTERS WASN'T THE HARD part. Luke simply laid his left hand on the shimmering black stone of the crypt wall. His hand's sprouted thatch of shadow web melded instantly with the stone's crystalline structure . . .

And they were there. He could feel them.

It was an unfamiliar sensation, vaguely analogous to sight—he sensed them in the stone the way one human might see another from a distance.

Getting their attention wasn't hard, either. They became aware of him in the same instant that he perceived them—and they knew he perceived them. He sensed their instant curiosity and puzzlement, and felt the interchange of lightning-fast pulses of energy between them like a conversation in a language he could not understand.

The hard part was actually talking to them.

They sent tentative, questing pulses toward him in what could have been a cautious hello, and he felt his own shadow web respond, but not like an answer. More like an echo, or a harmonic overtone—as though the dark mirror of his nervous system was warping into some kind of resonance with their signal. To communicate with them, he would have to send his mind fully into the shadow web alongside his nerves, into his internal void that swallowed even the memory of light. He'd have to join them in the dark.

In the Dark.

To bring his consciousness into resonance with the Melters would require that he not only stare into that abyss, but dive into it headfirst. To drown himself in the void. To let the dark close over his face and seep into his ears and eyes and down his throat and entomb him in the empty, meaningless end of all things.

But—

The Melters were at the core of this. Everything came back to them somehow. Meltmassif was their body, or bodies, or the medium in which they lived; meltmassif was the active ingredient in the Pawn Crowns. It was the control crystals and the deadly interlock inside each Pawn's brain. It was the underlying structure of Blackhole's entire base. It was the shadow web that Blackhole had used to infect Luke with despair.

It was what he would use to steal Leia's body.

It was dark where they were. Not just dark, but Dark. And he was afraid.

Afraid that the Dark really *was* the truth. The only real truth. That everything else everyone pretended was important was only a deception, a distraction, a game to keep your mind off the eternal oblivion to come. He had spent aeons in the Dark and he knew its awful power.

Everything dies, it would whisper forever in his heart. *Even stars burn out.*

But if his nerve failed him now, he'd be leaving Leia in that Dark. Alone. Forever. The Dark would swallow her as if she'd never existed. What chance would she have to escape? She wasn't even a Jedi. How would she find light?

Because that's what Jedi do, isn't it? Luke thought. *That's what we're for.*

We're the ones who bring the light.

So he gathered his courage and focused his mind to open a channel into the Force, because if he was going to dive into the absolute negation of light, he'd better bring along some of his own.

He allowed his consciousness to touch the event horizon of the shadow web's black hole, and let himself slip across the threshold and fall forever into the Dark.

NICK KEPT GRIMACING AS HE SHED THE SHADOWSPAWN robe and tried to stuff his aching body into a spare flight suit. Aeona watched him, wincing in sympathy at each grimace. "Hey, are you hurt?"

"Huh?"

"You look like you're in pain. Do you need bacta?"

"Depends," Nick said. "Can bacta cure a bad case of Too Old for This Crud?"

"Awww." She slipped an arm around his shoulders. "You're just a kid."

"Yeah. A kid who's spent a few days getting clubbed by a pack of drunken Gamorreans."

She nodded fractionally toward where Skywalker

knelt, his left hand half-buried in the stone. "When are you going to tell him?" she said softly.

"Tell him what?"

"About Kar," she said. "You heard what Solo said about the man who took Princess Kissy-Face. It was Kar. It had to be."

Nick frowned. "It wasn't Kar. It was Blackhole."

"Using Kar's body."

Nick looked away. "Yeah."

"I wouldn't put even a Jedi up against Kar."

"Me, neither," Nick said. "If I had a choice."

"So?"

"So I'm trying to figure my play," he said. "Telling the truth might be the wrong move here. Skywalker—he's not like his dad. Kindhearted, you know? If I let him know Kar's another one of Blackhole's victims, he might hold back. Going in soft against Kar will just get him killed."

"Again: So? Is he one of our favorite people?"

Nick looked her in the eye. "He's saved both our lives two or three times already, and we haven't known him three hours. You think the galaxy will be a better place without him in it?"

Aeona shook her head, just a bit, then nodded over at the kneeling young Jedi. "Okay, sure. He's a great guy. But Kar's your *family*. He's the closest thing to family you've got left."

"Yeah. But Kar is—well, you know him. He's not exactly a good guy."

"Neither are you."

Nick nodded. "And if I could get Anakin Skywalker's children out of here alive? Even one of them? That's worth Kar's life. Mine, too."

"Not to me it isn't. And I bet not to little Jedi Pretty-Boy, either."

"That's why I'm not leaving it up to him."

"Oh, sure, you're doing him a big favor: making him kill an innocent man."

"Kar? Innocent? You're kidding, right?"

"If Skywalker was gonna kill him for Haruun Kal, or Kessel, or Nar Shadaa, I could see it. I wouldn't lift a finger to save him. But Kar's not the villain here. He's a victim."

"That doesn't matter to me."

"If you say so." Aeona gave him a skeptical look. "But any stakes you care to wager, three to one says it'll matter to Skywalker."

HIS SENSES WERE USELESS HERE IN THE DARK.

Here was no sight, no sound, no touch, no awareness of his body. He had only an inchoate awareness of being part of some kind of indefinable field of energy—or perhaps he *was* the indefinable field of energy. The only perception he could summon beyond simple awareness of his own existence was of certain modulations in this energy field: unreceivable signals, untouchable textures, unseeable colors. Irretrievably alien. Cold and ancient lives that had never experienced the beat of a heart, the touch of a hand, the taste of air. Impossibly distant, unreachable, born of vanished stars.

Stars, he thought. *Yes. That's it: stars. That's where they come from. That's where we meet. Because that's what I am, too.*

Everything in the universe is born of dying stars. Every element is created in the fusion furnace of stellar cores. Every atom that exists was once part of some long-vanished star—and that star was part of others before it, an unbroken chain of ancestry back to the single cosmic fireball that had been the birth of the universe.

It is the death of stars that gives the universe life.

With the idea of stars on which to hang his imagination, he could bring his situation into a kind of focus. Instead of a formless field of barely perceptible energy, he visualized himself as part of a stellar cluster, vast and dim; those alien modulations of energy became distant stars.

Though every true star is functionally the same—a fusion furnace in space—each is also an individual. One may be larger, another hotter; one may be nearing the end of its life cycle, collapsing in upon itself or expanding to destruction, while another might be freshly forming by aggregating the dust and gases of ancient supernovae. In Luke's imagination, he could read their individual spectra the way he might recognize a human face: they looked tired, and old, and far apart, burning themselves out in the endless Dark.

But he, too, was a star, and the light that shone from him was the Force.

Each and every distant star on which he fixed his attention, however dim it was, instantly brightened as his light fed its own. They drew near, attracted by his energy, captured by his gravitational field, growing ever brighter as they approached, burning hotter, giving off bursts of exotic particles like gusts of delighted laughter. They fell into orbit around him, becoming a new system of infinite complexity wheeling through the Dark in joyous dance.

Here we are, in the Dark, he thought. *And it's not empty. It's not meaningless. Not with us all here.*

It's beautiful.

And each one he had touched with the Force remained linked to him by pulsing threads of light as they basked gratefully in its power; they had been trapped in this freezing Dark for so long, their only light coming from the burning away of themselves and their kin, forever fading until one by one they would wink from existence . . .

With that, Luke discovered that he knew them now.

Not as though they had told him about themselves; not as though there was any communication at all. Luke didn't need to be told. He was part of them now, joined to them by the Force. He knew their lives as if they were his own, because in the light of the Force he *was* those lives, and they were him.

He knew them as they knew themselves: a corporate entity that was also an array of individuals, nodes of consciousness in a larger network of mind. They had—been born? been created? altered? evolved?—first become aware of themselves (themself?) as alive on Mindor's rocky, airless sister planet, which Luke knew only as Taspan II; they had no name for the planet that Luke could comprehend. There they had lived for untold millennia, basking in Taspan's unfiltered glare, in fear of nothing save the changes that could be wrought in the meltmassif that was their home by radiation from Taspan's occasional starspots and stellar storms.

They did not have any comprehension of the cause of the Big Crush; the Imperial weapons research facility on Taspan II had been entirely outside their concern. In those days, they hadn't even known what humans were; they'd never had experience of noncrystal-based lifeforms. The Big Crush itself had been no disaster for them; on the contrary, the planet's destruction had simply scattered its crust into a vast cloud, with orders of magnitude more surface area to absorb the energy of the star. For the Melters, the Big Crush had been an all-too-brief Golden Age; their culture/mind had blossomed throughout the system, celebrating their accession to Paradise.

For these particular Melters, the Golden Age of Paradise had come to an abrupt and catastrophic end, as the chunks of their shattered home planet had drifted across the orbit of Mindor. Captured by its gravity, they had fallen to its surface in each and every rock storm, and soon found that their new home was less a home than a prison. An oubliette.

A cosmic extermination camp.

Many, many individual Melters had been lost as their rocks had burned away in the atmosphere, and the radiation-absorbing qualities of the vaporized meltmassif screened the survivors from Taspan's life-giving rays. The survivors were slowly dying of energy asphyxiation.

They were drowning in the Dark.

Each rockfall brought new Melters into Mindor's lethal gloom, and every meteor that burned away deepened the shadow that was killing them.

That shadow also cut them off from the rest of the Melter community out among the asteroids; they simply did not have the power to drive a signal very far into the planet's atmosphere. All they could do was wait, struggling to survive, and try to comfort the new victims falling into this planetary prison every day.

Comfort was what the Melters had originally sought from humans, as well; the human nervous system produced a tiny trickle of energy in the general wavelength of the Meltermind, which drew Melters to humans the way a glow rod attracted cave moths.

Cave moths, Luke thought. Perhaps that was what had happened to him at the cave . . . something in the meltmassif had been stealing light from inside him . . .

When these organic life-forms, these tiny flickering candle flames of warmth and light in the permanent midnight that was Mindor, had started shooting Melters with stun blasts that randomized the microcrystalline structure of meltmassif, the Melters had begun sequestering them in self-defense. There had never been malice in their attacks at all; they didn't even understand that their captives were dying—they were unclear on the whole concept of organic death. It wasn't murder, or war, or even violence, because they really didn't comprehend any of those concepts, either. Their campaign against humanity had been, to them, merely pest control.

As all this information filtered through his consciousness, Luke at last became aware that the stellar cluster of which he was the center was itself moving, rolling through the Dark as though in orbit around some vastly more massive gravity source, something so huge and dark that it could be seen only by its effect on the stars of the Melters in his cluster. One by one they were peeled from his cluster, stripped away to spiral into decaying orbits around the inescapable void until one by one they flared with a last brief burst of light as they slipped over some invisible event horizon and vanished forever.

An event horizon of the Dark, consuming the last of the light in his universe . . .

Oh, he thought. *I get it. It's a black hole.*

Some kind of metaphor for how Blackhole—how appropriate that old code name seemed now—was controlling the Melters, he figured; Blackhole must be luring them down somehow, cutting them off from each other so their only source of light was what he chose to feed them . . .

Even thinking about it seemed to increase the imaginary black hole's gravity gradient; he found himself drifting closer and closer to the event horizon, gathering speed as his spiral orbit tightened, more and more of the stars around him falling away, some to vanish into the black hole's insatiable maw, others breaking free into higher orbits until he was entirely alone, no star left between him and the black hole . . .

Except one.

One star like none of the others still swung through an orbit lower than his: a blue-white supergiant, far larger, far brighter than any his imagination had so far produced. This one did not feed upon his Force light, but shone with its own, as brilliant and powerful as his. It fell in a tightening tide-locked gyre down the black hole's gravity well, and as it fell the relentless pull of the void was stripping a huge jet of energy and mass from it, a fountain of star-stuff ripped from its heart and sucked down across the event horizon to vanish forever in dark beyond the Dark.

And he knew this star was Leia.

He reached out to her, but there was nothing to grasp, nor any hand to grasp it; he'd had some crazy half-formed idea to grab her and slingshot around the black hole and out again, because he'd half forgotten that this was only a vision after all, only a metaphor, and if he tried to stretch it into reality it would shatter. So instead he brought his light to bear, focusing a beam of the Force upon his sister star.

Leia, hang on, he tried to send. *Don't give in to the Dark. I'm coming for you. Hang on.*

He felt no response, only overwhelming sadness and crushing despair and that empty, lost meaninglessness at the end of the universe, and he couldn't even tell if this came from her or from himself. He tried to focus the Force on her, to make his beam of light a conduit for strength that might save her, even as the tiny crack of light he'd found in one imaginary pebble had saved him—but somehow his light could not add to hers. He burned a different color, but no more brightly.

He remembered too well that terrible void, the endless *lack* that was deeper than any darkness. If only there were some way he could show her that all the light she'd ever need shone from her own self . . . but that was only a metaphor.

Wasn't it?

What Ben and Yoda had called the dark side wasn't *actually* dark; it had nothing at all to do with the visual spectrum. The phrase *dark side of the Force* was just an expression. An evocative shorthand to express a broad range of negative characteristics.

A metaphor.

They could have called it *the evil side,* or *the death-and-destruction side,* or *the enslaving-the-whole-galaxy side.* But they didn't.

They called it the dark side. But they'd never seen dark like this. Or had they?

Maybe they *had* been here, at the end of all things— or at least glimpsed it. Maybe they had seen the truth of the Dark. Maybe that's why they never talked about a "light side." Because there wasn't one.

But, Luke thought, gazing upon the brilliant blaze that was his sister, *just because there's no "light side" doesn't mean there's no light.*

He had thought he was bringing light with him into the darkness, by holding on to the Force. Now he saw that the Force's light didn't shine on him. It shone *through* him.

He *was* the light in the darkness.

He saw it now, and it made sense to him at last. That same light shone through Leia, and as soon as he understood that, he began to sense other lights, pinprick stars far out in the dark. Some of them he recognized: Han, and Lando . . . Wedge and Tycho, Hobbie and Wes and the rest of the Rogues . . . Nick, and Aeona Cantor, Lieutenant Tubrimi and Captain Tirossk and so many, many others, sailors and marines, even the impossibly distant spray of vanishingly faint stars that must have been the stormtroopers, for even they were lights in the darkness. All of them were stars.

And every star, every life, was a thing of beauty.

And Leia couldn't see them. She couldn't even look their way, not anymore. Her star was tide-locked to the black hole—its gravity would not allow her to turn her face away. He couldn't even get her attention.

And the black hole was *aware* of him now; the abyss he'd stared into was now staring into him. He felt its emptiness that nothing could fill, its bleak hunger that could never be satisfied. In his mind, it swelled toward him like jaws opening to swallow the universe, capturing every scrap of light and hope and love that Luke could channel from the Force. The longer he stared, the more he lost, and nothing he could do would help Leia at all.

Once that maw closed around her, she would be lost to the Dark forever.

All right, he thought. *I guess I'll have to do this the old-fashioned way.*

He opened his eyes. Han was crouched at his side, his face dark with fear. "Hey, buddy—you all right?"

Luke said, "No."

Han's mouth drew into a flat line. "And Leia?"

"She's alive."

"And?"

Luke let the shadow in his heart show in his eyes. That was all the answer Han needed. "Okay, then," he said with a grim nod. "What now?"

Luke stood. "Nick," he said.

Near one of the *Falcon*'s landing skids, Nick gave a guilty start. "Uh, yeah?"

"Who is Kar, and what is it you don't want me to know about him?"

Nick's jaw dropped. "You—how did you—I mean, what?"

Luke's expression never flickered. He waited.

"Oh." Nick lifted a hand to the band of scar around his temples. "I get it," he sighed. "What do you want to know?"

"Everything you can tell me in five minutes or less,"

Luke said, "because that's about all the time we have to win this fight."

WITHIN A SECOND AFTER CRONAL HAD GIVEN THE ORDER to engage, the stormtrooper who had received that order triggered a relay that initiated a preprogrammed series of instructions to the crews tending an array of gravity stations buried deep below the surface of Mindor. No one beyond the troopers actually posted to them even knew these gravity stations existed. Arranged in a broad ring around the Shadow Base, they were substantially different from those out among the asteroids—both in technology and function. Rather than the fairly standard gravity wells projected by the stations out in the system, these buried stations generated a phenomenon much more along the lines of the gravity slice that had destroyed the *Justice;* the technology involved, like that of the gravity slice, was the product of the Imperial weapons-development facility on Mindor's sister planet, the one that had been destroyed in the Big Crush.

In fact, the phenomenon produced by these buried stations was precisely what had *caused* the Big Crush.

The stations powered up. Planes of invisible energy spidered through the rock between them, beneath the vast volcanic dome of the Shadow Base; where these planes intersected, they produced lines of gravitational gradient on the order of small black holes, instantly consuming the rock they touched and producing a titanic blast of extremely hard radiation that flashed the surrounding rock into superheated plasma. This released more radiation to vaporize more rock, in a growing cascade that soon sliced through the surface of the planet above in a ring around the base.

To the troopers who crewed the ring of ground-defense turbolaser towers, this was instantly lethal; the radiation flarewall came out of the ground at a shallow angle that touched the towers and vaporized them in a fraction of a second. The Republic marines and trooper infantry, dug in and fighting on the surface around the ion-turbo STOEs on the dome itself, had a second or two to look up into the blinding white that surrounded them before it melted their armor and burned every exposed soldier to fine black ash, while the empty crater left by the dome's departure filled almost instantly with molten lava that boiled over and spread over the ground on all sides, consuming everything that had survived the initial blast.

The only effects felt by Fenn Shysa and the Mandalorian mercenaries, grimly fighting room-to-room through the gravity-gun emplacement, was the sudden loss of comm channels and a deep rumbling vibration like a distant groundquake, followed by a subtle increase in perceived weight, as though every man had instantly gained a kilo or two.

To the pilots of Rogue Squadron, dogfighting over the base, it looked like the entire volcanic dome had been cupped in a huge bowl of impossibly bright light that swiftly darkened as the ionizing radiation ignited the atmosphere in a firestorm that sucked sand and dust and rock upward to mask its glare. The next thing they noticed was the shrieking of cockpit radiation alarms—and that the radiation seemed to have cooked their positional sensors: Though the sensors insisted that their starfighters were still high above the planet, their eyes told them they were falling swiftly toward the dome.

It was Wes Janson who first shouted the truth over the comm. "Wait, I get it! We're not falling toward the base—it's coming *up at us*!"

Characteristically, the most comprehensive grasp of the situation, as well as its most succinct analysis, belonged to Lando Calrissian. From the bridge of the *Remember Alderaan,* hovering with the rest of the task force in a sea of vast impact craters below the horizon, he watched the radiation flare and the mushroom clouds . . . and then watched the entire volcanic dome rise from the mushroom cloud and accelerate toward space.

He understood instinctively what was happening. The volcano itself was a solid mass of radiation-resistant stone; the base would be entirely impervious even to the gargantuan power of the stellar flares. All the bad guys would have to do was cruise away, beyond the perimeter of the gravity wells; then they could use the volcano itself as a radiation shield, to shelter whatever smaller craft they might want to use to flash away into hyperspace.

Using skills fine-tuned by a lifetime of living by his ability to instantly assess odds and opportunities, he reflected with part of his mind that it was actually a pretty nifty idea. He filed it away for future consideration; after all, there were a number of systems where intense stellar radiation made conventional ships too dangerous to use. But a flying shield, to provide cover for ships moving in and out?

There were some definite possibilities here.

Then another part of his brain—the part that ignored odds and opportunities to focus directly on threats to life and limb—reminded him that none of these "definite possibilities" would ever come to pass if his ship was destroyed along with the rest of the Rapid Response Task Force, which was an increasing likelihood, because the ion-turbo emplacements and that insanely dangerous gravity gun were on the upper curve of the dome, which meant they had just lifted off along with the rest of the base. Which meant that once the base achieved orbit, a simple half-barrel roll would aim those weapons back down at the surface of Mindor.

At anywhere on the planet's surface. Including the craters where the *Remember Alderaan* and the rest of the Rapid Response Task Force were currently hiding. A hiding place they could not leave, because to swing around to the sunside of the planet would expose the ships to the stellar flares and destroy them just as conclusively.

Lando's comprehensive grasp and succinct analysis of the situation required only four words.

"This," he said, "is a problem."

CHAPTER 16

WATCHING THE FLYING VOLCANO SLOWLY ROTATE AS IT rose into Mindor's night sky pricked beads of sweat across Lando's brow. The lieutenant at TacOps reported an estimated eighty seconds to the firing window for the nearside ion-turbo cannons, and only twenty seconds more for the full array, including the gravity gun. "Fenn," he muttered into his personal comlink, "give me some good news. I mean it."

When this request reached Fenn Shysa, the Protector commandant was lying flat behind the remnants of a blast-shattered wall within the gravity gun's infantry bunker, along with the mercenary commander and six commandos, all shrouded in smoke and covered in rock dust and all doing their best to impersonate several hundred bloodthirsty Mandalorians. This was for the benefit of two full companies of stormtrooper heavy infantry who were holding a pair of redoubts to either side of a blast door that looked like it could withstand a good-sized fusion bomb. The purpose of this impersonation was to distract the stormtroopers from the *actual* several hundred bloodthirsty Mandalorians, who were about to cut through a wall on the redoubt's flank. Any second now.

Or perhaps any minute now.

He hoped.

"There's nothing good to tell, Lando!" Fenn had to shout to hear himself over the whine of blasterfire and the rolling crashes of thermal dets and heavy weapons. He stuck his rifle up over the rubble and sprayed fire blindly into the smoke. "This place is armored like a Hutt's treasure vault—our breaching charges barely even leave scorch marks! Maybe your marines have something heavier?"

On the *Remember Alderaan*'s bridge, Lando rubbed his eyes; from what he'd seen, he didn't figure any marines had survived except the ones already fighting within the ion-turbo emplacements. He took a deep breath. "All right, Plan B."

He snapped out a series of orders that had his entire bridge crew staring at him blankly, mouths agape. "You heard me," he said. "Do it!"

The bridge officers jerked back to their panels. Lando turned to C-3P0. "What are you waiting for?"

"Me?" The droid pressed a hand to his chest. "What am *I* supposed to do?"

"This ship has Mon Cal systems. The interdiction ships are Corellian," Lando explained as patiently as he could manage. "They don't talk the same language."

"Well, of *course* they don't." C-3P0 gave a burst of static that sounded suspiciously like a contemptuous sniff. "I've never met a Corellian system that had *any* manners at *all*, whereas *Remember Alderaan*—despite her somewhat coarse sense of humor—is a system of *exceptional* refinement. Even elegance—"

"Yes, fine, whatever," Lando said. "Those Corellian ships also don't have the calculating power to pull this off—we need to give them access to *Alderaan*'s processor array."

"My goodness! That would require the services of—"

"The most capable and sophisticated protocol droid

ever constructed," Lando finished for him, with an encouraging smile. "Get to work."

C-3PO gasped. "General! Me? What a lovely thing to say! Really, I am *most* gratified—"

"Be gratified while you work." Lando turned away and again triggered his personal comlink. "Fenn, I need you to fall back."

There was silence for a second or two, then a grim, *"How far?"*

"All the way. When that gravity gun opens up, we'll hit back. Massively."

"Have you seen the armor on this place? It'll take you hours to pound through!"

"If we shoot the armor."

Another pause, then: *"I scan. Lando, don't wait for us."*

"Fenn—"

"We'll never make it. Do what you have to. Save the fleet."

"You don't understand what's about to happen—"

"We're Mandalorian. This is what we live for. This is how we die."

"*Stop* it! I *hate* that garbage!" Lando chewed the inside of his lower lip for a second or two, then took a deep breath to keep a grip on his courage. "TacOps: Are *Lancer, Paleo,* and *Unsung* reaching position?"

"Scan reports affirmative."

"When the Slash-Es hit their marks, execute at will."

THE TRANSPONDER ALERT IN WEDGE ANTILLES'S COCKPIT blared a warning: he was in the kill zone of friendly fire. A quick check of his short-range scan showed three converted Corellian freighters on approach through Mindor's shadow toward the flying volcano. Not far behind them, the four surviving Slash-Es were strung out in a curiously slanting sort of line. He couldn't guess what they were up to, and he didn't have time to figure it out; all three of the converted freighters were already swinging broadside and going into slow barrel rolls: an old navy trick to deliver maximum suppressing fire. Their main cannons had fire rates restricted by their ability to shed waste heat and recharge their capacitors; the barrel roll let them continuously bring fresh guns to bear while the recently fired guns were repowering.

Wedge triggered his general comm as he yanked his X-wing through a slewing arc that shot him away from the flying volcano. "Republic fighters: Break off and fall back! This is hot space. Repeat: We are in hot space!"

Starfighters scattered like roachrats surprised by sunlight. The *Lancer,* the *Paleo,* and the *Unsung* opened up with synchronized fire, blasting broadsides in precise sequence to maintain a near-constant rain of supercharged plasma on the ion-turbo cannons and the gravity gun. This was done less to inflict actual damage than to act as a particularly violent counterscan measure; radiation scatter from the ongoing barrage prevented the emplacements' targeting scanners from locking on.

Two of the ion-turbos had been successfully spiked by Republic marines; the other three opened up full-bore with counterbattery fire back along the vectors of the incoming blasts. Silent explosions lit up the flanks of the three Corellian ships; soon they were firing through clouds of their own vaporized hull armor. Then the central dome, over the gravity gun, dilated like the pupil of a vast, pale eye.

"Everybody hang on to something!" Captain Tirossk shouted over the comm, rather unnecessarily. *"Here it comes!"*

The gravity gun opened fire.

A sharp-eyed observer, looking in precisely the right place at precisely the right time, would have been able to actually *see* the flight of the gravity bombs. As they hurtled through the plasma storm created by the synchronized turbolaser blasts, their tiny event horizons swallowed all manner of highly charged particles that released a continuous stream of hard radiation as they fell out of the universe forever. That radiation in turn charged the plasma around it, creating instant blue-white flash-streaks straight as a laser.

The gravity gun unleashed such a blast every three seconds, spraying them all through a narrowly spiraling arc without any attempt to target specific ships. It didn't have to: even a near-miss could literally tear a ship apart.

Which was exactly what the spray of gravity bombs did to the *Unsung*.

The bridge crews of the *Lancer* and the *Paleo* could only watch helplessly as the *Unsung* was twisted and wrenched and finally ripped apart; though hundreds of kilometers separated each of these ships, the other two were also jolted by wave after wave of gravity shocks.

The breakup of the *Unsung* left a brief gap in the suppression fire. Alarms screamed as hostile target locks acquired the two remaining ships. "Prepare to increase fire rate fifty percent," Tirossk rasped. "Resynchronize with *Paleo*." When the fire-control coordinator protested that this risked burning out the turbolasers, Tirossk only shrugged. "They'll be burned out for sure when the ship blows up. Execute."

The spray of gravity bombs streaked on, and more came in their wake. They hurtled toward the cluster of capital ships still huddled helplessly in Mindor's shadow: ships without shields, with no armor or weapon that could protect them.

Ships whose only defense was the ingenuity of General Lando Calrissian.

The lead ship in the array of Slash-Es was the *Wait a Minute*, under the command of Captain Jav Patrell, a grizzled veteran who had been serving on, later commanding, interdiction ships for thirty-five Standard years. When his navigation officer announced detection of the first oncoming gravity wave, Patrell didn't hesitate. "All ships," he said. "Execute."

As his bridge crew turned crisply to their tasks, Patrell's XO leaned close and half whispered, "You really think this can work?"

"Of *course* it'll work!" Patrell snapped, which was an impressive display of confidence, given that he was, at that precise moment, entirely certain that there was no way in any Corellian hell that anyone could actually pull this off. His certainty was the product of long experience; in all his years of service aboard Corellian-made inderdictors, he'd never seen any indication that the artificial gravity wells they projected could be tuned or timed with the precision this sort of stunt required.

However, none of his thirty-five years' experience included an operation controlled by the main processor array of a Mon Calamari battle cruiser.

As the first of the stream of gravity bombs passed *Lancer* and *Paleo*, the gravity-well projectors of *Wait a Minute* began to pulse. The interaction of the two powerful gravity sources dragged each bomb a few degrees off course, at which point the next Slash-E pulsed its own projector in a similar sequence, further diverting the bombs' trajectories so that they would not only miss the task force, but avoid the planet altogether. The final two Slash-Es, however, were stationed on the *opposite* side of the gravity bombs' path; the first's task was to direct the bombs back toward the planet. Not *at* the planet, but along a tangential parabola that would allow the final Slash-E to drag them into a trajectory that had been precisely plotted by the titanic processor array that was the brain of *Remember Alderaan*.

All of Captain Patrell's training had insisted that the

gravity-well projectors of interdiction ships were *never* to be activated any time the ships were deep within a natural gravity well, such as that of a planet, because the projectors themselves created much too powerful a gravity field of their own. For Mindor, it was equivalent to having four medium-sized moons suddenly pop into existence entirely too close to the planet's surface.

The first groundquakes began only seconds after *Wait a Minute* initiated the sequence, as whole sections of the planetary crust were sequentially lifted and dropped and twisted and wrenched. These quakes were exacerbated by the close passage of the stream of gravity bombs as their altered trajectory became a slingshot maneuver described by General Calrissian as "Right back atcha, scumball; see how *you* like it."

In roughly eight and a half minutes, the first of the slingshot gravity bombs would reach the near vicinity of the flying volcano and begin to rip it to pieces.

Unfortunately, the movement of the gravity gun and the physics of gravity waves meant that all the calculations included a small measure of uncertainty.

It was that uncertainty that caused the second in the crooked line of the Slash-Es, the *Hold 'Em*—instead of diverting one particular gravity bomb farther from Mindor and the task force—to divert the bomb toward *Hold 'Em*'s own hull, just forward of the portside projector array. *Hold 'Em*'s captain had just enough time to understand the sensor readings and remark "Whoops . . ." before the gravity bomb's impact.

The point mass of the gravity bomb lanced through *Hold 'Em* almost without resistance, but the effect of its passage was very much like that of the gravity slice that had cut free the flying volcano: an instantaneous burst of high-energy radiation powerful enough to vaporize a hole so big that a fair pilot could have flown an X-wing in one side of the ship and out the other. The shock wave blew the ship in half and sent the remnants tumbling away from each other.

Even before the radiation flare from *Hold 'Em* had died, Captain Patrell was on comm. "General Calrissian," he said calmly. "We have a problem."

"So I see." Lando was already watching the laser-straight streak of blue-white radiation that marked the path of the first of the gravity bombs to enter Mindor's atmosphere. The impact lit up the distant planetary horizon like a fusion bomb. "I'm taking the rest of the task force back up into orbit; it's our best chance to survive. Except—"

Except that *Remember Alderaan*'s ultrasophisticated sensors had already detected a widening gravitic anomaly, spreading through the planet's crust from the huge crater left by the volcano's departure, and the ship's brain had already calculated that in approximately two Standard hours, the planet would no longer be a planet. It would be an expanding spheroid of newly formed asteroids . . . and every impact of every gravity bomb would shave those hours ever thinner.

When the planet broke up, there would be no more shadow to shield the Republic ships from Taspan's ever-increasing flares.

As the task force left the atmosphere, Lando could only stare back down at the impact flares. It didn't seem possible. Luke was down there somewhere. And Han, and Leia. And Lando had just helped blow up the planet.

His only consolation was that he wouldn't live to regret it. None of them would. He turned his gaze on the flying volcano and thought about the slingshot stream of gravity bombs, eight or ten of them on their way, and his lips peeled back off his teeth. "And you won't live long enough to celebrate."

He snapped out another string of orders, and the surviving ships of the task force swung into formation for full assault. *Remember Alderaan* soared into orbit, with four battle cruisers fanning out to its flanks. Two hundred starfighters spread through the formation, then kicked wide to come at the flying volcano in a tightening noose that kept their guns toward the enemy and themselves clear of the capital ships' field of fire. The three remaining Slash-Es split the difference, tugging gravity bombs as far from any ships as they could manage.

"Let's not give them a chance to even guess we're about to feed them their own weapons," Lando said. He turned to his XO. "Fire."

The entire task force rained destruction upon the flying volcano. With no shields of its own, without even armor, great chunks of the volcano flash-burned into clouds of supercharged plasma—a vast glowing shroud that swallowed turbolaser blasts and detonated proton torpedoes. But that was all right, Lando decided, because all that really mattered now was the flight of eight or ten gravity bombs heading right back where they came from.

Before the planet broke up and Taspan's star storm consumed the task force, he would have the satisfaction of watching the flying volcano pulverized by its own weapon. He didn't anticipate being especially comforted by that, but it was all he had left to look forward to. All any of them had left.

This is a lousy place to die, he thought. *It's a lousy place for the Republic to lose Luke and Han and Leia and Chewie. And the Rogues. And me.*

At least we're taking the bad guys with us.

He found himself contemplating, with a kind of awe, all the stories that would end here, in this little backwater system six jumps off the Hydian Way . . . He wondered briefly how the holothriller producers would tell this story. He had a feeling they'd try to make it into something grand and glorious—some legendary Last Stand of the Last Jedi, with a dash of the Romance of Doomed Lovers and a splash of Reformed Gambler Goes Out as a Hero . . . instead of what it really was.

We just got beat, he thought. *They outplanned us. Suckered us in. And we went for it headfirst because we thought we were invincible. We thought the good guys always win.*

Of all of them, Luke was the only one who had never suffered under that delusion. Well: not *never.* Han had told him once that something in Luke had changed after Bespin. Somehow Luke understood—in a way that Lando never had, that Han and Leia and Chewbacca had simply never grasped—just how dark a place the universe really was.

Lando guessed that was where Luke got his humility. His kindness. His gentle faith that people could change for the better. That must have been why he rarely smiled, and almost never made jokes. Because that goodness was all he really had. It was his lifeline. The rope to which he clung, dangling above the abyss.

And we all clung to him, Lando thought. *He was our hope. As long as Luke Skywalker was alive, we always figured somehow everything would turn out okay.*

That's what the Republic was losing today.

Hope.

Given what was going on dirtside, Luke was probably already dead. And even if by some miracle he was still alive, what could he possibly do? Had there ever been a good reason to burden one man with the hope of the whole galaxy?

Though this question was both rhetorical and silent, he got an answer nonetheless, as the lieutenant at ComOps said, in a voice hushed and hoarse, "General Calrissian, I'm picking up a signal . . . a ship on intercept

course . . . General! Transponder signature confirmed—
it's the *Millennium Falcon*!"

Lando felt as if the universe had shifted a couple of
degrees to the right. "What?"

Was it *possible*?

"They're broadcasting, sir. On all bands."

"Put it on speaker."

" . . . *Skywalker. All Republic ships, disengage and
withdraw. All Imperial forces: Group Captain CC-1000
is hereby promoted to air marshal. Air Marshal GC-
1000: You are now in command of all Imperial forces in
the Taspan system. You will order deactivation of subspace jamming, power down all gravity stations, and execute unconditional surrender with all available speed.
When surrender is complete, you will assist in the evacuation of noncombatants.*

"*Repeating: This is Luke Skywalker. All Republic
ships*—"

"Cut it off." For what seemed like a long, long moment, Lando could only stand and stare into space. Had
he really heard this? Did Luke actually *believe* he could
simply *order Imperial stormtroopers to surrender*?

That was beyond preposterous. It was completely
bloody *insane*.

"Sir?" TacOps said. "TIE fighters are withdrawing."

Lando said, "What?"

ComOps looked over his shoulder. "*Wait a Minute* reports that the gravity gun has ceased fire." He blinked.
"Subspace comm is operational."

"What?"

NavOps could only shake his head. "Mass-shadows
diminishing—the gravity stations are shutting down, sir!
Jump window projected to open in twelve minutes."

And Lando found, to his astonishment, that his feet
were striding forward and taking the rest of his body
along with them, and his hands were gesturing, and his

mouth was snapping off orders about jump coordinates and rendezvous points and search-and-rescue priorities, while his mind was still, for the most part, doing nothing except saying, *What?*

FENN SHYSA PRESSED HIS BACK AGAINST THE BULKHEAD and scowled down at the red-blinking charge meter on his blaster rifle. Ten shots. One grenade. Maybe just enough to last until Lando's counterstrike vaporized them all.

He exchanged a grim look with the mercenary commander who stood in an identical posture on the other side of the blown-open hatch between them. The mercenary commander was at his side because in the proudest Mandalorian tradition, he would cover his men's retreat or die in the attempt. Fenn Shysa, though, wasn't there because he was a commander. Or even because he was commandant of the Mandalorian Protectors, or because he was Lord Mandalore. He was there because he was Fenn Shysa.

He'd discarded his helmet at some point—a glancing hit had disabled his heads-up display, and the malfunction had triggered the autopolarizer to black out his visor altogether—and now he had a fresh burn streak along his temple where a near-miss had set his hair on fire. The haze in the bunker flickered and flashed with scarlet streaks of blasterfire, and it smelled like smoke, roast meat, and lightning.

The blasterfire through the doorway paused for just an instant, only long enough for a pair of thermal dets to tumble in and skid across the floor. On the dets' first bounce, Fenn swung through the hatch and went right, launching his anti-armor grenade on the run. As blasterfire out of the smoke tracked him, the mercenary commander slipped in and went left a millisecond before the blast of fire from the paired thermal dets roared through the hatch behind them.

Fenn located the focal point of the blasterfire. He ran in a tight arc, holding down his rifle's trigger, not aiming, putting fire on their position to keep their heads down and spoil their shooting as he threw aside his empty rifle and turned his tight arc into a straight-line charge, just wide of the line of fire pouring at the stormtrooper position from the mercenary commander. He charged partly because he still had his gauntlet blades, and if he could get into hand-to-hand he could rearm himself with the blasters of dead enemies—but mostly he charged because he was Fenn Shysa, and if today should bring his death, he would fall with his teeth in the throat of the man who killed him.

But before he could get there a new source of blasterfire erupted from a different angle and lanced through the smoke. Fenn clenched his jaw and kept running, because he could take a hit or two and still bring down a few men before he fell—but the blasterfire didn't strike him; it didn't seem to even be *aimed* at him. The bolts flashed high, directly over the helmets of the stormtroopers toward whom he charged, and were accompanied by authoritative shouts to surrender; but he was ready to die, so he ignored the shouts and put his head down and didn't even slow until he reached the first of the stormtroopers ahead and hooked his left hand's fingers under the jawpiece of the nearest and drew back his right fist to plunge his blade into the trooper's throat—

And stopped.

The trooper wasn't fighting back. He wasn't struggling at all. He simply stood with his empty hands raised and waited to see if Fenn would slaughter him like a fattened grundill.

Fenn blinked, unable to believe what he was seeing.

He was even less able to believe what he saw next, which was a black-armored stormtrooper stepping through the hatchway from which had come the surprise attack. He tensed and gathered himself, but the stormtrooper lifted an armored gauntlet, empty, palm forward.

"Ni dinu ner gaan naakyc, jorcu ni nu copaani kyr'a-mur ner vod," the stormtrooper said.

Fenn Shysa could only stare in disbelief.

The guy's inflections were kind of weird—he had a definite Coruscanti accent—but his meaning was absolutely clear, and his use of Mando'a was flawless.

Honor my offer of truce, for I would not willingly shed my brother's blood.

"What?"

"Lord Mandalore. Emperor Skywalker sends his regards," the stormtrooper said in Basic. He wore the rank flash of a group captain. "The situation has changed."

Fenn's mouth fell open. "Emperor . . . *Skywalker?*"

The situation has changed appeared to be the understatement of the decade.

"We have secured the surface-to-orbit emplacements," the group captain said. "General Calrissian requests that you help us evacuate the civilians. Several thousand civilians, whom we were ordered by Emperor Skywalker to protect."

And in the end, Fenn Shysa could only blink some more and wonder if maybe he'd taken a couple of shots to the head and just hadn't noticed. Or something. But nonetheless he and the mercenary commander followed the group captain back through chamber after chamber choked with rubble and stinking of ozone and charred flesh, back to the scene of the battle at the twin redoubts that guarded the massive blast doors. The group captain clicked a brief code into the door panel, and the enormous slabs of durasteel began to grind open.

In the interior control room of the gravity gun, several dozen stormtroopers stood in ranks as orderly as if they were presenting for inspection, their hands clasped on top of their heads. Their rifles had been stacked with millimetric precision in the center of the room; on the deck beside them, their sidearms were arranged in a perfectly spaced grid. Behind the weapons stood a pyramid of gleaming black stormtrooper helmets, which reminded Fenn unpleasantly of the stacks of severed heads built by the Jaltiri tribals of Toskhowwl VI.

"I can't—this is *incredible*," he said. "We couldn't even get *close*—we were tryin' to cut through the walls and gettin' *nowhere*—"

"That's because you didn't have the override codes for the blast doors," the group captain said reasonably.

"And they just *surrendered*?"

"At my order." The group captain sounded as though this sort of thing happened every day. "I am their superior officer. No stormtrooper would dream of disobedience."

"If they had?"

"This might well have presented some difficulty, as I and my men have been instructed by Emperor Skywalker to minimize further bloodshed. I'm grateful that I didn't have to make the decision."

"Group Captain—"

"Air Marshal," the stormtrooper corrected him with firm but quiet pride. "I have been honored with a battlefield promotion from the emperor himself."

"Emperor *Skywalker*," Fenn said slowly, struggling to beat this conversation into something resembling sense.

"The chosen heir of Palpatine the Great," the fresh-minted air marshal said primly. "Haven't you seen *Luke Skywalker and the Jedi's Revenge*?"

"Um . . ."

"It's a dramatization, of course."

"Of course."

"But it's based on actual events."

"Uh-huh."

"It's very powerful. A masterpiece," the air marshal told him. "It changed my life."

Fenn still couldn't get his mind around it. "When a fella says a holodrama changed his life," he said, "he's usually just exaggeratin'."

"I'm not exaggerating."

"I'm startin' to believe you."

"Now, if you would summon your men and follow me," the air marshal said as he turned and walked briskly away. "Though General Calrissian's forces are doing their best to delay or prevent it, catastrophic destruction of this facility may commence as soon as six minutes from now."

He had barely gotten the words out when the floor seemed to drop half a meter, then spring back up to slam them all off their feet. At the same time a terrific roar came up from the floor and out from the walls and battered them like invisible mallets crushing the breath from their chests. The echoes of the roar shook the dome until its armor shrieked and twisted and started to tear, and chunks of permacrete ripped loose from the walls and fell from the ceiling . . .

When the roar finally subsided to a mere grinding rumble, Fenn managed to sit up, coughing permacrete dust from his throat. "A bit optimistic about that *six minutes,* weren't you?"

CHAPTER 17

THE FIRST OF THE GRAVITY BOMBS WAS A DIRECT HIT: its impact blasted seven or eight hundred meters of the leading edge of the flying volcano into a bunch of high-velocity asteroids streaking through a cloud of expanding plasma. Two entire banks of the massive gravity-drive thrusters that the flying volcano depended upon for maneuvering were destroyed, and the central coordinating nexus was damaged, which destabilized the remaining three banks. These three banks of gravity-drive thrusters began to swing and blast in random directions as their autocompensators tried and failed to discover a configuration that would continue to guide the base along its programmed trajectory.

The resulting stresses began to rip the Shadow Base apart.

This process substantially accelerated with the arrival, in brisk succession, of the rest of the gravity bombs. The three remaining Slash-Es raced in at a steep deflection, overdriving their gravity projectors in a vain hope of dragging them far enough off course that the mountain had a chance to survive, but the bombs came in a great deal faster than they had gone out, having picked up considerable velocity in their slingshot around the planet.

Which meant that some 3,426 civilians—citizens of the Republic who had been violently kidnapped and forced into slavery, who were currently crowded shoulder-to-shoulder in what had once been the Sorting Center—had roughly four minutes to live.

In slightly less than those four minutes, the breakup of the Shadow Base would rupture the pressure seal around the Sorting Center and expose them all to hard vacuum. Further, the only landers available to shuttle evacuees away were not only far too few to hold more than a tenth of their number, but were also currently moored on the *exterior* of the flying volcano. To reach them, the evacuees would have to cross hundreds of meters of that selfsame hard vacuum—without the benefit of environment suits.

Han stared through the cockpit's transparisteel, his face bleak as empty space. "They don't have a chance."

"They *do* have a chance," Nick insisted from the seat behind Chewie's seat. "The same chance *you* had. They've got a Skywalker on their side."

"You think that's enough?"

"It was for you," Nick pointed out. "Skywalker's got a plan. He's always got a plan." He turned to Luke and lowered his voice. "Uh, you *do* have a plan, don't you?"

"As a matter of fact," Luke said, "I do."

Luke had, before he had ever assumed command, familiarized himself with every detail of every ship that would form any part of the RRTF. So he knew that three Corellian frigates attached to the task force had been converted from heavy freighters. He also knew that some of their original equipment had been preserved in its original configuration, to avoid a ridiculously expensive refit.

One piece of this original equipment was a conveyor bridge, intended to transfer cargo to or from another ship out of atmosphere. It was essentially a framework supporting a moving belt some six meters wide and a hundred meters long, enclosed in a force tunnel to maintain atmosphere, and carrying multiple small artificial gravity generators, insuring not only that the cargo being transferred would stay in contact with the belt, but also that any transfers would take place "downhill."

Lancer and *Paleo* were equipped with conveyor bridges; they were also the closest to the flying volcano. *Lancer,* in fact, was able to match trajectories and deploy its conveyor bridge with pinpoint accuracy in less than two minutes.

At the coordinates Luke had given, *Lancer* discovered only a broad, flat plain of solid rock. Captain Tirossk was understandably reluctant to risk his crew by bringing his ship so close to a flying mountain in the process of shaking itself to pieces simply to deploy a conveyor bridge that nobody could possibly use. He growled over the comm, *"Once I anchor the bridge and pump in atmo, what then? Will the rock just magically open up and let people out?"*

And because the Captain of *Lancer* occasionally indulged a guilty pleasure by viewing holothrillers such as *Luke Skywalker and the Dragons of Tatooine,* when Luke replied simply, "Yes. It will." Tirossk discovered, against all his better instincts, that he believed it would.

Han Solo didn't share that faith. He didn't have any faith to spare. He hunched over the *Falcon*'s controls, glaring out through the cockpit's transparisteel at the Shadow Base as it swelled entirely too slowly, his knuckles white on the yoke, his teeth clenched as though he could make the ship go faster by pure force of will. Now he twisted to look at Luke, who crouched behind Chewbacca's seat. "What, your new Melter friends? How do you figure to pull that off when we're a good two minutes out from you getting that hand on the rock?"

Luke said, "Artoo, I need a signal boost."

The astromech, socketed behind Han's seat, extended a datajack toward Luke like a trusting child offering a hand; in the same moment, the comm port on his dome slid open and his parabolic antenna popped up. Luke gripped the extended datajack, and Han watched a thatch of those glossy black crystals grow out of Luke's hand and thread themselves into the datajack's ports.

Han grimaced. "No offense, Luke, but that *really* creeps me out."

"Imagine it from my side."

"I'd rather not."

Luke didn't quite smile. "Now I need a second or two to concentrate."

The *Lancer* swung into position, and its conveyor bridge extended like a tongue going for a taste of the rock. An instant after the bluish shimmer of the force tunnel flickered into existence around it, the rock dimpled and began to melt away, retreating like a time-lapse image of a glacier in high summer. Light sprang upward from the hole, which shaped itself perfectly to the force tunnel. The conveyor bridge extended farther down into the hole, all the way down to the civilians and stormtroopers and Mandalorians waiting there.

First onto the bridge came a pair of Mandalorian mercenaries. They leapt up and grabbed the moving belt, flipping their bodies expertly through the ninety-degree gravity shift; for them, the artificial gravity's orientation made the bridge seem entirely level, the *Lancer* now appearing to cruise serenely alongside the volcano instead of hovering above it. They strode briskly in the opposite direction of the belt's motion so that they could stay in place and assist others through the transition.

A dozen pairs of Mando commandos spaced themselves along the conveyor bridge, while the balance of them helped organize the civilians on the cavern floor.

Solicitous stormtroopers assisted any who were too in-capacitated by age, injury, or disease to make their own way. Mandos along the bridge reminded everyone to "keep walking. Do *not* run. If you fall and can't get up, move to the side and someone will assist you." In this fashion the Sorting Center began to swiftly empty, de-spite the pitching and jouncing of the cavern's floor from the ongoing destruction of the Shadow Base.

None of them knew, either, that the convulsions they felt were substantially less than those experienced by other parts of the base. They also had no way to know that the atmospheric integrity of the Sorting Center was being preserved by a large contingent of Melters, who not only kept the cavern tightly sealed, but manipulated their meltmassif to minimize the shocks through the floor. Though all could see another part of the cavern's vault bulge, and droop, and belly downward like a vast droplet of glossy black slime.

One of the largest such droplets turned entirely liquid and drained away, revealing a Corellian light freighter.

In the instant that the *Falcon* settled onto the cavern floor, a HatchPatch blew off, opening a gap where its belly ramp should have been. The ship's freight lift slammed down as well, and through both openings flooded refugees, both Mindorese, organized by a human man named Tripp, and Republic, commanded by a Mon Calamari lieutenant named Tubrimi.

In seconds, the *Falcon*'s holds were empty of people.

In the cockpit, Luke laid a hand on Han's shoulder. "Are you good with this? I'm depending on you."

"I don't like it," Han said.

"I know. But this is how it has to be," Luke said. He triggered the comm. "Air Marshal—you and your men will board immediately. One minute to skids-up."

The reply came instantly. "*As you command, my lord emperor!*"

Han made a face. "Someday you're gonna explain this *Emperor Skywalker* bumblefluff, right?"

"No," Luke said. "No, I don't think I will."

IN THE ABSOLUTE BLACKNESS WITHIN THE SHADOW EGG, Cronal had only one problem left.

The Shadow Egg, as he had mentally dubbed it in the instant of its creation, was his improvised cocoon of meltmassif in the Cavern of the Shadow Throne. It hovered where the Shadow Throne had once stood, held aloft by the repulsorlifts that had once supported the Throne. There was no longer a lava-fall behind it, nor a lake of molten lava below; whatever remained of the volcano's lifeblood, once the Shadow Base had cut free from the planet, had spilled from its underside in a rain of fire. The Shadow Egg bobbed gently in midair as the shock waves of the Shadow Base's ongoing destruction passed over it.

This ongoing destruction was not Cronal's problem; it was not a problem at all. He had counted on it. Had the Republic forces not hit upon their idea of deflecting his own gravity bombs back at him, he would have been forced to blow the Shadow Base up himself.

The Battle of Mindor was to have only one survivor.

Nor was he concerned that all his preparation for his new life had focused upon impersonating Luke Skywalker rather than his sister; one useful lesson he had taken from working with Palpatine was the value in flexible planning. He would, as Leia, simply fake amnesia—traumatic brain injury would be an ideal explanation for any stumbles or fumbles he might make upon meeting the princess's old acquaintances—and then discreetly hire one of the countless hacks who scripted holothrillers to make something up. He would, he anticipated, even have this holothriller produced. He already had a few ideas for a title: *Princess Leia and the Shadow*

Trap, for example. Or, perhaps, *Princess Leia and the Black Holes of Mindor.*

Nor was he worried about making an escape from his own trap, once the transfer of his consciousness was complete. Buried in meltmassif not far from the Election Center, he had secreted a custom craft to make his escape as Luke. Though in appearance it was a very ordinary-looking Lambda T-4a, its hull was layered with so much additional shielding that there was no cargo capacity at all, and virtually no room for passengers. The cockpit was altogether fake; a pilot and at most two or three others could be packed into a tiny capsule cocooned in additional radiation shielding in the center of what would have been, in an ordinary shuttle, the passenger compartment.

All necessary planning had been done. All difficulties had been anticipated, and all contingencies had been covered. Except one.

The blasted girl simply *refused* to *break.*

The incrystallation had gone flawlessly; the raw power of the Vastor body had enabled Cronal to propagate a shadow web of crystalline nerves throughout her body with the speed of frost spidering across super-cooled transparisteel. With only a short time available—and no ready supply of thanatizine II—he had proceeded without drug suspension. After all, this was but a mere girl who had, through an accident of genetics, an exceptionally powerful connection to the small fraction of the Dark that Jedi had ignorantly named the Force. He should have been able to overwhelm her by brute strength alone.

He had taken her sight, cut away her hearing, erased her senses of smell and taste and touch. He had stripped her kinesthetic sense, so that she was no longer aware of her own body at all. He had shut down the activity of certain neurotransmitters in her brain, so that she could no longer even remember how being alive had felt.

She wasn't fighting him. She didn't know how. He wouldn't let her remember what fighting was.

She just wouldn't let go.

She had something that her brother had lacked, some inner spark of intransigence that sustained her against the Dark. He couldn't guess what this spark might be; some sort of primitive, girlish emotional attachment, he presumed. Whatever it was, it must be extinguished once and for all; she must sleep forever. The problem was how to do it without killing her outright. The melt-massif shadow nerves would contain only his consciousness; he needed her brain to be fully functioning to maintain autonomic functions. He hadn't gone to all this trouble to simply trade his decaying body for one that was already dead.

This was taking far too long. The boy Jedi had been ready to let himself slip away in a fraction of the time; of course, the boy had given him more to work with. He carried with him an inner darkness that would no doubt have astonished his sister, had she lived long enough to discover it. Had Skywalker not damaged Shadowspawn's control crystals, none of this would have been necessary in the first place. But as the situation stood, he could only drive his will deeper into the Dark—to gnaw away her resistance with the single-minded intensity of a Klepthian rock otter chewing into a basalt clam's shell.

But when he finally did break through that resistance, he found her brain not weak and quivering, but hard like a burnberry stone, and shining with a brilliant white light that was not imaginary at all. That light stabbed him like a knife in the eye, and drove him reeling back.

He took that stone in the palm of a hand made of the Dark, and with a Dark rock hammer he struck it . . . and the imaginary hammer splintered in the imaginary hand. He came at the stone like a gem harpy, and swallowed it into a crop powerful enough to pulverize diamond, but it burned its way out. He made fists of whole galaxies and brought them together to crush this one tiny star, but when their cataclysm faded back into the Dark, the tiny star shone on.

"What is *wrong* with you?" he shouted at the star in frustration. "What are you, and why won't you *die*?"

"I can tell you that." The voice came from everywhere, or nowhere: a young man's tenor, with the flattened, nasal accent of the far Outer Rim.

Cronal jerked upright in the absolute blackness inside the Shadow Egg.

"If you'd made friends with the Melters, instead of making them your slaves, you might have discovered all kinds of things they can do for you." The voice was coming from *inside* Cronal's head. "As for where I am, well . . ."

The interior of the Shadow Egg suddenly flared with light: blue-white light, from a crackling energy discharge that spidered across its inner shell. An instant later the shell collapsed, splashing around Cronal's ankles and draining off the repulsorlift platform that had supported the Shadow Egg.

Twenty meters away, on the ledge that curved outward from the tunnel mouth, stood a slim young man in a Republic flight suit who held, loosely and casually in one hand, a lightsaber of brilliant green.

LUKE TRIED TO KEEP HIS BREATHING SLOW AND STEADY, while his heart thumped against his rib cage like a trapped slashrat trying to break free. For an interminable stretching moment after the meltmassif egg had collapsed, all Luke had been able to do was stare blankly and think *Look at the size of him . . .*

Kar Vastor crouched like a sabercat coiled to spring. One of his enormous hands rested on a blob of melt-massif. His lips had peeled back to reveal teeth long and curving and sharp as stilettos. Luke blinked, and blinked again. *Each of his biceps is bigger than my head . . .*

And around him in the Force swirled a storm of dark-ness unlike any Luke had experienced since the Em-peror's death: darkness that could snuff his own paltry light like a candle.

But fear could have power over him only if he let it. He breathed deeply, slowly, and with each exhale he opened himself so that all his fear, all his tension and ap-prehension, his every care and concern drained out of him and flowed away.

How would Ben handle this?

That thought steadied him. He imagined Ben at his side, and held the old Jedi's kindly smile of warm know-ing firmly in his mind. "Blackhole," he said, and the calm solidity he heard in his own voice reassured him even more. "You have one chance to do this the easy way."

Blackhole's response was a low snarl that somehow, in Luke's brain, translated itself into words. *The easy way,* he growled, *would be to swap. Give yourself to be my body, and I'll let your sister go.*

Luke shook his head and hefted his lightsaber. "If you fight me, you will be destroyed."

Blackhole's snarl took on a mocking edge. *You think you can take me, boy?*

"I've killed too many people already today."

Then how will you destroy me?

"You remember Nick, don't you? Your puppet Shad-owspawn? And his girlfriend. Her name's Aeona. See, Nick knows all about you."

Bring him out so he can watch you die.

"Oh, he's not with me. We dropped off Nick and Aeona on the way here. They're in that custom shuttle of yours."

What?

"I told you: Nick knows all about you. Did you think I was lying? He and Aeona are on their way already. On their way to your *real* body."

Vastor went very, very still.

"I bet if you close your eyes and concentrate, you can feel where he is. I'm pretty sure you can. Because he can feel where *you* are. Go ahead, give it a try."

The eyes of the Vastor body went vacant. Luke, calm now, serene and centered in the Force, could also feel Nick's location humming in the meltmassif that shadowed his nerves: far, far off, hurtling through space, dodging asteroids and looping around a wide arc that would bring it into an orbital intercept with one particular asteroid—one particular chunk of rock left over from the Big Crush, one chunk that was not like the others, despite its absolutely ordinary appearance. No eye could have picked it out among the countless others that swarmed it on all sides; no instrument could have detected the slightest anomaly.

But Nick didn't need instruments, and he didn't need to see it to know where it was.

This chunk of rock—of pure meltmassif, in fact—was very far indeed from ordinary. Within its hollowed core were hidden engines, and a powerful hyperdrive, and the life-support chamber of a very old, very frail man, who from his perfectly concealed position had used a device forged of Sith alchemy not only to control this system, but also to terrorize the galaxy.

"Do you understand now?" Luke asked. "In a few minutes, a very, very angry man will arrive at your life-support capsule. This man does not share my reservations about killing you. I'm pretty sure he's already trying to decide whether he should blast you to atoms or cut his way in and beat you to death with his bare fists.

"So this is what I mean about the easy way. Walk away. Withdraw from the Vastor body and return to your own. Your gravity stations are powered down. You still have time to jump out of the system before Nick gets to you. But you don't have very *much* time. So I'll tell you again: If you fight me, you will be destroyed."

The Vastor growl lowered to a threatening rumble. *I still have the girl.*

He reached up to the shapeless mass of meltmassif; he laid his hand upon it and it slumped to liquid, and then that enormous hand lifted Leia by the neck. She dangled from his fist, limp, lifeless—only through the Force could Luke tell she still lived. Vastor growled again. *She can still die,* the growl said. *You both can.*

Luke sighed. "All right, forget the easy way." He took three running steps to the lip of the ledge and jumped.

The Force carried him high over the abyss that had once been the lake of molten lava. He flipped in midair, to make himself into a spear with a lightsaber for a blade. Vastor dropped Leia and vaulted away with a contemptuous grunt as Luke's flight ended with his lightsaber blade driving into the platform.

Luke somersaulted to his feet astride Leia's unconscious form and lifted his blade to garde. "I warned you not to underestimate my powers."

Are you mad? You were never even close to me, fool!

"I wasn't aiming at you."

Vastor's eyes flicked from Luke's face down to the lightsaber hole in the platform, which was now spitting sparks and gouts of smoke that smelled very much like a damaged repulsorlift burning out. Vastor's eyes widened, *"What have you DONE?"*

With one last gush of black tarry smoke, the repulsorlift shorted out completely, and the platform plummeted like the several tons of rock and obsidian it was, to the empty bottom of the formerly lava lake. But instead of falling the several hundred meters to the rocky bottom of the lava lake, after only twenty or so it landed, *very* hard, on the dorsal hull of a Corellian light freighter that had been hovering there ever since Luke had slipped out through its topside hatch and leapt to the wall, to make his long, slow climb up to the ledge above.

The impact knocked Vastor off his feet; Luke, with Leia in his arms, landed as softly as a Force-using feather pillow.

Vastor sprang to his feet, needle teeth bared in a feral snarl. *I will kill every last one of you!*

"No," Luke said, "you won't."

A slight sideways tilt of his head invited Vastor to look around, which he did. Which was when he saw the full company of black-armored stormtroopers on a ring ledge about three meters above him, all with weapons aimed at his gigantic chest.

"Air Marshal Klick," Luke called upward. "Tell Kar Vastor your orders."

The black-armored officer stepped forward crisply. "Kar Vastor, I have been directed to prevent, by any and all necessary means, any attempt on your part to do harm to that ship, to the woman, or to Emperor Skywalker."

Emperor Skywalker. Vastor's growl dripped loathing.

"I implore you to remain still, and take no aggressive action," the air marshal said. "The emperor wishes us to minimize bloodshed."

Luke, meanwhile, had taken a couple of steps to one side, where the dorsal access hatch promptly opened to reveal enormous hairy arms, into which Luke delivered his sister.

"Worrough?" Chewbacca asked solicitously, cradling her as though she weighed nothing at all.

"No," Luke said. "She's not all right. Take her below and tell Han to get ready to take us out of here."

He turned back to Vastor. "Now it's your turn, Black-hole. Go back to your own body. You might still make it into hyperspace before Nick kills you."

Vastor lowered himself into a crouch. *I understand now. I understand how you have defeated me.*

It is because I lost my way. I have been trying to create. To build, when I should have destroyed. I abandoned the Way of the Dark, and the Dark abandoned me.

"I don't care," Luke said. "All I care about is whether we're going to have to kill you. Now if you'll just abandon that body, we can all go home."

I will. But not yet. First, answer a question for me, Skywalker.

Luke shrugged. "If it will end this, sure."

Oh, yes. This will end. And very shortly. Answer me this: Why is the armor of my stormtroopers black?

Luke frowned. He'd never thought about it; he'd sort of assumed it was merely a style. An element of uniform, to set them apart from Palpatine's stormtroopers.

I'll give you a hint: It's not just paint.

Luke squinted up at the company of black-armored commandos above while with his mind he reached into the Force. Even with all the Force perception he could muster, he could detect nothing unusual about the armor beyond its color. And the color was, well, just black. Wasn't it? Black with faint opalescent high-lights, kind of a pearly glitter. It reminded him of something . . . but he couldn't quite bring it to the surface of his consciousness, because there was something nagging at him, a kind of tickle that grew to an itch that swelled into actual pain . . . but it was a pain he didn't really *feel* so much as sense, as if it were happening to someone else.

It was his shadow nerves, that's where he felt it, in his internal crystalline network of . . .

He couldn't breathe.

The ceramic base of that black armor, its fundamental structure, was not ceramic at all.

He could only stand and blink, and mouth a single word: *meltmassif.*

As if in confirmation, Vastor collapsed, just crumpled, folding to the deck like a dead man.

"Han . . . ?" Luke said uncertainly. "Han, I think we need to go."

"*Luke!*" his comlink crackled. "*There's something wrong with Leia—she's, I don't know, she's having some kind of seizure or something. Luke, what do I do?*"

"I don't know," Luke said as he watched Vastor's body do the same: writhe in slow, twisting convulsions like a Riddellian bloodworm baking on a hot fry-rock. There came a clatter from above: blaster rifles slipping from stormtrooper hands to bounce on the stone of the ring ledge. The stormtroopers, each and every one, began to buckle at the knees. They twisted and jerked, bucking in slow motion, clutching at their helmets with gauntleted fingers as though to claw out their own eyes.

"Han," Luke said. "Go. Go *now.*"

He reached out with the Force and slammed shut the *Falcon*'s hatch just as the Vastor body lurched to its feet and reached Luke in one lightning bound. Impossibly powerful hands seized Luke's shoulders as Vastor lifted him like a doll, and shook him and roared rage and bloodlust into his face, and there was nothing human left in Vastor's eyes. He sank his teeth into Luke's throat, and bit down.

And on the ring ledge above, the stormtoopers started to scream.

CHAPTER 18

AIR MARSHAL KLICK COULD NOT IDENTIFY THE SOUND.
Even through his consuming agony, pain so intense that
he could no longer stand, he was quite certain that he'd
never heard this particular sound before, and right now
he couldn't guess what it might be. The agony, however,
he understood very well.

The inside of his armor had turned into needles.

Big needles.

They stabbed every centimeter of him from the soles
of his feet to the crown of his head. And they didn't stop
once they had pierced his skin. Instead, they grew, lanc-
ing deeper into his flesh; they seemed to enter his blood-
stream and splinter off, tearing at him from the inside.
They went up his nose and in behind his eye sockets,
drilling right through the bone of his skull and slicing
into his brain. Inside his brain they didn't hurt—no pain
nerves—but he could feel them by what they cut away.

They cut away his honor, and his discipline. They cut
away his devotion to the emperor, and his pride in his
men. They cut away his memory, and his dreams, his
hopes, and his fears. The needles in his brain destroyed
everything he had ever been, but they didn't leave mere
emptiness behind . . .

Each of those empty parts of him boiled with savage
unreasoning rage.

His final thought as a conscious being was *Ah, that's what the sound is. It's me.*

Screaming.

The sound of his own screams was all he took with him into the dark. Then there was only rage, and a burning need to kill someone.

Anyone.

THE COUCH NICK WAS STRAPPED ONTO WAS BARELY EVEN a couch at all; it was more like a padded shelf in a slight widening of the crawlspace tube that extended back from the shuttle's lone pilot's chair. Nick lay with his eyes closed, watching the dark star in his head.

Watching was not exactly what he was doing. The sense he used was not sight, though the dark star appeared to his vision as a patch of deeper night in the infinite black between the stars. Nor did he touch it, though he could feel how cold it was, how it was a bottomless abyss that swallowed all the warmth in the universe. Nick's ears rang with an utter lack of sound, and in his nose and mouth was only corruption and decay.

But he did his best to ignore those sensations, because none of them would help him kill that evil son of an inbred ruskakk.

When Nick closed his eyes and turned his whole mind to the task, he simply *knew* that this dark star of hunger and decay was straight ahead, on the shuttle's current course. He knew it was moving, and when it smeared into a streak of jump radiation, he knew that too.

"He's gone into jump," Aeona said from the pilot's chair. "Unless there's more than one of these asteroids with a hyperdrive."

"Yeah," Nick said. "It doesn't matter."

"The navicomputer says his vector's wrong for the jump-out point."

"He's not going for the jump-out point. He's making for deep space."

"Then how are we supposed to *find* him? Guess?"

"I can find him," Nick said. "He can run, but he can't hide. Not from me. Get on his vector and jump."

"How far?"

"Just outside the system."

He could hear the shrug in her voice. "You're the boss."

"If you only knew how long I've been waiting to hear you say that."

He heard the tapping of codes being punched into the navicomputer. The rising whine of the hyperdrive sped them toward jump . . . then he heard the whine drop as the hyperdrive spun down.

Nick sat up so suddenly he whacked his head on the crawlspace's ceiling. "What's going on? Why didn't we—"

"Fail-safe cut in." Aeona's voice was tight. She twisted to glance at him over her shoulder, and the look on her face made his stomach twist. "We're in a gravity well."

She checked the shuttle's sensors. "Mass-shadows all over the place," she said, low and slow and grim. "They've repowered the gravity stations."

"What? Which ones?"

She lowered her head. "All of them."

"No way," Nick snarled. "No fraggin' *way*!"

"All those ships. All those people. On both sides." Again she twisted to look at him over her shoulder. Her eyes were haunted. "None of them are getting out. Not one."

Nick felt hollow inside, as if somebody had reached down his throat and pulled out his guts. He turned half-blind eyes to the meters-thick custom shielding that so nearly filled the entire shuttle. "Just us," he said. "No-body else."

Aeona nodded. "I think we're the only ones who have a chance to live through this."

LEIA STILL WRITHED AND TWISTED IN THAT HORRIBLE slow-motion convulsion, despite Han and Chewbacca's best efforts to calm her and hold her still. "Take her to the cockpit and buckle her into your chair so she can't hurt herself," Han said. "I'm going after Luke."

"Howergh!"

"He'd go back for me," Han replied grimly. "In fact, he *has.*"

"Argharoo-oo hrf."

"I'm not keeping count." He sprinted for the gang-way and clambered up to throw open the dorsal access hatch. When he poked his head out, all he saw was Luke's tame stormtroopers up on the ring ledge, writhing and howling in incomprehensible agony.

"Hey, bucket-heads!" Han shouted. "What's wrong with you guys? Where's L—uh, where's your emperor?"

All he got in reply was more howling, so he went up another rung on the gangway and peered around. The wreckage of the *Falcon*'s dorsal quad turret made him wince; all that was left was a flattened mass of crumpled transparisteel under great big gleaming chunks of what looked like obsidian. He made a mental note to bill the repairs to Lando.

Another couple of steps up the gangway raised his angle of vision enough that he could see the crown of the big man's shaved head over the wreckage and rubble. One step more showed him Luke's limp, unresisting form hanging from the big man's grip while that son of a Pervickian dung camel *chewed* on Luke's *neck*—!

Han cleared the hatch in a single leap, and by the time

his feet touched the hull his blaster was in his hand. "Hey, monkey-breath! Chew on *this*!"

But he couldn't just fire from the hip; Luke was in the way and Han knew stun blasts were useless against the Vastor body. In the fraction of a second that it took him to bring the DL-44 up to eye level to align the sights, the big man's right hand came free of Luke's shoulder with a weird *ripping* sound. Luke's shoulder, where that hand had been, showed black and glistening like the handful of crystal hairs back in the Melter crypt, and Vastor's hand was full of the same—and while Han was trying to make sense of that, some invisible force snatched his blaster away.

I have got to learn to hang on to that thing with both hands! Han bounded forward, swept up a jagged hunk of obsidian the size of his doubled fists, and charged, cranking the black glass rock back over his shoulder as if he was going to hurl it overhand—but he hurled *himself* instead, leaping up onto the rubble, then down again in a headlong dive with the chunk raised high until a scarlet blaster bolt slashed past his face and blew the hunk of obsidian right out of his hand.

He almost went face-first into the hull armor but managed to turn his crash into a clumsy somersault that left him flat on his back, dazed and gasping and staring up at the business end of his blaster. Which was in Luke's hand.

Luke said, "Didn't I tell you to go?"

While Han was still blankly mumbling, "Yow. Nice shooting. I think," the enormous Vastor-thing moaned like someone in terrible pain or fear or both. One huge hand slammed against Luke's chest, and for all Han could tell, it was like *Vastor* was the one in trouble and trying desperately to escape. An instant later, Vastor ripped his mouth free of Luke's neck—and his *mouth* was full of those black crystal hairs. The wound in

Luke's neck wasn't bleeding, it was sprouting a thatch of that same blackly glistening fur that was writhing and twisting and growing like it was *alive*. Vastor gasped like a drowning man and yanked his other hand off Luke's arm, and before Han could manage even a faint guess as to what was actually going on, Vastor whirled, took four or five running steps for momentum, and made a great big flying leap right off the ship.

Han had no idea if Vastor had fallen to his death, or if he'd caught a grip on the wall, or had maybe even started flapping his arms and flew into orbit. He could only stare up at his young friend and murmur plaintively, "Luke, what the hell?"

"You would have killed him," Luke said distantly.

"Oh, you think? We kill bad guys. It's what we do."

"I don't," Luke said. "Not if I can help it. Not anymore." He looked down at Han with a faint start, as though he'd been lost in a daydream and only now realized where they both were. Wearing a faintly bemused half smile, he flipped the DL-44 end-for-end and offered its grip to Han. "Here. You'll need this."

"For what?" Han asked, just as he was starting to realize that the shaft around the *Falcon* had suddenly gone quiet.

The stormtroopers had stopped screaming.

"Uh-oh."

He snatched his pistol out of Luke's hand and popped to his feet as blasters opened up on all sides to rain plasma upon them in a roaring flood. Luke's lightsaber flared to life and lashed out in invisibly fast arcs that sent bolts out and away in a fan, blasting into the rock of the shaft walls. Choking red-black smoke billowed out from the points of impact, shrouding them in gloom so dense that the *Falcon*'s exterior floodlights only gave off a yellow-brown glow.

"Stick close." Luke's voice was tight with concentration. "I'm not used to having to cover somebody else."

"Don't have to tell *me* twice." Han squeezed himself into a substantially less-than-Han-sized space at Luke's back and had barely time to wish that he knew a Jedi who was just a *little* taller before the *Falcon* bucked as if it had been kicked. The ship bounced off the shaft wall hard enough that Han had to grab Luke's shoulder to stay upright. "Chewie, *dammit*!"

"Not his fault," Luke said tightly, still carving smoke with his blade to catch stray blaster bolts. "The ship didn't move. The shaft did. The mountain's breaking up."

"Oh, *great*! Any *more* good news?"

"Yes," Luke said. "We're being boarded."

Dark shapes hurtled down at them through the gloom—stormtroopers jumping off the ring ledge. Han snarled something wordless that expressed vividly how he felt about having Imperial boots touch his ship and slipped his blaster over Luke's shoulder, snapping off a pair of double taps that caught two troopers while they were still in the air. The bursts blew them backward far enough that they fell short and tumbled into the shaft below, but dozens made it onto the hull. There were plenty more where they'd come from, and Han had a strong feeling that a stand-up fight against a hundred-some stormtroopers was a losing proposition under the best of circumstances. Which these circumstances weren't.

"Make for the hatch!" Han fired twice more, dropping one dark silhouette and knocking another spinning off the rim of the hull, while Luke fanned away a flood of return fire. "Let's see how these sons of monkey-lizards like open space and hard vacuum!"

"You first," Luke said.

"That's *another* thing you won't have to tell me

twice." Red-glowing spheres sailed in through the smoke: thermal detonators. Some bounced away, but four or five maglocked themselves to the hull. "Uh, Luke?"

"I've got them." With his left hand, Luke swung his lightsaber in a dazzling flourish to spray blaster bolts randomly through the smoke, while his right hand stretched out toward the dets. All of them suddenly jerked themselves loose and flipped over the edge of the ship. Multiple detonations bounced the ship off the wall again. "Go, Han! Go *now*!"

Han took three steps, then threw himself into a flat dive that became a belly flop and sent him skidding and scraping over the lip of the hatch. He pulled himself in with his free hand and pivoted around his grip to land on his feet on the deck below. "I'm in! Luke, come on!"

More dets went off and lit the smoke with bloody flame, and there came no sign that Luke had any intention of following him. Han scrambled back up the gangway. "Luke, don't be an idiot!"

"I'm going after Vastor." Luke leaned into the gale of blasterfire as he worked his way toward the ship's edge. "Go. Save Leia! Don't wait for me."

"We're not leaving without you! And if you're going after that huge crazy thunderbucker, I'm coming with you! You'll need me!"

"*Leia* needs you. Stopping the bad guy is *my* job. Your job is to save the Princess."

"And since when do I take your orders?"

Luke threw him a glance. For one brief instant his face lit up with one of those old sunny farmboy grins Han hadn't seen since Hoth. "Watch your fingers."

"What?"

The hatch slammed down on Han hard enough to knock him down the gangway. He landed hard, rubbing his ringing head. "*Luke!*"

He hauled himself back up the gangway, but the hatch controls were dark, and the manual dogs were frozen. He snarled and pounded at them with the butt of his blaster, but then it occurred to him that the hull above was crowded with old-line Imperial troopers, the kind who *specialized* in cracking ships, and any of them who weren't busy trying to kill Luke would be busy trying to peel the hull so they could flood inside and kill Han and Chewie.

And Leia.

"Hope you know what you're doing, kid," Han muttered. It was as close to a good-bye as he could let himself say.

He jammed his blaster back into its holster and pelted headlong for the cockpit. "Chewie! Change of plan!" He skidded into the accessway. "The stun field, Chewie! Charge 'em up!"

"Growf! Heroo geeorrough?"

"He's not coming," Han vaulted into his seat. He hit the antipersonnel trigger himself and was treated to the gratifying sight of a couple of stormtroopers falling past the cockpit's viewports with blue energy still crackling over their black armor. Maybe on some other day he would have stayed and fought it out, but Leia, strapped into Chewbacca's copilot chair, writhed and moaned and twisted Han's heart.

"Luke's doing his job. We have to do ours," he said.

He heeled the ship over, pointed her mandibles straight down at the shaft's bottom, and kicked in every erg of energy her damaged thrusters could produce. The ship streaked toward a wall of solid rock. Han lit up the quad in his one remaining turret and held down the trigger; the stream of laser bolts chewed into the rock but didn't blast it away.

"Strap in," he said through his teeth. He tightened his

grip on the control yoke. "This ride's gonna start with a bump."

THE TASPAN SYSTEM EXPLODED INTO A HURRICANE OF death.

None of the Republic's warriors could see the whole picture, but what each of them saw was horrifying enough.

Lando Calrissian, on the bridge of the *Remember Alderaan,* watched over the shoulder of the NavOps officer as his sensor readout showed gravity wells sprouting and spreading throughout local space like Turranian flesh fungus on a three-day-old corpse, and all he could say was "No, no, no, this can't be *happening*!"

Wedge Antilles and the pilots of Rogue Squadron stared in frozen horror as thousands of TIE Interceptors streamed out of the asteroid fields, hurtling toward the Republic ships at maximum thrust. As each one slipped from the shadows of the asteroids into the full harsh glare of Taspan's stellar flares, the fierce radiation turned their ships into brilliant stars plunging toward destruction even as the pilots inside them were being roasted alive. They came on without maneuver, without tactics or even formation; the lead ships vanished in silent fireballs as Republic starfighters and the guns of the capital ships laced space with annihilating energy, but the TIEs behind them just came on and on, flying through the wreckage of their comrades, throwing themselves on unswerving suicide runs into the Republic ships clustered in Mindor's shadow.

Wait a Minute was the closest to the leading edge of the swarm. Its point-defense guns destroyed dozens of incoming TIEs, but finally one slipped through; after the first impact took out two of his turrets, Captain Patrell ordered his ship into rolling fire, but another TIE hit only meters away from the first, and two more hit after that.

The ship broke up and finally exploded, and the storm of TIEs just kept coming.

They streaked straight through the wreckage field and curved toward the next-closest ship, and by that time Wedge and the Rogues and all the remaining Republic starfighters had thrown themselves into the suiciders' path and lit up space with the fireballs from hundreds of exploding TIEs. The Imperials didn't even bother fighting back; Wedge didn't need his tactical navicomputer to calculate the chance that any Republic ship could survive this storm.

There wasn't one.

In the crowded hold of *Lancer,* the screaming of the stormtroopers had raised hairs on the back of Fenn Shysa's neck. He didn't have any idea what was going on, but he understood all too well the fundamental rules of combat, one of which was *When you don't know what's happening, what's happening is always bad.*

As the troopers had fallen into seizures, Fenn had jumped atop a cargo container and roared in Mandalorian, *"Secure their weapons! Now!,"* which was the main reason the slaughter that followed wasn't much, much worse—but it was still bad enough.

The mercenaries had leapt to their task like the disciplined warriors they were, deploying in staggered array to keep clear lines of fire open so they could cover each other and, if necessary, shoot the convulsing stormtroopers. Unfortunately, no amount of training or discipline could allow a small cadre of soldiers to instantly control several thousand panicked civilians.

Some of those civilians had enough military experience to understand that the most useful thing they could do was get themselves out of the way; they dived to the deck and pulled down other civilians around them, but still there were more than a thousand who stood frozen, screamed, or tried to run.

Those were the first to die.

The seizures stopped as suddenly as they had begun; the stormtroopers who had not yet been disarmed leapt to their feet or simply rolled into firing position and opened up on the crowd; the mercenaries returned fire, and within a second or two the entire hold was filled with a haze of blasterfire and the stench of burning flesh. The disarmed troopers still had the fist blades that were integral to the gauntlets of their armor, and they fell upon the nearby civilians like Nomarian thunder sharks in a feeding frenzy; they cut and chopped and hacked at their victims, while their fellows took fire from the mercenaries and responded with grenades lobbed at random into the screaming mob.

"Down blasters!" Fenn roared; the mercenaries were inflicting almost as many civilian casualties as were the maddened troopers. *"Down blasters and up blades!"*

And because he was the sort of commander who believed in leading by example, he leapt from the cargo container to land hard on the back of a black-armored trooper and punched his own fist blade through the back of the trooper's neck. Before that trooper even knew he was dead, Fenn had rolled to his feet and stabbed the next one in the kidney, and as that trooper whirled to face him, the Protector commandant jammed his blade in deep under the man's chin. He let the dead man fall and looked around for his next target.

He had plenty to choose from; he didn't anticipate running short in the foreseeable future—a future that would be, in Fenn's experienced judgment, exactly as long as the rest of his life.

The Shadow Base was now breaking up in earnest; one of its damaged gravity drives had already ripped free, spinning away and taking with it a kilometer or so of the base's rock. The remaining two gravity drives swung through opposing cycles of thrust-angle that were ripping what was left of the base in half. On the base's surface, the Republic marines found that their docile prisoners were docile no longer. With no regard for their own lives, or for anyone else's, they mobbed their captors, the troopers in front absorbing fire until the ones that followed could swarm over the dead and dying.

There was, in the whole of the Taspan system, only one faint reason for any hope at all.

Deep within the remains of the base, in the heart of the Election Center itself, Kar Vastor could find nowhere else to run.

KAR CROUCHED, HIS BARE BACK AGAINST AN ICY WALL, in a stone chamber filled with the dead. Corpses in long robes littered the floor, and the room stank of corruption; the only light came from blue spark-chains that crackled across the ceiling. His heart hammered against his ribs, and his breath rasped in his throat. His teeth were bared in an involuntary snarl, and his fingers scrabbled against the stone at his back as if he could somehow dig his way through. All from fear of the small blond man.

The same small blond man who now stood on the far side of the piles of dead bodies, inoffensive and mild, his expression friendly, his hands, empty of weapons, spread wide in invitation.

Kar did not know where this place might be, or how he had come to be here; he had no memory of having been anywhere like this maze of stone peopled only by dead men. He knew only that he had never felt such terror.

Not as a child, lost and alone in the lethal jungles of his homeworld; not in the dock of the Galactic Court on

Coruscant; not even in the infinite deadly dark of Kessel's spice mines. He had come back to himself in the midst of battle, blind with rage, surrounded by armed men on a starship's hull. He remembered seizing this little man in his unbreakable grip; he remembered sinking his needle teeth into the little man's throat, biting down like a vine cat strangling an akk wolf.

And he remembered what the little man had done to him.

The hands that scrabbled against the wall at his back still sprouted the black crystal hairs. His mouth was full of these crystal hairs, stiff and sharp as needles; when he worked his jaw, they cut and slashed at his palate and punctured his gums. And he could feel them *inside* him, throughout his body, an infection of dead *stone* within his living flesh . . .

He snarled wordless animal sounds. *What are you?*

The small blond man started toward him. "I'm not your enemy, Kar."

Stay back!

"I can't. Too many lives depend on me."

I'll kill you! Kar gathered himself to spring. *I will rip your head from your body. I will feast upon your guts!*

"It's all right to be afraid, Kar. This is a frightening place. Things have been done to you here that should never be done to anyone."

It's so . . . dead. Something broke inside him then; his rage and terror fled, and he sagged to his knees. *Nothing but stone and corpses. Everything dead. Dead within. Dead without. Dead forever.*

"Not everything." Though the small blond man had to step over corpses to reach Kar's side, his expression of sympathy and compassion never flickered. "You're alive, Kar. I'm alive."

That means nothing. Kar's eyes burned as if he'd dipped his face in sand. *We mean nothing.*

"We're the only meaning there is." The small blond man extended a hand. "Trust me or kill me, Kar. In the end, it'll come out the same. I will not harm you."

What are you? His snarl had gone plaintive. *What do you want from me?*

"I'm a Jedi. My name is Luke Skywalker," the small blond man said. "And I want you to take my hand."

DEEP IN HYPERSPACE, CRONAL REACHED UP FOR THE Shadow Crown. His life-support chamber was buried within an asteroid of meltmassif; with the Shadow Crown to focus and amplify his control, he could part the stone that shrouded his chamber's viewports and so enjoy the infinite nothing of hyperspace.

He loved gazing into hyperspace, the nothing outside the universe. The place beyond even the concept of *place* . . . Ordinary mortals sometimes went mad, succumbing to the delirium of hyper-rapture, from gazing too long into the emptiness. Cronal found it soothing: a glimpse into the oblivion beyond the end of all things.

To him, it looked like the Dark.

It would be some consolation for the frustration he had faced these past days. How was it that everywhere he turned, there seemed to be a Skywalker waiting to bar his path?

Still, the Skywalker boy's weakness had been a gift. How fortunate he was that Skywalker had lacked the strength of character to simply kill him.

Even in Cronal's wandering through the trackless wastes of hope where he had lost his way, he still had managed to deliver a blow to the infant second Republic from which it would never recover. Not to mention that he still had the advanced gravitic technology made possible by the properties of meltmassif, and he had the Shadow Crown itself.

Yes, he had lost his best chance to acquire a young,

powerful, and influential body to carry his consciousness, but he still had his original body with all his powers intact. In a few days—long enough to be certain that every Republic ship still in the Taspan system was crewed only by the dead—he could return, harvest the meltmassif from the asteroid clouds, and begin anew.

He would not repeat his mistake, however. Never again would he seek to build rather than destroy. Never again would he create anything but engines of ever-greater destruction.

Never again would he forsake the Way of the Dark.

His rule of the galaxy would be no mere Second Imperium, it would be the Reign of Death. He would preside over a universe of infinite suffering whose only end would be oblivion, meaningless as life itself.

He would author the final act in the saga of the galaxy.

With that dream to comfort him in his temporary exile, he lowered the Shadow Crown upon his head and sent his will into the Dark beyond darkness, to take control of the mind in the stone.

But where there should have been Dark, he found only light.

White light, brilliant, blinding, a young star born within his head. It seared his mind, blasting away even his memory of darkness. He recoiled convulsively, like a worm encountering red-hot stone. This was more than light; it was *the* Light.

It was the power to drive off the Dark.

This was inconceivable. What could heat his absolute zero? What could banish his infinite night?

You should know. The voice of the Light was not a voice. It spoke without speaking, communicating not with words, but with understanding. *You invited me here.*

Skywalker? This light was *Skywalker?*

In the instant he thought the name, Cronal *saw* him: a shape of light, absolute, uncompromising, kneeling within the Election Center in the darkest heart of the Shadow Base, his hands solemnly interfolded with the massive paws of Kar Vastor. He had linked his shadow nerves to Vastor's, and through the intimate connection between Vastor and Cronal he had somehow stretched forth to touch the Shadow Lord himself.

In the Dark, Cronal saw Skywalker smile. *Thank you for joining me here. I was a little worried you might get away with that silly crown of yours.*

This was *impossible*. This must be some hallucination, a twisted product of his Darksight run amok. He was in hyperspace! Hyperspace did not, *could* not, interact with realspace—

I was with Ben Kenobi in hyperspace when he felt the destruction of Alderaan.

No wall can contain the Force.

The Force, the Force, these pathetic Jedi kept nattering on about the Force! Did any of them even faintly comprehend how naive and foolish they were? If any of them had ever had so much as a glimpse of the real power of the Dark, that glimpse would have snuffed their tiny minds like candles in a hurricane—

Was my tiny mind snuffed? I must have missed that part.

Cronal could sense gentle amusement, like a tolerant uncle indulging a child's tantrum. Fury rose within him like molten lava climbing a volcanic fault. This simple-minded youth had fooled himself into believing his paltry light could fill the infinite Dark? Let him shine alone within eternal night.

Cronal opened himself wholly to the Dark, cracking the very gates of his mind, expanding the sphere of his power like an event horizon yawning to swallow the universe. He surrounded Skywalker's light, and with a shrug of power he consumed it.

In this arena, minds naked to the Dark contending in nonspace beyond even hyperspace, there was no question of age, or health, or physical strength. Here the only power that counted was the power of will. Skywalker and his so-called Force could never match Cronal's mastery of the Way of the Dark.

On this level, Cronal *was* Blackhole. From his grip no light could escape.

Escape? Me? Did you forget that you're the one who's running away?

Cronal suddenly felt, unaccountably—and unpleasantly—warm.

At first he dismissed this unwelcome sensation; he was too experienced a servant of the Dark to be distracted by a minor malfunction in his life-support settings. But gradually he became aware that his body—specifically, his body's skin—did not seem to be warm at all. It was, in fact, chilly. And damp.

As though he had broken out, somehow, in a cold sweat.

He turned his mind back to the Dark, and became again the ultimate black hole. He examined the abyss of darkness he had become and found it to be flawless. Perfect. The ultimate expression of the absolute power of the Dark.

This boy, this infantile Jedi-ling, had thought his meager light could stand against that power? Cronal's black hole had swallowed every last lumen; Skywalker's light was gone forever. His puerile Force trick of light had done to Cronal nothing whatsoever.

That's because I'm not trying to do anything to you. I'm doing something through *you.*

What?

How could Skywalker still speak?

A creeping dread began to poison Cronal's smug satisfaction. What if Skywalker was telling the truth? What if the boy had been so easily vanquished because he had *intended* to be? He had already used his tiny gift of the Force to forge a link through Kar Vastor to Cronal . . . what if his light had *not* been destroyed by falling into the black hole that was Cronal's mind?

What if his light had simply passed *through*?

That's where you dark siders always stumble. What's the opposite of a black hole?

Cronal had heard this cosmological theory before: that matter falling into a black hole passes into another universe . . . and that matter falling through black holes in other universes could pass into ours, bursting forth in pure, transcendent energy.

The opposite of a black hole was a white fountain.

He thought, *I've been suckered.*

The Sith alchemy that had created the Shadow Crown had imbued it with control over meltmassif in all its forms; to drown Skywalker in the Dark, Cronal had opened a channel into the Crown. Through the Crown.

Through the Shadow Crown, Skywalker's light could shine upon every crystal of darkness.

Every shadow stormtrooper. Every gravity station. Every millimeter of the shadow web of crystalline nerves in his body, and Vastor's, and—

And Cronal's *own*!

With a snarl, he yanked his mind back into his body; it would require only a second to pull the Crown from his head.

Or it would have, if he could have made his arms work . . .

In the shimmery glow from the viewscreens within his life-support capsule, Cronal could only sit and watch in horror as his skin began to leak black oil. This black oil flowed from every pore, from his ears and nose and mouth and eyes. This black oil drained even from the channels within the Shadow Crown.

And not until the last drop of it had left his body could Cronal even take a breath.

He did not, however, have time for more than a single breath before the meltmassif rehardened, encasing him wholly in a sarcophagus of stone. The asteroid of melt-massif around his chamber melted, and its shreds vapor-ized as they fell from the hyperdrive zone. Very soon, the hyperdrive itself fell away, as it had been mounted on the stone, rather than on the chamber.

The chamber, no longer within the hyperdrive's pro-tective envelope of reality, simply dissolved.

Cronal had enough time to understand what was hap-pening. He had enough time to feel his body lose its physical cohesion. He had time to feel his very atoms lose their reality and vanish into the infinite nothing of hyperspace.

HAN SAT ON THE POLYFILM SURVIVAL BLANKET UNDER the *Falcon*'s starboard mandible, hugging his knees and waiting for the sun to rise. Leia lay on the blanket beside him, breathing slowly and easily now. She looked like she was only asleep.

He didn't think he should wake her up.

The only word Leia had been able to speak had been *light*. She'd kept asking for light, even with every light source within the *Falcon* dialed up to maximum. She must have been talking about a different kind of light.

And when Han had gotten the grim news on their situation from Lando, he'd figured that he might as well give her what she was asking for.

Everyone was going to die anyway. There was no es-caping this trap. The choice was between being killed by the breakup of Mindor or being roasted alive by Tas-pan's stellar flares.

So he'd set down the *Falcon* on the shattered battle-field, spread the blanket, and made Leia as comfortable as he could. Chewbacca had hung back; he watched over them from the *Falcon*'s cockpit, out of respect. Humans, he understood, often wanted privacy at times like these.

Han had stayed at Leia's side as her seizures quieted; he stayed at her side as her every pore oozed black and shiny meltmassif, as it drained off her and puddled on the blanket. And he would stay at her side as the groundquakes strengthened and the killing sun rose over the horizon.

He would be at her side when the planet exploded.

A bitter irony: she had suffered so much from being forced to watch her homeworld destroyed. Now she would die in very much the same brutal fashion as had her family and all her people.

That was why he figured he probably shouldn't wake her up.

But the Force again displayed that nasty sense of humor; Leia stirred, and her eyelids fluttered. "Han . . . ?"

"I'm here, Leia." He felt like his heart would burst. "I'm right here."

Her hand sought his. "So dark . . ."

"Yeah," Han said. "But the sun's coming up."

"No . . . not here. Where I was." She drew in a deep breath and released it in a long, slow sigh. "It was so *dark*, Han. It was so dark for so long I couldn't even remember who I was. I couldn't remember anything."

Her eyes opened and found his face. "Except for you."

Han swallowed and squeezed her hand. He didn't trust his voice.

"It was like . . . like you were *with* me," she murmured. "You were all I had left—and I didn't need anything else."

"I'm with you now," he said, his voice hoarse, unsteady. "We're together. And we always will be."

"Han . . ." She pushed herself up to a sitting position and swiped a hand across her eyes. "Is there anything to eat?"

"What?"

"I'm hungry. Is there any food?"

Han shook his head, baffled. He nodded around at the stormtrooper corpses that littered the field. "Nothing but, y'know, Imperial ration packs. And they're probably stale."

"I don't care."

"Are you kidding?"

She shrugged, and gave him a smile that even now, even here, minutes from their deaths, made his heart race and his breath go short. "We'll make it a picnic," she said. "We'll have a picnic and watch the sun rise. One last time."

"Yeah," he said. "Yeah, that sounds good."

He stripped some ration packs off dead troopers, and they sat together, shoulder to shoulder, eating in silence as the horizon began to blaze as though the planet were on fire.

"Well, one thing's for sure." Han pushed an echo of his old half grin onto his face. "This is one meal we'll never forget as long as we live, huh?"

Leia smiled, though her eyes sparkled with tears. "Always the joker. Even now. Even here."

Han nodded. "Well, y'know, we always get romantic when we're about to die. It was getting repetitive."

The ground beneath them spasmed once, then again, and Leia said, "*I* think we should respect the tradition."

"You do?"

"Kiss me, Han. One last time." She lifted a hand to his cheek. Her touch was warm and dry, and impossibly precious to him. "Once for all the kisses we'll never get."

He gathered her into his arms and lowered his face to hers—and then a great Wookiee yelp of joy that echoed all the way from the cockpit yanked his head up and popped his eyes open. "What? Chewie, you're sure?"

Chewbacca pounded on the cockpit's transparisteel and waved both his arms, frantically beckoning. Han sprang to his feet and lifted Leia as though she weighed nothing at all. "Han—what is it?" she gasped. "What did he say?"

"All those other kisses you were talking about?" His eyes alight, he pulled her toward the *Falcon*'s freight lift. "He said if we move fast, we might get every one of 'em after all!"

ONE BY ONE, INSIDE HIS HEAD, LUKE FELT THE STARS wink out.

Linked through Kar to Cronal, through Cronal to the Shadow Crown, and through the Crown's ancient powers of Sith alchemy to every Melter mind in every scrap of meltmassif in the galaxy, Luke had shone upon them with the light of the Force. This light had drawn them as moonlight draws a shadowmoth, and they found that its inexhaustible flood could fill them to overflowing. Never again would they feed upon light; there would never be the need. They would forever shine with light of their own.

And so they came out from every place the Dark had put them.

Luke felt them go.

He felt them leave the gravity stations. He felt them leave the Shadow Crown, and Cronal's body, and Leia's and Kar's and his own.

And he felt the stormtroopers, in all their thousands throughout the system. He felt every single man who wore Cronal's black armor. He felt the uncontrollable rage and bloodlust, the almost-mindless battle frenzy that the crystals in their brains had triggered and now sustained. He felt the damage that had been done by the brutal force of the crystals' growth.

He felt what the crystals' exit would do.

He did not look away. He did not withdraw his perception. He owed these men that much. Enemies they might be, but still they were men.

None of them had wanted this. None had volunteered for this. None had even cooperated. This had been done to them with casual disregard for their humanity; Luke could not allow its undoing to be the same.

So he stayed with them as the meltmassif in their bodies and their brains liquefied. He stayed with them as it poured forth from their every pore. He stayed with them as the exit of the meltmassif triggered their deadman interlocks.

He stayed with them while every stormtrooper in the entire system, all at once in all their thousands, sagged and shuddered.

And died.

Luke felt every death.

It was all he could do for them.

WHEN HE FINALLY WITHDREW HIS MIND FROM THE Dark, Luke found himself in darkness of the wholly ordinary sort. The flicker of the energy discharge had fled from the chamber that had once been the Election Center.

He knelt in darkness, and from that darkness came a long, slow growl that the Force allowed him to understand as words. *Jedi Luke Skywalker. Is it done?*

By reaching into the Force, he could feel the surviving Republic ships jump away as the artificial mass-shadows of the destroyed gravity stations shrank and vanished.

He felt the final breakup of the Shadow Base, and the final destruction of Mindor under the killing radiation of Taspan's flares.

All gone, now. Everything was gone.

No more shadows.

"Yes," Luke said. "Yes, it is done."

Is this where we die?

"I don't know," Luke said. "Probably."

How long?

Luke sighed. "I don't know that either. I sealed the chamber when I came in, so we'll have air. For a while. But I don't know how thick the stone around us might be, now that the mountain's broken up. I don't know how much radiation it can block. We could be cooking right now."

And there is no one who can come for us.

"Their ships can't protect them. Not from radiation like this."

Then this will be where our lives end.

"Probably."

I do not like this place. I do not know how I came to be here, but I know I did not choose this.

"None of us did."

This is a bad place to die.

"Yes."

Granted a choice, I would not die beside a Jedi.

"I'm sorry," Luke said. And meant it.

I have known Jedi. Many, many years ago. That knowing was not a gladness for me. I believed I would never know another, and I rejoiced in that belief.

But it is a gladness for me to be proven wrong.

I am happy to have known you, Jedi Luke Skywalker. You are more than they were.

"That's—" Luke shook his head blankly, blinking against the darkness. "I mean, thanks, but I barely know *anything*."

So you believe. But I say to you: you are greater than the Jedi of former days.

Luke could only frown, and shake his head again. "What makes you say that?"

Because unlike the Knights of old, Jedi Luke Sky-walker . . .

You are not afraid of the dark.

R2-D2 CLUNG TO THE SURFACE OF A TINY ASTEROID AS it rolled along its slow spiral descent toward the stellar sphere of Taspan.

The asteroid was roughly spherical, its diameter perhaps half that of the *Millennium Falcon,* and it had a very slow rotation, slow enough that the little astromech could drag himself along the asteroid's dark side by clutching the rock with his manipulator arms. In this way, R2-D2 kept the asteroid between himself and the radiation bursts from Taspan's stellar flares—bursts that could permanently fry his circuitry in less than a second.

In this way, R2 calculated that he could maintain operational capacity for an additional seven-point-three Standard hours, after which time his asteroid would pass between Taspan and a particularly dense cloud of other asteroids, which would reflect enough hard radiation onto his asteroid's dark side that he would—he estimated with 89.756 percent certainty—experience sudden catastrophic system failure.

Permanent shutdown.

Should he through some fluke survive that transit, he was reasonably certain—83.973 percent—that he would survive an additional two-point-three Standard hours.

He was not distressed by the prospect of shutdown; he had spent several seconds calculating his overall chance of personal survival before he had judiciously overridden the *Falcon*'s trash-ejector system and had it bump him into space less than a second before the ship had blasted free of the disintegrating Shadow Base. That chance had been so tiny as to defy the description *probability;* he had, he calculated, roughly the same chance of remaining operational as he did of undergoing a quantum phase transition that would instantaneously transform him into a Lofquarian gooney bird.

However: He had been instructed more than once, very firmly and in no uncertain terms by Princess Leia herself, to take good care of Luke Skywalker. Considerations of personal survival were irrelevant to his assigned task.

He did not concern himself with survival. Every minute or so, however, he spent a millisecond or two accessing a few directories in his very, very extensive library of recordings of his adventures with the only droid in his long, long existence who he could truthfully label *my friend:* C-3PO. He did not anticipate that he would miss C-3PO; he did not anticipate that he would be capable of missing anyone or anything. He did, however, experience a peculiar sensation in his social-interaction subroutines every time he accessed these particular directories. It was a sensation both positive and negative, and it was largely impossible, to R2's considerable puzzlement, to quantify.

He supposed, after much computation, that he must be regretting that he would never see his friend again, while at the same time he was taking considerable comfort from the knowledge that his friend was, and would be for the foreseeable future, quite safe.

Somehow that seemed to make him more able to focus on the task at hand.

When the *Falcon* had departed without Luke on board, R2 had known exactly what to do, and he had done it. Once free of the trash ejector, he had tuned his sensor suite to register Master Luke's personal chemical signature—his scent—and tracked Luke's progress through the Shadow Base, right up until the trail had ended abruptly at a stone wall. Having no instructions or programming that appeared to offer him any useful alternative courses of action, he had settled in to wait.

R2 had waited while the gravity stations depowered, and while the fleet departed. He had waited through the breakup of the Shadow Base, and through the explosion of the planet. And he was waiting still.

He was entirely—one hundred percent—certain that Luke had been on the opposite side of that stone wall, which was now part of the surface of this tiny asteroid.

Luke was inside this ball of rock, and though Luke's own chance of personal survival was only fractionally greater than R2's—which was to say, for all practical purposes, nonexistent—the astromech would continue to clamber along the asteroid's dark side and keep himself functional until he could do so no longer, because there remained a very slight, but measurable, chance that he might still be able to somehow help.

A peculiar motion among the starfield attracted his attention. One particular asteroid—one point of *very* bright radiation reflected from Taspan—moved somewhat more *across* the system's plane of the ecliptic than along it. Further: This bright point's motion was clearly retrograde; its heading was against the general direction of the asteroid field. Finally: This point of light did not travel with the consistent velocity that would be expected from a body whose motion was subject only to the laws of orbital mechanics; on the contrary, it accelerated, then slowed, then sped up again.

There was only one probable explanation.

Activating the telescopic zoom feature of his optical sensor, he was able to confirm his calculation: This object was indeed a ship.

Specifically, a Lambda T-4a shuttle.

R2-D2 opened the comm hatch in his dome and extended his parabolic antenna. He aimed it precisely—after calculating the lightspeed delay—at where the shuttle would be when his transmission would arrive, and began to broadcast a distress beacon code with all his considerable energy. Once he had established contact with the shuttle's brain, he was able to explain the details of the situation and trust that the ship's brain would be able to communicate the pertinent facts to its pilot.

The shuttle's vector shifted to an intercept course with gratifying alacrity. The shuttle swung around to the asteroid's light side, extended a docking claw, and seized the asteroid, drawing them close enough together to enclose the asteroid in its hyperdrive envelope. Then it made the jump to lightspeed.

R2-D2 spent the hyperspace transition reviewing his calculations, but they were impeccable.

The designs of an evil but brilliant man had been thwarted. Luke would survive, Princess Leia and Han Solo had escaped, C-3PO was assuredly safe, and R2-D2—to the best of his self-diagnostic subroutine's ability to determine—had not, in fact, undergone a quantum phase transition into a Lofquarian gooney bird.

The odds against this outcome were literally incalculable.

The universe, R2 decided, was an astonishing place.

DEBRIEFING

GEPTUN RAN A FINGER UNDER HIS UNIFORM'S COLLAR and grimaced at finding it damp. Really, Skywalker kept his quarters unpleasantly hot. He continued to pace the length of the sitting room, however, despite the undeniable fact that this was only causing him to sweat even more. He continued to pace because simply sitting, he'd discovered, was intolerable.

How was it possible he could be so nervous? Imagine, at such an age, after such a long and varied life, to find oneself very nearly overcome with what could only be described as *authorial vanity*.

He was entirely flabbergasted at how desperately he wanted—how badly he *needed*—Skywalker to like the story.

The expression on Skywalker's face when the young Jedi returned to the sitting room hinted rather broadly that in this, as in so many other things, Geptun was destined to be disappointed.

Skywalker practically threw the holoreader at him. "What is this—this *garbage*?"

"Ah." Geptun lowered himself onto a settee with a long, slow sigh. "It's not to your taste, then."

"My taste? My *taste*?" Skywalker flushed bright red; veins stood out on his forehead from the effort he expended in controlling what was clearly considerable anger. "It's *terrible*. It's the *worst* thing I've ever *read*!"

"Ah." Geptun leaned forward and slowly, a little sadly, retrieved the holoreader. "Well, then. I'm sorry you don't care for it. I'll just be, well, on my way, then."

"You will *not*." Though not a large man, Skywalker seemed to tower over him. "I hired you to *investigate*. I hired you to write a report. An *indictment*. Instead you bring me *this*? It reads like one of those blasted holothrillers!"

"Well . . . yes," Geptun said. "There's a reason for that."

This brought Skywalker to a full stop. "What?"

"I have, well . . ." Geptun coughed. "I've already sold the holo rights."

Skywalker sank into a chair. The flush drained from his cheeks. "I don't believe it."

Geptun's initial disappointment had faded already, and he was constitutionally incapable of shame. "Did we not understand each other? Why do you think I agreed to do this in the first place?"

"For money," Skywalker practically spat. "But I'm not paying you for *this*."

"Suit yourself. The holothriller production company paid me *ten times* what you agreed to pay—and that was just for the production rights; I'm also getting points on the back end. They like it so much they've already optioned my next two Luke Skywalker Adventures."

"Next *two*—? Please tell me you're joking."

"I have been known to joke," Geptun said. "But rarely about business, and *never* about money."

"You were planning this," Skywalker accused. "This was what you planned to do from the *beginning*."

"Oh, yes. Yes, indeed."

All Skywalker's anger had fled. Now he only looked

tired. Very tired, and much older than his years. "Did you even bother to investigate?"

"Of course," Geptun said. "Verisimilitude is vital. I stand behind every word."

"Verisimilitude? I did *not* defeat Kar Vastor in single combat—I didn't even *fight* him. He was terrified, and confused, and aside from one, well, bite, he just ran away. I didn't cut off his arms with my lightsaber, and I don't even know what a 'vibroshield' *is*."

"I did take some liberties," Geptun said. "Call it artistic license."

"It's—it's just so . . ." Skywalker shook his head helplessly; for a moment Geptun feared he might start to cry. "You make me look like some kind of *hero*." The word dripped loathing.

"You *are* a hero, General. Trust me on this, if nothing else. In my lifetime, I've known exactly four actual heroes, and one of them is you."

"Don't call me General."

"I beg your pardon?"

"I've resigned my commission. I'm no soldier. Not ever again."

"Ah. And what *are* you, then?"

Skywalker's eyes went hooded. "All those men . . . I killed them. All of them."

"You had no choice."

"There's always a choice."

"If that is so," Geptun said, "then you made the right one. *That's* what this story is about. Don't you understand? You are more than a man, now. You are a symbol of everything that is good in the galaxy. In this horrific civil war, don't you see how much good that image of you can do? You give people hope. You set an example that they can aspire to live up to. Just by *existing*, you make people want to be better than they are."

"But it's not me. It's just some made-up guy using my name. A holothriller hero. A storybook prince."

"If you say so."

Skywalker lowered his face into his hands, and for a long moment he just sat there, silent, motionless. Finally he said, "You didn't write anything about my good-byes with Nick."

"No. Too anticlimactic. The story needs to end with a nice, neat wrap-up. I like your little astromech droid. I think I'm going to end with him."

"On the shuttle, later, after I asked Nick about an investigator and he told me about you, just before Nick and Aeona took off . . . Nick reminded me that I'd never told him what my 'best trick' was. You know what I told him? I told him he'd just seen it."

Skywalker lifted his face from his hands, and his eyes were dark. Wounded. Haunted by shadows. "My best trick is to do one thing—to make one small move, even a simple *choice*—and kill thousands of people. *Thousands*."

Geptun nodded noncommittally. After a moment, he said, "One of those heroes I mentioned liked to occasionally say *Jedi are not soldiers. We are keepers of the peace.*"

"Keepers of the peace," Skywalker murmured. "Yes. Yes, I like that. I think that's right. We are the light in the darkness."

"A poetic metaphor."

"I'm not surprised you like it; you made it up. But I think . . . I think it's not just a metaphor. I think it's the plain truth."

"And all I'm doing," Geptun said, "is sharing that light with the whole galaxy. I would think you'd want to play along."

"I suppose . . ." Luke took a deep breath, sighed it out. "Maybe you're right. How much harm can it do?"

"Well . . ." Geptun shifted on the settee. He had an uncomfortable feeling that he was about to do something he abhorred: tell the truth.

Something about Skywalker just seemed to bring that out of him.

"Let them tell their stories," Skywalker said. "Let them make holothrillers and whatever else. It doesn't matter. None of the stories people tell about me can change who I really am."

"Yes," Geptun said heavily. "But they can change who people *think* you are. And that, my young friend, can do considerable damage. Look at *Luke Skywalker and the Jedi's Revenge*."

Luke nodded thoughtfully. "I guess . . . I guess if people are going to tell stories about me anyway, I should make sure they're telling the right kind of stories."

"You'll never have cause to complain of mine, at least. Just don't start believing your own press."

"No fear of that," Luke said. "I'm not much of a reader, and holothrillers bore me. But there are a couple of changes you need to make."

"Do I? My producers rather like it as is."

"And if I were to visit them and talk it over, they might change their minds. They might change their minds about making the production at all."

"Oh, please. After all the money they've sunk into it already?"

"I can be," Luke said mildly, "surprisingly persuasive."

"Ah, yes, I suppose you can." Geptun sighed. "Very well. What changes?"

"You made the deaths of the shadow troopers seem almost like an accident. Like I didn't know it would happen. But I did. I knew what I was doing. The story has to say so."

"Well . . ."

MATTHEW STOVER

"That lightsaber versus 'vibroshield' fight? That goes too. It's stupid. Besides, who wants to watch me cut up one more villain with my lightsaber? Don't you think that's getting pretty old?"

"Perhaps," Geptun allowed, "we can work a little bit of truth in there."

"And then there's Aeona Cantor. She's *not* my love interest—she's *Nick's* girlfriend, and that's the whole story. Anyway, she's not my type. Too abrasive. And I don't like redheads."

"I'll make a note of it. What did happen to Nick and Aeona? And to Kar?"

Luke shrugged. "Nick thinks Blackhole is still alive."

"Really?"

"That's what he said. He and Kar figure they have a score there that needs settling. And if Blackhole really is still alive, having Nick and Kar and Aeona on his tail will keep him busy enough looking over his shoulder that he won't have much time to stir up mischief. Now, look, in the story—some of these similies you use are . . . well, I'm not exactly a literary critic, but . . ."

Geptun sighed and reluctantly reached for the holopad. He had a feeling this would be a long, hard process.

Rewrites, he decided, sucked.

Read on for an excerpt from

Star Wars: **Fate of the Jedi:** Backlash

by Aaron Allston

Published by Century

The rainforest air was so dense, so moist that even roaring through it at speeder-bike velocity didn't bring Luke Skywalker any physical relief. His speed just caused the air to move across him faster, like a greasy scrub-rag wielded by an overzealous nanny-droid, drenching all the exposed surfaces of his body.

Not that he cared. He couldn't see her, but he could sense his quarry, not far ahead: the individual whose home he'd crossed so many light-years to find.

He could sense much more than that. The forest teemed with life, life that poured its energy into the Force, too much to catalogue as he roared past. He could feel ancient trees and new vines, creeping predators and alert prey. He could feel his son Ben as the teenager drew up abreast of him on his own speeder-bike, eyes shadowed under his helmet but a competitive grin on his lips, and then Ben was a few meters ahead of him, dodging leftward to avoid hitting a split-forked tree, the recklessness of youth giving him a momentary speed advantage over Luke's superior piloting ability.

Then there was more life, *big* life, close ahead, with malicious intent—

From a thick nest of magenta-flowered underbrush twice the height of a man, just to the right of Luke's path ahead, emerged an arm, striking with great speed and accuracy. It was humanlike, gnarly, gigantic, long enough to reach from the flowers to swat the forward tip of Luke's speeder bike as he passed.

Disaster takes only a fraction of a second. One instant Luke was racing along, intent on his distant prey and enjoying moments of competition; the next, he was headed straight for a tree whose trunk, four meters across, would bring a sudden stop to his travels and his life.

He came free of the speeder-bike as it rotated beneath him from the giant creature's blow. He was still headed for the tree trunk. He gave himself an adrenaline-boosted shove in the Force and drifted another couple of meters to the left, allowing him to flash past the trunk instead of into it; he could feel its bark rip at the right shoulder of his tunic. A centimeter closer, and the contact would have given him a serious friction burn.

He rolled into a ball and let senses other than sight guide him. A Force shove to the right kept him from smacking into a much thinner tree, one barely sturdy enough to break his spine and any bones that hit it. He needed no Force effort to shoot between the forks of a third tree. Contact with a veil of vines slowed him; they tore beneath the impact of his body but dropped his rate of speed painlessly. He went crashing through a mass of tendrils ending in big-petaled yellow flowers, some of which reflexively snapped at him as he plowed through them.

Then he was bouncing across the ground, a dense layer of decaying leaves and other materials he really didn't want to speculate about.

Finally he rolled to a halt. He stretched out, momentarily stunned but unbroken, and stared up through the trees. He could see a single shaft of sunlight penetrating the forest canopy not far behind him; it illuminated a swirl of pollen from the stand of yellow flowers he'd just crashed through. In the distance, he could hear the roar of Ben's speeder bike, hear its engine whine as the boy put it in a hard maneuver, trying to get back to Luke.

Closer, there were footsteps. Heavy, ponderous footsteps.

A moment later, their origin, the owner of that huge arm, loomed over Luke. It was a rancor, humanoid and bent.

The rancors of this world had evolved to be smarter than those elsewhere. This one had clearly been trained as a guard and taught to tolerate protective gear. It wore a helmet, a rust-streaked cup of metal large enough to serve as a backwoods bathtub, with leather straps meeting under its chin. Strapped to its left forearm was a thick durasteel round shield that looked ridiculously tiny compared to the creature's enormous proportions but was probably thick enough to stop one or two salvos from a military laser battery.

The creature stared down at Luke. Its mouth opened and it offered a challenging growl.

Luke glared at it. "Do you really want to make me angry right now? I don't recommend it."

It reached for him.

SEVERAL DAYS EARLIER
Empty Space Near Kessel

It was darkness surrounded by stars—one of them, the unlovely sun of Kessel, closer than the rest, but barely close enough to be a ball of illumination rather than a dot—and then it was occupied, suddenly inhabited by a space yacht of flowing, graceful lines and peeling paint. That was how it would have looked, a vessel dropping out of hyperspace, to those in the arrival zone, had there been any witnesses: nothing there, then something, an instantaneous transition.

In the bridge sat the ancient yacht's sole occupant, a teenage girl wearing a battered combat vac suit. She looked from sensor to sensor, uncertain and slow because of her unfamiliarity with this model of spacecraft. Too, there was something like shock in her eyes.

Finally satisfied that no other ship had dropped out of hyperspace nearby, or was likely to creep up on her in this remote location, she sat back in her pilot's seat and tried to get her thoughts in order.

Her name was Vestara Khai, and she was a Sith of the Lost Tribe. She was a proud Sith, not one to hide under false identities and concealing robes until some decades-long grandiose plan neared completion, and now she had even more reason than usual to swell with pride. Mere hours before, she and her Sith Master, Lady Rhea, had confronted Jedi Grand Master Luke Skywalker. Lady Rhea and Vestara had fought the galaxy's most experienced, most famous Jedi to a standstill. Vestara had even *cut* him, a graze to the cheek and chin that had spattered her with blood—blood she had later tasted, blood she wished she could take a sample of and keep forever as a souvenir.

But then Skywalker had shown why he carried that reputation. A moment's distraction, and suddenly Lady Rhea was in four pieces, each drifting in a separate direction, and Vestara was hopelessly outmatched. She had saluted and fled.

Now, having taken a space yacht that had doubtless been old when her great-great-great-grandsires were newborn, but which, to her everlasting gratitude, held in its still-functioning computer the navigational secrets of the mass of black holes that was the Maw, she was free. And the impossible weight of her reality and her responsibility were settling upon her.

Lady Rhea was dead. Vestara was alone, and her pride at Lady Rhea's accomplishment, at her own near success in the duel with the Jedi, was not enough to wash away the sense of loss.

Then there was the question of what to do next, of where to go. She needed to be able to communicate with her people, to report on the incidents in the Maw. But this creaking, slowly deteriorating SoroSuub StarTracker space yacht did not carry a hypercomm unit. She'd have to put in to some civilized planet to make contact. That meant arriving unseen, or arriving and departing so swiftly that the Jedi could not detect her in time to catch her. It also meant acquiring sufficient credits to fund a secret, no-way-to-trace-it hypercomm message. All of these plans would take time to bring to reality.

Vestara knew, deep in her heart, and within the warning currents of the Force, that Luke Skywalker intended to track her to her homeworld of Kesh. How he planned to do it, she didn't know, but her sense of paranoia, trained at the hands of Lady Rhea, burned within her as though her blood itself were acid. She had to find some way to outwit a Force user several times her age, renowned for his skills.

She needed to go someplace where Force users were relatively commonplace. Otherwise, any use by her of the Force would stand out like a signal beacon to experienced Jedi in the vicinity. There weren't many such places. Coruscant was the logical answer. But if her trail began to lead toward the government seat of the Galactic Alliance, Skywalker could warn the Jedi there and Vestara would face a nearly impossible-to-bypass network of Force users between her and her destination.

The current location of the Jedi school was not known. Hapes was ruled by an ex-Jedi and was rumored to harbor more Force sensitives, but it was such a security-conscious civilization that Vestara doubted she could accomplish her mission there in secrecy.

Then the answer came to her, so obvious and so perfect that she laughed out loud.

But the destination she'd thought of wouldn't be on a galactic map as old as the one in the antique yacht she commanded. She'd have to go somewhere and get a map update. She nodded, her pride, sense of loss, and paranoia all fading as she focused on her new task.

TRANSITORY MISTS

Jedi Knight Leia Organa Solo sat at the *Millennium Falcon*'s communications console. She frowned, her lips pursed as though she were solving an elaborate mathematical equation, as she read and re-read the text message the *Falcon* had just received via hypercomm.

The silence that had settled around her eventually drew her husband, Han Solo, to her side; his boyish, often insensitive persona was in part a fabrication, and he well knew and could sense his wife's moods. The chill and silence of her complete concentration usually meant trouble. He waved a hand between her eyes and the console monitor. "Hey."

She barely reacted to his presence. "Hm."

"New message?"

"From Ben."

"Another letter filled with teenage talk, I assume. Girls, speeders, allowance woes—"

Leia ignored his joking. "Sith," she said.

"And Sith, of course." Han sat in the chair next to

hers but did not assume his customary slouch; the news kept his spine rigid. "They found a new Sith Lord?"

"Worse, I think." Finally some animation returned to Leia's voice. "They've found an ancient installation at the Maw and were attacked by a gang of Sith. A whole strike team. With the possibility of more out there."

"I thought Sith ran in packs of two. Vape both of 'em and their menace is ended for all time, at least for a few years, until two more show up." Han tried to keep his voice calm, but the last Sith to bring trouble to the galaxy had been Jacen Solo, his and Leia's eldest son. Though Jacen had been dead for more than two years, the ripples of the evil he had done were still causing damage and heartache throughout the settled galaxy. And both his acts and his death had torn a hole in Han's heart that felt like it would last forever.

"Yeah, well, no. Apparently not anymore. Ben also says—and we're not to let Luke know that he did— that Luke is exhausted. Really exhausted, like he's had the life squeezed out of him. Ben would like us to sort of drift near and lend Luke some support."

"Of course." But then Han grimaced. "Back to the Maw. The only place gloomy enough to make its next door neighbor, Kessel, seem like a garden spot."

Leia shook her head. "They're tracking a Sith girl who's on the run. So it probably won't be the Maw. It may be a planet full of Sith."

"Ah, good." Han rubbed his hands together as if anticipating a fine meal or a fight. "Well, why not. We can't go back to Coruscant until we're ready to mount a legal defense. Daala's bound to be angry that we stole all the Jedi she wanted to deep-freeze."

Finally Leia smiled and looked at Han. "One good thing about the Solos and Skywalkers. We never run out of things to do."

CORUSCANT
Jedi Temple

Master Cilghal, Mon Calamari and most proficient medical doctor among the current generation of Jedi, paused before hitting the console button that would erase the message she had just spent some time decrypting. It had been a video transmission from Ben Skywalker, a message carefully rerouted through several hypercomm nodes and carefully staged so as not to mention that it was for Cilghal's tympanic membranes or, in fact, for anyone on Coruscant.

But its main content was meant for the Jedi, and Cilghal repeated it as a one-word summation, making the word sound like a vicious curse: "*Sith.*"

The message had to be communicated throughout the Jedi Order. And on review, there was nothing in it that suggested she couldn't preserve the recording, couldn't claim that it had been forwarded to her by a civilian friend of the Skywalkers. Luke Skywalker was not supposed to be in contact with the Jedi Temple, but this recording was manifestly free of any proof that the exiled Grand Master exerted any influence over the Order. She could distribute it.

And she would do so, right now.

DEEP SPACE NEAR KESSEL

Jade Shadow, one-time vehicle of Mara Jade Skywalker, now full-time transport and home to her widower and son, dropped from hyperspace into the empty blackness well outside the Kessel system. It hung suspended there for several minutes, long enough for one of its occupants to gather from the Force a sense of his own life's blood that had been in the vicinity, then it turned on a course toward Kessel and vanished again into hyperspace.

JADE SHADOW
In Orbit Above Kessel

Ben Skywalker shouldered his way through the narrow hatch that gave access to his father's cabin. A redheaded teen of less than average height, he was well muscled in a way that his anonymous black tunic and pants could not conceal.

On the cabin's bed, under a brown blanket, lay Luke Skywalker. Similar in build to his son, he wore the evidence of many more years of hard living, including ancient, faded scars on his face and the exposed portions of his arms. Not obvious was the fact that his right hand, so ordinary in appearance, was a prosthetic.

Luke's eyes were closed but he stirred. "What did you find out?"

"I reached Nien Nunb." Nunb, the Sullustan co-owner and manager of one of Kessel's most prominent mineworks, had been a friend of the Solos and Skywalkers for decades. "That yacht did make landfall. The pilot gave her name as Captain Khai. She somehow scammed a port worker into thinking she'd paid for a complete refueling when she hadn't—"

Luke smiled. "The Force can have a—"

"Yeah, so can a good-looking girl. Anyway, what's interesting is that she got a galactic map update. Nunb looked at the transmission time on that to determine that it was pretty comprehensive. In other words, she didn't concentrate on any one specific area or route. No help there."

"But it suggests that she did need some of the newer information. New hyperspace routes or planetary listings."

"Right."

"And she's gone?"

"Headed out as soon as her yacht was refueled. By the way, its name is *She's a Chancer*."

"Somehow appropriate." Finally Luke did open his eyes, and Ben was once again struck by how tired his father looked, tired to the bone and to the spirit. "I can still feel her path. I'll be up in a minute to lay in a course."

"Right. Don't push yourself." Ben backed out of the cabin and its door slid shut.

SEVERAL DAYS LATER
Jade Shadow, In High Dathomir Orbit

Luke stared at the mottled, multicolored world of Dathomir through the forward viewport. He nodded, feeling slightly abashed. Of *course* it was Dathomir.

Ben, seated to Luke's left in the pilot's seat, peered at him. "What is it, Dad?"

"I'm just feeling a little stupid. There's no world better suited to be the home of this new Sith order than Dathomir. I should have realized it long before we were on our final leg here."

"How so?"

"There are a lot of Force-sensitives in the population, most of whom are trained in the so-called witchcraft of Dathomir. There's not a lot of government oversight to detect a growing order within the population. There are lots of individual, secretive tribes." Luke paused to consider. "Jacen was here for a while on his five-year travels. I wonder what he learned and whether it relates to the Maw . . . And there are mentions in ancient records that there was a Sith academy here long, long ago."

Ben nodded. "Well, I'll prep Mom's Headhunter and get down there. I'll be your eyes and ears on the ground."

Luke gave his son a confused look. "I'm not going down with you? I'm feeling much better. Much more rested."

"Yeah, but there's a Jedi school down there. The terms of your exile say that you can't—"

Luke grinned and held up a hand, cutting off his son's words. "You're a little bit behind the times, Ben. Maybe you need your own galactic map updated. More than two years ago, when the Jedi turned against Jacen at Kuat—"

"Yeah, and we set up shop on Endor for a while. What about it?"

"We pulled everyone out of the Dathomir school at the time. Jacen's government shut the school down. The Jedi have yet to reopen it."

Comprehension dawned on Ben's face. "So there's no school, and it's legal for you to visit."

"Yes."

"That's kind of getting by on a technicality, isn't it?"

"All law is technicality, Ben. Get authorization for landing."

DATHOMIR

Half an hour later, Luke had to admit that he was wrong. *Most* of law was technicality. The rest was special cases, and he, apparently, was a special case.

He stood on the parking field of the Dathomiri spaceport. Perhaps "spaceport" was too generous a term. It was a broad, sunny field, grassy in some spots, muddy in others, with thruster scorch marks here and there. Dull gray permacrete domes, most of them clearly prefabricated, dotted the field; the largest was some sort of administrative building, the smaller ones hangars for vehicles no larger than shuttles and starfighters. A tall mesh durasteel fence surrounded the complex, elevated watchtowers dotting its length, and Luke could see the wiring leading to one of the permacrete domes that marked it as electrified. The spaceport facilities offered little shade, so the Skywalkers stood in the darkness cast by *Jade Shadow,* but even without the heat of direct sunlight, the moist, windless air was still as oppressive as a blanket.

Luke poured thoughts of helpfulness and reasonability into the Force, but it was no use. The man before him, nearly two skinny meters of red-headed obstructiveness, would not yield a centimeter.

The man, who had given his name as Tarth Vames, again waved his datapad beneath Luke's nose. "It's simple. That vehicle—" His wave indicated *Jade Shadow.* "Neither it, nor anything with an enclosed or enclosable interior, can be inland under your control or your kid's." He turned his attention to Ben, who stood, arms folded across his chest, beside his father. Ben glared but did not reply.

Luke sighed. "Is any other visitor to Dathomir operating under that restriction?"

"Don't think so, no."

"Then why us?"

Vames thumbed the datapad keyboard so that the message scrolled downward several screens. "Here, right here. An enclosed vehicle, according to these precedents—there's about eight screens of legal precedents—can be interpreted as a mobile school, especially if *you're* in it, especially if its presence constitutes a continuation of a school that's been here in the past."

"This is harassment." Ben's words were quiet, but loud enough for Vames to hear.

The tall man glowered at Ben. "Of course it's not harassment. The order came specifically from Chief of State Daala's office. Public officials at that level don't harass."

Ben rolled his eyes. "Whatever."

"Ben." Luke added a chiding tone to his voice. "No point in arguing. Vames, are you also prohibited from answering a few questions?"

"Always happy to help. So long as it's within latitudes permitted by the regulations."

"Within the last couple of days, have you seen any sign of a dilapidated yacht called *She's a Chancer*?" Luke knew the yacht had to be here; he had run his blood trail to ground on Dathomir, and the girl had not departed this world. But anything this man could add to his meager store of knowledge might help.

Vames entered the ship name in his datapad, then shook his head. "No vehicle under that name made legal landfall."

"Ah."

"Dilapidated, you say? A yacht?"

"That's right."

Vames keyed in some more information. "Last night, shortly after dusk, local time, a vehicle with the operational characteristics of a SoroSuub yacht made a sudden descent from orbit, overflew the spaceport here, and headed north. There was some comm chatter from the pilot about engines on runaway, that she couldn't cut them or bring her repulsors online for landing."

Ben frowned at that. "Last night? And you didn't send out a rescue party?"

"Of course we did. As per regulation. Couldn't find the crash site. No further communication from the vehicle. We still have searchers up there. But no luck."

"Actually, that *is* helpful." Luke turned to his son. "Ben, no enclosed vehicles."

"Yeah?"

"Rent us a couple of speeder bikes, would you?"

Ben grinned. "Yes, sir."

Fate of the Jedi: Outcast

Aaron Allston

THE EXTRAORDINARY NEXT EPISODE IN THE STAR WARS GALAXY BEGINS HERE . . .

The Galactic Alliance is in crisis. Worse still, the very survival of the Jedi Order is under threat.

In a shocking move, Chief of State, Natasi Daala, orders the arrest of Luke Skywalker for failing to prevent Jacen Solo's turn to the dark side. But it's only the first blow in an anti-Jedi backlash fueled by a hostile government and a media-driven witch hunt. Facing conviction, Luke must strike a bargain with the calculating Daala – his freedom in exchange for his exile from Coruscant and from the Jedi Order.

Though forbidden to intervene in Jedi affairs, Luke is determined to keep history from being repeated. With his son, Ben, at his side, Luke sets out to unravel the shocking truth behind Jacen Solo's corruption and downfall. But the secrets he uncovers among the enigmatic Force mystics of the distant world Dorin may bring his quest — and life as he knows it — to a sudden end. And all the while, another Jedi Knight, consumed by a mysterious madness, is headed for Coruscant on a fearsome mission that could doom the Jedi Order . . . and devastate the entire galaxy.

Century · London

Fate of the Jedi: Omen

Christie Golden

**The second novel in a bold, new Star Wars story arc –
Fate of the Jedi!**

The Jedi Order is in crisis. The late Jacen Solo's shocking
transformation into murderous Sith Lord Darth Caedus has cast
a damning pall over those who wield the Force for good. Two Jedi
Knights have succumbed to an inexplicable and dangerous
psychosis. Criminal charges have driven Luke Skywalker into
self-imposed exile. And power-hungry Chief of State Natasi
Daala is exploiting anti-Jedi sentiment to undermine the Order's
influence within the Galactic Alliance.

But an even greater threat is looming. Millennia in the past, a
Sith starship crashed on an unknown, low-tech planet, leaving
the survivors stranded. Over the generations, their numbers
have grown anew, the ways of the dark side have been
nurtured, and the time is fast approaching when this lost tribe
of Sith will once more take to the stars to reclaim their
legendary destiny as rulers of the galaxy. Only one thing stands
in their way to dominance, a name whispered to them through
the Force: Skywalker.

Century · London

Fate of the Jedi: Abyss
Troy Denning

**The third novel in a bold, new Star Wars story arc – Fate
of the Jedi!**

Luke and Ben Skywalker arrive in the mysterious part of space
called The Maw in search of more clues as to what caused Jacen
Solo's fall to the dark side. But they are not the only ones
exploring The Maw: a Sith Master and her apprentice arrive –
determined to kill Luke. And they're not the only ones with
plans for Luke Skywalker. There's a powerful being hiding in
The Maw, enormously strong and purely evil . . .

Century · London